Daughter's Justice

Thaddeus Nowak

www.thaddeusnowak.com

Published by Mountain Pass Publishing, LLC.

ISBN: 978-0-9852851-3-5

First Printed: March 2013
Second Edition: February 2014

Set in Adobe Garamond Pro
Cover art by Mallory Rock
Maps by Thaddeus Nowak

Daughter's Justice

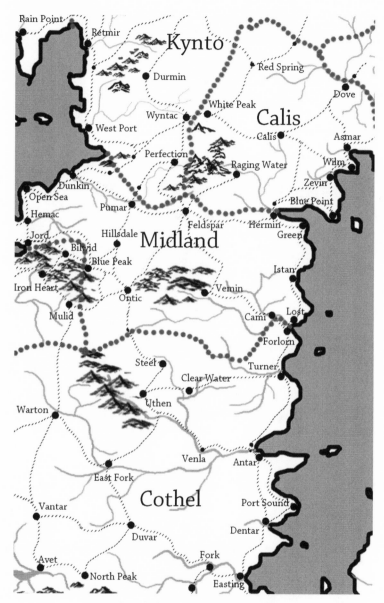

Map of Cothel, Midland, Kynto, and Calis.

Acknowledgements

I would like to thank the many people who have helped make this work possible. My wife Sherri, my best friend Chad, my brother Joe and his wife Samantha, my other brothers Dave and Dan and their wives Jenni and Linda, and my parents. I would also like to thank my friends Priya S., David J., and Alysia B. as well as the others who have inspired and offered advice. Any errors left in the work are entirely mine.

Chapter 1

The wagon's constant rocking from side to side finally stopped and Stephenie sighed. She looked up from where she was propped among the leather packs at the two story wattle and daub building. A sign over the door proclaimed it Dom's Inn. It was an unimpressive building and had a significant tilt in the right wall of the second story. However, the smell of food set her mouth watering, and for something to eat, she could easily ignore the building's state of disrepair.

She slowly crawled to the back of the wagon where Sergeant Henton waited to help her down. She detested being injured and showing weakness. Injury was something she had always hid from others, but the Sergeant had seen her with significantly worse looking wounds. He had fed her when she had been nearly starved, bandaged her left forearm after it had been burned through to the bone by lightning, and carried her onward when she had overused her body and could not walk. It angered her to know her current state was far worse. Visibly, she looked generally healthy, if not too thin. The trouble was her very bones ached and her muscles just did not have the strength and stamina they should. The ten days of riding in the back of the wagon had allowed her no real recovery, though she did have to acknowledge that she could now at least stand and walk short distances on her own. However, that was a far cry from the twenty to thirty miles a day of forced marches she had been able to perform less than a month earlier.

Stephenie gave a small smile to Private Oliver, a sandy blond who had come up beside Henton to offer a second hand. She shook her head at both of them and made a point of sliding off the wagon without aid.

"Private Beth, you really need to let us help you."

"Yes, Sarge," she almost snarled, but kept her tone from being insubordinate. Ever since Henton had first called her Beth in an effort to conceal her identity, she had told him repeatedly that she did not think of herself as a Beth. It had done nothing to stop his use of the name.

He smiled at her, as if to say, just try and stop me. Then he turned to Corporal Will, who was in the driver's seat and had turned to watch the excitement. "Corporal, you and Private Berman take care of the wagon, everyone else, grab the gear and follow me."

Stephenie did not bother reaching for her pack; she knew it would be removed from her hand before she could lift it. However, she did grab her sword and slowly strapped the belt around her waist. She straightened her leather armor and pulled the belt tight, which was now in a second set of holes they had punched so the belt would stay up. While never having been much more than a thin girl, she had never weighed as little as she currently did. This, despite the last ten days of eating enough to feed fifty people. It was just another odd thing that made her certain there was something very wrong with herself.

Once Sergeant Henton and the other five privates pulled all the gear from the back of the wagon, Will and Berman drove the two horses forward and around the side of the Inn. The wagon was in poor shape, with damage to the side rails, the support structure, and the bed. However, Stephenie was very glad for it. Without the wagon, she would have to walk and that would demonstrate just how weak she really was. At least with the wagon, she could conceal it to some degree.

Henton signaled the squad to move forward and Stephenie fell in directly behind the twenty-seven year old man, whom despite all their differences, she had found she respected more than nearly anyone else. He was ten years older than her and while quite different in personality from her brother, she found herself wishing he could have been a second brother to her. He had accepted what she was and while it challenged his beliefs, he chose to give her a chance for the sake of the country at large. It was not something that many others would have done.

Inside the inn, the main room held four tables near a fireplace built into the left-hand wall. A counter with a variety of dried goods and supplies stood in front of the right wall. An older woman, whose grey hair was speckled with bits of brown, eyed them cautiously as they filed in through the door.

Henton took a step forward and nodded his head. "Ma'am. I am Sergeant Henton and we are in need of rooms, food, and stabling for two horses."

The woman frowned at Henton. "You be a long way from the main roads. What are you doing this way with a wagon?"

Henton shuffled slightly and took another step forward. "Ma'am, we are returning to Antar. The King has need of supplies and a reasonably fit wagon is one of them. However, the main roads are a bit crowded and His Majesty, King Joshua, thought it would be a good idea for some of us soldiers to pass through some of the smaller towns and spread news of the war."

"The war's done. We had runners come through declaring Duke Burdger as holding Antar. Then a few days ago, more runners say Prince Joshua survived the battles in the Greys and is returning to Antar."

"Ma'am," Henton nodded, "I can confirm with my own eyes that King Joshua is indeed returning to Antar with several thousand soldiers and citizens of Cothel. The Senzar invaders were routed. Their leadership and most of their witches and warlocks were destroyed in the Grey Mountains."

"By one of Elrin's spawn they said. Elrin's evil turning on itself. The get of that traitorous bitch who fled the country with the treasury." The old woman squared her hips, "Now His Majesty thinks to take even more from us? His father, a good man, until he led us into this stupid war, which killed so many while robbing us of goods and supplies. What kind of spawn came from that Queen? We know at least one is a demon of Elrin."

"Careful woman," Private Tim said, stepping in front of Stephenie, his hand on the handle of his sword. "Less than that's been considered treason."

Henton raised his left hand. "Ma'am, I am sure you were just posing observations. I can tell you that His Majesty, King Joshua, is a true and good King. He did not abandon his people and wants to return peace and prosperity to the country."

"By having the likes of me provide you room and board at my expense."

Henton shook his head. "Ma'am, if that was your concern, we may have gotten off to a bad start with a simple misunderstanding." Henton pulled out a coin purse. "We intend to pay the normal rate for three rooms, all the food we eat, and the stabling of our horses. The King knows everyone has given a lot and the Senzar have taken even more. He does not want to take anything if he has a choice."

The older woman softened her expression. "Well, then, as long as you don't go professing loyalty to that demon witch, we can just assume it is true that her curse came from her mother selling her soul to Elrin when she carried the child."

Henton nodded his head. "Fair enough, ma'am. Princess Stephenie did save thousands of Cothel's sons, brothers, and women from the Senzar heathens. She drove them from the Grey Mountains and killed thousands of the enemy. And speaking as a follower of Felis, I will not exalt her deeds to you; however, I will say that leave the evil of the mother where it lay and do not blame the children. The only daughter that cared for the traitor, who is no longer our Queen, was Princess Regina. That princess fled north with her mother to that forsaken country, Kynto."

The old woman took a deep breath, but did not gainsay Henton further. "Three rooms and food."

"We will need a fair amount of food. However much you cook, I am sure that nine hungry soldiers can easily eat it all."

"Have a seat, I'll have the food prepared." She left the main room through a door in the back wall.

Stephenie, sorely feeling the effort of standing, moved toward a spot next to the fireplace. She slid into a chair and slouched to avoid having to hold herself upright.

"Beth, we don't have to stay here with that kind of attitude."

Stephenie looked up and met Tim's brown eyes. She found the seventeen year old to be almost too intense most of the time. The private had thrown himself completely into the army life and had trained hard, making himself one of the strongest and fittest soldiers Joshua had at hand. His dedication to her and nearly zealous defense of her honor, despite what she was, had earned him a place as one of her personal guards. She trusted him as much as any of the other five men Joshua had added to what remained of Henton's squad from *The Scarlet*. However, she wished he could scale back his drive from time to time. "Tim, it's all good. We'll see worse before we get to Antar. It's why we are going this route in the first place."

Henton cleared his throat. "And next time you want to interrupt my conversation, consider the fact that you are a private and I am a sergeant."

"Yes, Sarge. I should have held my tongue. I will do better next time."

Henton sat down next to Stephenie. "Good. Go help Will and then come back for some grub." The Sergeant did not bother to watch as Tim put down the packs he was carrying and left. Instead he turned to Stephenie. "You going to be okay?"

"I'm starving. I can't seem to get enough food."

"What's Kas have to say about it?"

"I'm a freak."

"I'm serious. You've gone through all of our rations and you seem to still be losing weight."

"He thinks something is out of whack with my body. Ever since I woke up after that night, I seem to be constantly consuming food. My body might be using it to rebuild itself, but it's not going to my hips, that's for sure."

"You need—"

Stephenie interrupted Henton with a shake of her head and a quick glance at the kitchen door. She could sense the old woman returning. She knew there were three other people in the backroom, she suspected they were male, but her ability to sense much more than the vaguest of surface emotions from people near her had not improved. Kas called her mentally deaf, and from what she could tell, he was right.

When the woman returned, she was carrying several loaves of bread under one arm and a pot of stew in the other. "You need bowls or do you have your own?"

"We've got our own, thank you, ma'am."

"Well, three rooms, food for nine, and stalls for two horses will cost you forty square."

Stephenie watched as Henton swallowed what she expected was an angry retort. That much money was a lot even for a larger city. Obviously the woman wanted to test just how much King Joshua's or Henton's word was worth.

"Well ma'am, that is a fair sum. I assume you took me at my word that my men are hungry and will eat a lot. I won't let them eat you out of home, but be forewarned, for that amount, we expect breakfast in the morning after a large feast tonight."

The woman pursed her lips and nodded her head, "Fair enough."

Henton counted out forty small square coins and handed them over. It was a good portion of what was left of their minted coins, many of which had been provided by Henton's original squad. She still had several pieces of gold and silver, the remains of coins from the Dalar empire, long since dead and forgotten, the last set of which Joshua had melted into lumps of metal before he had left the Greys ahead of them. She had almost lost a number of those coins to some Senzar soldiers, and that could have led to more difficulties. As lumps of gold they were not as valuable, but they would not be traced to any specific country or time.

Paid, the woman went back to working on counting goods behind the counter as Will, Tim, and Berman came in through the front door. "Wagon's stowed, Sarge. Horses in the hands of a stable boy." Will sat down across from Stephenie, who was already eating from a loaf of bread as Henton loaded up her bowl with stew. "We're going to have a crowd of people tonight."

"Well, spreading news is part of our job," Stephenie said with a full mouth.

Having grown used to her consuming all the food around, the others started digging into the bread and stew the moment she received her bowl from Henton. As Henton started to fill his own bowl, he called over to the woman behind the counter, "Ma'am, as I mentioned, we've been underfed for a while. If you can bring another round or two of food, we'd be much appreciative." Frowning, the woman reluctantly returned to the kitchen as Henton sat down to eat.

They were only into the second course of food, Stephenie her fourth, when many of the town's people started to file into the tavern. Some of the men greeted the old woman as Ava, others simply moved to sit at nearby tables, but most people remained standing, clustering into small groups. It was not long before the room was filled with a mass of people and the odor that came with so many working men and women.

Stephenie had opened herself up a little more than normal, allowing the mental energy into her mind. However, the muddled mess of noise still meant little to her. Kas bemoaned her lack of mental sensitivity frequently and while it was useful when she had been around people as they died, it was frustrating to know that a normal person with the ability to use magic would be able to easily pick up surface thoughts, not just strong emotions. Of course, most normal mages had been systematically killed over the last thousand years and the only ones left in her part of the world were minimally skilled and untrained. *And dead if anyone discovered what they were.*

She put the thought aside and continued to eat mechanically. She was sensitive enough to know the room was full of apprehension, anger, and a bit of fear. The war that Cothel had been fighting was just barely over and the victory not entirely decisive. It was not unlike the other small towns they had passed through.

Henton stood, drawing her attention, but the strips of beef continued to move from her plate to her mouth. "Good evening." Henton turned so he could briefly meet the eyes of everyone in the room. "My name is Sergeant Henton. I am glad that so many of you decided to visit with us. I wanted to pass on the latest news."

"The war truly over?" someone asked from the back of the room.

Henton nodded his head. "The Senzar forces are in retreat. The immediate threat to Cothel appears to be over for now. His Majesty, King Joshua, decided not to pursue those retreating. While the actions of Her Highness, Princess Stephenie, had freed many thousand soldiers and citizens of Cothel and neighboring countries, it was decided that it was not in the best interest of Cothel to pursue them at this time.

"I can tell you that the Princess killed between six or seven thousand of the Senzar, including most of their witches and warlocks. She killed their leadership, leaving mostly lower ranking soldiers."

"What of all those we heard were in the countryside as well as those back in Esland? They control most of that country."

Henton turned in the direction the question had come from. "Those that were killed were in a valley in the Grey Mountains. They were after lost artifacts, which appear to have been destroyed as well. The top leadership was there. However, you are correct, there are still many Senzar west of the Greys. At this time, they don't appear to be wanting any more conflict from us. We think they are stretched pretty thin."

"We should never have been fighting this war." The statement was followed by a number of affirmative comments.

Henton shook his head. "I cannot comment on what the late King did and his reasons for doing so, may he live on with the gods; however, King Joshua's focus is securing Cothel and bringing it back to prosperity."

"After his traitorous mother stole everything? He going to tax us to death so he can rebuild? He going to draft those few of us left to fight more battles? Duke Burdger took the crown."

"Joshua does not plan to tax you to make himself live comfortably. He will only do what is needed. Regarding Burdger, the Duke took over before he knew Joshua was still alive. I am sure the Duke, who was friends with our late King, will welcome His Majesty's return."

Stephenie sensed a good deal of doubt from the crowd at that statement. She looked around, pausing in her eating. The people definitely were frightened and she understood that. She wanted to allay everyone's fears. She just did not know how to do that and she hated to feel helpless.

A sudden sharpness of fear and perhaps anger drew her attention; the more intense the emotion, the more readily it stood out to her. She noticed a young man next to an older man who was in a fine set of clothing.

A whispered chain of comments spread quickly though the crowd: "It's her!"

"Who?"

"The Witch."

Henton stopped talking as the mood of the crowd changed palpably in an instant. The man in fine clothing moved to the front of the town's people, the holy symbol of Felis on his chest.

"Is it true?"

"It is!" the young man who had been next to him said from within the safety of the crowd. "I was on the top of the ridge. I saw her face; her red hair. That's the demon spawn that brought the mountain down. And that sergeant was always with her."

"Sergeant?" the old man questioned. "I ask as a priest of Felis, is this true? This woman the witch?"

Stephenie slowly rose to her feet, sending everyone in the room back a step. She wished this irrational fear of what she was did not exist.

Henton bowed his head to the priest. "It is true, she is the Princess." He raised his hand to prevent comment, "but as one of Felis' loyal men, I submit that she has never performed an evil act."

"That is not for you to decide. Witches must be destroyed to prevent the spread of Elrin's evil. Allowing her to live is spreading his tainted influence."

Corporal Will rose to his feet and pushed his way in front of Henton. "Enough of this crap! I am so sick of everyone wanting to hurt Steph. She destroyed the Senzar heathens. She saved the country!" Turning to the young man, "She saved your life and you want to judge her?" Will shook his head and turned back to the priest. "Henton is as a devout follower of Felis as I've seen. When we served on *The Scarlet*, a ship in His Majesty's fleet, his closest friend was a Holy Warrior of Felis. You cannot question Henton's faith."

"I was questioning his judgment."

Will took a breath. "Why do you burn witches?"

"To remove Elrin's taint from their soul."

"Exactly. This young lady's soul has been purified. I was there, I saw it happen. She burned in a holy fire and was remade." Will took a step closer to the priest and held out his arm. "Read me. Prove what I say is true."

The priest frowned, but took his holy symbol in one hand and grabbed Will's arm with the other. After a moment, he nodded for Will to continue.

"The Senzar had shot her with arrows and threw curses and spells at her. She had fallen to the ground, her legs crippled, but she fought on to save those she was trying to protect. I was certain she would die at their hands, but then suddenly her entire body erupted in flames. The flames covered her from head to toe. It was so bright I could see her clearly from where I stood on the top of the ridge. Her clothing and everything she was wearing was burned away. The Senzar tried to retreat. These Elrin-loving demons were fleeing her.

"Then suddenly the mountain roared, exploded, and destroyed the invaders. Those Senzar warlocks and witches were destroyed in an explosion of fire and rock." Will looked around the room. "When I reached her, we found her whole. Naked and in a crater of melted rock. She had many scars before; one on her cheek from an early childhood injury and others on her arms and legs from all the weapons training she had. But when we found her, they were all gone. The arrow wounds she had just taken, gone. Her body was perfect. The only mark is a black hand print on her left breast, just over her heart." He nodded his head in her direction. "She was remade and purified by the gods. Felis' holy warriors had fallen to the Senzar. Their holy symbols and the statues of power stolen and used against us. The same can be said of Ari's, Duman's, and several other gods from where the Senzar had marched. So I ask you, could not the gods have decided to take one of Elrin's own and purify her and use her as a weapon against the invaders? She survived purification by fire and was remade. I do not believe Elrin ever had a hold on her, but after that fire, if there was ever a bit of taint, it is gone."

Will held up his chin, "What say you, priest?"

The old priest removed his hand from Will's arm and looked toward Stephenie. "Your words were spoken true."

A murmur of surprise ran through the crowd and a low cacophony of comments drowned each other out. Stephenie wanted to walk over and shake Will. His interpretation of events was skewed. She had never heard him put forth that view of the events before and it worried her that others might start to believe the things he just said. *I am NOT some chosen warrior for the gods.*

The priest drew Stephenie's attention again. "Is this true? Are you separated from Elrin? Would you submit to another trial by fire?"

Stephenie took a deep breath and moved forward. This time the crowd did not retreat. "I have never worshiped Elrin. I was born like this, with these powers. Yes, I was surrounded in fire when I fought the Senzar and yes, I have healed and," she turned to glare at Will, "it seems more people have seen the mark on my breast than I originally thought." She turned back to the priest. "I personally have not drawn conclusions about those events. However, having been covered in flames once, I do not think I really want to do it again."

"Then the curse of Elrin was drawn to you by your mother as the rumors have stated. It would make sense, the traitorous..." the priest paused.

"Traitorous bitch is how I refer to her. She's no longer my, nor Joshua's mother."

The priest nodded with a slight softening of his expression. "It would hold with her behavior. You have given me pause and something to consider. However, only the High Priest in Antar can make a proclamation regarding your status. It has always been something that is conceived of as possible, but there is no record of someone surviving purification by fire. If true, it would mean that Elrin has no power over you."

"I have only ever acted to try to do what is best for Cothel and her people."

Stephenie turned just before the man on her left jumped forward. "We cannot suffer a witch!" he screamed, a dagger in his hand. Private Tim moved forward as well, trying to draw his sword. *No more, damn it!*

Almost instinctively, she drew energy from her surroundings, the air, the wood of the floor and tables, and even the people around her. A slight chill followed the drawing of the energy, but it was so minimal it would scarcely be felt. Directing the energy through her body, she created a field around Tim and the man with the dagger. It was irregular in shape, matching their form. Kas had only recently begun teaching her how to control complex fields, but unlike reading thoughts, this was something for which she had an affinity.

The two men froze in mid-stride, confronted with a wall of energy that repelled their forward motion. Sensing and almost visualizing the pressures they exerted on the force, she kept what Kas referred to as a modified gravity field only strong enough to keep them where they were.

"I am sick and tired of people hurting each other. I am not here to hurt anyone. I am simply going back to Antar. If everyone will be kind enough to cease hostilities, at least until we leave in the morning, I think everyone will be much better off in the end." She looked to the priest as she released Tim, whom she had already sensed had stopped his effort to move forward.

"Your Highness. I never trained as a Holy Warrior, but I do know what you just did is not considered easy. At least, not without injuring people. Your corporal has given me things to consider and I will be sending word to Antar regarding these events. I will give you the benefit of the doubt, at least until the High Priest can comment." The old man turned his head to look at the people in the room. "Until we hear otherwise or have cause to know differently, we must consider that perhaps Elrin does not possess this one. Leave her and her soldiers to their own and they will leave in the morning."

"Thank you."

The priest nodded his head. "I pray to Felis that I am not making a mistake. But so far, your actions today do not speak of evil. And I do not think we could do anything to you even if we wanted to. Anyone that can bring down a mountain, as young Arvin described several days ago when he returned to us, is not going to be endangered by a small group of townsmen."

Stephenie hesitated, wondering just how much of the priest's proclamation was due to fear as opposed to actually believing she did not intend to harm anyone. "Thank you for the trust. We will not do anything to invalidate it." She released the man with the dagger, who's face was a mask of anger and fear. However, three other men grabbed his arms and pulled him back into the crowd. "If there are no other questions, my friends and I will finish our food and then retire to our rooms for the night."

Chapter 2

Stephenie crawled into the old and rickety bed that was leaning against the wall. She was in the middle room of the three that her group were using; her personal guards had divided up and taken the two on either side of her's. She told them they should all try and get some sleep, but Henton insisted that one person in each room would remain up through the night. For Stephenie's room, that would be Kas.

She smiled, sensing her friend floating beside her. He was never far from her, but he had been a bit more emotionally distant of late. "Kas," she whispered and then waited for his form to slowly materialize. It started as just the hint of a blue-green glow, then his face, shoulders, and chest appeared in a very translucent image. "Kas," she demanded a little louder and with a bit of mental command directed at him. She had not yet figured out how to direct mental communication. The ghost would only hear her thoughts if he was listening to her mind.

With a huff, the rest of his form materialized and shifted into the firm opaqueness that Stephenie preferred. While she could sense him clearly without seeing his form with her eyes, she noticed that he appeared to have more cohesion when he decided to be visible.

"Kas, I really need to talk to you," she said in the Old Tongue. She was teaching him Cothish and he had picked up many words and phrases over the last ten days, but to have a full conversation, she needed to use the old Denarian language. "Did you pick up anything that Will said this evening? I wanted to strangle him. How in the world could he start making out like I am some gift from the gods? Or that the gods had anything to do with me?" She balled up her hands, "remade in order to defeat the Senzar, really, Will? Where did he come up with that shit?"

The ghost walked over to her bed and sat down, this time the covers moved slightly and Stephenie grinned at the effort he was making to behave more like a person with a body. "I caught only part of what was said. His manner of speech is rather quick."

"I'm so sorry for how frustrated I must have made you when we first met. I really was the brain-damaged simpleton you called me. I've explained things to Will and the others, but even Henton is reluctant to believe. Sometimes I think he is willing, but..."

"Stephenie, you must learn to let it go. They are your friends and protect you. However, getting them to understand may be too much to expect. Besides, whatever he said seemed to quiet the townspeople for the most part and it is better not to kill those whom you wish to eventually like you."

"But Will is going to try to make it out like I am some sort of warrior for the gods. I just know where he's going to take it. I don't believe in fate and destiny, but I could see it in his eyes. I could even feel it from him. I think he really believes I am some chosen person. The mark you left when you tried to freeze my heart, they think it is something special!"

"Stephenie, you still carry that mark because you wanted to. The more I think about what happened, the more I am certain you were able to somehow direct the excess energy into healing yourself. Even rebuilding and remaking your body based on some internal ideal you have, which removed the old scars and injuries, but, since you are so adamant that we belong together and you associated the mark with me, you subconsciously left it."

"I have feeling there again," she said, grinning at him from where she sat, knowing deep down that he was right.

Kas smiled back at her. "I've seen you playing with your breast."

She shook her head and frowned at him. "You must have been a pervert a thousand years ago, watching me when I'm not looking." She could not keep the grin from growing on her face as his eyes took on a mischievous light, showing a little brown through the blue-green of his luminescence. Stephenie wondered if he could produce a more natural color all the time, but had resisted asking. "But I've not been playing, just poking to see if it had fully healed."

Kas' form flashed out for a brief moment and he reappeared with his body standing and facing her. "Levity aside, we need to discuss a more serious topic." He paused for just a moment, blinking out and back, but not moving position. "You are not getting better. I think your ideal you used to reform yourself must not have been correct. Either that, or your body is somehow stuck in a mode that it is constantly rebuilding itself. You are not regaining your strength of muscle. I am worried about you. What you did on the mountain is beyond my understanding. The fact that you even lived is unbelievable in itself, but if you continue to deteriorate, I fear you may die and one does not just become a ghost as you know."

Stephenie raised her eyebrows. "What do you want me to do?"

"Get better," Kas said, lowering his head before floating closer to her. "Magically speaking, you seem to have recovered completely, if not improved." Pride filled his eyes. "I was quite impressed by the field you created tonight. Very well done."

She smiled and leaned back against the wall. "Thank you. I was glad you held back from doing anything. People have enough problems with me...knowing about you would make it worse."

"You are capable of protecting yourself, but you are not healing. Your constant need to eat is worrying. Regardless of how much of a pig you make of yourself, you are still gradually losing weight. You seem to survive when you are not eating, as if your body's consumption of the raw materials slows, but the moment you eat something, it picks back up. I would need you to take more detailed measurements and record data over time, but it seems you lose more weight when you eat more."

"Measurements?"

"Your size, how much you eat, and such."

"I am not an experiment, Kas."

"No, but we need to understand what is going on. Your body should always be slowly rebuilding itself, but it is almost as if you are stuck in a high-intensity mode. Like your body is fighting a disease or injury."

"Well, perhaps that is why I'm so achy all the time. Any suggestions? Aside from prescribing this to my fat sister Regina?"

"This is not a joke. I think this is dangerous. You could end up doing a lot of damage to yourself in the long run. Plus, you are miserable."

"I jogged and marched from Antar all the way to the Greys. That was five hundred miles and I did it while injured and half starved. Now I can't hardly walk two dozen feet. I made it up those stairs using my powers to support my body." She took a deep breath. "So yeah, I'm miserable and very scared. I really am. But what can I do about it? I don't know how to fix it."

Kas nodded his head and sat down next to her again. "When we get back to Antar, I will go to the library. I will need to check on the situation to make sure the ghosts in Arkani are still quiet. I will see if I can find anything that might talk about this. Otherwise, you might have to let me into your mind again and I can try to determine what is going on. But—"

"That's too risky for you. I don't want to harm you. I love you."

"So you keep saying."

"Kas. Don't make light of my feelings."

He looked at her and shook his head. "I have no body. I have no way to truly care for you. It frustrates me."

"But you do love me as well, yes?"

"Stephenie. Yes, I do love you. Are you happy?"

She smiled. "Now I am. And no more talk of me until we know more, okay?" She reached out with her mind, drew in energy, and pulled her pack from across the room to her hands. Putting it behind her, she shifted it until it was more comfortable than leaning against the wall. "Let's work on you learning more Cothish. There's nothing to be done about me for now."

Stephenie was awakened early in the morning. Henton had procured food directly from the kitchen and store room before anyone else was awake. He justified taking the food as having paid for it already and not wanting to risk someone trying to poison them. That was the preferred way to kill a witch or warlock. The idea was to overwhelm the witch's body trying to deal with the damage from the poison and so prevent the witch from fighting back with magic. The other ways were to sacrifice a number of people to tire out the witch or to use holy warriors to bring more power than the witch had. Since her body was already working overtime, getting poisoned would be a significant risk, even if her powers did not seem diminished.

At first light, they were on the road and heading out of town. "Steph, we probably need to think about trying to get to Antar as quickly as possible. I don't want those people sending word ahead of us to get a mob ready to take us. Perhaps we should also cut and dye your hair."

"No."

"You don't want to cut your hair or no to Antar?" Henton's voice was filled with disbelief.

"I will not cut and dye my hair." She sighed, knowing it seemed unreasonable, but she knew Kas liked her red hair long and she would not do anything that might give him another argument that she should find someone with a physical body.

"Do you get your powers from your hair?"

Stephenie turned to John, who's blond hair was pulled back in a long pony tail. "No," she said with a bit of skepticism. "Why would you ask that?"

"I heard old stories. Once people learned about you, there were lots and lots of stories going around camp. Some merc from the northeast had said witches get their power from their hair. That is why they never cut it. Didn't apply to warlocks for some reason."

Stephenie shook her head and then smiled at the crazy lack of logic some legends had. "I've not heard that before. Let me set you straight. No, my hair is not the key to my powers."

"So it must be key to your vanity," Henton said, his tone harsh enough to silence the others. "I am serious, Steph. We don't need you recognized. It is going to be hard enough to blend in. Nine soldiers with a wagon are easy to spot."

"Then it matters little that my hair is long and red. Leave it."

Henton huffed, but said nothing further on the subject.

"That spell you cast on me," Tim said, coming up next to John. "That was something else. I couldn't move forward. You just froze me in place."

"It wasn't a spell," she said, knowing a bit of frustration was leaking into her voice. Henton, Will, and Douglas had been with her on her journey to the Greys and had the benefit of her explaining what Kas had taught her. She had not had much desire to explains things to the five soldiers added to their number, but it was something she needed to reconcile now that they had seen her perform magic. "Nothing that I do is really a spell."

"See, I told you, she's not like the witches. She's different."

"Will, I am just like the priests and witches and warlocks. The difference is, I have Kas to help teach me things that most everyone around Tet appears to have forgotten." She moved forward in the wagon, using her powers to help her move smoothly up into the bench seat. "Okay, everyone, I am going to explain some things, so listen up."

Henton cleared his throat, "We should keep the scouts ahead and back a little. Clustered this close we won't—"

"Kas is watching. He's about a hundred feet above us and can see...well...more sense than actually see, in all directions around us. We're safe for now."

She waited for Henton to come in closer so she could talk in a normal tone. "Some of you have heard this before, but I want to stress this, what you call witchcraft, they used to call magic, but really it is just the manipulation of the energy that is already stored in everything around us. Light and heat are forms of that energy. The force that holds you to the ground and makes things fall is another form of energy. Long ago it was called gravity. It's a little different than light and heat, it is a force that causes things to be attracted to each other, not just for things to fall to the ground."

"Like Oliver to any pretty woman," John joked and Oliver grinned.

"Well, okay, perhaps." Stephenie shook her head, wanting to say 'More like Fish to water,' but Fish's death was too recent to joke about. "The force is actually fairly weak, unless the objects are large.

But, there is some amount of it between your hand and the sword or your butt and the back of a horse, at least until it throws you.

"It's a weak force, as I mentioned, but I can create a field that changes that. What I did to you, Tim, was simply create a field around your body that worked the other way; it repelled you. I made it just strong enough to keep you from moving forward. I would have had to constantly modify the field if you had struggled, otherwise you might have pushed through it. If I made it too strong, it might have crushed you."

"Like you did to the Senzar mages who attacked us on the way to the Greys," Douglas remarked.

"Right." Stephenie put aside the memory of the cracking bones and the pain, anguish, and fear the people she had killed felt as they died. "I also had to leave room for you to breathe and a way for air to reach your face, otherwise, you'd have died because you would not have been able to breathe. It takes a lot of concentration and constant adaptation to get it right and keep it working. It's not just some words you utter that does everything for you."

"So, not a spell. Then why do witches always cast spells?"

Stephenie turned to Oliver and his cocky grin. "I discussed that with Kas. We suspect that the whole concept of spells might have come when people who have the ability to use magic accidentally did something that put their mind in the right state to make it happen. They thought it was what they did or said. Then over time, they got so hung up on the chanting or what they did with their hands or what they burned, that in the end, that was the only way they could repeat the state of mind. Some of the things might have been early learning techniques and people eventually lost understanding. For instance, I found moving something was initially easier if I moved my hand, because then I am doing something with more than just my mind. But truly, I don't need to do that."

Tim raised his hand. "And so selling my soul to Elrin won't get me any power. You have to be born this way, right? That was what you said before."

"That's right. One of my ancestors had this ability."

"But no one else in your family was a witch or warlock?"

"Not that I have heard of. Kas is a little bit at a loss to explain it. But the other day he asked me if we still bother to breed good qualities into animals."

"You mean like we breed good hunting dogs. Choose a good bitch and stud to get a fast and smart dog." Oliver's grin widened.

Stephenie did not need her extra sensitivity to emotions to know Oliver's thoughts were back on his own reproductive exploits. "Kas didn't compare me to a dog. He chose horses, but the theory is the same. Sometimes you get what you expect, other times, you get something you don't expect, something from deep in the animal's past."

"So you're some odd freak of chance that happened to spring up?" Will asked, his eyes daring her to challenge him.

"I love you too," she said, shaking her head. "Enough about me and my odd hang ups. My hair stays, it's not a key to my power or undoing, and to answer the unasked question, apparently no one discussed good breeding practices with my parents before I was conceived."

"Hey, I think you came out just right."

"Here, here!"

Stephenie smiled despite herself. Henton had remained quiet and reserved as always, but she could sense admiration from the others and it felt good to know there were at least a few people who actually liked her for herself.

Stephenie opened her eyes. The change in Kas' presence had awaken her from her uneasy sleep on the ground. They had passed through two towns earlier in the day, Douglas buying supplies ahead of their arrival. However, Henton had decided to press on until nightfall, fearful that word of their travels would precede them. In the end, the decision was made to sleep in an abandoned field.

Nearly two dozen men approaching from the north, Kas' voice echoed in her mind. *They are not very organized. Not soldiers, but, they are bent on conflict.*

Stephenie rolled out from under her blankets and quickly moved over to Henton, shaking his shoulder, and bringing him instantly awake. "A couple dozen farmers and town's men coming from the north." He nodded his head and quickly went to wake the others on his left, motioning for Stephenie to move to the right. A couple moments later, everyone was awake and armed.

"We don't want to hurt anyone badly," Stephenie said as she forced herself forward using her magic to move her limbs. "These people have families and maiming someone won't help make them accept me."

"Ma'am, they're coming to kill you, being nice to them seems a little stupid."

Stephenie refrained from glaring at John. The light from the Mother Moon was bright enough everyone would be able to see her expression. Instead, she simply shook her head. "Be careful and don't get hurt," she added just loud enough for the others to hear. Sensing the mass of men growing closer, she raised her voice. "We know you are coming, so let's just take a moment and have a conversation."

The mass of men who had been slowly moving forward paused a moment, then a couple of men barked some quiet commands that drove the men forward again.

"We won't suffer a witch," one of the attackers finally shouted in defiance. "You soldiers walk away from the witch and we'll overlook your sins."

"She's already been cleansed," Will shouted back, earning a silencing look from Henton.

"We just want to confirm your claim. If your claim is true, she won't mind a second burning."

Stephenie looked into the blue eyes of the man who had emerged from the trees. Her night sight was always exceptional, and in this moonlight, she could see as well as she did during the day. The man's voice had trembled slightly and while she could only sense the barest of emotions, the group of men were terrified. "Go back to your families. We've done you no harm and don't want to cause your loved ones more loss."

"Take them before she casts a spell to addle your minds!"

Stephenie watched in dismay as the men charged forward, a few with swords, most with pitchforks or sharp farm tools. Several screamed, yelling angry, fear-filled challenges as they massed into clumps.

Henton and the squad formed up in a silent and composed response. They came around both sides of Stephenie to protect her. She moved one step forward, staying just behind Douglas and Henton. A heavy sword held loosely in her hand.

The initial clash of weapons showed the differences in skill and discipline. Henton, a seasoned marine sergeant, easily defected the pitchfork aimed at his chest. Stepping to the side, he casually disarmed the uncertain youth. A quick punch to the boy's jaw sent him backwards into an older man who had crowded too close.

Stephenie watched as Douglas turned aside one man's sword and barely dodged a scythe. Oliver automatically moved forward and kicked out the right leg of the man with the scythe, allowing Douglas to concentrate on the first man.

Blocked from the conflict by Douglas and Henton, she reached out with her senses, trying to place where all her friends and their adversaries had moved. Berman and Tim fought to her left, while John and Will were being drawn off further to her right. Her men were better, but they were following her desire to avoid hurting their attackers, who outnumbered them more than two to one.

Douglas grunted under the blow of a mace formed from a tree limb. He staggered back and Stephenie reacted instantly, allowing the energy surrounding them to course through her body and she threw Douglas' attacker back a dozen feet, knocking over two more of the twenty-three assailants.

To her right, pain from Will drew her attention; one of the three men surrounding him had landed a solid blow. Stephenie reached out with her mind and launched Will into the air. Almost instantly, he was twenty feet over the heads of the startled men around him. Stephenie angled his flight behind their line.

The attacking men, regaining their composure, started to move toward John, who was only just holding his own against two other men. Anger filling Stephenie, she drew more energy through her. Kas would complain about her lack of subtlety in creating a low-powered field to guide the energy instead of drawing it all through her body, but she did not have the time.

Unleashing the energy, which had made her hands tingle, she flung all the attackers back off their feet. Barely keeping the force in check, the sixteen men she hit sailed more than a dozen feet, several colliding with trees and each other. She felt several sharp spikes of pain from a couple men, but no one seemed to die.

"I told you we didn't want to hurt you or anyone else. Go back to your homes and be glad you still have your lives!" Stephenie stood and watched with barely contained rage as the farmers and town's men scrambled to their feet and retreated into the night. She could see several limping or holding their sides, but none appeared to be severely injured.

Turning, she rushed to Will, who was standing with the help of Douglas. "Where are you injured?"

Will looked over and gave her his innocent grin. "That was amazing. Throw me again."

Stephenie straightened. "I thought you had been hurt."

Will leaned into Douglas and struggled with the straps on his leather armor. After a moment, Stephenie moved closer and helped. "I took a hit to my side. Bastard had half a tree."

"You don't look like you're bleeding."

Henton moved in to also help Will get out of the armor and handed the boiled hide to Tim. "I don't see any bleeding either, but we'll need to watch for bruising. I wish we were on *The Scarlet*, I'd 've had Nermin heal you, but I think even if we hadn't lost most of our priests to the Senzar, we'd have a hard time getting one to help us now."

Stephenie looked to Henton and then to Will, her heart racing, knowing the problem was that they had thrown their support behind her and that marked all of them. "I...I could try to heal you."

Will smiled and winked his left eye. "I'm fine, really. The fat man just caught me off guard. I took far worse swinging to the mast on that Mytian pirate ship."

"Perhaps," Henton mused, "but you'll be taking it easy with Steph in the back of the wagon."

"Really Sarge, I'll be fine." Will tried to stand up tall, but could not hold back a cringe of pain. "Well, perhaps you can fly me into the wagon?"

Stephenie shook her head, but then smiled at the twinkle that came into Will's eye. "Yeah, I guess I can, Corporal Lazy."

"We should move out. Most of the night is gone anyway and we're all awake."

"Ma'am, can I ask why you waited to fight back?"

"And what of Kas?" Oliver asked, trying not to look like he was avoiding the ghost who had materialized next to Stephenie. "He'd have frightened them away sooner."

Stephenie looked around, feeling the lack of strength in her limbs. Her magic was the only thing holding her upright. "We've, meaning Henton, Will, Douglas, Kas, and I, have talked about that. Scaring these people will not win me friends. They don't trust power like that and I can't blame them. I had really hoped that they would have turned away when a couple of them were knocked down. I didn't want to use my power at all, but keeping Kas a secret is even more important."

Henton handed the rest of Will's armor to Oliver. "We should all try to minimize talking about what Steph can do. Whatever we say will get exaggerated in retelling. Why don't you get Will's bed role picked up. Tim, get the horses ready."

"You going to fly me into the wagon?" Will asked, his puppy dog eyes looking up sheepishly.

Stephenie turned away from him, then drew in the energy and lifted Will easily the forty feet into the back of the wagon.

"Can you fly me as well?" came a chorus of voices from Oliver, John, and Berman.

"No she will not," Henton snapped as he walked away. "She is not standing around for your entertainment. We don't want to wear her out."

Sticking out her tongue, she bounced Henton a foot into the air, making him stumble and her giggle. She had to use her powers to keep him from falling to the ground. "I think we can have a little fun as we pick up the camp."

Chapter 3

The ten of them continued to ride, march, and float toward the east for the next five days. Stephenie would have liked to drive everyone a little faster, since riding in the wagon was not a very entertaining pastime. The old wagon bounced and shook, keeping her from being able to read, so all she could do was sit and think. However, considering the condition of the back roads, the old horses were doing good to cover ten miles a day.

A couple of the privates, Oliver and John primarily, continued to complain about the long days and how tired their feet were. Stephenie had tuned them out days before and was startled back to attention when Henton finally broke his silence.

"Enough. If you two don't stop the griping, I'll have you jogging in place for a turn of the glass once we find a place to camp." He shook his head. "We were jogging from before sunrise to well after dark without a break for days on end when Steph led us to the Greys, our current pace is slow even for us lazy, ship-bound marines. I don't want to hear any more griping from you land grunts. You are supposed to be used to this."

"Yes Sarge," came their subdued reply.

Shaking his head, Henton picked up his pace and quickly outdistanced the wagon.

When Oliver looked at Stephenie, seeking approval or perhaps forgiveness, she shrugged. She was hopeful they would stop the complaining, but Henton's response had been a little harsher than she would have expected. She knew the fact they had been dodging pursuit and attempted poisonings from locals was weighing on him. It had put everyone on edge for too long, but he was normally more reserved.

"We're not heading back to the Grey's, are we?" Tim nodded his head toward the mountain range that was just now visible through a gap in the trees.

"Those are the Uthen Mountains," Stephenie responded after a brief look. "We've been heading east, not west."

Tim frowned. "I was never very good off the main roads."

"Well, you just have to look for the position of the sun and know what time of day it is. Or look for certain stars if it's night."

"And overcast days like today?"

"There are lots of tells. For..." Stephenie lifted herself up to peek over the drivers seat, Douglas, Berman, and Kas were moving quickly toward them with several bags of supplies over their shoulders. However, the anxiety she felt from Berman was high.

"What's happened? Do we have to avoid this town as well?"

The three of them, joined by Henton, quickly came over to the wagon. "Your Highness, we've heard some news."

Stephenie frowned at Berman's use of her title, as did Douglas.

"Steph," Douglas injected, "we've heard reports of what's going on in Antar and it sounds bad."

Stephenie used her powers to move over the edge of the wagon and land on her feet. "What's happened?"

"It seems Burdger didn't want to hand the crown back to His Majesty. He's got himself locked up tighter than a clam. Your brother's camped around the castle, but it's been a stalemate they say. Nothing's happening. At least for now. Burdger's been going on about how the country's coffers were emptied and that your brother has no money to pay anyone. The people we talked to thought we were troops that might be going to relieve Burdger."

Stephenie's fists were clenched and she felt the hairs on her arms rise as energy coursed through her body. Slowly she released the energy, afraid she might accidentally hurt one of the men. "Damn it! If they have relief coming, he can't risk bringing down the walls. Plus, we wouldn't have the money to rebuild them right now." She nodded her head for Douglas to continue.

"Well, they say the High Priest has not thrown in with Burdger, instead, he's ordered all the priests to remain neutral and only heal injured people and to not get involved with direct conflict. However, he's still locked in Antar castle with Burdger."

Stephenie's mind raced. Switching to the old Denarian tongue, she turned toward Henton and Kas, "I need to talk with you. I need to throw some ideas around about how we can help."

Henton nodded his head. "Sure." He turned to the men, "okay, we're going to push on. The holiday is over; we go as far as the horses can take us each day."

Stephenie drew upon her energy and launched herself into the back of the wagon and Henton grabbed the side rail and pulled himself in next to where Kas had appeared.

The next seven days were torture for Stephenie and the men. While they were still fearful of attacks from farmers and villagers, Kas' scouting allowed them to avoid any confrontations. Then each night, Stephenie insisted they work through multiple scenarios while she rehashed all the things they did not know. When she was not working with the men, she worked herself raw, practicing the attack the Senzar had used against her in the Greys. The fields were complex, forming a narrow beam of focused gravity speeding at a target, but the effect was as deadly as a ballista bolt.

The daylight hours were the hardest for Stephenie. Physically drained to the point of total exhaustion from her nighttime activities, she lacked the strength to do anything more than bounce around in the back of the wagon while obsessing over what was happening in Antar.

"Steph, it'll be all right," Will said as the tired horses pulled them up another hill. He had toned down his natural charm and Stephenie was grateful. She liked his sly smile most of the time, but she was tired of people trying to cheer her up.

She glanced in his direction, but said nothing as she turned back to watching the buildings they passed along the road. They were not in Antar yet, but in one of the many smaller towns and villages that existed just outside the largest city in Cothel. They had passed through Ivar earlier in the day when they crossed the large bridge over the Uthen River. The guards there simply assumed they were another squad of soldiers coming to Cothel to join the siege.

The people they passed along the road no longer identified them as anything except common foot soldiers and Stephenie could see the relief in Henton's eyes when he talked with her over the last couple of days. His emotions were still quite muted to her senses, but she had noticed how the threat of being lynched had taken a sharp toll on him.

As the wagon passed another cluster of scattered buildings at the top of the hill, Stephenie looked forward and out across the valley before them. Antar was in the distance. It was a large mass of homes, businesses, and green spaces. More than one hundred years of relative peace allowed the city to grow well outside the original walls that were just noticeable as lines through the city.

Immediately to the south of the city, and on higher bluffs, sat Antar Castle, overlooking both the city and the Sea of Tet. Stephenie heard people say it lorded over the city, held aloof by a steep and rocky approach. However, she had always believed it had a more benevolent air, protecting and watching. Today there was no joy in its sight; an army of soldiers camped around the castle. *At least it is an army commanded by Josh.*

The last time she had seen the castle had been from within its walls and at that time, it was her uncle's soldiers that had camped outside the walls. Those soldiers had helped her mother betray the country, stealing the war supplies, the treasury, and anything of value not built into the very foundation of the castle.

"Let's get to Josh," she said just above a whisper. She hoped Douglas and Tim had been able to get through to her brother and get them an escort past the sentries. She did not want to announce her presence for fear of the reaction. When in the Grey Mountains, the soldiers she freed had mostly declared their support for her, but that was more than a month ago and time and distance may have changed their opinion.

Without an escort, there was also the potential someone would think they were common soldiers and demand that they report in with the rest of the stragglers that were arriving. She could not risk either the delay or discovery.

To Stephenie's relief, as they grew closer to Antar and the massing of soldiers, a group of horsemen wearing the gold and black crest of the wolf, which was the mark of Joshua's personal guard, approached and stopped them. After a quick appraisal, Sir Walter turned his horse around and motioned for them to follow him. The five horsemen escorted the wagon deep into the encampment and to King Joshua's tents.

Joshua's tents were large, but not as large as their father's had been. However, like their father's tents, these tents were not gaudy or overdone, just a series of large practical structures. Her father's tents had been primarily used for meeting with advisers, leaving only a modest area for his personal space. Based upon the number of people she sensed in the tents, she suspected Joshua had adopted a similar theme with these smaller structures.

Outside of the main flap to the larger center tent, eight guards stood and Stephenie noted the colors of at least five families. Taking a deep breath, with Kas invisible beside her, she moved herself forward. Once through the outer flap, she could hear the discussion taking place in a backroom of the main tent. The argument for retreat was being made strenuously by what sounded to be an older man.

When Stephenie entered the backroom, everyone became instantly silent. She noted many familiar people around a table, but only a couple of them held something other than a mask of carefully schooled indifference. They all had played at politics for far too long to allow their emotions to come to their face. However, even Stephenie could easily sense the chilling of their mood on her entry.

"Steph!" Joshua exclaimed, moving to quickly embrace her. "Your trip here safe enough?"

She nodded her head and was forced to steady herself with her powers. After a long hug, Joshua held her at arms length and looked her over. She knew she was dirty and in need of a bath, so she was not surprised to see a little scowl cross her brother's face.

"You not eating?"

"I am, we were just trying to get here as quickly as possible. I heard Burdger was holding the castle against you."

Joshua nodded his head toward the table and Stephenie followed him over to see what the group of people were discussing. She noted Lady Rebecca Cole watching her closely from the other side of the table, the symbol of Felis proudly displayed on top of her blouse. She was the only other woman here, but her femininity was offset by the fact that she was a Master Priest of Felis, one of eight who were supposed to report directly to the High Priest.

Rebecca had lived in Antar castle for the last five years and it was not a secret that Joshua often spent a fair amount of time in her company. Stephenie worried what Rebecca would now think of her. A Master Priest of Felis and a witch were often on opposite sides of any conflict. For Stephenie to have hidden her nature for the years Rebecca had known her, would put Rebecca in an awkward position to explain why she did not know.

"Your Majesty, perhaps Princess Stephenie would like to refresh herself from traveling." Duke Yaslin Forest's voice held a sharp edge of disapproval. "After we are done with the meeting, you could catch up on her trip. We have some important decisions to make."

Stephenie knew it had been his voice that was arguing strongly for a retreat before she had entered. She had met the aging man a few times, but never really cared for him. Duke Yaslin held the lands to the north along the Sea of Tet. He rarely traveled from his castle in Turner and when he did, he always treated everyone else as though they did not have the first clue of how to do anything. Although Stephenie never wanted to have anything to do with him, the Duke had supported her father strongly in his policies.

"Stephenie is a Princess and is the reason many of us are alive today. I will not send her away as if she was a child."

Yaslin bowed his head. "Of course, Your Majesty. I merely thought she might like a bit of rest."

"I've had plenty," she said, looking across the maps scattered about the table. She recognized Antar and the castle. Another set of maps showed the western duchies and the small markers would seem to indicate unfriendly troops to the immediate west and south, coming from East Fork and Dentar.

After a moment more of silence, Duke Yaslin cleared his throat. "As I had been sayi—"

"Your Majesty," Duke Tallow interrupted. "Burdger's baron's have been demanding we hand Her Highness over to them. They intend to burn her. If they find out she is here, they will send even more troops. She's the very reason half of them have turned on you."

Stephenie's breath caught in her throat; she had not expected the barons would react that strongly to her.

Duke Yaslin cleared his throat again, "As I was saying, our men cannot hold out against Burdger's reinforcements. They may not be huge in numbers, but do you really expect your men, who come from all over the country, to fight their countrymen to the death in front of Antar? It would destroy their morale and since we can't even pay them, it's likely they would simply surrender. Antar is too large and the old walls not maintained. We could not retreat into the city. The only course is to give up Antar and head north. Turner is a fair distance, but once we are there, we can hold against Burdger and his barons..." He looked specifically at Stephenie, "and, we could secrete her further into the north country, out of sight and away from you."

Baron Frank Willow shook his head. "The reinforcements are still at least four or five days out, we have time to try and negotiate with Burdger."

Stephenie glanced at the short man. He was Joshua's age, but four inches shorter than her. It made others discount the man rather frequently.

Yaslin turned his glare on Baron Willow, "Burdger knows the reinforcements are coming. He's got no reason to negotiate. We can't do anything to him. Although we've got a handful of priests, they've already said they will only heal those that are injured. The High Priest has prevented our loyal priests from acting, but we can't count on Burdger's to do the same."

"But at least the High Priest won't use his powers against us. So we can wait a little longer to try and reason with Burdger."

Joshua cleared his throat. "Rebecca, if we were to assault the castle, do you think the High Priest will remain neutral?"

"Joshua, you know I cannot say with any certainty. However, it is my feeling that as long as we don't force any of the priests into the battle, he will stay in the temple and not get involved."

"And what of your involvement here?" Yaslin's acidic voice whispered across the table.

"Burdger has Lord Evans to advise him. He's a holy warrior of significant skill. I do not see why I cannot advise my long time friend."

"And the fact that you are the last Master Priest alive?"

Stephenie could not repress the grin that rose to her lips at the look Rebecca gave Yaslin. She needed no words to silence the aging duke.

Joshua brought the conversation back to focus. "Yaslin, how long will it take to muster the men to retreat?"

"It would take us at least two days to pickup and leave with any order."

Joshua frowned. "We are also waiting for word from Duke Marks. If he and his barons have men to spare, they could pressure Burdger to keep his men to the west to protect East Fork." He sighed, "I had hoped to already hear from him, but we still might get a rider this evening. That could factor into our decision." Joshua took a deep breath. "Okay, let's adjourn for some food then we will discuss the other factors after we eat."

The various people around the table bowed their heads and departed with a 'Your Majesty.'

Stephenie waited until the others had left and were out of hearing. "Josh, I thought Burdger was our friend. He and father always got along so well."

Joshua smiled, but Stephenie could see the pain and desperation in his eyes. "He thinks he can do a better job of running the country than I can. He's been atop the walls shouting to the soldiers about how the treasury was emptied by Mother. He's been telling our soldiers that even if they take the castle from him, that no one will get paid because we have no money. He's been trying to convince them to turn against me."

Stephenie ground her teeth, "The bastard's not any better than Elard. The father and son are alike."

Joshua took Stephenie over to a series of chairs and sat her down. "How was your trip?"

Stephenie shook her head. Her limbs ached, but her mind was racing. "If he doesn't have that many men, we could sneak in through the weakness in the east wall."

Joshua shook his head. "He's got somewhere between seventy-five and one-fifty. Not enough to repel a real attempt for long, but too many for a small force to sneak in and do anything. He'd pick our men off." Joshua leaned forward. "He's got enough food, and the wells will hold him for months. We can't tear down the walls; if we do, then we'd have no defense once we took it."

Stephenie rose and walked back over to the maps and stared at the markers. "Four days wouldn't give us time to rebuild even if we could afford it." She frowned. "These markers show you have about twenty-five hundred men. There are at least five hundred coming from the west and what, another five hundred to a thousand coming from the south." Stephenie turned back to Joshua. "Where'd they get those numbers?"

Joshua rose, but did not come to her side. "We don't know the numbers for certain, but not everyone sent the troops father had requested. We sent almost all of our own, but it seems some of the other dukes and barons held a fair number back. Mostly men from those dukes and barons that didn't come to the front with the rest of us." He stared at the table, "We lost a lot of allies to the Senzar. Which means our enemies are stronger." He dropped his gaze, before turning toward Stephenie, "truly I think we'll have to retreat."

She turned to face him. "And, I'm a problem. I probably should be sent away. We don't want more trouble to be caused by my being here. Perhaps that would reduce Burdger's support."

"I will not, I repeat, will not exile you. You are the last family I have left and they will just have to get used to you being a witch."

Stephenie swallowed and turned back to the table. She could sense his protectiveness, but the word 'witch' was a heavy word to hear spoken aloud by her own brother. She could tell by his voice, despite his love for her, that what she was still bothered him to admit aloud.

Putting that out of her mind, she stared at the table without focus for several moments, then lifted her head. "Josh, if we could get over the walls, there isn't a building in there we can't get into. I would imagine they've found several of the secret passages in the main keep because Mother discovered me spying on her. But, I doubt they would have found all of them. We get past the wall, we have Burdger." She turned to face him again. "How many soldiers does he have on the gatehouse and the walls at night?"

"Eleven on the walls by our count. The gatehouse has always been something that could be held with just a handful. I would imagine Burdger only has a few there. Why?"

"Well, if they are not expecting magic, then perhaps I can get the gates open before anyone notices and you can rush the castle."

"And how do you plan to do this? You brought down a mountain, I believe you could bring down the walls with ease, but we need those walls intact. Plus, you look terrible and I won't risk having you fall into their hands. They'd kill you the moment they got the chance."

Stephenie smiled and tried to force herself to look energized, despite how weary her body felt. "Josh, I'm not stupid. Plus, I doubt I could even bring down one of the walls. What happened in the Greys I don't understand, but it is likely that what exploded were the artifacts that were buried in the rubble." She shook her head. "What I will do is take my men and get us to the top of the gatehouse. We can come down from the roof and take out the guards. I should be able to open the doors from there."

Joshua stepped closer. "And the portcullises? They are both down and both doors are shut and barred."

"Once inside, we can hold the gatehouse, open the doors, and raise both of the portcullises. If you have people ready to rush the castle once I open the doors, we can take them by surprise. Perhaps even keep too many from getting hurt on either side. That would help keep people from feeling bad about our taking the castle back."

Joshua stood, still shaking his head. "No. It would take too long to raise the portcullises. You'd need a dozen men to do that alone. They would wake the remainder of the forces and fill us with arrows from the walls."

"Not with my magic. I can lift them quickly. I've been practicing with heavy boulders on the way here. If you have a handful of men ready to go. Perhaps a couple hundred ready to rush the castle as soon as the doors open, you can take them before they can muster those that are sleeping."

Joshua shook his head. "I will not risk you."

Stephenie crossed her arms. "I crossed Cothel with only a couple of men to rescue you. Don't get over-protective with me. I wouldn't suggest it if I didn't think I could do it." She sighed, dropping her arms. "Josh, we don't have time to come up with anything better and if the High Priest or Burdger learns I am here, they may not keep the priests out of the conflict. We have to take them before word spreads about me. We have to do it as soon as it gets dark. It is the best way to avoid too many people getting hurt. We can't start a civil war."

"Steph..."

Stephenie raised her hand and looked at the tent wall in the direction of Joshua's army. "I've got another thought as well." She turned back to Joshua. "We can't tell the bulk of the troops what we are planning, too much chance someone might get word to Burdger. Instead, tell the men to start preparing to retreat and pack up their tents. Burdger might even relax more if he thinks you are getting ready to leave. Have a small force you trust ready to go and leave some people in charge who know the plan, when the time comes, they can order the others to drop what they are doing and charge the castle. No need to wake sleeping soldiers. It will be a second wave and you'll have the castle before morning."

"This sounds risky."

"What other option do we have? Retreat and run away? You'll lose more support the longer you wait. People will start to feel perhaps Burdger and that bastard Elard should be in charge."

Joshua shook his head, but finally relented. "I'll agree, but only if you take some of my men. Your soldiers are good, but I'd feel better with people I know can handle things."

"No. My men know me and we trust each other. We've been working on plans since we heard Burdger had the castle. I don't need someone who might not take well to what I am going to do."

"Steph, you are being very demanding that we do all of this your way."

She smiled, through most of her life, she was always Joshua's student; if felt good to be the one coming up with the plan. "You should know me by now." She grew more serious. "We need to do this just after dark, it will give us enough cover and reduce the time for things to go wrong. I just need some time to rest, get something to eat, and explain everything to my men."

Joshua nodded his head slowly, but Stephenie could sense his growing excitement of the plan. "Okay, you stay here and use my tents. That will lessen the chance of someone seeing you. I need to start arranging everyone else anyway." He smiled at her, then gave her a big hug. "It is good to see you again. Don't allow yourself to get hurt; I love you too much to lose the last of my family."

Joshua's personal tent was barely large enough for Stephenie and her eight guards to crowd together. While his clothing was scattered about the enclosed space, it was not as messy as she had thought it would be. *Of course, he has less things here.*

"I am uncertain this is the best option," Kas said in the Old Tongue as she leaned back on Joshua's cot.

Henton, sitting with the others on the thick carpet that was covering the ground, looked up. "I would agree. You are still far too weak to use a sword. What if you have to face someone?"

She looked back and forth between Henton and Kas, no one else in the room could understand the old Denarian language generally used only by priests and royalty. As normal, the men sat quietly, waiting for their discussion to conclude. "This is one of the possibilities we've been planning for. Plus, we don't have a choice. Josh needs to move this forward. He doesn't have the time or resources to wait out Burdger, and if Burdger gets wind I am here, he might convince the High Priest to put priests on the wall, so we have to work fast."

"And after days of hard travel, we go into battle?"

"Henton, I assume you are simply trying any angle you can to dissuade me. Our march was not that hard and the five of us went into battle after more exhausting efforts than that."

"Fine. I give up trying to protect you."

Sighing, she pushed herself up from the cot, walked over to Henton, and knelt down. Grabbing his hands, she looked into his face. "Please don't. I know I put you into difficult situations, but I do need you." She looked around at the others and switched to Cothish,

"I need all of you. I really do. I know I am asking a lot, but we are needed and we can do things others cannot."

"No offer to let us back out if we don't want to do it?" Douglas asked solemnly. "You always offered that before."

She rose slowly to her feet. "Douglas, if you want out, just ask. But you all knew what I was before you volunteered back in the Greys. So, really, this should not be a surprise."

Douglas smiled. "Everyone always takes me so seriously. I promised you before the Greys, I'm with you 'til the end."

Stephenie shook her head, but smiled. "You all say I frustrate you. I can't tell where I stand with you guys sometimes." There was a chorus of comments affirming their support from most of the men. "Will? Henton? Your thoughts?"

"I'm in," Will said, snacking on the last of the meat he had grabbed when the food first arrived. "You know better than anyone else what you are capable of."

Henton stood, grabbed Stephenie's wrist and led her back to the cot. "Of course we are all committed. I just wish you would not risk yourself so much. Now, everyone, get some sleep! We will have a long night."

Chapter 4

It was well after dark when Joshua returned to his tent. His approach woke Stephenie from her light sleep, and she was on her feet before he actually entered the inner tent. She shook Henton's shoulder with her powers, waking him as well. "Are you ready for us?"

"Well, fortunately, the Mother Moon is not yet in the sky and her little red bastard, Mestecarn, won't light the sky much either. I've got over three hundred people sitting quietly and the captains and lieutenants are ready to order the rest of the troops to attack. We've kept the plan as secret as possible."

"Okay. We are ready here." Stretching her shoulders, she strapped a sword over the dark clothing Joshua had provided them earlier. She considered leaving the blade behind, but other than herself and her companions, no one really knew she would not be able to wield it.

Henton had roused the others while Joshua was talking and everyone followed the King out of the tent and into the night air. Stephenie breathed deeply, enjoying the smell of the sea blown in from a strong westerly breeze.

Joshua turned to Stephenie and pulled her into a tight embrace. "Take care, little sis. I want you to come back in better shape than how I left you last time."

She looked up into Joshua's brown eyes, her unnatural night vision allowing her to see the dark flecks in the brown. "You keep yourself safe. This will be pleasant compared to when five of us went to rescue you from the Senzar."

He hugged her again and she leaned into him as he kissed her forehead just as their father had often done. It left her content and empty all at the same time. Fighting back a tear that was threatening to burst forth, she pulled herself away and turned to her men.

"Okay, we have to be quiet. Just like when we were playing, only everyone at once."

"The guards changed perhaps one turn of the glass ago. You can hopefully run to the gatehouse without too much trouble."

She turned to Joshua and smiled. "We'll save the running for later." Looking back at her men, she nodded her head as she drew energy into her body. The power coursing through her tingled; using magic was satisfying as nothing else she had ever experienced. With a final nod of her head, she wrapped a field of energy around her men's legs and lower bodies and then pushed them up into the air. She heard Joshua's startled gasp as they rose quickly to fly high over the tops of the tents.

Closing her eyes, she reached out with her mind and visualized the ebbs and flows of the energy around her, in the ground, and most importantly, the gatehouse, with the pair of guards on its roof. She sensed, but for now ignored, the three other guards walking the northern wall.

Flying well above the height of the gatehouse, she angled their approach, subconsciously following the trajectory of a trebuchet's projectile, which she had always been good at aiming. Making slight adjustments as they neared the top of the large gatehouse, she slowed their descent at the last moment, landing everyone directly behind the two guards who were giving Joshua's force only a causal appraisal.

Henton moved as soon as they were on the roof. He grabbed the nearest man around the neck, his own large arms knocking the breath out of the soldier and preventing the man from crying out in alarm. Will and Tim grabbed the second man as Stephenie directed her concentration to putting a small field of force over the man's mouth, blocking his breath as Will pulled the man to the slate roof.

After a moment, both men were tied, gagged, and placed against the crenelations so that they would not be visible should anyone be looking from one of the far towers.

Using hand signals, Stephenie motioned for her men to head toward the small structure on top of the gatehouse that held a door leading to the interior floor. The gatehouse was the most secure building in the castle complex, but as long as those inside did not expect someone attacking from above, she had high hopes for this part of the plan going well.

She sensed Kas rise up through the stone below them. *There are five men, all at the far end, sitting quietly.*

Stephenie resisted the urge to smirk at Kas; she had already sensed the same. However, she felt his care and concern for her in his brief mental contact. *Thank you,* she thought back in response, allowing her own sense of what Kas meant to her flow back to him. A moment later, he drifted back through the roof.

Stephenie raised five fingers and pointed toward the front of the gatehouse. Henton nodded and started down the stairs. It was his one demand that he would not relinquish; she was to be the last to enter the gatehouse. She had tried to argue that she should be the first to enter, but gave in when it became obvious Henton was not going to relent.

The others filed into the narrow stairs that led down to the main floor. She could sense Henton already running across the floor as she entered the spiral stairs. She quickly descended the stone stairs two at a time with help from her powers and came out into the large room as cries of alarm were ringing from the mouths of four of the guards. Henton had tackled one man and had him around the neck as the others tried to engage the remaining men.

Fearing Joshua's safety, Stephenie immediately drew upon the energy around them and slammed the four soldiers against the wall and blocked the air to their mouths. She could feel their building panic as they struggled to breathe. Monitoring the emotions coming from the men, as soon as they passed out, she released each one to slump to the ground.

Will, Douglas, and Tim had rushed forward and were already binding and gagging the men who had collapsed, and Oliver was helping Henton get control of the last man. By the time Stephenie reached the middle of the room, the last man was face down and being tied hand and foot, a gag already in his mouth.

"John, Berman, Oliver, go down the east stairs. Hurry, get the door to the top of the wall barred and make sure it holds. Don't forget the one at the base of the wall either."

The three men took off and were quickly through the heavy wooden door. Stephenie turned back to Henton. "Once he's tied, I want you on the north winch. Tim, you take the south winch. I'll free the bar from the doors first, then pull up the portcullises. You wind up the slack as fast as possible, I'll hold it until that's done. Then you need to slide those support beams into the openings so the portcullis' weight is spread across the floor." She turned back to the others, "rest of you down the west stairs and hold those doors. I can sense people coming to check the east ones."

"Steph, can you get those bars without seeing them?"

She glanced at Henton, who had moved to the winch and was covering his left eye with one hand. "I can sense the energy in them through this stone and wood floor. Besides, I know this place very well. I know exactly what it looks like."

She took a deep breath and was reassured by Kas moving closer to hover invisibly by her side. Closing her eyes, she visualized the tiny threads of energy spreading out from her mind and body, reaching through the floor and down into the large open area below them. The large, reinforced doors were closed and locked in place with five hundred pound bars. Winches and pulleys were normally used to move the squared off logs. Breathing out slowly, she used her control threads to draw energy not through her, but to form fields to direct and channel the energy around the beams. The first beam resisted her effort, remaining firmly in place. Breathing in, she concentrated on how the fields of energy looked and noticed a slightly denser area near the blocks that supported the beam. Realizing someone had added metal pins through the blocks and into the beam, she channeled energy to pull those pins free. Once that was done, she resumed the work of lifting the bar. This time it lifted easily.

Tipping it on its end, she leaned it against the side of the gatehouse. Each portcullis stood a few feet behind each pair of doors, providing just enough room to leave it down with the doors open.

The sounds of men on the east side demanding the gatehouse door be opened could faintly be heard through the stone. Ignoring the fear she felt growing, she shifted focus to the southern door and beam. Quickly removing the pins, she more dropped, than set, the beam aside.

She took a deep breath and opened her eyes. Henton and Tim were each at their winches and ready, but her insides were feeling raw and burned from the energy she had drawn through her body.

"You can do this," Kas said softly. His own limited powers vibrating the air to generate sound.

"I know. This just takes more concentration than I thought." Closing her eyes again, she reached out with her mind and this time tried to lift both portcullises at the same time. She felt them budge and start to move. The chains rattled and the wood creaked, but the massive objects moved very slowly. Henton and Tim started to pull up the slack and then tried to offer help by pushing on the winches. However, each winch was typically operated by half a dozen men. Individually, they would not be able to do much.

She heard more calls of alarm from outside the gatehouse and knew that time was running out. Giving up on the subtle approach of using control threads to direct the energy, she opened herself up and pulled all the energy directly through her body. At first the wave of power felt exhilarating, but a moment later, the pain was intense. She released the fields that were keeping her standing and she sunk to her knees.

Exhaling both breath and raw energy, she pushed the power to do what she wanted, generating a gravity well above each portcullis, drawing it upwards and out of the way of Joshua and his men. As the energy coursed through her, she felt both of the massive wood and metal grids rise into the air. They moved so quickly that the heavy chain started to get in the way and jam in the pulleys. Almost subconsciously, she directed separate fields of energy to address the chains, pulling them up and over the large steel pulleys tied into four foot thick tree trunks that supported each portcullis.

Henton and Tim scrambled to frantically turn their winches as Stephenie fought to maintain control and simply hold the heavy objects stationary.

Henton pulled up the last of his slack first, engaged the locking mechanism, and started to push the nine-inch by nine-inch beam through one of the openings in the portcullis. The beam would spread the weight over the floor and take the strain off the pulleys. Kas, using his powers moved the second one.

Feeling her limbs tremble from the effort, Stephenie released the power from the first portcullis. At the same time, Henton and Kas rushed to the south end of the gatehouse to help Tim, who was still winding up the slack chain.

Beneath her feet, she could barely sense and hear soldiers rushing through the deadly passage of the gatehouse; her insides were too raw to draw enough energy to sense them clearly. However, through the small murder holes in the floor, she could see the quick passage of armored men.

Looking up at Henton who was waving his hands, she realized they had secured the second portcullis and she released the energy she had been using. Coughing on the blood in her mouth, she reached up with exhausted arms to pinch her nose shut so blood would not run down her face and onto her clothing.

"Kas, find Joshua and make sure he's safe!"

I am not leaving. You overextended yourself. Subtlety Stephenie, subtle control of the energy. Channeling it all through you is sloppy and dangerous.

Taking a deep breath, she forced herself to her feet. "Kas, Joshua is out there and I can sense there is fighting going on. Watch him. Otherwise, I'm going out there."

Kas cursed in what Stephenie assumed was Dalish, his native tongue, then dropped through the floor, never having become visible.

Henton was at her side and took her in his arms to steady her. Taking another deep breath, she shook her head and spit out the blood that was in her mouth. Her nose had stopped bleeding and she was not feeling anywhere near as bad as when they had been caught by the Senzar before they had rescued Joshua.

"You need to rest," Henton said in the Old Tongue.

She shook her head no, drawing in power to keep herself on her feet despite the pain. She turned toward the men they had captured. The one Henton had tackled and one other was awake. She sensed the other three were still unconscious. "We are all from Cothel," she told them. "We don't plan to hurt you, so just sit quietly and once

Joshua—King Joshua, is back in the castle, we'll let you go." The two men stared at her with a mixture of fear and loathing. She shook her head and turned away.

Switching back to the Old Tongue, "Henton, make sure they stay under control and the doors hold. I'm going up top to make sure things don't get out of hand."

"Steph, don't draw attention to yourself. Your popularity is questionable. You do too much and people's opinions might get worse."

She nodded her head, forced herself up the stairs, and on to the roof. She hated Henton for pointing out what she already knew. She hated the loathing coming from the men they had captured, which was discernible even to her mentally deaf and worn senses. She was going to have a lot of challenges dealing with the people of Cothel. It was unlikely that they were going to suddenly start accepting her, especially if she did things to draw attention to herself and just how powerful she was. The stories of other people seeing her bringing down a mountain was one thing. To see her do something directly was different.

King Joshua watched the gatehouse doors with a great deal of trepidation. His little sister was in that solid stone building and could be fighting for her life. He had never dreamed of allowing her to put herself in such danger. He had never expected her to rescue him from the Senzar and he never expected to be king when he was only twenty-four years old. He always knew one day he would have to take the throne, but he had hoped his father would pass that burden to him when he was much older. Having to pick up the pieces of a country torn apart by conflicting interests was something he had never anticipated.

"Steph," he mumbled under his breath. She had always been precious to him and he knew their father had loved her despite what she was. They had allowed her to be self-reliant and somewhat isolated because she was a witch. Something convention said made her evil and dangerous, but neither of them had ever wanted to turn her over to the priests. They could not face the fact that she would have been burned to death. They had never wanted or expected her nature to become public knowledge, but now that it was, their concealment put their own standing into question. *Well, I guess just mine now that father is gone.*

The fact that Stephenie was born that way meant their mother had committed some great sin against the gods while carrying Stephenie and so Stephenie was cursed with Elrin's taint and the curse their mother should have borne. With their mother betraying the country, many people accepted that. However, many of those people would now want to kill Stephenie so the curse would rebound to their mother, the real evil.

"Except Stephenie says..." he sighed. He wanted to believe Stephenie and her explanation that Elrin did not exist. However, she also said that Felis and the other gods were not what everyone believed. That he just could not accept. He was just glad she had not repeated those things to that many people. His only hope for her salvation from the people of Cothel was that she had fought the Senzar heathens and sent their army into retreat. She had saved several thousand soldiers who saw the holy warriors and priests fall before the Senzar and even saw the Senzar steal the power of the gods for their own use. He hoped that they would sway opinion enough to allow the people of Cothel to make an exception for the commandments that had existed for as long as anyone could remember.

Commotion on the walls near the gatehouse drew his attention. When the outer doors seemed to move slightly, he sent the runners to alert the captains to start ordering the mass of soldiers to attack. When the groan of the portcullises moving sounded in his ears, he offered a prayer to Felis for Stephenie and then led the charge toward the gatehouse.

Three hundred and thirty-eight darkly dressed men followed him, the only sound of their approach was the creaking of their armor. He hit the door hard and pushed, several men joined him and the large doors parted. He slid through the narrow opening as subsequent men further opened the doors. Repeating the process with the second set of doors, he charged onto the castle grounds that he hoped would once again be his home.

A group of startled guards were charging in his direction. Once they noticed the size of the invading force, the guards turned, crying out alarms. Joshua overtook the eight men quickly, hitting the first man with the flat of his sword and sending the man to the ground. The others turned and Joshua yelled for them to surrender.

Several arrows rained down from the keep. A few cries of pain rang out into the night. Joshua ignored the arrows and charged forward toward the guardhouse that was attached to the old tower that Stephenie had called home for years. Several dozen men followed him while others overwhelmed the handful of guards they had chased.

Before he reached the door to the guardhouse, another group of men came around the edge of the old building. They had been in the area of the chapel, which was blocked from view by the old keep, Stephenie's tower, and the guardhouse. There were a dozen men, with the leading man dressed in a fine jerkin. Joshua immediately recognized Lord Elard's slightly crooked nose.

Duke Burdger's son, seeing the larger force, turned and retreated behind the men who were with him. Joshua gave a one word command of "guardhouse" to the men behind him while he rushed toward forward. He knocked aside the sword of one guard and dodged around another as he pursued Elard around the corner.

With Joshua on his heels, Elard turned, "Joshua, you can't win."

"Elard, I've got more men than you. Surrender before someone gets hurt." Joshua kept Elard in his peripheral vision while he parried away the blow of one of Elard's guards who had broken free of the men with Joshua. He could hear commotion from the guardhouse behind him and would allow this guard one more thrust before he would change tactics to disable instead of trying to disarm the man.

"Never. You can kill my men, but I will not surrender to you."

Joshua barely dodged a thrust from a second of Elard's guards. Using his short sword in his off-hand, he nicked this second soldier's hand. The attack drew the first guard in, hoping to take Joshua down with a quick thrust. Joshua, anticipating the move, stepped aside, and punched the man in the side of the face. The force of his fist, enhanced by the weight of his sword, staggered the man. Off-balance, the guard was easy for Joshua to push out of the way and into the path of the second guard. Two dozen of Joshua's soldiers come up and overwhelmed the rest of Elard's men, pulling them to the ground.

Elard stepped back, but did not turn and run. Joshua was before him with both swords ready. "You still want to fight me?"

Elard spit at Joshua's feet and then threw his single sword to the ground. "You demon-loving bastard. Your rule won't last."

Joshua turned away as eight men took Elard and removed his other weapons as they bound his hands behind him. "Bring him." Joshua turned and walked back to the guardhouse where there were several men standing at the door.

"We've got nearly fifty men here. They're under control."

"Good. Keep them under wraps." Joshua looked to the walls and saw many of his men having swarmed them as well as more of his people at the base of the towers on the north wall. He turned back to the gatehouse and saw a river of men in his colors streaming into the castle's grounds. It meant that the captains had started the second wave.

"Your Majesty. The Duke is on the top of the keep and demanding to speak with you."

Joshua nodded his head and started in that direction, a group of two dozen men now surrounding him. "How many casualties so far?"

"A few injuries from arrows, not heard if anyone has died."

Joshua nodded and continued toward the large keep, which was considered new because it was only a couple hundred years old. The old parts of the castle complex were made of grey stone and had many more architectural details. The new keep, and other more recent construction, were tan in color and had sharp lines and flat facades. Differing from his sister, Joshua preferred the new keep over the old.

As Joshua grew closer, several of his men stepped ahead of him, holding shields at the ready in case the men on top of the four story keep decided to shoot arrows down at the mass of men now occupying the castle grounds. "Burdger!" Joshua shouted up. He could see several men among the crenelations that adorned the top of the keep, but could not tell which one was the Duke with the distance and the darkness.

"Joshua. I am very disappointed in you. You should have more sense than to press this."

Recognizing the voice of the older man who had been friend and occasional adviser to his father, Joshua turned to the four men that might be the Duke. "Me? Burdger, I am King. How do you think I felt when me and my father went out to defend Cothel and its allies from aggressors only to return and find someone we trusted has taken our home and then refuses to allow us entry. It is treasonous."

"Treasonous? Like your mother? Your family lost the right to rule when she stole the treasury and abandoned you and the rest of us to die."

"The bitch is no longer my mother. I have stated so more than once. Blame Kynto and King Willard as well, they consorted to undermine us. I think your family line has direct ties to his grandfather, no? And if my memory serves, your own father strangled his wife over a failed game of tables. Can we hold you responsible for those crimes?"

"That is nothing compared to the destruction of the faith of a people. Besides, how will you pay all these soldiers? There is no money here. They will starve and go without. You plan to tax everyone to rebuild your grand house?"

"Burdger, at this rate, I will confiscate your assets and use those. However, I would rather not do that. I appreciate that you stepped in to help bring order to the country when things looked bad. But we cannot fight each other. We have to be strong as a country now more than ever. If we battle each other, the Senzar might come back or just as likely, our neighbors to the north and south might decide to put us in order."

"I thought your demon witch of a sister destroyed the Senzar. Is that not what you've been claiming?"

"These men bled with me. Fought with me. We saw the Senzar slaughter our holy warriors and priests, taking the power of Felis for their own. My sister destroyed a large portion of their army, freeing thousands of us from slavery. She routed them and sent them running back to the coast. However, they are not gone. They could return. Do not make this an issue of my sister. That is not why you won't relinquish your hold on my home. It is greed and self importance. I am growing tired of your constant refusals. I offer you one more chance to yield. Remove yourself from the field and for the sake of our past friendship, I will overlook what has occurred here."

"Because you know you cannot do anything to me. The other dukes and barons will rally to my aid."

"Burdger, I have your son. If I declare you a traitor, your whole family will be stripped of its title and lands. Any of your family that has taken up arms against me will be executed. We have managed so far to harm very few. I am not certain, but it may be that no one has yet died. I can take the keep when I choose, but I would rather work with you and be at peace instead of see more good people die. This is no time to put brother against brother and father against son."

"Release my son and we can talk."

"I've tried to get you to talk for the last ten days. You and your men will come out of the keep and leave my castle now. You will leave your bows and arrows. I will allow your swords and armor, but nothing else. You will send dispatches to those troops on their way here. Once I have confirmation that those armies have disbanded and are returning to their homes, I will release your son. If you do not comply, I will execute him for being a traitor."

"He's done nothing to you!"

"He led men against me. I offered him the chance to surrender and he said he'd rather see his men die than surrender. A truly noble act."

Joshua waited several moments, but Burdger made no reply. "If I wanted to kill you, I would have taken the castle ten days ago. I want peace, not more blood." He looked back and motioned for Elard to be brought forward. "And bring a torch so he is visible."

Elard sneered, but refrained from spitting. "My father will see you dead."

Joshua looked back to the top of the keep. "What is your decision?"

"Very well. We will return the castle to you. However, the women should be allowed to keep their clothes and possessions. They are not a part of this."

"Burdger, I will permit that. However, all of their belongings will be searched. I will not have you remove more than is reasonable by hiding it under the skirts of women. Tell your men to come out with their swords sheathed. Their bows should remain where they are. We will search them as well and then allow them to leave."

"When will you release my son?"

"When I have confirmation those men you have coming to your aid have returned to their homes and your own men stationed here are heading back. I will allow you fifty men for your protection. Not a person more."

Chapter 5

Stephenie passed through the mass of soldiers toward the large tan keep. Kas had told her Joshua was in that area and while she was now able to recognize people she was familiar with by their mental signature alone, her exhaustion and the number of people crowded around her prevented her from being able to filter out the noise.

A few people recognized her as she and her guards pushed their way forward. This sent a rush of whispers and comments through the soldiers and within moments the soldiers started parting before her. Whether out of fear or respect, she was too tired to be able to tell.

When she reached Joshua, he was standing with a group of his advisers. Lady Rebecca was among the group and Stephenie noted that her approach had been watched. Stephenie gave the Lady a short bow of her head, which Rebecca returned.

Joshua's smile was forced. "Steph, I figured you would remain in the gatehouse for now."

"Sorry Josh, but I heard you have Elard as a prisoner."

"I do."

"He should be tried for treason. Before we rescued you, he spotted us in Venla. He sent a dozen men to take my head and kill Henton and the others. When that didn't work, he had men following us on horse for days."

Joshua looked around at the others, obviously taking note of who was present. "Steph, let's discuss that later. We are trying to clear out Burdger's men and make sure the castle is secure."

Stephenie hesitated, she had vowed that Elard would pay; however, looking at the concerned faces of the advisers, she was not sure how much support she would get. "Okay. Just don't let him go. Not until you've heard my full complaint."

Joshua smiled. "That you can count on."

"I'll make sure the tower and old great hall are clear. Then check on the state of my rooms." She waited for Joshua to nod his head and then she headed toward what had been her home for many years. Joshua was already back to addressing concerns of one of the nobles with him.

Exhausted, Stephenie forced herself up the steps to the old great hall. The large double doors in the middle of the hall were currently open and she walked through into the dimly lit building.

Inside the great hall were numerous fire places and long lines of tables, worn and well used. The new great hall, which was actually attached to the outside of what had been the original southern curtain wall, had new tables that were made with sharper lines and square legs. These old tables were dark with stains and worn smooth from years and years of use before being retired into obscurity.

Stephenie looked up at the rafters and the roof many feet above their heads. In the growing light of the rising Mother Moon, she could see points of light where hail and weather had broke through the slate tiles. It was something she had planned to demand her father fix. However, he was now dead and there was no money left in the kingdom's treasury.

"This is something! You lived here?" Will asked as he followed Henton into the hall. The other men, with the exception of Douglas, looked around in awe.

"This was my favorite hall," she said. "I lived up in the tower. It was away from others and I found it to be relaxing."

Henton walked ahead of Stephenie. "It also worked my legs, all those stairs you forced me to climb several times a day. I guess it was good practice for all the marching we've done since then."

Stephenie paused a moment; there were several of Joshua's soldiers still in the hall and down in the old kitchens to the south. "I am glad you did, but at the time, I'd have rather you not have been there."

"So recent, but it feels like years ago."

Stephenie's breath caught in her throat as she looked toward the door to her tower, having the same thought and then ones far worse. The last time she had been in this room, she had killed a man. It had been the first time she had ever really harmed someone. She knew she had not intended to do it. At that time, she had not yet met Kas and was as blinded as everyone else with regard to just what she was. She had known herself to be a cursed witch, damned by Elrin and her mother. The thoughts of those days left her hollow.

"Your Highness," one of Joshua's soldiers said as he approached her. "The tower appears to be clear; but, we haven't checked everything in detail. Someone could be hiding if they found a clever place to stay."

"Thank you. I will check the tower with my men." She turned to the others. "Will, John, Oliver, and Douglas, can the four of you go back and get our supplies. If I can, I want to sleep in my own bed for once. Ask Josh or one of his lieutenants to have cots and some extra blankets brought to the tower. There are some rooms we can all use and keep out of everyone else's way."

The four men nodded their heads and then left quickly.

"Okay, let's go check out my room."

Stephenie led them up the single step to the high table at the north end of the hall. She paused for a moment, then turned her head away and continued through the large door that led into the tower's spiral staircase. The stairs rounded upward to the left for the first five levels, following the outer wall of the tower. To the right, they descended into the catacombs under the keep. In both directions, they were wide enough to allow heavier furniture and supplies to be carried to each of the various floors. After the fifth level, two separate sets of narrow and tightly winding stairs provided access to the upper floors and the roof.

As they walked up the lower stairs, Stephenie tried to reach out with her senses, looking for the presence of any people, but the world was muted to her. She did notice Kas quickly ascend through the ceiling and disappear out of her range. When she reached her room on the fourth floor, she was breathing heavily and leaning on Henton's arm. In her room, Kas was waiting, visible and fully opaque.

"There is no one above us," he said in the Old Tongue. "I presume this to be your floor, as it is the only one with a bed."

Stephenie smiled and wanted to reach out and squeeze him. For too many days he had refrained from taking on a visible form. "Indeed." She turned to the others behind her. "Okay. This is my room and while I trust all of you, I would rather you knock and ask before entering. I'm a bit particular about my personal space. But for now, feel free to see what is left of it."

Using the light from the lamp Henton was carrying, they explored the room. The tapestries she had on the walls were ripped down and laying on the floor. They were never more than utilitarian, lacking any real style or flare. Her heavy wooden bed was still against the center dividing wall, which separated her bed chamber from what had been her closet and storage room. However, the mattress was torn and thrown to the floor.

She looked at the dressers and frowned at the state of the drawers. All of the drawers were scattered about the room and several were broken. Her desk was overturned and ink stained the floor and walls. Any clothing she had left in the room was torn, stained, and scattered about. "Mother had already taken anything of value. What was the point of doing this?"

"We can help clean things up Steph," Henton said. "Come on men, let's pick things up." He put the lamp on the floor and moved in front of her. "Tim and Berman, help me get the mattress back on the bed."

Stephenie could sense the concern coming from the men. *They must fear I'm going to become incensed.* Taking a deep breath, she walked through the doorway into her backroom and looked around. This had been where all of the things she actually valued were kept. The book case was knocked over, but this room had been nearly empty when she had left. She was angry, but too tired to give any more than a detached response to the wonton destruction.

She bent down and picked up the book case, pushing it against the dividing wall, but not over the section of the floor she could pull up and use to escape. The rope and clothing were no longer concealed in the opening in the floor joist, but she knew she could now float herself down into the storage room on the floor below without trouble.

"You okay?" Henton asked, coming into the room with her. "Do you need me to get you anything?"

She forced a smile and shook her head. "No. I'm not as furious as you might expect. I knew it wouldn't be the same. It just irritates me that people can be so petty sometimes."

"We can get some people to bring up fresh things in the morning. I just wanted to make sure you were not overtaxed with what you did so far this evening."

She smiled again at Henton's evasion. "I'm fine. I just need some rest. When Will and the others get back, you can set up in the storage room on the second floor. There are a couple of fireplaces on that level and unless Burdger found a bunch of supplies, that room has been empty for a while. Should be big enough for everyone. We can look at what's available for additional space in the morning."

Henton nodded his head and followed her out of her back room. "Okay men. Let's give Steph some time to rest. We'll head to the second floor and set up a watch. Two on at all times and we'll keep everyone, save for His Majesty, out of the tower."

"Nite Steph," Tim said as he filed out of the room with the others.

Henton, long used to Stephenie's assurances that she did not need much light to see, picked up the lamp and shut the door on the way out. With Kas' glow and her eye sight, the room was clear to her.

"Stephenie."

She turned toward Kas as she sat on the bed to pull off her boots. "Yes."

"I would appreciate it if you refrain from ordering me about like one of your servants. If it is someone that will obey your every command that you want, you would be best to seek someone other than myself."

"Kas," she said, panic filling her. She rose to her feet, one boot discarded on the floor. "I—"

"I am only here because I want to be," he interrupted. "I am not bound to you. Your ancestors killed me after all."

"Kas, please. I am sorry." She paused, searching for something to say, knowing her tone with him in the gatehouse had been too brisk and too sharp. "I was worried about Josh. He's all the family I have left. I did not mean to hurt you. I love you, Kas."

Kas appeared to take a deep breath, then he turned and moved about the room, his feet and legs fading slightly as he lifted them from the floor. Eventually he stopped in front of her. "I am sorry as well. I know you are under stress. However, I do not want to be simply treated like someone you can command. I am here because I care for you. Love you...in what little way I can. And I have said this before, but it bears saying again, I will put your life and welfare ahead of all others. That includes your brother. I will allow others to die if it is a choice between you and them."

"Kas, I don't want anyone else to die because of me. And you know that I would sacrifice myself to protect you."

Kas sighed. "That my dear, Stephenie, is part of the problem. I am dead. You should never have stayed on those mountains. You should have fled. How can I protect you when you risk yourself too much. I do not know what to do about you."

Stephenie closed her eyes as tears started to leak out. "Kas, please don't leave me. I promise, I will treat you better. I swear I will never order you about again. Please, you are the only one who truly understands me."

She felt pressure on her shoulders and looked up. Kas' arms were resting beside her head and he was making the effort to generate a field to mimic his touch. "Stephenie. I am not planning to leave you. I am just growing frustrated. I cannot touch you, not truly, and I see how easy it is for the others to give you a hand or offer a shoulder for you to lean against. What am I to do?"

She reached up and put her fingers through the edge of his cheek. "I will find a way to make this work, Kas. I swear, I will find a way."

He moved away from her and sat down in her chair. The second chair that Henton had brought up weeks ago, when she was still a prisoner, was broken. The pieces now stacked next to a fireplace by one of her men. Stephenie sat down on her bed and looked at him, her eyes still moist with tears.

"I need to go back to Arkani. I need to find something to fix what is wrong with your body. You cannot rely on using magic to augment everything you do."

"How long will you be gone?"

"I do not know. I wish the necklace was still available. I would at least know if you were in danger or if you moved somewhere."

"Sorry, Kas, that melted and burned up with the rest of what I was wearing."

"I will try not to take too much time. But, there are many books in the library, and I am not sure how long it will take for me to go through enough to find something useful. Plus, I need to ensure the ghosts are not becoming aware. That would not be good for you, or anyone else in your city above ground."

"If I need you, I will try to come to you."

"Do not. Your presence will disturb things. I will try to check on you once per day. However,..."

"You are not so good with time anymore and the lights in Arkani are not working correctly." Stephenie forced a smile and wiped away some of her tears. "If you are gone more than three days in a row, I will come down there."

"It would do no good. Please, for your own safety, remain here. I will not leave you Stephenie. I do love you and I can hardly stay angry at you. I just want you to be safe and it scares me since I can do so little to ensure you remain safe."

"Kas, you do more than anyone else. Far more than you can imagine. I will try to listen to you more. I promise. But I cannot help but try to keep the others safe."

Kas smiled, then faded and dropped through the floor.

Stephenie looked over at the door. Now without Kas' illumination, she had to rely on her mental senses to clearly see the large block of wood used to bar her door. Reaching out with her powers, she lifted the bar and then set it into the metal brackets. Years of habit could not be easily ignored. With a bit of effort, she removed the other boot and then crawled into her damaged bed.

Henton was standing the morning guard duty on the tower stairs with Douglas when the door between the tower and the great hall opened. Two soldiers followed closely by King Joshua entered and turned to go up the stairs.

"Sergeant," Joshua said in greeting.

"Your Majesty," Henton replied, bowing in as close to a proper manner as his tired body allowed. Douglas performed a less graceful one, having never being called to duty to protect an ambassador or anyone else of rank. "Her Highness I believe is still asleep."

"That is fine," he said in Cothish and then switched to the Old Tongue to keep the conversation private, "I will talk with you a bit first anyway."

"Your Majesty," Henton said, coming down the stairs so he was not looking down on his king. "How may I serve?"

"How did the gatehouse go last night? From what I heard, it appears to have gone without problem. I must confess I had doubts about Steph being able to pull it off. It seems I need to reevaluate what she's capable of."

Henton nodded his head. "I had doubts as well and they nearly caused the operation to fail. I will not doubt her again." Seeing the confused expression on Joshua's face, he elaborated. "I did not think she was strong enough. But I was not really considering what she can do. I insisted on myself and the men going first, thinking we would protect her. However, we had to cross the gatehouse floor and that meant those inside were alerted to us and started to call out an alarm. If Steph had not come down the stairs as quickly as she had, they would have gotten the alarm sounded." He met Joshua's eyes, being nearly equal in height. "She simply took the four men that were left and slammed them into the wall, then prevented them from making any sound while the rest of us tied them up. Had I listened to her and let her go first, I would not have this black eye and they would've had less warning than they did."

Joshua clasped Henton's shoulder. "I think she will change the way we have to think about many things. The holy warriors we've always used in battles could knock men from walls and start fires and crush people without difficulty. But when I saw the nine of you lift off the ground and fly so effortlessly to the gatehouse. I could scarcely believe it." He took a deep breath. "But, she is my sister, and I also don't want harm coming to her. She seemed well enough when she came to me asking about Elard. No permanent damage from what she did last night?"

"Not that I am aware of. I think she did more than she should have, but her determination is unmatched."

"What of that thing? Her dead friend? He still around?"

Henton smiled. "Kas. Yes, he's seldom not with her, though he does not have to be visible to be around. I think it takes effort for him to fade out of sight completely, but one word of warning..."

"Yes?"

"Don't refer to Kas as being dead. Steph will not appreciate it. In fact, you might find yourself ducking for cover. She will insist very much that he is alive, just without a living body."

"I don't like that ghost. It makes me uncomfortable. You have some influence with her. Try to make her see reason. She should find someone with a body—a living body."

Henton raised his eye brows and then realized who he was questioning.

"You think I am wrong?"

"No Your Majesty. Kas makes me uncomfortable as well, but you assume too much of my influence. Stephenie gets what she wants. The only one that might be able to sway her opinion is Kas and to be honest, I don't think he's got that much influence if her mind is set."

"I see."

Henton swallowed, still uncertain about Joshua. They had talked a while when in the Grey Mountains waiting for Stephenie to wake after she brought down a mountain peak. However, he never seemed to have as easy of a rapport with Joshua as he did with Stephenie. Henton considered that perhaps it was because Joshua had always been raised to be King, while Stephenie, the youngest daughter, had always known she was extra. "If I may, I have heard them talk and they have even included me somewhat, though most of the time, it is just the two of them." Henton wished for something to drink. "What I am trying to say is that Kas makes her laugh and smile and giggle and tease. She has a light heart when he is around. I don't think she would take that well to anyone else."

"Even you?"

Henton raised his eyebrows again. "Your Majesty, I am a commoner. I admit that I care for her, but..."

"Henton, you have gone well and beyond any expectations for someone in the military. You have a knighthood in your future. In fact, you've already earned it. I just don't have any funds to grant you at the moment. However, I can make the appropriate announcements regardless and simply owe you the trappings."

"Your Majesty. I am honored. But she sees me as an older brother. Not to detract from you," he quickly added. "She idolizes you and has been focused solely on your rescue and safety. However, she has no desires for me or any of the men who have traveled with us."

Joshua nodded his head and then smiled. "Be at ease. I was just wanting to see where things stood. I would never try to force her into something she didn't want. I think you are correct when it comes to Kas. She'd probably not take well to me insisting she give him up."

"I think she would tell you to bugger yourself," Henton said, dropping in to Cothish for the vulgarity. "No offense, Your Majesty."

Joshua laughed. "She grew up with myself and soldiers. That would be the kindest of what she would tell me to do. But I don't think anyone would take her at this point, even if she would consider it. They would fear her and no one would want to risk the ire of Felis' priests."

"What of yourself? Her presence here could cause you trouble. You have a priest as an adviser and I am not sure what her opinion is, but she definitely seems weary."

"Rebecca is, but she's willing to consider things. The High Priest is another story. I am trying to find a way to get his blessing. If that happens, then perhaps things can settle down. The soldiers mostly appear ambivalent or support her. The general populace less so. They didn't see what we went through at the front, and so they cannot be expected to understand as easily. They worry me. My father's primary support was from the people. We will have trouble if we lose them."

"Perhaps you should talk to my Corporal Will. He has some interesting ideas."

"I will." He looked around at his guards and then back to Henton. "Steph alone upstairs?" he asked, switching back to Cothish.

"Yes."

"Okay. The four of you can remain here. I need to talk with my sister."

* * * * *

Stephenie forced herself out of bed using only her muscles. She groaned from the effort, but managed the feat. She took a short walk around the room and tried to stretch without falling over. Giving up on that, she opened her mind and did what she had been doing for too long now, used her powers to help move her body.

She began going through the remnants of clothing and started tossing destroyed bits into the nearest fireplace. She had only managed to clean one small section before she sensed Joshua coming up the stairs. Smiling, she reached out with her mind to remove the bar from the door and pulled the door open as he reached her landing.

He carefully stepped across the threshold and into the room, turning his head to look for her. "You opened the door from over there?"

"Josh," she said, coming quickly to him and wrapping her arms under his to give him a big hug. "I am so glad everything worked last night."

She leaned against him as he returned her hug. Then slowly she stepped back. "Any serious injuries?"

"A few arrow and sword wounds the priests are seeing to. Five people died, three of ours and two of theirs. I am pleased that there were so few. We would not have been able to do as well without your help."

Stephenie shrugged. "I only did what was needed." She sat down on her bed, leaving the chair for him. "Any news on Jenk, Samuel, or Doug? Were they locked up in the dungeon?" She blurted out, unable to wait any longer to hear if her prior personal guards had been found.

It was Joshua's turn to shrug. "There were a few people in the cells when we took over, none of which I think should be freed, but I have not reviewed their cases. Burdger, despite not handing the castle back to us, was being fairly reasonable to the people."

"Elard would not be. That bastard only thinks of himself."

"Which is why I would not let him pursue you those years ago. I would not want him as a brother. He's locked up for now, but he'll have to wait." Joshua paused. "I suspect the others were likely killed before Mother left. The details are sketchy, but it was reported a large number of bodies were removed from the dungeon and tossed off the cliffs when she left."

Stephenie closed her eyes, but did not fight the tears that came. *I am sorry Doug. You deserved better.*

"Steph, I've got a question for you and Kas." Joshua looked about the room. "He here?"

Stephenie shook her head. "He's gone to try and find out what's going on in Arkani. He wants to make sure the ghosts are not becoming aware."

"What about you?"

"I'm fine."

"No you're not. I've been talking to some people. I would like Lady Rebecca to take a look at you."

Stephenie raised her left eyebrow. "Really? You want a priest of Felis to look at me? I doubt she would do more than request a trial."

"Rebecca has been open minded about you. She doesn't like the situation, but she's not advocating for your death."

Stephenie watched Joshua for a moment, wondering how much their relationship had changed now that he openly admitted knowing what she was. However, weakness was not something she was good at sharing. Finally, she spoke, "Yes, I've got something going on, but Kas is going to be the only one who I would trust to find a cure. Perhaps it will fix itself over time." She smiled. "I'll let you know if it becomes serious. You've got a lot to deal with."

She could tell Joshua wanted to argue more, but he changed the subject instead. "We have a money problem. The bitch took everything. Burdger wasn't lying about that."

"I mentioned that to you when we were in the Greys."

"I know. I was hoping that I'd be able to get some of Burdger's money, but the bastard either managed to smuggle it out or has hid it where we have yet to find it. I've got some trusted people searching, but there are lots of places to hide things here in the castle." He leaned forward. "Which made me think, what about the gold from that city under Antar? Can you and Kas get us more?"

Stephenie sat up straight. "I don't know. Kas doesn't want me going to the city, he thinks it will be dangerous. We don't want to rouse the ghosts. They've been locked up for hundreds of years and have basically lost all awareness of the world around them, just reliving bits of their lives over and over. If we disturb things, it could wake them out of the trance they are in, and they won't know how much time has passed. They will just see all of us as the invaders that sealed them in the city to slowly die. It would not be something we want to unleash on Antar."

"Can't Kas get the gold for us? That way it won't be you going back into the city."

Stephenie took a deep breath. "Perhaps. I'll ask him, but I can't promise anything and we'd still have to melt down anything. We don't want people to realize the jewel of the Dalar empire didn't die a thousand years ago. The Senzar were after old artifacts. We don't want them coming here.

Joshua nodded his head. "Anything at all can help. I need to be able to pay the troops and if I can do so quickly, that can buy us time until I can raise some money. I just don't know how the dukes and barons are going to react. We know Burdger was ready to make himself king. If we have lost the support of too many, it will be hard."

"What about Uncle? Any chance he'll give us back some of the money?" Stephenie suspected she would know the answer, but the prospect of asking Kas to rob his dead countrymen was not sitting well with her."

Joshua shrugged. "I'm waiting for a response from him. I asked for assistance when we first arrived, just to see what he would say."

Stephenie frowned as she reached down and picked up one of her boots. "I might know where some money is. I'll want to replace it; give it to Jenk, Samuel, and Doug's families when we can. Doug said they were saving to buy a public house, I think they had saved up a fair amount. That might help a little. I've also got a bit left from what we took from Arkani." She pulled on the one boot, and then walked over to her desk behind Joshua and handed him the pouch that was sitting on the old wooden surface. "It's not enough to do much, but it could cover a couple people's pay."

"Thank you, Steph," he said, rising from the chair. "This will help. Let me know about what you and Kas can do. I need to know what I have to work with."

She smiled at him. "You should have taken me with you. I hated being here with Mother so damn much. She was planning to cut out my heart and eat it."

"You mentioned that." He pulled her close and hugged her. "But if we had taken you, then you'd never have met Kas and come to save us."

Stephenie slowly pulled away. "Just don't get 'all things happen for a reason' on me."

Chapter 6

Stephenie climbed the outside steps to the guard barracks attached to the south side of her tower; the interior door between the tower and barracks had long ago been walled over. Going to the barracks was bittersweet. She had laughed and joked with her friends in the tired and worn building, but now many of those friends were gone. Most specifically, the three men who had been her personal guards before things had escalated with her mother.

She pushed aside the heavy wooden door and entered the dark room that smelled of sweaty men. There were a number of people in the long room filled with bunks and chests. Conversations started to die as soon as those inside noticed her. Within a few moments, everyone was staring at her, and a chill had settled in the room.

Stephenie swallowed and was thankful that Henton, Will, and Tim were immediately behind her. She nodded her head to the closest man, it was someone she did not recognize.

"Princess," a man halfway down the room said to break the silence. The brown haired man moved forward, his dirty clothing still in his hands. He bowed when he was a dozen feet from her. "It is an honor to see you. I wanted to thank you for everything you have done."

A man standing between the stacked bunk beds rushed forward. Stephenie belatedly realized he was Lieutenant Rintar, a man she had trained with regularly. He leaned his face into that of the brown haired man. "You want to thank her? She's one of Elrin's demons!

Worshiping that damn god of the elves! Spreading lies and hiding among us! A deceitful witch!"

The brown haired man, who was about the same size as Rintar, dropped his clothing and pushed Rintar back. "You weren't there. She saved our lives and killed the Senzar. She's a hero!"

The lieutenant held his ground. "That doesn't change what she is." He nodded his head as two other men came up behind the brown haired private, daggers drawn.

"Stop!" Stephenie shouted. "Do not fight because of me."

Lieutenant Rintar turned around to face Stephenie; his eyes narrowed. "I refuse to live and work in a place that allows a tainted witch to roam free."

She held her left hand out to keep Henton behind her. "Rintar, we trained together and laughed over mugs of ale..."

"And you were casting curses all the while. It explains why you were always so good. I knew there was something off with you. Damn witch!"

"She's not a witch," Will said, frustration rumbling in his voice. "She's been marked by the gods. She's been purified in fire and carries the mark of Catheri."

"Will, please..." Stephenie pleaded.

Henton had put his hand on Will's shoulder to restrain him.

"No, I'm not going to have them talking bad about you."

"She's a witch and should burn!" Rintar shouted.

"She already burned," said the brown haired man, unaware of the men behind him.

Stephenie tensed, ready to draw in more power and put a stop to anyone getting hurt, though she knew that would likely make matters worse in the long run. "Please, I don't want—"

"I will not remain here if you are in this castle. If your brother won't do what's..."

Stephenie turned her head, slightly startled by Lady Rebecca's appearance behind her. She had been so focused on the men behind the brown haired man that she had not been paying attention. Now that she was aware of Rebecca, she also sensed the dozen men right behind the master priest.

"You would challenge the High Priest?" Rebecca asked with a raised eyebrow?

Lieutenant Rintar bowed his head. "No Priestess." He looked up, glared at Stephenie, and then turned his focus back to Rebecca. "But, she's a witch. How can we be expected to live with that thing here?"

"The High Priest is preparing to examine her and wants her to remain in the castle until he does so." Lady Rebecca glanced to the other men who had lowered their daggers. "I can understand that you may all be a little confused, but His Majesty has only been able to take back the castle last night and things are still a little chaotic at the moment. However, that does not give you right or cause for hostilities. Things are being handled and will be addressed. When it is possible, what needs to be shared with everyone, will be announced publicly."

"My apologies Priestess. I only wanted to do right by Felis. I..."

"...allowed yourself to become emotional," Rebecca completed. "Why don't all of you take some time to think about your behavior? I will see fit to overlook what has happened here, provided this is the end of it. Any further contention of the issue of Her Highness must wait for the High Priest to hear the charges and make his proclamation."

The soldiers in the barracks nodded their heads.

"Good." Rebecca turned to Stephenie. "Your Highness, if you would come with me."

Stephenie marveled at the range of subtle expression Lady Rebecca was capable of in her eyebrows alone. She knew the priests and priestesses were trained to have commanding personalities. Much of the power the priests of Felis commanded was through personal influence. Rarely did they resort to overt displays of power. However, since she had started to learn magic from Kas, she had noticed Rebecca and others using small amounts of power all the time. In fact, Rebecca seemed to have tendrils of energy touching many of those in the room, though none of them appeared to connect to herself. The purpose of those energy threads eluded her so far; *something for me to remember to ask Kas about.*

"I was actually doing something for Josh," Stephenie whispered, remembering Rebecca's command to go with her. "I was looking for something."

Rebecca turned back to the others in the barracks. "If you would do us the kindness of allowing us the use of the barracks for a little while, we will not keep you from your rest very long."

The soldiers nodded their heads and filed out of the barracks. Most avoided looking at Stephenie or her guards. The brown-haired man, however, did offer a reassuring smile as he passed. Once they were gone, Rebecca turned back to Stephenie. "I had hoped to catch you in your rooms before anything like this occurred. What is it you are looking for here?"

Stephenie looked at Rebecca. Though the Master Priest had just saved her from getting personally involved in a conflict, the fact that her loyalties would be to the High Priest scared her. *Hopefully, the worst would be that I need to make a quick break for it.*

Stephenie cleared her throat, her muscles throbbed because of the tension she was feeling. Only her magic kept her from trembling. "Money that my personal guards had saved. I wanted to give it to Josh to help pay the soldiers, provided when we can, we give the proper amount to Samuel, Jenk, and Doug's families."

Lady Rebecca nodded her head. "Where would this money be hidden? I would imagine anything of value would already have been removed from their chests. Most likely by your mother's men after she took them prisoner and most certainly by Burdger's men that followed."

Stephenie nodded her head and forced herself to breathe deeply. *Mother, you will pay for what you did.* "Doug hid the money in the wall." Without further discussion, Stephenie walked over to where Doug and Jenk had shared a bunk and started to examine the stone wall. Even with her excellent sight, nothing looked obvious. Closing her eyes, she opened herself to the energy around her, sensing the energy potentials in the air and the stone and even in people. Focusing on the wall, she noticed an area where the density of the energy was less, as if there was a void in the wall.

Opening her eyes, she used her power to create a weak gravity well just a couple inches from the stone she suspected and was rewarded by the stone easily falling into her outstretched hand. Inside the opening was a deep void with five leather pouches. She quickly removed the coin-laden bags and handed them to Henton as she replaced the stone.

"Is that all?" Rebecca asked from the aisle between the bunks.

Stephenie nodded her head. "We need to count it and make sure the amount is recorded, but that is all for now."

"Then if you would, the High Priest wants to speak with your guards. The priests by the door are waiting to escort them. I would also like to speak with you in private."

Stephenie caught the slight change in Henton's posture. Will and Tim were less capable of hiding their concern. "My men have done nothing wrong," she demanded.

"Nothing will happen to them," Rebecca said quickly. "The High Priest is wanting to discuss you, not them." She turned to Corporal Will. "William here is of significant interest, considering he is the reason a messenger has been waiting in Antar to speak with the High Priest. The siege had delayed that message, but the man rushed to see the High Priest even before first light. It seems your claim that Stephenie is marked by the gods has spread somewhat. Did you discuss that with some of the soldiers when you were in the Greys?"

Will cleared his throat. "Yes ma'am. But I have spoken no lies. Only what we have seen."

Rebecca smiled. "You are not in trouble. The High Priest wants to hear your story personally."

Will, Henton, and Tim turned to Stephenie. It was subtle, but Stephenie interpreted the raise of Henton's eyebrow as meaning he would protect her as much as he could. She gave him a quick smile and nodded her head to the three of them. "Please, answer the High Priest's questions. I'll be fine."

Henton handed her back the money and headed to the door to be escorted out by the waiting priests. Stephenie stood silently with Rebecca until they had left. "Okay, now what?"

Rebecca smiled and indicated the door with her head. "I was hoping to speak with you privately. Is there some place you would feel comfortable talking?"

Stephenie refrained from making a rude comment, knowing that it would not be helpful. Her future was in the balance and if she needed to make a quick escape, she could not afford to get herself locked up in the temple or somewhere with attentive guards. "There are some offices in the old kitchens off my great hall. I call it mine because no one else really uses it."

Rebecca smiled. "Josh calls it your great hall as well. However, I suspect there will be soldiers garrisoned out of the hall as we sort through who we have room for and who should go down into Antar. We need enough in the castle to protect her in case Burdger decides to lay siege, but we can't have too many or we'll run out of supplies. Besides, having another large group of troops close by would deter someone camping at the doorstep. Assuming we can keep them loyal and not have them turn on us." Rebecca held out her hand. "Come, let's talk about other things."

Stephenie led Lady Rebecca into the old kitchens and a small office that had belonged to the head cook before the new kitchens were built by her grandfather. The room was dusty and dimly lit by one narrow window high up on the wall. Seeing an old oil lantern, the master priest called out to Felis and ignited the wick. It took a moment of sputtering, but the flame held, providing illumination.

Stephenie sat in one of the four chairs and quickly said, "Okay, you have me here. What is it you want to talk about?"

Rebecca smiled again; it was not the proud smile of victory, but one of consolation. She took a seat across from Stephenie. "May I call you Stephenie? Or perhaps Steph? I don't want to assume too much familiarity if you have not given me leave to do so."

"Rebecca?" Stephenie asked and Rebecca nodded yes. "Most of the people I know call me Steph. It used to be only my mother who would call me Stephenie. Regina just called me a stupid chit. However, Josh said you know about Kas, and Kas calls me Stephenie, so it doesn't bother me anymore. You can call me either, just not a stupid chit."

Rebecca's smile softened. "Steph, I wanted to talk to you in a nonofficial sense. Complaints started coming as soon as word got out that you helped in the taking of the castle. Both from servants that stayed in the castle as well as from some of the soldiers that have been in Antar. They do not like your presence here, and they keep coming to the temple and demanding the High Priest do something. They came all through the night and even more this morning."

"This is my home. I've lived here all of my life. They've known me forever. I've not changed. I'm the same person I was before they found out."

"That may be true, but what you are and what you represent is unpalatable. Your sudden appearance here, after the stories that have been spread by the soldiers who were in the Greys, scares them. They know the fault is from your mother, but most people, noble or otherwise, would have been taken into custody and burned, not allowed to live as an honored resident here in the King's castle."

Stephenie's jaw tightened; she wanted to scream. She had grown too used to Henton and the others simply accepting her. Deep down she knew this would happen. Her life was forfeit the moment she demonstrated her powers when escaping her mother. "So you're giving me a warning that I should leave the castle before they come for me?"

Rebecca shook her head. "No. The High Priest wants to meet with you. The report I mentioned from the west, it appears other soldiers from the Greys are spreading a similar story as the one your Corporal William has."

"Damn it, Will, what have you started?"

Rebecca raised her eyebrows. "Steph, you might want to be less harsh. It has given the High Priest pause, and he needs to validate the claim. If it is true, that might avoid some trouble." Rebecca took a deep breath. "Between us, as I cannot take an official position without leave of the High Priest, I believe you may have been purified with fire and the gods have cleansed you. Josh filled me in extensively on the events of that night and his descriptions match exactly the report the High Priest was given."

Stephenie closed her eyes and shook her head.

"What is it? You disagree?"

"I know Josh has confided in you. So you know that I do not believe in Elrin or Felis or any of the other gods."

"Stephenie, your belief, or lack there of, does not mean Felis and the other gods do not exist. It simply means you do not believe while many others do. Perhaps it is what allowed the gods to remove Elrin's tainted influence from you." Rebecca raised her hand to stop Stephenie from interrupting. "However, because I do not want to see Josh hurt, and I have always admired you and don't want to see you come to harm, I suggest that when you do talk with the High Priest and his other advisers, you do not make those claims. Instead, denounce Elrin. If you do not believe in him, then it can do you no harm. I will, in turn, keep what I know in confidence. Though it divides my loyalties between the High Priest and your brother, I believe it is what Felis would want me to do."

"So, when am I to meet with him?"

"It may be a day or two, depending on what research he will order based upon his interviews with your soldiers." Rebecca leaned forward and Stephenie detected a trace of ice in her voice. "I want to stress to you that you do not want to run away at this point. It would be construed as a sign of guilt and it would force the High Priest to rule against you. Which would put his relationship with Josh in trouble, and if they had a falling out, Joshua would likely lose the throne."

Henton sighed. He had sat for what seemed like an eternity in a small room off the main temple. The sun had long ago stopped shining in through the small east facing window high up on the wall. Based on the rumbling in his stomach, it was well into the afternoon and perhaps even the early evening. While he was not a stranger to hunger, especially with Stephenie eating most of the supplies on their journey to Antar, he was feeling his irritation rise. The mug of water they gave him after first asking him to wait was empty, and while he loathed to feel anger at any of Felis' priests, the treatment he was receiving was not what he had expected.

He sighed again. Most of his discomfort was fear for Stephenie. Witches were burned, as were those who aided them. The fact that she was a princess would not normally save her or any of those who had helped her. It was a weight he had borne their whole trip back.

He feared for Will and Douglas as much as for Stephenie. The others he worried for as well, but since Fish died, he found himself holding back when it came to the five who had joined them in the Greys. It was not something he was proud of, but simply the reality of it. His deceit in hiding his knowledge of her powers had caused Zac to turn on them and Fish had died because of that. At this point, he did not feel ready to bring more people under his wing. However, His Majesty had insisted on the additional men, all of whom volunteered to protect her, so he could hardly refuse to have them join his squad.

Rising, he paced the room again. Aside from the two wooden chairs and a small table, the room had a small painting of a pastoral scene with a soldier working a field. One of Felis' primary tenets, care for the land, but be prepared to protect it. The scene was not one he personally identified with, being more at home on a ship than on a farm, but it was intended to be a relaxing painting.

He glanced toward the door, detecting the quiet foot steps of someone walking down the hallway on the other side of the wooden barrier. Fear and doubt washed over him as the door opened. He knew he had done the correct thing in helping Stephenie, but people in power did not often agree with a pragmatic appraisal.

"Sergeant Henton, follow me."

Henton bowed his head slightly to the young priest, not likely even twenty years old yet. The air of disapproval was heavy in the priest's eyes and Henton held his tongue. There would be no point in arguing his case to this man.

The young man quickly led Henton down a series of hallways and finally into a small office. The room was filled with fine furniture and a thick carpet. Sculptures and paintings lined the walls, but the muted frames and simple lines of the furniture held a reserved air, acknowledging the power contained in the room, without shouting about it.

An older man in fine robes sat behind the large desk. Several piles of neatly stacked papers covered the dark walnut surface. He met Henton with strong eyes, but the dark lines and wrinkles in his face spoke of waning strength. Henton knew the High Priest was one hundred and three years old, but the man looked as if he was only in his late fifties. The power of Felis had preserved him, keeping him strong well after almost all men would have fallen from age.

"Sergeant, please have a seat."

Henton bowed deeply to the High Priest as the young priest left. Meeting the High Priest was something Henton had always dreamed of doing, just not under these circumstances. "Your Excellency," he added as Henton straightened. With an air of dignity that belied the fear in his gut, Henton crossed the room and sat in front of the most powerful man in Felis' church.

"I apologize for how long you had to wait. I wanted to speak with your soldiers before speaking with you. I know this must seem rather harsh, but I trust you understand the circumstances."

"Your Excellency, I expect this is my inquisition. Though, to be honest, I did not expect that you would be leading it."

The High Priest allowed a partial smile to come to his face. "The circumstances are most unusual." He leaned forward. "You probably know the Princess the best." After a moment, he raised his eyebrows.

Henton breathed deeply, not sure where the conversation was heading, but had no intention of being jerked around, even by the High Priest. "I am sorry, I was not aware that was a question."

The High Priest frowned. "All my information indicates she confides in you more than anyone else, is this not so?"

Henton could only hope the others had not spoken of Kas. The ghost's existence would not help Stephenie and so far, only a handful of people knew Kas existed. "I try to advise her as best as I can."

The High Priest sat back and pursed his lips. He glanced to a large stack of papers to his right, drawing Henton's attention. He looked back at Henton, his sharp eyes measuring and gauging. "You are a contradiction. A very significant contradiction and so that means something is amiss." He put his hand on the stack of papers. "Do you know what these are?"

Henton shook his head no. The pile was several inches high even after the weight of the High Priest's hand compressed the stack.

"They are reports about you. Did you know that Lord Nermin, your friend from *The Scarlet*, reported on you extensively?"

"I did not, Your Excellency."

"He did." The High Priest lifted the first page and glanced over it. "A most faithful and honorable soldier. Someone who is an enormous asset to Felis and Cothel." The High Priest picked up another page. "A man I would trust with my life and soul. Sergeant Henton is quiet, he does not seek out conversation with the sailors regarding his beliefs, but when asked, honors Felis most strongly."

The High Priest set down the paper. "Did you know we had intended to make you a soldier for Felis?"

"I was aware. Nermin tried to convince me a couple of times, but I did not feel it would be the best role for me."

"Indeed. We could not understand why and even questioned Lord Nermin about it, wondering why he would praise you so and then support you so strongly in remaining where you were."

"Your Excellency, I was performing a valuable service. I was teaching and protecting young marines. And to be honest, I prefer the sea to land."

"And despite your faith, you do not advocate Felis openly?"

Henton hesitated a moment, then decided to be frank. "I have found that those who seek to tell others about their beliefs are trying more to validate their own than trying to help others. If someone comes and wants to truly talk, I have no trouble discussing almost any topic. But I don't want others forcing their opinions on me and so I won't subject others unwillingly to mine either."

The High Priest smiled. "So Nermin had reported, and while I don't entirely agree, I can see some validity in that position." The High Priest leaned forward again. "Now then, for someone who is so honorable and faithful, why the contradiction? You know witches are evil and spread Elrin's influence, what possessed you to protect and aid the Princess when you were obligated to turn her over to the holy warriors?"

Henton paused, "Your Excellency, you may see fit to burn me, but I have never seen Stephenie commit a wonton act of evil. For as long as I have known her, she has always tried to protect Cothel and help those she could. Aside from a lack of holy warriors to turn her over to, I felt she was the best chance to save the country. If you burn her, you will be destroying a truly good and honorable lady. You would be making a grave mistake."

"I see. What of Corporal William's assertion she is purified by the gods? Is she Catheri's warrior?"

Henton paused a moment, but could not bring himself to lie about his beliefs. He could lie about a great many things, but his conscious would not permit stretching this truth. "She does not claim to be. She's told Will a number of times to stop, though it has not stopped him."

"What about you? What is your opinion?"

"Your Excellency, I am not in a position to judge that. She was consumed by fire, that I did see. The very rock below her was melted. The steel of her weapons and brass of her buckles gone as if they had never existed. Her body was engulfed in bluish-white flame. It hurt the eyes to watch it. I felt the heat from afar and when it was gone, she lay there naked, battered and beaten, but whole. Her flesh unbroken. She remained unconscious for more than two days, then she simply woke up. She said her bones felt as if they exploded and her body felt like it burned from the inside, but she does not remember much else.

"She has no idea why she lived and no one can explain it. She is special and I will continue to protect her with my life, but I cannot say for certain what happened and why. I do know that most of the gods, or at least the priests of the gods, claim that a witch or warlock who can survive a burning whole is to be considered cleansed. But I do not think she was ever tainted to begin with."

"I see." The High Priest sat back in his chair. "Do you wish to add anything further?"

Henton shook his head no. He was not certain what had made him so bold in his statements. Even when drinking he had always been able to hold his tongue, at least for the most important things. Looking into the High Priest's eyes, he suspected the old man had used some power on him. The trouble was, he could not be certain of what the High Priest would do now.

"Thank you for your time Sergeant. Please go back to protecting the Princess for the current time. Your report will be duly noted. Let Stephenie know that it will likely be a day or so before I will meet with her. In the mean time, all of you will need to remain in the castle."

"Your Excellency, I worry over the safety of our food. Will you permit me to send a couple of the men into Antar to purchase supplies for our own use?"

The High Priest paused a moment and then nodded his head. "I will provide instructions permitting it. I have already made a proclamation that Stephenie is to remain unharmed and free to move about the castle until such time as a council can interview her and review the claims of her cleansing. However, it would be prudent to take precautions. Not everyone in the castle is likely to be as loyal as we would desire."

Chapter 7

Stephenie stepped back from her window. She was a prisoner in her tower once again, only this time it was of her own choosing. She would not admit it aloud, but the reaction of the soldiers she had once laughed with, was too sharp and painful to endure. Using the rationale that she needed to keep to her rooms to prevent her presence from causing trouble for Joshua, she avoided having to discuss the situation. Even Henton did not press her.

Worried about the safety of the food for all of them, over the last three days Henton had Will and a couple of others make several trips into Antar to buy supplies with some of the money they had recovered from the barracks. Disguised, they left the castle each time with groups of sympathetic soldiers in case someone thought to lynch them for offering their support to a witch. Fear for their safety twisted Stephenie's stomach in knots each time they were gone.

On the first day of her isolation, Joshua had visited, but after an argument over the release of Elard, Joshua had not returned, and Stephenie was more than happy that he had stayed away. While she understood the reality of the situation and that Duke Burdger would tear the country apart if Elard was not released, she could not forgive Elard's calculated attempt to have her and her men killed.

That first night, still angry at Joshua, when Kas returned from Arkani, they fought over the situation in the castle and his demand that she leave for her own protection. Her arguments about Joshua's position as king being risked were unconvincing to Kas, and he returned to the library, where he indicated he'd have to spend more time if he was to find a cure for her condition. He had come back each evening since, but had said little, only claiming he wanted to make sure he was not wasting his time if she should have been killed during the day.

Frustrated at Kas, Joshua, and everything else, she glared at the desk on the other side of the room. Biting her lip, she released the power she had been constantly drawing into her body. She felt her legs tremble as the gravity fields she had been generating faded away. *I'm a damn warrior. I can do this!* Moving her left leg forward, she tried to take a step, but wobbled. Quickly compensating with her right leg, she stumbled and instinctively reached out with her mind to keep from falling down.

Primal rage escaped her lips and she hurled the mug in her hand against the wall. With her augmented strength, it exploded into a cloud of tiny ceramic fragments that scattered across the wooden floor.

Hating her loss of control, she flung herself face first on her bed and sobbed into the quilt. Despite everything, she was not getting better and the doubt that she would ever improve filled her.

After several minutes, she realized Henton had come into her room and she silently cursed herself for not having replaced the bar earlier. She wished he'd simply go away. Sniffling back her tears, she refused to acknowledge his presence. After a moment, she involuntarily took a sharp breath as she sensed him move over to her bed and sit down next to her.

"This can't go on much longer. I've let you lock yourself up for nearly three days, but no more. You need to stop moping about. The men are starting to get worried." When he got no reaction, he continued. "Word is expected back today on Burdger's troops. If they've turned back like they were supposed to, Elard will likely be released tonight or tomorrow."

Stephenie turned her head to face Henton and glared at him through bloodshot eyes. "I don't want to hear about Elard."

Henton nodded his head, not showing any reaction to her snarled comment. "I know you made your case with your brother and frankly, even as an ignorant marine, I don't see how His Majesty can do anything except release Elard. We don't have the forces to withstand a long siege and I'd rather not die strung up by the bastard Duke after he tears down the walls."

Stephenie closed her eyes to try to stop her tears. "I know that, but I want him punished for trying to kill all of you."

"Do I need to send Douglas in to talk to you? Revenge at the expense of everything else is stupidity. I thought you and he had talked about Elard before and you said you'd put it from your mind."

"You heard our conversation all those weeks ago?"

Henton nodded and then swallowed. "Has Kas come back today?"

Stephenie took a deep breath and struggled to push herself up. Using her magic, she tucked her legs under her as she shook her head. "When I saw him yesterday morning, he said he's piled up some coins, but mostly he's been reading." She closed her eyes and shook her head as tears ran from her eyes. Shaking, she leaned forward into Henton, placing her head on his chest. "Kas is so angry at me. What if he decides not to come back? What if he can't help me?" Henton wrapped his arms around her. "There is something really wrong with me," she sobbed. "I don't want to die."

"You've survived the impossible. You just have to give Kas some time. He's as dedicated to you as any one of us and he's got a lot more skills and knowledge than the rest of us combined. He won't abandon you because of an argument."

She shook her head, feeling the coarseness of his shirt on her face. "I can sense it in him. He doesn't think I'll survive either."

"You have to give him time. He's worried. We all are. But, no one's giving up on you."

"What's the point? Even if I don't die right away, the High Priest is likely to order me burned. Then Josh and the rest of you will do something stupid and you'll all eventually get killed. It would be better if I just died from what's happened to my body, then no one else gets hurt."

Henton grabbed her shoulders and held her at arm's length. "Get your head on straight soldier. You don't get to have the easy way out. The High Priest just might declare in your favor."

Stephenie avoided Henton's eyes and shook her head. "Why is he waiting so long to talk with me then? He's just looking to find a way to have me burned without angering Josh."

Henton shook her and she looked up to meet his eyes.

"You have a lot of people working hard to protect and support you, don't start acting stupid."

"It's been days since he talked to you. What did the others say to make him wait so long? What'd he ask you? What'd you tell him?" She pleaded with every bit of her being, "do you even think I'm not some cursed demon spawn?" She tried to wipe away the tears with her shoulder, "I know how devoted a follower you are."

Henton shook his head and pulled her back to his shoulder. "You're worried about what I am thinking? Steph, I simply told him the truth. I told him that you're the most honorable, selfless, and loyal person I have had the privilege to meet and that there is nothing evil or unholy about you. If I didn't think that about you, I'd not have supported you."

"What about in the back of your mind? No thoughts that I'm some demon of Elrin?"

"I know you are not."

Stephenie closed her eyes and allowed herself to feel the warmth coming from Henton's chest and arms. She could not remember the last time she was actually held by someone. For all her life, her mother had never wanted anything to do with her and that meant the nannies that had been assigned kept their distance as well. Joshua was seven years older, so holding her was not something he had done, and while her father had held her when she was young, it was likely five or six years since she had truly been held by anyone.

She pulled slowly away from Henton. She wiped her eyes and forced herself to meet his gaze. "You know I would not be here today if you had not decided to help me. You've saved my life many times. If I have not said how important you are to me, I want to say it now."

"Steph, I know how you feel."

She nodded her head and looked away, knowing Henton did not want to discuss that subject any further. "Kas thinks I started to transform my body. Perhaps an instinctual response to trying to pull that much energy."

"He keeps telling you to be subtle and not draw it all through you."

Stephenie met his eyes, "Don't you start as well. I'm doing what I can, but you don't just pick up a sword and become a master of the blade. The both of you need to give me a chance to learn what I am doing."

Henton raised his hands to surrender and Stephenie had to smile at his expression. "Anyway, he thinks I am caught: not fully something else, but not fully me. To get back to normal, I need to learn how to transform myself."

"How can I help?"

Stephenie shrugged. "Kas can't even help, not really. It's usually something that requires lots and lots of practice and only a small number of people ever master it. And almost never with anything living. Supposedly, living transformations were more often done by elves than humans, but even for them, that was not common."

"I see."

"So, now you know why I have a feeling I won't survive. If I simply died now instead of later, it'd save both Josh and the High Priest from having to deal with me and everyone else's reaction to me." She turned away at Henton's disapproval and then took a deep breath, "Josh is coming up the stairs."

Henton nodded his head, rose from her bed, and walked toward the middle of the room so he would be in full view of someone approaching the door. After a moment, Joshua reached the landing outside the door and pushed the door open before coming into the room.

"Steph?"

"Josh," she said sharply, still angry and irritated that he would be able to plainly see that she had been crying.

"Your Majesty," Henton said with a bow. "If you will excuse me, I will leave you to talk."

Joshua shook his head. "I expect Steph would fill you in later, so you might as well stay." Without looking at Henton, Joshua walked across the room, grabbed the chair, and set it down in front of Stephenie. Once he was seated, he looked her in the eyes. "You okay?"

"Perfectly."

"Don't lie to me. I know you're mad about Elard, but you have to understand, I don't have a choice. The barons and some of the dukes that support Burdger will attack if I don't release him. Perhaps it doesn't matter, since they're threatening to attack if I don't turn you over to them as well." He shook his head. "Even the dukes and barons that supported father, the few left that were not killed in the Greys, they want more control of the government in exchange for money to pay my troops. And worse, they are not certain that having you around is the best choice." He shook his head, "As you can see, I am having a rather bad time of things, so I'd ask that you leave Elard out of it for now."

"All of the barons and dukes?"

"Most of them. They smell blood and know we've not paid anyone since we got back. I can only delay by offering up the excuse that most of the war records were lost when the Senzar overran father. But, the people are going to want to be paid sooner rather than later, especially if they are going to be expected to fight or provide us with supplies. I'm afraid I'll be handing a lot of control to the barons, and it won't just be those that support me.

"This could easily be the end of us. They start taking more and more control and nothing good will ever get done for the country. The majority of them can't agree on anything, except perhaps that this might give them a chance at more money and power. But right now I need their tax money to keep the country running."

"Josh—"

"And uncle has been a bastard." Joshua pulled a folded letter from his shirt and handed it out to her. "You can read it later if you like, but basically he said he would send the money back with troops to help me if I turned you over to him. He said Mother wants to make sure you're safe."

"Bullshit. She wants to cut my heart out and eat it, not that that would do her any good." She opened the letter and started to quickly scan the page. "He won't send the gold even if you send me," she added as she read.

"That much you can be certain of, Steph. And don't worry, I would never consider giving you to him" He pursed his lips. "His response was written before you arrived, but it is obvious someone informed him you were not with me at the time I sent the original message."

She lowered the letter. "Could have been any number of people in Antar that sent him a message. We still have trade with Midland and Kynto, no?"

"We do. But it worries me how quickly information gets to him. He'll know you are here by now or within a few days. Messengers can cover a lot of ground if they have horses and people to switch off. I will expect he will try to undermine us if we don't agree to hand you over. The threats are clear in the letter and father always said Willard was an evil son of a bitch." He sighed and shook his head. "We need money to stabilize us. Has Kas got any? If I can start paying people, I can hold off the barons and we won't look so weak to Uncle."

Stephenie swallowed; she could feel the stress and frustration coming from Joshua. And for once, she could even sense a little bit of annoyance coming from Henton, but she wondered if that was directed at Joshua for pressing her for gold. "What would you have me do? Until Kas comes back, I can't go to Arkani and what about the High Priest? If he can't find me, he'll think I ran off and declare me guilty."

"Kas can't bring it up with him?"

"No. He can move things for short distances, but it would wear him out to try to bring up enough gold to do what you need."

Joshua pursed his lips and then nodded his head. "I can have Rebecca cover for you for a time, as long as you were not gone for too long." He leaned forward and softened his posture. "Look Steph, I don't mean to nag you, but for me to be able to protect you, I need to have a stable base of power and unfortunately, money is the key to that. If the High Priest thinks I'll fall anyway, he'd be a fool to declare for you. If there is a chance we will survive this, he'll have motivation to defend you."

Stephenie nodded her head. "I'll see what I can do."

Chapter 8

The light outside had faded when Stephenie and Henton followed Kas down to the lowest level of the tower and the old storage rooms that had long ago ceased their usefulness. The low ceilings were made even lower by the raised cedar flooring. In a back storage room, she allowed Henton to kneel down and lift a section of the floor that concealed an old wooden door that was sunk into the underlying stone floor.

"It appears Mother must have wanted to simply cover over the passage and leave," she said, noting that the decaying door had not been replaced.

"So this is where you escaped through?" Henton asked as he lifted the door and swung it open to reveal a set of stone stairs going down into darkness. "I was quickly kicked from the castle. They wanted nothing more to do with me and to be honest, I was happy to be away from the Kyntians. They lacked a sense of decency for the most part."

Stephenie nodded her head. "My uncle's forces are mostly mercenaries. He hires them from a number of places, a lot from within the country. He doesn't rely on his nobles to provide forces. Instead he taxes them heavily to pay for troops that are as loyal to him as money can buy."

Henton raised his eyebrows. "I did not know that. Sounds like something that can be trouble."

"Yeah, but he doesn't have nobles with armies to challenge him like my brother does right now." She adjusted the nearly empty pack on her back. "I'm not advocating that model for a number of reasons, not the least of which being, if he was as broke as my brother, he'd have a bunch of mercs in control of his country." She turned back toward the passage, "Anyway, let's get going. I can't be gone too long."

Kas drifted ahead of her and down the stairs. "If you are done talking about other things, you should know your exit was not simply forgotten. Of course, one might say it was fortunate that someone had the foresight to build a stone wall to keep people from passing further into the catacombs."

"Foresight indeed. That was me they were trying to kill by making sure I could not come back to the surface." To Henton she added, "Josh and I explored this maze of passages once when we were younger, but we didn't find much at that time and the other passages were always more interesting."

She held up one of the light stones she had received from Kas the first time she had been to Arkani and led Henton down the stairs. The stone's warm glow provided enough illumination to show muddy foot prints on the stone stairs. Once they had descended far enough, she used her powers to shut the trap door behind them. Kas' presence had already drifted far ahead, so she hurried their pace to catch up.

Once they grew close to where he had stopped, he turned away from them, arms crossed, and nodded his head to the hastily constructed wall. "You will need to break that down, should you want to go further."

Kas' tone tightened her jaw, but she said nothing. Instead, she examined the wall. A number of randomly sized and shaped stones were packed in with lots of mortar. The stones were obviously brought in from the outside due to their lighter color, a contrast to the darker stone of the squared off passage.

"So Mother, what was your plan? I die, you get the curse, or at least that is what you believe. Obviously you didn't want me to escape, but this wall is crap." She scratched her worn fingernail across the mortar and part of the sandy mixture broke free. "This would only delay someone a while, not stop them."

Henton took a closer look as well. "Perhaps that's all she intended, to delay you long enough for her to pack up and leave. It didn't take long after that night for her to go."

Stephenie nodded her head. "She had been waiting on confirmation that the Senzar would release Islet in exchange for betraying my father and the country." Thinking about Islet's smile and sometimes sweet expression left an ache in her heart. *I am sorry we could not have done anything to help you.*

"Well, if you insist upon going down to the city, you will need to remove that barrier. From the surface, there is not another way around this point."

Stephenie sighed. She wanted to mend things with Kas, but his tone was salt in her wounds, made fresh by thoughts of her sister only a year and a half older. They had abandoned Islet to the Senzar, who had taken her prisoner. Although many people understood that the Senzar would not have released Islet while there was a potential that Cothel would be able to cause them any trouble, it was still painful to know they could not help her. It was for that reason, she could not give Kas what he was demanding, the abandonment of the last of her family, and one of the very few who had loved her, even knowing what she was. Feeling tears threatening, she fought back her emotions. *We will work this through*, she repeated to herself.

Taking a deep breath, Stephenie drew in a small amount of energy and worked to form fields outside of herself, channeling the bulk of the energy through the fields she generated and not through her own body. She sensed a force building and pressing against the wall before her. Breathing out slowly, she adjusted the fields slightly and was rewarded when a sudden lurch of gravitational energy slammed into the center of the wall. Stones and loose mortar were blown away from them, flying hundreds of feet down the passage with a loud clatter. A cloud of dust followed after the stones as Stephenie's force sucked air past the three of them.

With another deep breath, she released the fields and glanced over at Kas, whom she caught with a momentary smile. She looked at him hopefully.

"That was well done," he said as he drifted ahead of them. "Very well done," he added softly.

Stephenie smiled, sensing a slight breaking of the cold that had been slowly growing in their conversations since they left the Greys.

* * * * *

Kas led them through the maze of passages that seemed to branch off in a multitude of directions, like a giant ant nest. He avoided the small wooden walkway where she had originally fallen when her mother's soldier had tackled her. Instead, he took them down a series of levels with small rooms that had at one time been used by merchants even before Antar Castle existed. A few bits of decayed trash, now nothing more than lumps of damp and unidentifiable mass, littered the floors of those carefully carved out rooms. Otherwise, there was generally nothing of interest outside the fact that this was once a prospering underground city.

Eventually, he led them through a tall passage under what had been the walkway that collapsed under Stephenie. The stench of rotting flesh was overwhelming and she turned her face away from the corpse of the soldier who died over two months earlier. The body was partially buried under broken planks of wood, but enough of his corpse was visible to give her nightmares.

Kas led them away from the body and out of the passage into a huge chamber. "This was used for large gatherings and on most days merchants would line the walls. The walkway above was intended simply to get a better view of the room."

Stephenie stood in awe of the room. There were thirty large, milky white pillars that ran the length of the enormous room in two rows. Grey flecks in the stone shimmered in the light from her crystal. The floor was a deep blue with geometric lines of lighter grey stone. The thirty foot high walls matched the grey lines in the floor and met the ceiling in a series of fan vaults.

"I'd never have believed this existed if I had not seen Arkani." She moved slowly across the floor, pieces of broken stones were scattered about, with the primary mass of debris on the right hand side of the room. "Those hurt my feet."

"That is what the Denarians left when they collapsed the main passage to a series of residential areas. Once they were sure we would never escape Arkani, the bastards apparently decided to leave everyone else to die the same way, trapped in their homes. At least for them, they were not sealed in by magic and when they died, they truly died."

"I am sorry for what happened."

Kas looked at her for a moment and then softened his expression. "The Denarians may or may not have been your ancestors, but regardless, you are hardly responsible. Don't take my irritation to heart. However, know that we risk the burning hatred of many ghosts who could awaken and are not likely to take the time to realize how many generations have passed since we died. I nearly killed you before I was even aware of what was happening and only stopped because you reminded me of Sairy."

Stephenie nodded her head and wondered how much time Kas spent thinking about his wife who had died well before he had been sealed in Arkani. Ghosts, he had explained, would lose touch with the world around them after years upon years passed and there was less and less to keep their focus. Falling into something of a trance, they would relive memories again and again, unaware of anything but the memory of what they had lost. Something changing in their environment could disturb that pattern and just as a hungry bear wakes from hibernation, that ghost could lash out at anything or anyone nearby. After more than a thousand years, nothing would seem familiar to them.

Looking into his face, she had a sudden thought, *he must fear that if I die, he will truly be alone again.* Angry at herself for some of the things she had said, she reached out her hand. "I promise, we will be careful."

"What do the carvings on the columns mean?" Henton asked, drawing away Kas' attention. "And what did you use for light down here, Steph's crystal isn't bright enough for me to see from end to end, regardless of what she can see."

"Those half pillars in the corners used to have glowing orbs on their tops. The arched ceiling would had several as well, illuminating the whole chamber." After taking a brief look at the pillar that Henton had been examining, he turned away. "The horses represent horses and the people are people. As far as I know, it was intended to simply be a pretty carving. Not everything is done to have special meaning."

Stephenie grinned. Kas' tone had been a bit sharp, but able to sense his mood, she felt some of his playfulness coming back. Seeing

Henton's expression, she quickly spoke up. "Kas enjoys inventing answers to questions he doesn't know the answer to."

"Well, if you insist on asking stupid questions, I will do my best to provide an amusing answer." He drifted toward the far left hand wall. "Let's get to Arkani. The two of you will need to remain away from the city wall. I don't want your presence to disturb anything."

As they approached the far wall at the long end of the massive chamber, Stephenie's stone illuminated a large multicolored plaque embedded in the stone above the exit. She recognized the crest from the doors to Arkani, even if the large plaque was much smaller in size.

"You made it through all this in complete darkness?" Henton asked quietly as Kas drifted even farther ahead.

Stephenie nodded her head, slightly overwhelmed by what she was only now seeing for the first time. "I was always worried something would come out of the darkness and get me. Bugs and spiders and such. I never expected there to be such beauty in the darkness."

The passage from the market chamber to Arkani was long and sloped downward with no real side passages. Eventually it ended, opening up high in the wall of a large, natural cavern. An old wooden bridge, now crumbling with rot and missing several sections, wound its way along and down the outer edge of the cavern to the paved area that stood before the large stone doors of Arkani.

The bridge originally had a covered top with open sides to provide a view of the natural cavern as well as the unnaturally smooth wall that formed the outer dome of the city. In that smooth stone, were the massive doors that came to a peak thirty-five feet off the ground. The panels of the doors were filled with geometric patterns of deep blues, greens, and reds. Raised scroll work and lettering reflected a pristine gold even in the dim light of the stone Stephenie carried.

The paved area before the doors extended to the foot of the wooden bridge and into a natural tunnel to the left of the doors. That dark passage was at one time the primary road that ran several miles between the surface and Arkani. Collapsed by the Denarians in two locations, Stephenie had barely managed to crawl through narrow openings in the debris when she left the last time.

Kas drew her attention. "The bridge was enchanted at one point to withstand rot from all the moisture dripping from the ceiling. However, time has allowed the magic to fade and sections to collapse."

She wanted to ask Kas how something could be enchanted to hold magical properties, but he had already drifted through the bridge and down to the base of the flow stone on which part of the bridge had been constructed.

Without waiting for Henton to comment, she drew in energy and flew the two of them from where they stood, high up in he chamber, to the base of the flow stone and into a rubble field where Kas was waiting. "The last time, I fell through that first missing section and bounced down and cut up my arm on one of the sharp rocks sticking out."

Henton looked over the steeply sloped mass that had the appearance of wet, rippled glass. The occasional chunk of a sharp rock stood out at odd angles, where they presumably landed after falling from the ceiling before being absorbed into the larger flow stone. "I've never seen anything like that before."

"It forms over centuries as mineral rich water leaves small deposits," Kas said. "These stalagmites," he indicated a field of one foot high columns of stone growing from the ground, "were not here when I lived. Though, they may someday reach the ceiling if enough time passes."

"I just hope the ceiling doesn't fall down and meet them," Henton said, looking up into the darkness, not able to clearly see the stone roof above their heads.

Kas shrugged. "It is unlikely to collapse, but if it does and it crushes you, I do not expect you will suffer long."

"Thanks," Henton grumbled.

Kas turned and they all faced the magnificent doors. "Trying to save ourselves from the invasion, those of us inside reinforced the protective magic on the walls and doors." He shook his head, "the Denarians, unable to gain entry, decided to do the same and the combined magic created a seal that even death could not escape." Kas turned to the right and moved through the boulder field, avoiding the paved area. "Please stay away from the walls as much as possible, I don't want someone to sense either of you." After a short distance, he stopped next to a larger boulder.

Stephenie could see the narrow crack in the smooth wall of Arkani on the other side of Kas. The light from her stone drowned out the subtle reddish glow reflected from the city's lights. It had been that initial glow that had originally drawn her attention in the total darkness. The single crack in the city wall was only a couple feet wide and a few feet high. It was large enough for Henton, if he tried to move through it, but she knew the angle and jagged nature of the opening made climbing through the thick wall a difficult challenge.

"I have been storing the valuables I collected over here," Kas said, drawing her attention. "You should take the time to practice manipulating matter. Or at least the shape of it. To actually transform matter will be a much greater task."

"What do you want me to do with matter?"

"I've told you before, matter is made up of very small pieces. It might look solid, but it is not. There are fields that hold all these small pieces together. If you can weaken those fields, you can allow the pieces to move around each other, just as if it were a syrup or a liquid." The empty leather backpack that Stephenie had given Kas days earlier to gather the coins rose from the ground into Kas' hand. "You can weaken those fields with heat, yes. Just like changing ice to water. However, heat can destroy things and in order to learn the next steps in healing your body, you need to learn to break down these fields without exciting the matter with heat." A few coins floated into the air and formed a pile on top of a rock. "Your challenge will be to weaken the fields, then merge the coins together into a bar. I don't need to remind you that we must hide all trace of the Dalar empire, so all markings must be removed from the coins. You don't want someone thinking this city still exists, find it, and then stir up the ghosts."

"That's a lot of coins," Henton commented, looking at the two piles beneath Kas.

Kas looked down, but then shrugged. "Arkani was rich. I have not counted, but I did separate the gold coins and the silver ones. Do not do anything using too much power; everything I read indicates this is another one of the more subtle skills, so raw power is not what is needed. Remember, anything too strong might draw attention."

Kas floated toward the crack, which was as far as Stephenie knew, the only break in the magical seal that had locked everyone in Arkani to slowly die of starvation. "I'll spend some time in the library and gather a couple of books that are important. I'll try to get some more coins as well."

"Wait. Can you show me how it's done?" Stephenie asked, hoping to have something she could mimic.

"I wish I could. I am far more limited in capability in this form. And even when I had a body, I lacked the skill. The master formers, those who formed the shape of the stone wall around Arkani and even most of the buildings in the city, had years of practice. One of the books I will bring may explain it better, but it was written in an older Dalish dialect and even I struggle with that. But you are able to sense fields unlike anyone I ever knew, perhaps that will be enough."

She nodded her head. "Be safe, Kas."

He nodded his head and continued to the crack. After a moment, the leather pack disappeared out of sight and Stephenie felt him drift out of her range.

"Steph, that's a lot of gold and silver, if you can, try to make small bars, not large ones. I've had to carry a chest of tribute once and it nearly pulled my arms out of their sockets."

She held out her hands in surrender. "You are assuming I'll be able to create this field in the first place."

Stephenie continued to stare at the pile of coins sitting on the jagged boulder. She tried to do as Kas had instructed, to create a field of energy that would loosen the bonds between the small bits of metal so that she could move the bits around without having to heat the gold. She wanted to take the stack of coins and form a solid column, but so far nothing had worked.

Exhaling, Stephenie closed her eyes, hoping she could visualize the process more completely with her eyes closed. However, all she could sense was the potential energy in the coins. She just could not feel or sense this subtle field that Kas had mentioned.

Frustrated, she sat back on her heels and glanced at Henton who she knew had been staring at her for what had to be at least one turn of the glass, most likely more. "You are going to get very bored watching me."

"Well, I've got nothing better to do for the time being. Besides, I enjoy watching you. You always give everything your full effort and that inspires me."

She shook her head. "My brain hurts, and not from drawing in energy. This is like staring at a flame until you are blind and then trying to see the wall on the other side of the room through it. This is just so damn frustrating. If it takes skilled people years to be able to do this when they have people to show them, then damn it, how am I going to do it on my own?"

He shrugged. "Be practical about it. There has to be steps to learning how to do it. Take small steps. Work backwards when you can. Someone had to discover it could be done in the first place."

Looking at all the piles of coins, Stephenie took a deep breath and directed energy at the nearest pile, allowing heat to build in the coins and melt the gold. Slowly the gold started to slump and she generated a gravity field to crush the gold into one solid mass. Once that was done, she reversed the flow of energy and drew the heat away from the gold. The effort gave her no insight into the fields. Angry at not being able to make any progress, she continued to draw out energy until frost formed on the bar that was only half an inch in diameter and a couple of inches long.

"I think that is cheating."

Stephenie looked over at Henton and shrugged. "Well, I had to do something." Using her mind, she tossed the ice cold gold over to Henton to place into one of the leather packs they had brought down to carry the gold back to the surface. She piled more coins on the stone, building a mass large enough to actually make a brick of gold. Again she heated the metal and formed it into a bar.

Breathing slowly, she closed her eyes and tried to focus on the gold and look at the whole mass. Very briefly, she thought she noticed a subtle pattern in the potential energy, as if it was as Kas described, not a single mass, but in fact a group of many objects. As the gold cooled, this distinction seemed to fade and she was not sure if she had only imagined the variances in the first place.

Opening her eyes, she used her powers to toss this bar to Henton, who dodged away instead of catching it.

"That was uncalled for." He picked it up and hefted it. "Weighs about twenty-five pounds. You want to kill me with this?"

"Sorry," she said, feeling quite stupid for thinking anyone would be able to catch something like that. Suddenly, the guilt was pushed from her thoughts. "Henton, don't move." She slowly rose to her feet, sensing a presence off to their right, just coming through the crack in the wall. This presence she knew was not Kas.

"What is it?"

Stephenie shook her head. She could see the faint glow of a humanoid form gliding in their direction. She could sense a general state of confusion and anger. The ghost seemed to be casting around, examining the situation. When it noticed her and Henton, it moved quickly in their direction.

"Stay behind me," she ordered, noting Henton's forward movement. "You can't fight this."

Remembering the last time she fought a ghost and the blisters that had been left on her shoulder from the icy touch of the ghost drawing energy out of her flesh, Stephenie unleashed a blast of raw energy at the ghost. Blue-white lightning leapt from her hand, through the dense area of energy that made up the ghost, and struck the smooth wall of Arkani, crackling and bouncing off the magically protected stone.

The ghost seemed disoriented for a moment, then came at her with more fury than before. It covered the distance in an instant. With only a bearded head, shoulder, and hand clearly visible, the man was reaching for her face.

Stephenie tried the tactic she had used when she was in the library, linking a channel from the ghost's energy to an area across the cavern and allowed as much energy to flow through that channel as possible. She paused, almost closing her eyes to get a better sense of the fields and the impact it had. The ghost had been relocated, but it had not dissociated.

Damn it Kas, how do you kill a ghost? She did not have time to wonder, as the ghost blinked its way across the cavern almost faster than she could follow. This time it went for Henton.

"Watch out!" she cried as Henton cursed, dropping low in a futile attempt to avoid the spirit. Desperate, she linked another channel to the ghost, this time drawing the ghost's energy toward her, hoping to draw it away from Henton.

The ghost slowed it's attack, which was basically an attempt to completely envelope Henton. Stephenie opened herself fully, gorging herself on the ghost's energy. She could feel her insides start to burn with the excess power coursing through her, but the ghost still seemed to have strength and was now trying to move away from both of them.

Not wanting to give it a chance to escape and possibly find the surface and some helpless person, she continued to draw in energy. She knew the energy was not just from the ghost; her link was not fine enough to isolate just the spirit's energy. Making it worse, she had the sense that the ghost was also drawing energy from the surroundings in an effort to sustain its existence and cohesion.

Tears streamed from her eyes and her limbs quivered from the pain of the energy burning through her. She sank to her knees, no longer able to control the gravity field she was using to stand.

Finally, unable to contain the energy in her body, she dumped it out trough her left hand, pointing it away from Henton and herself. Blue flames enveloped her hand and forearm, shooting out in a billowing cone at least ten feet long.

Unable to breathe, she took one last determined pull and tugged again at the ghost. She sensed his cohesion starting to break down, as what made up his personality was slowly ripped apart and drawn through her body. *I'm sorry,* she thought with some forced detachment to the man she knew had been called Rowlin. *I just can't let you go.* With one last struggle, the ghost's essence finally broke apart and passed through her tortured body, only to be broken down and shot out again as random energy.

Gasping for breath, Stephenie opened her eyes. She looked down and noticed the remains of her sleeve was on fire around her bicep. With a thought, she snuffed out the flames and then knocked the burnt fragments from her arm. She thought she noticed a slight iridescent shimmer from her skin, but after flexing her aching arm, her skin looked normal.

Still breathing heavily, she looked up at Henton, who was again staring at her. Realizing what he was thinking, she blurted out, "Please, don't tell anyone."

He shook his head as he scrambled over to her. "Are you hurt?"

On unsteady legs, she forced herself to her feet. The blood running down the back of her throat told her she had over extended herself, but the intense burning she had felt throughout her body had subsided and she was surprised she was not in more pain.

Henton took her left arm in his hands. "I don't see any burns." He met her eyes. "I don't suppose you can explain this." He glanced to a melted lump of gold on the stone. The coins she had stacked had liquified for a brief moment when the flames had washed over the rock where they had been sitting.

"I don't know," she said slowly, trying to think back to what she might have done with her arm. *I was dumping as much energy as I could, but other than that...* She shook her head. "I didn't do anything specifically."

Henton released her arm. "Steph, I don't think you need to worry about being burned. There's barely a mark on you and that was a very hot flame. I felt the heat from where I was twenty feet away. I'd suspect if they try to burn you, you'll walk out of the fire untouched. Even the hairs on your arm are fine."

She shook her head. "I don't know. That wasn't so much fire as raw energy." She turned away from him, frightened about the implications of what just happened. "I mean, crap, I burned my tongue this morning on tea I had heated. I hardly think I'm impervious to flame."

Henton turned her face to meet his eyes. "Steph, I think you would survive just fine. Not that I want them to try, but I'm not worried."

"You just want to see me naked." She shifted her shoulder forward to draw his attention to the burned sleeve. "Set me on fire so you can burn off all my clothing again. That what you want? Me standing about with a crowd looking?"

"Steph, I've seen you naked. Probably more than anyone else, considering I was the one to clean up after you in the Greys. Kas would hardly allow anyone else near you, and he couldn't really do it himself."

Stephenie blushed. Realizing just how exposed she probably was when she was unconscious for nearly three days. "Let's keep this to ourselves. I really don't want Will going even further with me being some chosen person. He's gone too far as it is. There's got to be some explanation that doesn't involve more signs from the gods."

Henton nodded his head. "I'll keep it between us, but..."

Stephenie turned her head back to the opening and smiled. A leather bag emerged from the narrow crack in the wall, followed immediately by Kas. "What happened? I felt a ripple from you using lots of magic. I said to be discrete."

"Kas," Stephenie's voice trembled slightly with relief. "I think I killed someone from Arkani. I am sorry, I didn't want to, he seemed confused, but when he noticed us, he came at us."

Kas blinked quickly to her side, the bag dropping to the ground where he had been. "Are you hurt? What happened?" Noticing her sleeve, he started examining her arm, which she allowed him to move around with the fields he was creating. He looked her over and then around the large chamber. "Are you sure you destroyed the ghost? When you were here last, I don't think you did more than drive that one ghost off."

"I pulled his energy through me this time instead of trying to push it away. I think it ripped his cohesion apart. It felt similar to how others have felt when they have died, but much quicker, no slow lingering."

"You have blood on your face. You are sure you are okay?"

Stephenie nodded. "Just a little overtaxed."

Kas relaxed some, but frowned. "I am glad you are safe, but this will cause trouble. I felt you from well within the walls. And if a ghost came out, obviously my rooting around for gold has disturbed others. It may not be safe for me to even go back to the library." He cursed in Dalish and shook his head. "How am I to find a way to heal you if it is too risky to get to the library?"

Stephenie felt her chest tighten.

Kas sighed and looked toward the pack he had dropped. "Perhaps we have enough. I just don't know. But, unleashing a few thousand ghosts won't help anything either. I will have to watch from out here for a while to make sure no one else comes out. I think you should head back to the surface. I will join you when I can."

He paused and then lifted her chin with a field around his hand. "This may not be as bad as it sounds. I was not finding much in the library as it was. I suspect that most of the abilities you need to develop were not shared in general libraries. Probably more in private collections and only shared with a select few apprentices. Any private collections in Arkani decayed long ago. The library only lasted because it was constructed to preserve documents."

"But Kas, I wasn't able to do it. I might have started to see something, but what I did, I did with heat."

"It will take time. We just have to make sure it does not take too much time." He nodded to the coins as he went to retrieve the bag he dropped. "Finish making the bars and head to the surface."

Chapter 9

Stephenie climbed the stairs to her room, exhausted and ready to sleep, but she knew Lady Rebecca was waiting in her room; the others had warned her. Containing her irritation at her personal space being invaded, she met the Master Priest, who was equally aware of Stephenie's presence, at her doorway.

"Stephenie!" Lady Rebecca's concern was evident in her voice, but her emotional presence was as muted as ever. "You're a mess and you're late."

Stephenie stifled a yawn, noting the amount of light coming in through the windows of the tower meant it was likely mid-morning. "Things took longer than expected."

"Are you injured?"

Stephenie shook her head as she walked across the floor of her room. "Who gave you permission to enter?" escaped her lips before she could rein in her thoughts.

Rebecca raised her left eyebrow. "Really? You want to get particular about me being in your room. I've been buying you time. The High Priest wanted to meet with you this morning. I've been hiding out here to avoid questions about where you are." She shook her head. "If you are not injured, were you successful as well?"

Stephenie nodded her head. "I left Henton watching the gold with the men on the second floor. Will's already on his way to notify Josh."

Rebecca grew hopeful, "How much?"

"The Dalar gold piece was larger than our full crown, so the six bars I made should make about ten thousand coins. It's amazing how many thumbnail sized coins you can squish together into a solid bar. There's about three silver bars as well."

"That's great! Josh should be able to cover the back pay and expenses and perhaps have a little more to keep things rolling. We'll need more of course, but that will be a huge help."

Stephenie frowned. "There was a problem, which explains my clothing. Kas remained near the city to watch in case any other ghosts become aware. I'm hoping it will be just that one."

"Do you think it is serious?"

Stephenie shrugged. "I can't say with regard to the ghosts, but it means no more gold from under Antar."

Rebecca took a deep breath and then closed the door. She drew Stephenie's attention to the bed with a nod of her head. "Well, we can't focus on that right now. You need to get cleaned up and changed. I've brought some clothing that would probably be the most appropriate, some water to wash up, and there is a little food. Unfortunately, I have a feeling you won't like this interview."

Stephenie held her breath and paused as the door to the High Priest's meeting chamber opened. She was afraid to use her powers to reach out and survey the room, for fear one of those in the room might notice, but so much of what she did was subconscious that it was almost impossible not to draw energy into herself. Kas had reassured her multiple times that most people were nowhere near as sensitive to energy fields as she was, and so far Rebecca had never commented on any of her usages of magic, but she was not certain if that was just politeness.

A man with cropped black hair and a short, but thick beard stood with his hand on the door. His eyes were hard and it did not take her powers to know he would not be a friend to her.

Looking past the hostile man, she took her first look upon a chamber she had never seen before. The outer chambers were as far as she had ever gone into the temple and if there were secret passages in the walls, she had never once felt the desire to know about them. She had met the High Priest a number of times, but normally in her father's or brother's presence and never in his private chambers. As a matter of self preservation, she had avoided all the priests as much as reasonably possible growing up.

This room was large, but not huge. It was about twenty feet by fifteen and with five other men in the room besides the High Priest and Lady Rebecca; the room felt quite constricting and worse than being trapped in a dark tunnel. The furnishings were plain, and this room was less an office than a small audience chamber. The High Priest was the obvious focus; his aged skin slightly yellowed and his blonde hair nicely cut and combed, but obviously thinning.

He sat in a gilded chair on a dais, raised a foot above the floor. Lady Rebecca stood to the left, just behind his chair. Another man Stephenie had seen once or twice stood to the right. Three other men sat in a line of chairs that formed a row against the wall perpendicular to the front of the dais. Directly before the High Priest was another chair, its thin wooden slats looking quite delicate and uncomfortable for long term sitting.

She expected Rebecca would not try to detain her, even if the High Priest ordered her confinement through the use of magic, but the other men, whom she could sense had power, would probably fight her and she did not want that to happen.

"Your Excellency," Stephenie said when she reached the middle of the room. The outer door had fallen shut after she entered. The black haired man remained directly behind her. Giving the High Priest a curtsy, she raised her eyes to meet his face.

The old man watched her for several moments and then pointedly motioned to the chair. Without further pause, Stephenie walked the rest of the way to the chair and carefully sat down. Her long skirt was simple enough that it did not billow around her legs as she sat.

"You have been accused of being a witch." The High Priest's tone was so conversational that it caught Stephenie off-guard.

Pausing for a moment, she nodded her head. "I am as I was born. I do not deny what occurred in the Grey Mountains."

"Do you think your saving thousands of soldiers, giving your brother back some semblance of an army, should sway my decisions?"

His tone had become instantly hard, tightening Stephenie's jaw. "I think all of a person's actions should be considered, but I will not presume to tell you what to think." Stephenie sensed a bit of apprehension from Rebecca, something she normally could never do with these self-disciplined people. Moderating her tone slightly, she continued. "I have done what I have done in order to save Cothel and her people. I have not sought to harm anyone, only do what I can to protect those that I can protect."

Stephenie glanced to her left and the row of three priests plus the black haired man that joined them. She could feel the tendrils of energy flowing into the holy symbol around the black-haired man's neck. She turned back to the High Priest whose quizzical expression indicated he might not feel the change in the energy currents in the room.

"I have never wanted to hurt anyone."

"You have called for Elard Burdger to be hung, is this not true?"

Stephenie leaned forward. "Elard ordered his men to kill those who were traveling with me and to remove my head and bring it back to him. He continued to send men to hunt down soldiers of Cothel with the intent to kill them so that he and his father could take the throne. He's a coward and a traitor. He did this not knowing what I am, well before I had reached the Greys."

The man to the High Priest's right moved forward, "You should keep your tongue, witch. Lord Elard is the son of a Duke."

"And I'm the daughter of a king!" Stephenie closed her eyes for a moment and steadied her breathing. When she opened them, she looked directly at the High Priest, ignoring the others. "I have asked for justice to be served in the case of Lord Elard, not for me, but for the soldiers he wanted killed. That does not make me evil."

The High Priest's brow rose slightly. "Elrin's taint would make you evil, but we have received multiple reports that, if true, would potentially be unprecedented." The High Priest held out his hand and the brown-haired priest closest to the dais rose and walked over, handing the aged man a folded piece of parchment. "I assume you know what this is," he said holding the parchment in his left hand.

Stephenie tilted her head slightly to the left, "A report from a priest in the town of Jebrim?"

The High Priest smiled slightly and nodded his head. "Exactly that. It indicates that there is a claim you have been cleansed by fire and the gods chose to remake you, removing Elrin's taint."

Stephenie said nothing. She hated to perpetuate Will's theory, but she was not so stupid as to throw away a potential chance at having the High Priest declare her no longer a witch.

"The perplexing issue is that you seem to still posses Elrin's powers. Of course, while it has always been said that someone favored by the gods would survive a purification, there has been no documented case of that ever happening before. Nor is there documentation on what to expect as the result. This means you would be something very special if the claims are true."

"Or that there was no purification performed," said the man to the High Priest's right.

"Lord Evans, if you will hold your peace." The High Priest's tone tightened the man's jaw, but he stepped back into place. "So, Your Highness, we need to understand just what occurred and what your standing really is."

"Your Excellency, I do not remember much of the actual event, aside from being in a lot of pain. I could swear all my bones had broken and I know others said I was covered in flames."

"Your Sergeant Henton witnessed the events. He submitted himself to my review after our first meeting."

Stephenie felt her stomach tighten. Henton had not mentioned that and he knew more about her and Kas than anyone. She feared what the High Priest might have learned if he read Henton's mind and what he would do with that knowledge. Rebecca had assured her that no one would try to read her mind, more out of fear of what she might be able to do to them, than out of respect.

"With the information from his first hand account and that of a couple of soldiers who had witnessed the events, or been available just after the events, I am willing to concede you were indeed set on fire. A very hot fire that melted metal and burned away all of your clothing." The High Priest moved forward slightly and motioned for her to lean closer. He studied her face and then leaned back. "You had a small scar on your forehead from hitting your head as a child. I see that is gone. It is said that all your other scars and wounds are gone. Is this true?"

Stephenie nodded her head. "Yes, as far as I have seen and remember, I no longer have any marks from old injuries."

"Yet you bear another mark, no?"

She hesitated, having a sinking feeling they would not be happy until she showed them her breast. "Yes, I have one mark left on me that I was not born with."

"A hand print. A hand print the corporal who protects you has been claiming is the mark of Catheri. It seems when he goes into Antar to purchase food for you, he spends time preaching to a number of soldiers, peasants, and burghers."

Stephenie, not aware of Will's activities, felt her mouth hanging open and quickly closed it. He too was obviously keeping secrets. It would mean Will's life would likely be forfeit if the High Priest declared against her. They would not want Will making her into a martyr.

"Were you not aware of that?"

Stephenie glanced to Rebecca, who's face was schooled to impassivity, but her eyes indicated she had not been aware either. "I did not. Please do not go after Will. I will have him stop immediately."

"We will decide what to do with him later. For now, we will verify his claim. Show us this mark."

Stephenie was glad Kas was deep underground; he would react badly to this. Having resigned herself to this likelihood after Rebecca's warning, she was glad Rebecca chose a simple dress with a large and open neckline, she reached up and pulled her left sleeve down so that she could reach into the collar and pull loose the binding around her breasts. Noticing the eager expressions of the men in the room, she set the binding in her lap and pulled the collar down far enough to expose her left breast and Kas' hand print.

The man with brown hair, who had handed the High Priest the document, rose and came over for a closer look. He eyed her breast for several moments, while Stephenie irritably stared straight ahead.

After a moment more, he squinted his eyes, "The color is a deep black, perhaps with a bit of blue undertone. Very vibrant. The mark appears almost claw-like, directly above her heart and partially over her breast. It looks to be solid in color, not like a tattoo with variations."

Stephenie caught his right wrist in her left hand as his fingers moved to touch her. "I don't need you groping me."

The man swallowed and nodded his head. She released him, barely noticing the red marks her strong grip had left.

Being careful to keep his hands close to his body, the man moved his head to get a look at different angles. Stephenie watched his face, but the man seemed only to see her small breast and the hand print. After a moment more, he looked up to her face and then looked away quickly. He stood, bowed his head to her, then turned back to the High Priest.

"Your Excellency, I have studied the records ever since word came to us. The claw of Catheri has been represented in many slightly different variations. There are of course no priests of Catheri alive today, since she removed herself from our world years ago due to the sins of man. However, this could definitely be a form of her mark. And the High Priest of Catheri, in the year 358, did declare Catheri would return when she was needed most. The stories being branded around that she claimed she would come in a revolutionary form cannot be substantiated. Though many people are claiming to have heard such a legend at some point in their lives."

"This is ridiculous," Lord Evans blurted out. "You expect me to believe a girl with, what looks to me, to be a tattoo on her breast, which could have easily been put there by any of her numerous lovers among these soldiers who are spreading this very rumor..."

Stephenie had risen to her feet, her expression silencing the outburst. "I don't know you, Lord Evans, but you better have your facts straight before insin—"

"Enough!" The High Priest was also on his feet. "Evans, I agreed to let you be here because I felt it was fair to give Duke Burdger's adviser an opportunity to see the facts. You are still a priest of Felis, which means your loyalty is suppose to be to Felis. Do not interrupt my adviser again or I will have you disciplined."

Lord Evans swallowed and nodded his head, but Stephenie could see the rebellion still in his eyes. "Yes, Your Excellency. I will hold my tongue. Forgive my overstepping of my place."

Stephenie's eyes narrowed in spite of herself. She realized that Lord Evans, while not a master priest, was the ranking priest in the Duchy of Lists and someone with a great amount of influence with lower priests in the west. Lord Evans' position on her would undoubtedly be political and not in her favor.

"Your Highness, please sit."

Stephenie looked back to the High Priest and nodded her head. She adjusted her left sleeve; the collar had already slid back to cover her breast. She sat down and the High Priest resumed his seat as well.

"Do you worship Elrin?"

Stephenie shook her head. "No. I have never worshiped Elrin in thought or action."

"Are you Catheri's prophet?"

She paused, "Some people would love for me to say yes, but if I am, I have not been made aware of it. I simply try to protect the people of Cothel, my family, and those who are close to me. I will go to war when someone threatens those I protect, but I do not seek out conflict."

"Will you denounce Elrin and the demon god's taint?"

"I will never advocate Elrin, now or ever."

The High Priest nodded his head. "Very well. I will have to review the situation. Please remain in the castle until I tell you otherwise."

Stephenie nodded her head. "Yes, Your Excellency."

"Good. I am sure you are quite aware that your behavior will reflect upon your brother. He has risked much in his unfailing support of you."

Stephenie felt her chest tighten again. If he turned against Joshua, they would all fall. She wished she had a better sense of his mood, but all she had was his tone and that had fluctuated during the discussion. *Josh, you should have told me to avoid coming back to Antar.*

"You are free to return to your rooms."

Stephenie nodded her head and stood. "Thank you, Your Excellency."

* * * * *

Stephenie walked out of the back rooms and into the larger temple chamber with her chest binding still twisted in her hands. She felt dread for what could happen, but as she quickly replayed every aspect of the conversation in her head, she felt her anger growing. The fact that those men simply assumed she would bare her breast for their pleasure, so they could have their beady eyes running over her flesh.

Straining the threads of the binding, she wished she had some female friends whom she could talk with. This was was not something she could tell Kas, Henton, or any of the others. The men would insist on taking action to protect her honor and that would simply make things worse. *To stop them, I'd have to tell them it wasn't a big deal and to not worry about it. But, it is, and I don't want to be forced to dismiss the insult to keep them out of trouble.* She suspected a woman would understand the rage within her, but would know to be subtle enough to not cause more problems. *A woman would be a silent confidant that would share my anger and be sensible enough to think instead of simply reacting. A woman would know to wait for revenge.*

Stephenie stopped. She calmly folded her bindings and tossed them behind a row of benches. There was not a place for her to put them back on and if she carried them out of the temple, the others would know what happened.

With the evidence gone, she stepped out through the large wooden doors that contained numerous inscriptions and carvings that indicated this building was the home of Felis. Henton and Douglas were waiting for her where she had left them, next to what had been the outer wall of the original castle and her great hall. Lady Rebecca's advice about leaving them outside of the temple was sound.

"Everything okay?" Henton asked, obviously picking up her mood.

She sighed, knowing there was no point in lying. "I just don't want to talk about it."

"Is he going to declare for or against you?" Douglas demanded.

Stephenie turned her head toward Douglas. He had not become any more talkative since she first met him, but he was no longer even slightly hesitant in sharing his opinion or concerns with her.

"I've no idea; save for the fact the High Priest didn't try to take me in his chambers. Perhaps that is good. But I don't know. Burdger had Lord Evans there to weigh in and there were a couple others I didn't recognize who seemed eager for me to burn. Who knows, perhaps they're all in line to be promoted."

Henton nodded his head, picking up her lead and changing the topic. "Lady Rebecca is the last Master Priest alive. The others are dead. They need to appoint more, but the number of qualified people are so few these days. I hope they avoid appointing bad choices just to fill the ranks."

Chapter 10

Stephenie remained in her rooms for the next day and a half. She had Henton get regional maps and reports on troop movements, which her brother had allowed him to borrow so she would have something to do. She did not want to go over to the new keep and irritate Duke Yaslin Forest and the handful of barons who had come to the castle. She knew they had not been pleased to see her in Antar and she worried about how much of a point of contention her continued presence would be.

From the reports, she could tell that while Burdger had upheld his end of the bargain for Elard's release, it would not take much to get the armies on the march again. Unfortunately, the only way she could see to counter that threat was to keep a large standing force in Antar. Doing that left the country on the verge of civil war; all that was missing was the actual fighting. What pained her was that everyone was using her as potential justification for bloodshed and killing, though the truth was far more base. She knew the truth was simply people who had some power wanted more, and they found a way to manipulate the general populace to support their goals.

Slowly, she pushed aside the most recent report and looked up; Lady Rebecca was coming up the stairs. She hoped the High Priest had finally made up his mind. For good or ill, she was tired of remaining sequestered and was almost ready to let Henton see if his prediction was true regarding her ability to withstand fire.

"May I come in?" Rebecca asked when she arrived at the door Stephenie had already opened from where she sat on her bed.

"Please, make yourself at home." Stephenie did not feel like rising. Her legs had lost so much muscle tone, she had completely given up trying to move about without her powers. Her clothing was all too large and yet somehow she continued to survive.

Rebecca entered and shut the door behind herself. "Can I get you anything?"

Stephenie glanced at the pile of empty plates and bowls sitting next to her wall. "I'm eating plenty."

Rebecca nodded, obviously not believing the statement, but unwilling to challenge it either. She pulled a chair in front of the bed and sat down. "Well, perhaps a little good news will help you."

Stephenie felt her arms start to tremble at the smile Rebecca gave her. "You mean a decision was made?"

Rebecca's smile grew to match Stephenie's. "Yes. Josh would have brought it to you himself, but he's stuck in council with the barons, and so I decided to bring it over to keep you from having to sit without knowing.

"Stephenie, you are declared cleansed. The first person on record in the whole world." Rebecca pulled a folded piece of parchment out of a pouch at her waist. "I thought you might want an official copy of the decree. The High Priest signed it this morning and copies are being made to distribute around the country. And even to other countries," she added. "He will be personally addressing the citizens in the Antar temple this afternoon. The turn out is expected to be quite a bit larger than normal."

Stephenie took the parchment and quickly scanned over the words, barely reading them. The document included a fair amount of background and justification for the decision, including testimony from several soldiers and Baron Arnold Turning, who had been on the mountaintop and had arrived in Antar only the day before, after he had first made a trip to his home.

"I don't think there is anything too personal or sensitive in there. The High Priest also left out any testimony from Joshua."

Stephenie looked up.

Rebecca smiled again. "He felt putting anything that Josh said into the document might be construed as the High Priest catering to your family."

"Thank you Rebecca," Stephenie said, her voice breaking. "I must say I was terrified of what you would think of me. I've been afraid of what Josh would do if they declared against me." She wiped away the tears of relief that had leaked out and breathed a sigh.

Rebecca nodded her head. "Actually, I've had rather little to do with the decision." She looked away for a moment and then back to Stephenie. "Steph, I want to be honest with you. A good deal of the decision was based upon the results of your friend William's effort to convince the general populace that you are chosen by Catheri. The fact that there was a significant favorable response helped make the High Priest's decision possible. If the response had been poor, he would not have been able to declare for you."

Stephenie leaned back, her tears dried up. "Truly?"

"Yes. Another significant factor is the High Priest and Duke Burdger do not share a great deal of ideological ground. If he declared against you, he would lose Joshua's support and gain Burdger's. That would tip the balance and most likely your family would fall from power and Burdger would take over, since many of the priests and holy warriors who were most loyal to the High Priest are dead, he lacks the power base to keep Burdger in check himself."

"Plus, there was the factor that Josh is able to pay the soldiers with all that gold your father had hid from your mother because he didn't trust her." Rebecca pursed her lips. "That is the cover story I suggested for the gold you brought up. It is giving Josh the chance to keep his soldiers for a little while longer. Which means the High Priest can in turn rely on Josh's support, hopefully until things can quiet down and tax money can come in to sustain Josh."

"His decision has nothing to do with me? Was it completely political?"

Rebecca gave Stephenie a forced smiled. "He is familiar with your history. The fact that you have always appeared to have Cothel's best interest at heart has helped his decision. But honestly, it was far from the most significant factor." She sighed and gave Stephenie a more honest smile. "With your position in the royal family, you should already know this, but at a certain level, all decisions become political. One hopes that the politics align with what is right, but that is not always what happens. I would like to say in this case, things have aligned. I truly believe you are a good person and I feel this was the correct decision, regardless of the politics. I am happy the politics worked as well."

Stephenie looked into Rebecca's eyes, but she could sense nothing from the Master Priest. She wanted to believe her, but she was no longer certain of Rebecca's intentions. Was Rebecca's support just a means to remain on Joshua's good side or did she truly think Stephenie was not evil? If the High Priest's decision was solely political and Rebecca knew it, she might still believe Stephenie was tainted by Elrin.

Stephenie smiled, hoping it looked genuine enough. "Thank you. That means a lot to me. I need to tell the others."

Rebecca rose. "The castle staff should be hearing the news as we speak, so you should be free to move about as much as you like."

Stephenie watched as Rebecca took her leave, heading quickly down the tower steps. She forced herself from the bed and quickly changed into cleaner clothing. As she finished pulling on a new shirt, she sensed Henton at her door, a smile on his face and a plate of food and a pitcher of water in his hands.

Stephenie had been summoned to Joshua's keep shortly after she had eaten with Henton. A green dress donated from Baron Arnold Turning's younger daughter was sent with the request and after Henton had helped her into the decidedly feminine, if slightly youthful, dress, she was escorted the short distance from her great hall to the keep. Henton, Douglas, Will, and Tim were asked to return after dinner and Stephenie was led inside to meet with the dukes, barons, and other nobles that had the previous day been highly opposed to her. The afternoon was a little stiff and Stephenie felt a decided pointlessness to the occasion. The false sentiments, well wishes, and 'I knew the High Priest would declare for you', sickened her stomach.

Not everyone was false. Baron Turning and his fourteen year old daughter, Isabel, who was thin enough to donate the dress, both seemed genuinely pleased for her. Though their conversation was constrained to safe topics, such as the weather, the dress, falsely claimed to be enhanced by Stephenie's fine features, and his pleasure of being able to finally show his daughter the grand city of Antar. Despite their meeting in the Greys, there was no discussion of the war, the Senzar, the gods, or politics, at least not with her.

Always considered something of an odd girl, she had been able to avoid these types of events most of her life. When dinner was announced and Stephenie was finally able to sit down, she was truly happy to see and smell the food covering the table, as it would give her something else to do with her mouth other than make small talk.

She glanced at Joshua, already seated at the head of the table next to Lady Rebecca. He was dressed in regal clothing and while he had talked her up to the group that had gathered, she had not had a chance to talk with him privately.

Baron Turning smiled at her from across the table, his blonde daughter looking sheepish among the rest of the crowd. Duke Yaslin Forest and five other barons also sat around the table, their faces still filled with smiles and cheer.

Hearing her stomach grumble, her brother stood and smiled at her. "Stephenie, my lovely sister, who has done so much to make today possible, I am pleased to once again have you join us for dinner. With the High Priest proclamation, we can all look upon you as we have always known you to be, pure of heart, honorable, and deserving of our respect and love."

"Here, here," came a chorus of voices from around the room and Stephenie could not help but to blush slightly. She had received plenty of praise on the practice field from the soldiers she had trained with before the war, but that was more camaraderie than anything else. Rarely did she have to listen to someone speak well of her to a room of other people.

"Thank you, Joshua. I truly only wanted to bring everyone home."

"That you did!" Arnold said loudly, raising his glass. "I've said it many times, but Isabel only had me left to care for her. I could not imagine leaving her so soon in life. You have my sword always."

Stephenie nodded to Arnold. He was only thirty, having been wed when he was fifteen to a woman his own age. Living on the northwestern side of the Uthen Mountains left the Baron's court etiquette a bit rough, but Stephenie liked him all the more for his frank comments.

"Well, let's not keep my sister any longer from her food. She's been sorely worried about a lot of things for so long that she's hardly been eating."

Stephenie smiled and was only barely able to refrain from using magic to pile her plate with food. Instead, she forced herself to use proper etiquette and allow the servants who had been standing quietly along the walls to come up and start putting food on their plates and filling their goblets with wine. Even before the serving girl was directly behind her, Stephenie sensed something was troubling the girl. When the dagger was drawn, Stephenie simply wrapped a gravity field around the girl's body.

The table erupted in confusion and anger as the girl stood motionless with a dagger ready to strike. Joshua started yelling for guards and the other servants quickly retreated from the table.

Stephenie rose and turned around. "Quiet!" she shouted over her shoulder. Before her stood a girl of probably thirteen or fourteen, tears streaming down her face. Stephenie sensed the girl had ceased to struggle and would collapse to the floor if released. Carefully taking the dagger from the girl's hand, she released the field and the girl slipped to the floor.

"Please, don't eat my soul!" the girl sobbed, her brown hair having fallen to cover her face. "Please!"

Stephenie knelt down to where the girl had slumped to her knees. "Why would you do this? Why would you think I would eat your soul? I eat beef stew and bread." Guards were already standing around them, as was Lady Rebecca.

The girl looked up, tears streaming from her eyes. "Please. Don't feed me to Elrin!"

Stephenie rose to her feet as Baron Yaslin cleared his throat. "If there are traitors in the kitchen, we can't trust the food. Someone will need to interrogate all the staff."

A pair of guards grabbed the girl and started to drag her to her feet. Stephenie could sense her complete terror. "Wait."

"What is it?" Joshua asked.

"Don't harm the girl. I want to talk to her."

"She'll be questioned," he said, anger in his voice as well as emanating from his being. "I won't have traitors trying to kill members of this household or its guests. We'll find out who is involved."

"Do not harm her," Stephenie said, enunciating every word.

"I will question her," Lady Rebecca said, gently taking one of the girl's arms from the second guard. "Then I will question the others and I will not hurt anyone. We don't know that she was working with anyone and it would not be prudent to accuse everyone in the castle of being a traitor without cause."

Joshua visibly calmed. "Thank you Rebecca. Question her and then take her to the dungeon for now."

Yaslin's voice was quiet, but it carried through the room. "I warned you that not everyone would accept the High Priest's proclamation. We have to be prepared for more of this."

Stephenie felt the truth of it bite deep into her being. She had been declared cleansed just half a day and already someone was trying to kill her. "I'll be back."

"Where are you going?"

"First to speak with my men, then I will talk with the girl, then I want to talk with you Josh." She knew her tone was brusk and not appropriate for how she should address her King, especially when there were so many ranking witnesses. It was imprudent, but it was already out of her mouth. She could feel the others in the room staring and wondering how her brother would respond and she hoped he would not feel the need to reassert himself.

"Yes. After Lady Rebecca is done, I will permit you a chance to deal with her."

Stephenie's mind was racing as she rushed down to the first floor of the keep. Forgoing any escort, she rushed back to her tower and found Henton and Will sitting in the great hall playing a game of tables. "Find Douglas, I'll get Kas," she said as they rose to their feet. "I need to talk to the four of you."

Kas had been in her room reading one of the books from the library and Douglas was quickly found, so she had only just changed out of the dress by the time the others arrived in her room.

"What happened?" Henton asked as everyone gathered around.

She had filled in Kas mentally already and repeated the events of the evening for the others.

"And what of the girl?" Will asked.

"The girl had no chance to do me, or really anyone, harm. She's terrified I'll eat her soul. But that's not what I want to talk about. It's a factor, but not the issue." She looked at Henton, Will, and Douglas, already aware of Kas' answer. "What would you say if I wanted to leave the Castle?"

"Where do you plan to go? It would be hard to protect you in Antar city." Will offered. "There are a number of your followers there, but there are others like that girl who'd try something regardless of what the High Priest said."

She forced herself to ignore Will's comment about followers. After a moment, she continued, "I'm thinking a bit further than that. I can't stay here. I'm a distraction and the nobles are using me as an excuse for war. I can't live with being the cause of that." She tried to contain a smile that was building. "Plus, I've got an idea to help Josh with money and remove a potential threat to Cothel."

"Are you thinking to banish yourself?" Douglas asked.

"I wasn't, but that might be a good idea."

Henton raised his hand. "Please, Steph, get to the point and I promise we will wait to ask questions. However, in general, if you plan to be on the move, we need to make sure we don't let people know who you are. I know the High Priest's proclamation means by his commandment you are safe, but he's not going to be able to enforce that."

"Yes, I would intend to make sure we sneak out of town and not let anyone know where we are going. Which is why I am talking to the four of you first. The other five we can bring in as we need them, and for what I am planning, we'll need them."

"And what are you planning," Kas asked in Denarian. He could follow enough of the conversation in Cothish, but would not yet speak in it in mixed company.

"I am planning to get back at my uncle, hinder his ability to harm us, and help Josh by leaving the country so he can deal with other issues and not have to address everyone's concerns about me. And in getting back at my uncle, I plan to bring back some of the gold he stole, fixing the money problem."

Will smiled. "Catheri's hand of justice is what you are."

Stephenie rolled her eyes. "I am glad what you've done helped cause the High Priest to find in my favor, but I don't want you preaching about me. I'm just the girl you helped escape her bitch of a mother to rescue her brother. Nothing else."

Henton looked up to Kas and asked in the Old Tongue, "You follow enough of that?"

"She wants to rob her uncle, the King of Kynto. I was waiting to hear just how she is planning to do that and live."

Stephenie smiled at Kas. "This brain damaged simpleton has a couple of ideas. But, I've never been to Kynto, so we'll have to make some of it up when we get there. However, my older sister Regina loved to brag about how much Mother loved her more and would regale me with tales of how wonderful my mother had it living in Wyntac castle. Plus, I've had a lot of time to think about things and I think what I have in mind will be possible."

Three turns of the glass later, Stephenie was back in the central keep and in her brother's office. "Josh, I want you to let the girl go."

"What? You can't mean that. She tried to kill you."

Stephenie crossed her arms and stared at her brother who was sitting behind his desk. "You let Elard go; this girl had absolutely no chance of being able to hurt me. She was talked into doing it by other people in Antar who obviously just wanted to cause trouble at this girl's expense. No one else in the castle is believed to have been involved."

"Steph, if we let her go, we'll be telling people she didn't do anything wrong. Yaslin and several barons saw her. She committed treason trying to harm a member of the royal family!"

"And so did Elard, except he had a much better chance of actually doing it. But more importantly, with Elard, he tried to kill Henton and the others. That's unacceptable. This girl, who's just turned fifteen, didn't know what she was doing and most importantly, didn't try to kill my men or anyone else in the castle. Just me, which she lacked any chance of succeeding at."

"Steph—"

"Don't tell me only those rich enough to have an army to back them up get to escape justice. Let this girl go. Banish her if you want, but don't execute her. Show the people you are fair to commoners as well as nobles."

Joshua shook his head. "This is a mistake. You are telling people it is okay to attack you if they think you are evil. The High Priest declared in your favor just this morning and at dinner you get attacked. What message is that going to send if she is not punished?"

Stephenie took a deep breath and clenched her jaw. She loved her brother and hated to give an ultimatum, but she was not about to see someone else die in her name. "Do not go against me on this Josh, I will not give in. Let the girl go or I will free her myself! Tell people I insisted because I believe she's simply misguided and not a threat. It's the right thing to do and you know it. I am calling in any favors you owe me."

Joshua rose and walked around his desk to Stephenie. He took her shoulders in his hands and looked into her face. "Okay, you win. And no it will not require any favors, I owe you my life many times over. The country does as well, which is why I really want to punish her for trying to kill you. She was attacking the country as well as this family. But, if it is that important to you, I will grant this to you." He raised his head to stop her interrupting. "But, know that this will cause trouble with the barons and dukes. They will use this to say we didn't punish her because we knew she was correct in trying to kill you. Many of them are not going to agree with the High Priest in the first place. I've already heard that several people think he's just a puppet for our family. And that was reported to have been said by some that support us. I'm fighting to keep from giving them more power and they will use any excuse they can." He shook his head. "One thing for sure, we don't want an aristocracy. That was the ruin of Rawnar; they are always arguing and nothing gets done. The people suffer for the greed of their leaders."

He let her go and sat down in the other chair in front of his desk. Looking up at her, he asked, "any chance for anything more from Arkani? Money is our biggest weakness at the moment."

Stephenie shook her head. "Kas has seen changes in the behaviors of the ghosts, though no others have appeared to fully wake." She sat down in the other chair, hating herself for manipulating the conversation in this manner. "You think things are really that bad?" Joshua nodded his head and she pursed her lips as if she was considering her decision. "Then I am going to go as well. I'm the reason for a lot of the trouble."

"What?"

Stephenie hesitated. "I've been thinking about this for some time, and today confirms it. And ironically, today is actually the first time I could leave without breaking the High Priest's commandment. I'd have left Antar earlier, except for what I feared it would do to your position, but now staying is worse than leaving."

"I won't let you go. You've done nothing wrong and I won't let you give in to the demands for you to be banished. The High Priest thinks you are not an agent of Elrin, no one else should continue to make those claims."

"Banishment? Who was demanding you banish me?"

"It's not important."

"I'd imagine our allies. Our enemies would demand I was burned." She shook her head. "It doesn't matter who, but if I leave, you have to fight far fewer issues. Tell the barons you've sent me away to avoid the issues surrounding me. I'm guessing some of them think I am trying to run the country through you."

Joshua did not respond immediately. "You'll be at risk if you are outside the castle."

"I'll take the men who want to come with me and I'll disappear into the countryside." She grinned. "Besides, I've been making plans that may fix our money problems."

"What plans?"

"A bit of justice if you listen to Will; Uncle needs to pay for what he's done. He's as much involved with what Mother did as anyone. I will take my men with me to Wyntac and we will steal it back."

Joshua stood up shaking his head. "No, that is a very bad idea. Assuming you could get the money, he'd hunt you down and kill you. He's a bastard and as corrupt as they come."

"No, Josh, he can't. Wyntac is near the border with Calis. Uncle can't march his troops into Calis and he's not about to tell anyone he's been robbed. That would make him appear weak and financially unstable. You know what that's done here; imagine if the majority of your army was mercenaries, not loyal citizens, and they suddenly thought they might not get paid. Sure, he'll try to send some people after us, but it can't be a lot, because then there would be a risk that they would find out what happened, and what he can't do, is let word get out.

"So, to avoid a revolt or an enormous demand on his treasury for advance pay, he'll keep it quiet. We just have to avoid a small force for less than a dozen miles to the border, take the money across Calis to the port of Wilm, and sail home."

"And how do you expect to storm his castle to get to the gold?"

"Mother," she said with a smile. "Regina always got to listen to all the good tales, then bragged to me about them. The vault is in the lower levels of the keep. There was an old square tower that predated the rest of the castle. With the exception of the top floor, it's been sealed off from the rest of the castle that was built around it. I fly the men and myself up, we go down to the vault, take the gold, I fly us out of the castle and over the city walls and we are in Calis when the sun rises. Who'd have thought that fat cow could give me something useful, eh?"

"Steph, Regina's your sister, even if she doesn't seem to be a good one."

Stephenie nodded her head and had the decency to pretend to look abashed, though she would never forgive her sister for the years of hate and malice. "I know. Anyway, Kas agreed to confirm what Regina said all those years ago and make sure it is safe. Then we'll adjust the plan from there. I just need a few things from you to make this work."

"I don't like this. You are too confident in how he'll react."

"I've given it a lot of thought and father always talked about why Willard was in the position he was in and why we should always try to avoid that if we can."

Joshua's shoulders slumped. "What do you need from me?"

"Some money and a ship." She nodded her head when Joshua waited for her to continue. "Wyntac is about five hundred miles to the north, about the same distance from here to the Greys where I went off on my own with just a handful of men. Give us a month to get there from here. We should be safe going through Midland and into Kynto. When we leave Wyntac, it's ten miles to Calis and then a couple hundred miles across to the Sea of Tet. If we take back enough money, we'll probably pick up a couple horses, but even still, let's say a week or so to cross Calis. A ship will take what, four or five days given a good wind. If you send a ship there in say about a month and a half and leave it waiting until we come, the ship might have to pay a bit for docking fees, but it will give us flexibility for when we arrive and when we do, we can set sail immediately."

"Steph—"

"Josh, I've been looking over maps and planning for a few days now. And based on how much you've been pressing me for money, I am sure the pressure is worse for you. We don't want to turn the country over to the barons and this can solve many things, including making Uncle less able to send men here to cause trouble."

Joshua thought for several moments. "The dukes are not really interested in giving more power to the barons. It would hurt them as well. It's even given Burdger some pause, since a few of his barons are waiting to see what happens with us before putting their full support behind him. Burdger wants to be king in whole, and he won't make concessions to the barons if he takes over. That means some of his support has waned a bit.

"However, you are correct, money is our biggest issue and what you, and Kas," he added, "have brought up has bought us time, but we will have trouble collecting taxes before next year and I don't know that we have enough to last. Definitely not if there is conflict."

"Then I should leave before first light. We don't want to waste any time. Besides the ship, I will need some funds to help get us to Kynto and I hope we can keep the cost down on the way back."

Joshua took a deep breath. "I don't like this, but I can see it in your face, you'll do it without my blessing if you have to." He rose and gave her a tight hug. "Get some meat on your bones and come back safely, even if it is without the money. Don't try to take it if you can't get away. Just having you gone from the castle for a while will help calm things and that could be enough."

Chapter 11

Morning came too early and Stephenie wished she had not spent most of the night explaining parts of her plans to the rest of her men. She had not told them the specifics, only that they would be leaving before dawn, heading out of Antar, and that she expected the trip to take about two months. Coming back to Antar in the autumn would hopefully keep the thoughts of war down, since most people did not like to fight in winter.

They were all to store their armor and uniforms in the tower, leaving behind any colors, as Stephenie and Henton were going to be traveling as merchants with their bondsmen. Stephenie would have liked to acquire new armor without any family or country marks, but there was not time and the very act of doing that would draw suspicion.

Will and Tim had gone into Antar to get additional supplies and Stephenie presumed Will had also taken care of his responsibilities for the church of Catheri he seemed to be setting up without her blessing. Despite everything they had discussed, Will was convinced she was a prophet of some sort. *If he starts worshiping me, that will be the end of it*, she swore to herself. So far, he had not treated her any differently, just remaining his charming self and trying to entertain her. If she was not so fond of him, she would have had him remain behind as punishment.

She breathed deeply and looked around at those gathered on the top of her tower. The moon had set already and the Sea of Tet was a vast void in the darkness. The sound of the waves crashing on the cliffs to the east formed a relaxing background din.

"Sarge, you wanna look the other way while I take these?" Will's grin was lost in the darkness to everyone but Stephenie.

She walked over to Will and closed his hand. "Put those away unless we really need them. Marching through the morning should wake you up. I told you last night we'd be leaving early. It's not my fault you got back so late."

Will started to complain but obviously thought better of it. He slipped the pills back into his pouch and let out a big sigh. Stephenie noted Douglas let slip an approving nod of his head. The pills Will carried had a kick that could wake someone up almost immediately, but it was rough when they wore off. Based on Douglas' response, she wondered if Will was using them more often now that they were back in Antar and he had a ready supply from his friend by the docks. She would have to ask Kas to keep an eye on him.

"Ready?"

"I still think horses would be nice," Peter said, rubbing his hand through his cropped hair.

"Private, you are about to find out just how far you can march in one day," Henton said, adjusting the pack on his own back. "You go on much more about horses, and I'll see to it that you end up with the worst guard shifts." Clearing his throat, he continued, "At this point, no more ranks. Just names. I hope you can all remember that Stephenie is to be called Beth. And since that's been hard enough, the rest of us will go by our own names. None of us are that well known, so it shouldn't matter."

"Yes Henton, I will keep my mouth shut about horses."

Stephenie was tempted to give Peter a smack on the back side of his head, but instead she looked toward where Kas was floating off the edge of the tower. With a nod of her head, she drew upon the energy around them and launched the group high into the air. The rush of wind blew her long red hair behind her and brought water to her eyes. Ever since she started entertaining the men by flying them about, she had grown to love the feeling of flight; it was exhilarating and gave her a sense of freedom.

Breathing deeply as the energy coursed through her body, she felt its toll and decided to cut the flight shorter than she might if she was on her own. Having already angled their path well above the wall and gatehouse, she let gravity and momentum help carry them away from the castle. She set them down more than four hundred yards north of the gate house, squarely along the road toward Antar.

The predawn light was not yet cresting the horizon, and the roads would be clear for at least one more turn of the glass. She planned to skirt around Antar and avoid most of the people before they were about their morning tasks. On foot and with the ability to fly over obstacles, such as the Uthen River, she no longer needed to worry about bridges and keeping to the roads. Instead, she headed west and would simply fly everyone over anything in their way. They would pick up the road again on the other side of Ivar and continue west toward the Uthen Mountains and then follow the range north through the cities of Uthen and Steel and then up into the country of Midland. From there, her planned route continued north through that country and across Kynto's southern border.

It would be a long journey, but Stephenie was not going to push as hard as she had done when they rushed to the Grey Mountains to save Joshua. This time she would take it easy and try for fifteen to twenty miles a day. *Provided my mind holds out from a day of actively moving my body.*

She looked back and Kas materialized his head into a vague translucence, but it was enough to see him smile at her. With that approval, she started marching faster, leaving Henton, Will, and the six privates pushing hard to keep up.

As the middle of the day approached, Stephenie turned away from the Uthen River and looked to the north and the thick forest that stretched across the land for leagues. The flowing water had reminded her of the last time she had marched west along this road and all the jokes Fish had told to keep everyone's spirits up.

"He'd want you to smile and not be sad over his death."

Stephenie turned toward Douglas, who always seemed to know what she was thinking whenever she was thinking bad things. She shook her head, "He'd rather we'd strip down and go for a swim."

Douglas grinned at her. "I'm willing if you are."

She punched his arm softly. "I bet you are." She hurriedly cleared the bad thoughts from her mind. "Whatever happened to the guy who thought girls shouldn't be soldiers?"

Douglas shrugged. "Anyone get any ideas about you, Kas will sort them out. I still think it makes the guys think about other things, but you were never really just a girl. You're much more."

"Thanks Douglas. You always know what to say."

They continued walking in silence for a while, just taking in the peaceful countryside. They passed a few travelers heading toward Antar and after casual inquiries from both sides about the state of the road ahead, continued walking.

Peter, and a couple of the others, had drifted behind the rest of the group which was now led by Henton and Will. Stephenie did not mind, as Peter was still grumbling about how far they were expected to march each day. She was content to walk with Douglas and Kas, who remained invisible beside her.

After a couple more miles, Stephenie turned her head, hearing the rhythmic thumping of galloping horses coming up the hill behind them. Even before the riders crested the top of the hill, everyone had started to move into the tall grass along the road. Too many riders tended to take offense at people on foot and these days the roads were often filled with men rushing about the country.

She saw the lead rider's head and shoulders, but only noticed the crossbow after it was discharged into one of her men at the rear of their line. She knew it was Oliver when his mind reacted to the sudden pain.

Disbelief was replaced by rage and power that burned through her body. The rider just behind the first also fired his crossbow. Almost instinctively, Stephenie released the energy in her and despite the distance, the bolt exploded into a million splinters before it could find its target. The gravity field blew the debris aside as it continued onward, blasting through the chest of the rider who had shot the bolt. Armor, bone, and entrails shot out of the man's back, like a fountain erupting. A moment later, the rest of the man's body followed to the ground as the horse reared in panic.

Stephenie heard, but ignored, one of the riders shouting for their surrender. With power coursing through her, time seemed to slow as her senses sharpened on the world around her. Seven of the eight men were still charging forward, two of them had channels of energy radiating from the medallions bouncing on their chests. The others were releasing their crossbows as Kas was rushing forward. *Not my men!*

Gorging on energy, Stephenie knocked away the additional crossbow bolts that had been released.

A gravitational wave rushed from one holy warrior, directed at her and her men, but she sensed the intent of the fields the holy warrior was creating even before they were fully formed and she easily countered the attack, allowing the energy to roll over them in a hazy shimmer. A heart beat later, the second holy warrior linked a channel to her and unleashed a bolt of lightning.

Instinct took over, she linked the channel of energy to the holy warrior's control thread. All magic users generate control threads that carry information back to their minds, even though most never realize these subtle threads even exist. Following the path of least resistance, the electricity that had been directed at Stephenie arched back at the closing holy warrior, striking him in the head and killing him instantly.

Kas' invisible form drove through the other holy warrior, drawing the energy from the man's flesh, freezing his mind and stopping his heart in one stroke.

Feeling Oliver's agony, fury poured from Stephenie in the form of a rapid series of focused gravity blasts. Nearly as one, the five remaining horse men had their heads blown apart. A few moments later, their bodies tumbled from their startled horses, which, no longer being driven forward, were slowing to a gradual stop.

Hearing and sensing Oliver's screams and anguish, Stephenie rushed to him and knelt beside the blonde haired man. Peter was next to him, holding his hand while Oliver's body was racked with convulsions. Noting the bolt still sticking out of his stomach, Stephenie knew they must have poisoned the tips.

"Kas, I need your help!" She pulled the wooden bolt free, hoping a bleeding wound might flush out some of the poison. However, the poison used by holy warriors and witch hunters was very fast acting. "I've never healed anyone else before," she said in the Old Tongue as soon as she sensed Kas near her.

"You need to make a connection with his mind. Just as you have healed your own body, allowing your subconscious to direct your efforts to what your body knows is wrong, you must let his mind and body direct you. Unfortunately, I fear I am unable to help much beyond that. I was never trained as a healer and aside from one's natural talent for healing oneself, I have not had experience with healing."

Stephenie tuned out Henton's sharp orders for the others to gather the horses and strip the bodies. "Kas, I have a hard enough time sensing emotions, let alone reading someone's mind. Help me."

"Concentrate on Oliver's presence. Your trouble will be that you also have to open yourself up. Mental communication goes both ways. There is always a risk of being overwhelmed by the other person. Your instinctual defenses will try to resist this, I have wondered if that may be a factor in why you have trouble sensing others."

Placing her hand on Oliver's arm, she closed her eyes. She knew enough from living near priests that physical contact made the effort of entering someone's mind easier. *Oliver*, she thought, hoping to direct her consciousness to the man before her. She sensed no change in what she knew to be his terrified and pain-filled presence. The poison was always brutal, crippling one with pain as it killed. It was the safest way to limit a mage's ability to fight back, but for someone without magic to fight the poison and hold to life, it meant that the agony would not have to be endured for long.

Oliver, she thought again, trying to force her way into his mind without success. Breathing slowly, she drew in more power and formed more threads between herself and Oliver's fading presence. *Please Oliver, I need to help you.* Slowly, she felt his mental barriers weaken and was startled by a dual awareness. She felt an incredible burning and a complete lack of orientation, but knew that was from Oliver.

Using her experience with Kas linking to her, she tried to keep her thoughts separate so she could concentrate. Using her instincts, she tried to tunnel her consciousness deep into his mind, to his subconscious so she could use her powers to provide energy to Oliver's body to fight the poison. She felt incredible resistance, but eventually was able to push further as Oliver's body continued to shutdown.

Panic filled her, partially from Oliver, but mostly because she knew she was running out of time. Exhaling the breath she had held, she released energy into Oliver, hoping his body would heal.

Raw screams filled her ears as both she and Oliver cried out in unison.

Why are you killing me? I don't want to die! Stephenie felt the thoughts more than heard the words as Oliver's mind finally broke down and stopped the coherent patterns she had come to understand as who Oliver was.

Collapsing onto Oliver's blood covered stomach, she felt the incredible emptiness of where her mind had just been. His pain had been her's. His certainty of death had filled her. His accusation that she was his murderer burned into her thoughts.

"Steph?" Henton finally said when she had failed to respond to his calling her 'Beth' multiple times. He carefully lifted her off the man she had failed to save. "Are you injured?"

She smeared away the blood on her face with her hand, but the metallic taste hung in the air. "I killed him," she whispered. "Kas, I killed him," she repeated in the Old Tongue.

"No, Stephenie, you did not. The poisoned bolt killed him and you killed his murderer."

She shook her head, tears coming from her eyes. "I felt him die. My attempt to heal him ended his life. He asked why I tried to kill him."

"Stephenie, he would have died if you had not tried. If I had been thinking, I should not have let you even attempt such an act on someone so injured. You absorbed too much of his emotional state from the link. He would have been confused, unaware of what was going on. He would not have been able to recognize you from anyone else. Now you are feeling the effects."

Stephenie closed her eyes. She would not gainsay Kas, but she had sensed the accusation. She knew Oliver knew it was her. He had died unable to understand why she would want to hurt him.

"You okay, Steph?"

She turned to Henton and nodded her head. "We need to bury him."

He nodded his head in return and then turned to the others that had gathered around. "Put anything of value into a pile, then throw the arms, equipment, and bodies into the river separately."

"What of the horses?"

"They're branded. We don't want to be caught on them. We'll take them into the woods and turn them loose, then they will be someone else's problem. Get Oliver on one of the horses, we'll bury him in the woods." Henton looked around, Douglas and Will were already moving, but the others were still standing still. "Move it, people, we can't have someone come by and see us standing around with a bunch of dead bodies on the bloody ground."

Henton helped Stephenie lay her blankets on the ground. It was only late in the afternoon and they were only a few miles away from where the attack had been, but her nose had been bleeding on and off since she had created a hole to bury Oliver and she had struggled to even keep moving for the last mile. He did not want her to push herself too far and do more damage.

"Just take it easy, we'll go through everything and get you some food."

Henton stood up when she nodded her head and he looked around at the men who were watching them intently.

"Sir, you think there are traitors in the castle? How'd they know where to find us? Should we go back?"

Henton turned to John, fear evident in his voice and posture. "Listen up, we don't know how they found us, but we are not heading back. We've got a mission to perform and we're going to perform it." He sighed and softened his tone. "I'm not ruling out a traitor, but we've been gone half the day. Those men were riding hard. The fact we left would be obvious to a lot of people and word might have gotten to someone purely by accident. We just don't know. However, we can be sure that when those men don't come back, someone will come looking for them and then they will know we were headed west."

"Well, as long as Steph's rested, we should be fine," Berman said. "She took them down just like the Senzar slaughtered us in the war. As long as there aren't too many, she'll kill them all before we can draw swords."

"Heck, she's better than the Senzar, she took down a mountain. To be able to kill with merely a thought," Tim mused.

Henton noticed Stephenie flinch at the comment, but he doubted any of the men noticed. "We need to be more careful. Oliver's loss is hard, but we have to keep going. We'll keep to the trees and off the main roads for now. Will, you take care of assigning guard shifts and getting food prepared."

Henton watched Will start assigning tasks to the others who quickly went about the work. Hefting the saddle bag full of things that were removed from the dead, Henton walked back to Stephenie and knelt down. "I think we've got a fair amount of coin from that. Probably quadrupled the money your brother provided. Might not run out now before we reach Kynto."

He watched as she slowly turned her head toward him. He knew she was in physical pain, but emotionally, she seemed worse than when she found out Fish had been killed. Of course, at that time, she had been unconscious, so she had not felt Fish's actual death.

Henton set the saddle bag aside and then sat down on the ground. "Look, bad things happen. Losing someone is terrible. And honestly, I'm beating myself up over it as well. We should have gotten off the road earlier in the day. Likely some of those people we passed were questioned by those men. We can't rule out a traitor, but aside from Will, Douglas, Kas, Josh, and Lady Rebecca, no one knows our destination. It'd be obvious we left, and we didn't cover our tracks as well as we should have. I'm at fault there."

She shook her head. "I've never been able to sense much from you. And only a bit from most other people. Do you fear me?"

Henton smiled and shook his head. "No. I trust you. Don't take too much of what they said to heart. They were admiring what you can do, albeit, in a rather thoughtless way."

"No, Henton, some of them fear me. I can feel it. They fear I could simply end their life if I took offense at something."

Henton took a deep breath and glanced toward the men who Will had arranged to be busy and away from the two of them. *Likely three, Kas is undoubtedly listening, even if his understanding of Cothish is limited.* He turned back to her; he did not doubt what she had said and based on how some of the men would cast an occasional glance in their direction, it was likely that Berman and John were the most fearful.

"Look Steph," Henton said, lowering his voice and switching to the Old Tongue. "I've been letting you down. I should have been working more to integrate the new guys. We've been excluding them from a lot and if I was one of them, I would feel like a second class person as well. I need to strap on some balls and fix that." He forced another smile at her. "First, I am not going to allow you to sulk over here by yourself. You want to build their trust and allay their fear, you're going to have to interact with them and treat them normally, even if you sense they are hesitant. Show them they have no reason to fear."

"But it's true, I can kill with a thought. I didn't hesitate to kill those men and then I killed Oliver while trying to save him." Her eyes started to tear up, so she wiped them with a sleeve covered in dried blood. "He thought I was trying to hurt him."

"Steph, everyone knows it was not your fault and you did what you could. You ever have any training at healing? No. So how can you expect yourself to excel at something when you don't have the time to learn." He softened his expression and then pulled her to her feet. "I'm not going to carry you, so you're going to have to walk to where Will's set up the camp. Let everyone grieve together. We've got a long way to go and can't let Oliver's death destroy your plans on the first day."

Swallowing, she nodded her head and walked over to where Will had placed the center of the campsite. Henton bent down, grabbed her blanket and pack, and the saddle bag before following after her.

He glanced over to his left, catching a glimpse of illumination. He felt torn, not really liking the ghost, but he knew Stephenie did. In the Old Tongue he mumbled, "You really need to spend some time talking with her like you used to."

Chapter 12

Stephenie woke with a throbbing headache and dried blood on her face. She forced her eyes open, knowing it was later than it should be if she wanted to stay on schedule. However, with the extra sleep, she was not feeling quite as hollow as she had the prior evening. Henton had been correct, she needed to engage with the others more. Ever since the five of them joined the group in the Greys, they had been held slightly at a distance. That separation, in spite of their loyalty, had left them somewhat uncertain.

After Henton dragged her back into the camp, she slowly joined in with everyone around the campsite and allowed herself to open up with the men as she had done with Henton's original group of soldiers from *The Scarlet*. At first it was hard, the pain of Oliver's accusation was still very fresh in her mind, but the more Tim and Berman told stories about Oliver, the better she felt. It helped put the anger and frustration aside as she listened to how the blond twenty year old had spent his time, often having disastrous, but thoroughly entertaining, failures in wooing young ladies.

And while she had few stories to tell about Oliver, or any of the others, she did talk about her own childhood growing up in the castle and the trouble she and her brother caused. That led Will to relay a wealth of stories at Henton's expense. Most of which, Will had heard from others about Henton's first year at sea, well before he made sergeant. Henton declared Will's primary source, Lord Nermin, unreliable and totally drunk that year.

The best part for Stephenie was that Kas had chosen to sit beside her, fully visible. While his understanding of Cothish was limited, he did his best to follow along and had, with Stephenie's help, relayed Will and Henton's reaction when he had first met them. After that, Stephenie translated back and forth a series of questions about Kas' past, leaving out any mention of Arkani or the city buried under Antar. At the end of the evening, she felt almost normal again.

Now in the morning light, some of the pain of losing another friend came to bare. *He was a good man,* she told herself. She had no idea if he still had family, but she would find out and make sure they were compensated, if they could be found.

Forcing herself up from the ground, she noted that Berman and John were also still asleep, but the others had already gathered up the rest of the campsite. Her stomach growled, as it seemed to always be doing.

"They had the last two watches," Kas said, materializing beside her. "Henton still wants to have someone stay up."

Stephenie shrugged. Henton had explained the need for soldiers to act like soldiers and not get soft and she had decided not to argue the point.

Aching for food, she walked over to Will who had already started cutting off hunks of cheese to go with the dried meat and bread he had set aside for her. "Thank you."

"Anytime."

Kas made a sound not quite like clearing his throat and Stephenie turned toward him, the food quickly going into her mouth.

Forcing her to practice Dalish, he asked very slowly, "You avoided the question last night, what do you plan to do with your mother?"

"Put a sword in her heart," Stephenie said even more slowly. The Dalish language had an unusual set of inflections that made her pronunciation of Kas' native tongue difficult. With Henton having listened secretly to their private conversations on their way to the Greys, they both agreed she should learn another language that no one else was likely to know. Switching to the Old Tongue, she added, "I don't even know she's with her brother, but I hope so."

"You pick up languages fast, but you need more practice."

"You more than me," she mumbled in Cothish over a hunk of bread. Her smile took any sting out of the comment.

Henton cleared his own throat and nodded to John and Berman. After they were awakened, he addressed the whole group. "We don't want a repeat of yesterday. We should assume that there will be more people hunting us and we will assume anyone who sees us might talk. So to minimize that, we'll be cutting across country and staying off any of the major roads. Instead of heading to Uthen and then up to Steel and into Midland, we'll head directly to Clear Water, then up to Steel." Henton nodded his head to Stephenie.

She looked around at the attentive faces. "For those who don't know, the land between here and the Midlands is a mix of farmland, forest, and bogs. Not overly difficult terrain for the most part, assuming we avoid the bogs, but we'll not have as many towns and villages along the way to resupply."

"Then the horses might not have been that big a deal," John mumbled barely loud enough to hear.

Choosing to ignore the comment, Stephenie continued. "We're about a hundred miles from Clear Water, so let's see if we can't work up to twenty miles a day after a couple more days of warmup. We'll plan to be there in seven days. Kas agreed last night to keep us on course and we'll make sure to stop at enough farmsteads and smaller villages to keep supplied."

"Would this help you?" Tim asked, holding out the two holy symbols that had been removed from the dead.

"You kept them?" Henton demanded.

Tim straightened, but somehow made himself look smaller. "Yes, sir. I wasn't sure we should throw them in the river. Felis might take offense. Also, I know the Senzar had used them against us, so I thought perhaps they could be of use to Steph, assuming Catheri doesn't take offense."

Still held out to her, Stephenie took the two silvery grey medallions into her hands. She turned them over. They were only three inches in diameter, with the front containing the raised image of a soldier and the back an image of a field. A small loop at the top had a steel chain run through the cold metal of the medallion. She had seen similar holy symbols before, but had never touched one. It tingled and almost felt alive below the surface of the metal.

She looked up as Kas materialized next to her, startling Tim and the others. "Destroy them," he said in accented Cothish. Then continued quickly in the Old Tongue, "They are an abomination. I will not have you contribute to the evil they represent. You are strong enough without a crutch."

Stephenie felt the chill radiating from him "Kas, I am not sure I know how to destroy them. I won't use them myself, but I do know they are not easy to construct and there are few enough priests left in Cothel, and too many of those are loyal to Burdger before Josh or the High Priest."

Kas radiated anger, causing Tim to step back. "These things are parasites. Like thousands of ticks, slowly bleeding their host to death to make your lives a little easier when those that use them should be able to use magic without that aid. They should all be destroyed!"

"Kas," she said, softening her voice. "I know that. I don't condone what these things represent, but I am trying to think about the overall good. We can't change everything overnight and people need healers and someone to protect them against threats."

"I died because my people chose to stand up for what is right! My parents, my family, the people of the Dalar empire...Sairy—died because we refused to simply stand aside and ignore the evil that represents. Your ancestors did not care because it was not humans or elves being bled dry! Just some nameless being in another world."

"Kas," she said again slowly, feeling as much as hearing his conviction. "I understand. I will try to destroy these I have, but please," she held out her hands, "please listen to me. The people of your time knew what these things were and you could not convince all of them. The people today are even more ignorant and they will only see it as a holy war. I grant you that there would be plenty of people today that would also take up the position that if it was not humans dying, who cares. I'm not one of those people, Kas, but at the same time, I can't start a holy war. That will just get a lot more people killed and galvanize everyone against us."

She took a deep breath, "We, meaning, you and I and everyone else we can get to support us, need to find a different solution. We can't provoke the rest of the world at the start of change. We have to convince them over time, with a plan."

Kas remained silent for several moments and then nodded his head as his form visibly softened. "Stephenie, please accept my apology. I...I should not have gotten so angry. You are correct. My people, a powerful nation, with many others to support us, could not overcome the greed and drive for power. I agree; right now we are just a handful, and I am not even in my time." He appeared to sigh. "I am sorry for yelling."

Stephenie smiled, despite her concern for his sudden melancholy. "It's okay, Kas. I had to be reminded very recently that I needed to wait for my revenge against Elard. We just have to wait until the time is right and I know you have been waiting a very long time. We will work to fix the problem, but we can't do all of it right now."

He shook his head. "I still feel bad. I pride myself on being rational. To lose control in that fashion. It is inexcusable."

"I love you, and so you get a few angry rants for free. Just don't make a habit of it," she added with a bigger smile. She turned to the others; even her lack of sensitivity to emotions and thoughts could not mask the fear coming from the men. Switching to Cothish, she searched for a way to explain the situation without revealing too much sensitive information about Kas' history. "That might have sounded bad, but Kas was concerned about me using the holy symbols. They have not always been considered that. A long time ago, people knew them to be devices that augmented a mage's powers, providing extra energy to the mage instead of having them draw it through themselves. The problem is, these devices slowly kill a being somewhere else to provide that power. He does not want the killing to continue. It's something he is very passionate about, since it is a big factor in the reason he and his people died."

She waited for a reaction, but everyone seemed frozen in place and afraid to move or say anything. Nodding her head, she met Tim's eyes. "You didn't do anything wrong. He's not angry at any of you, just frustrated and yelling at me, but everything is good."

Tim, still watching Kas carefully, nodded his head and swallowed.

Stephenie gave everyone a reassuring smile. "Just a bit of a lover's spat, nothing big. Actually, more just miscommunication than anything." Becoming more serious, she added. "We do have a long way to go and the longer we are here, the easier it is for someone to find us. So, I'll hold on to these while we get moving."

They marched for the better part of the day, but they still only made a small amount of progress. Less than twelve miles through the dense woods left Stephenie completely exhausted and bleeding from her nose.

The two days that followed were slightly better, but they had still only traveled about fifty miles from Antar. At their current rate, Henton guessed it would be five or six more days before they even reached the area around Clear Water, which would mark their halfway point to the border with Midland. Heading directly toward the border instead of following the roads did remove some of the distance, but the rough terrain more than canceled any benefit.

He folded up Stephenie's map and placed it back in the waxed leather pouch before putting it back in his pack. He hoped it would not rain, that would only make them go slower than they already were and the slower they went, the more stops they would need for food.

He sighed as he looked at Stephenie sleeping next to a clump of birch trees. The sandy ground here was currently dry and more hospitable than much of the ground they had covered that day, but if it rained, they would have to pick up their campsite or be flooded.

"Hey, Henton, got a few minutes?" Will asked quietly as he approached.

Henton nodded his head, aware most of the others were already asleep. Tim and Douglas were the only others awake and they were standing watch a short distance from the campsite. So far there had been no sign of additional pursuit, but he was going to have more warning than when Oliver was killed. "What's up?"

Will pursed his lips ever so slightly, which Henton knew to be trouble. Will almost never had to consider his words, something everyone had always envied when they would put into a port and try to meet the local women.

Switching to Pandar, the trade tongue, Will finally spoke. "I know I shouldn't ask, so tell me to sod off if I'm overstepping, but I know you can understand quite a bit of what Kas and Stephenie tell each other. I'm concerned about a few things and I'm hoping you can tell me there's nothing to worry about."

Henton looked around, but if Kas was close, they would never know it if the ghost did not want to be seen. Most of the men knew Kas could speak only a little Cothish and had not really started learning Pandar. Will's question was directly related to Stephenie's desire to learn Kas' native tongue, which Henton still did not even know the name of. "Will, I'm guessing you are getting very close to the line." Continuing in Pandar himself, he inclined his head. "What's your question?"

Will rolled his shoulders as he casually glanced around. "That thing with the holy symbol. I heard Kas demand that they be destroyed before he switched over into that Senzar tongue. What's he at? Steph...Beth was talking about how they were killing something. Kas has been good enough, but there are times I just don't trust his motivation."

Henton looked at Will, trying to gauge the man he had practically raised into adulthood. He suspected the others were likely talking about Kas' outburst as well, but none of them would come to him. "Let me ask you this, do you really believe everything you have been preaching about Catheri or are you just doing what you think needs to be done to help her?"

Will smiled. "You would question my conviction? Have I said or done anything that contradicts something else I've said? Do you not believe in her?"

Henton frowned; pinning Will down to an explicit position was nearly impossible. It was one of the most frustrating things about Will, but it also allowed him to be flexible, which was very useful in many situations. "Will, you know I believe in her, but I really wish you would be straight with me sometimes." Knowing there was no point in pressing his question further, he sat down on the blankets he spread out on the ground. "You would be better to talk with Steph, tell her your concerns, and ask your questions."

Will sat down next to Henton. "I have a feeling she doesn't want to talk about it." He pulled a small bundle of cheese from his pouch, unwrapped it, and held it out for Henton.

Hungry, Henton took a piece and put it into his mouth. "Yes, Kas wants her to destroy them, but she's worried about provoking people into thinking she's trying to start a holy war. Kas has a long history and knows a lot of things. There is a chance that much of what we believe today is wrong. Which means a lot of what has been fought about for generations might be for naught."

"How old?" Will leaned in closer, "I know you've heard a lot and I know there is something under Antar no one is supposed to know about. The gold for one, but is Kas being truthful? Some people might think he's an agent of Elrin."

Henton's jaw tightened. "And just who would be saying that? Almost no one knows about Kas save for us."

"And His Majesty, a handful of other soldiers who saw him in the Greys," he sighed, "and Lady Rebecca." He held up his hand. "I'm not saying he is, but he's definitely got a problem with the gods and the priests and he has a lot of influence on Steph."

"Will, I've seen things and heard plenty, and yeah, much of it challenges what I thought I knew; but, you have to trust her and trust Kas. I don't know what your angle is with this whole Catheri business, but Stephenie needs us to support her."

"I do, Henton. I just worry where all of this will go. I never really considered the consequences when we all went with her to the Greys. I feel like I am getting a late start, but I am just trying to navigate us through these waters, so we can come out on the other end."

Henton nodded his head. "I don't have an answer for you, but I'm committed to the course we are on."

Chapter 13

Stephenie pushed herself harder each day and in four days, they had managed Clear Water. It was not that her stamina was improving, only that she refused to stop each day until the sun was setting. After six more days, Stephenie was sure they were across the border into Midland. Although they had been traveling through dense woods and had not seen a town or village for two days, near the end of the day, they encountered a wide river. Based on the maps, she was certain it was the Yellow Snake River.

That night the rains started. It rained heavily over the next three days and nights, and while there were occasional breaks in the downpours, a continual dampness kept everyone miserable as their progress slowed to a crawl. Eventually, Tim acquired a scratchy voice, which led to a cough and fever.

With his worsening condition, and others threatening to become ill as well, Henton was finally forced to admit they needed to find a small town and risk being seen. As the sun was going down, they entered the town of Amil. While bigger than a village, having three public houses, with one attached to an inn, the town lacked a wall and was generally outside the main flow of traffic going north and south. Travelers normally went through Ontic, a day's journey to the northwest.

Had the sky been clear, from Amil they would have had an excellent view of the Miden Hills, the mountain range that occupied the center of Midland. The majority of the mountains on the northern side of the range could only just barely be considered mountains. Even in the southern range, only a few of the peaks were tall enough that snow survived the summer months.

Tired and hungry, they chose to stay at the Prancing Boulders, which was the inn with the attached public house. After negotiating a rate for at least three days, they put Tim and Douglas in one of the two rooms they rented. Everyone else, still wearing their wet clothes, went down to the public room to get some food and sit by the fire.

After eating enough for four people, Stephenie sat back and started to watch the other people in the common room. Their group made up only about a third of the people present. And while the locals were somewhat reserved around such a large group of strangers, they were generally kind and willing to please. Stephenie knew the dress and customs of Midland were not that different from Cothel's, but was surprised at some of the colors these more remote people were wearing. It was not that she objected to their choices, but she had a hard time looking away from the bright dyes.

She tried to listen to the conversations, but there were at least four native languages spoken in Midland and she had never learned any of them. However, even these people here spoke Cothish and Kyntian, as well as Pandar and sometimes all of those languages were spoken in the same sentence. She was able to keep up most of the time when the Midland words were left out, but the look of confusion in her companion's faces kept her giggling.

The variety of languages was a direct result of Midland being the only country around the Sea of Tet that had ports on both Tet as well as the Endless Sea. It made Midland a powerful trade partner or enemy, depending on the situation. Most of the trade between the Seas was along Midland's northern border, but everyone who made the country their home was proud of the power they had.

This evening, driven in by the many days of rain, the locals were especially festive, given to energetic dancing and boisterous laughing. Stephenie watched two older men who sat in the far corner. They were taking turns playing a fiddle, drum, and some type of flute or recorder between them. The music was something that provoked movement and her foot had been tapping since they started.

Feeling a bit nostalgic about the times she had spent with Joshua and the soldiers around fires in the training fields, she sat back and allowed herself to relax. She glanced over to the dark corner, opposite from the musicians and thought of Kas who was silently watching without visible form. *I feel so bad for him, excluded from everything. Tied to me, yet even we are separated by miles.* She sighed, *if only I could get him a physical body.*

She took a deep breath and tried yet again to reach him mentally. It was something she had been trying to do every night and despite her failures, she was certain she was getting closer to understanding what it took to open the link between herself and someone else.

Breathing out, she allowed her eyes to lose focus on Will and the others who were dancing with the locals in a space created by pushing aside half the tables. Opening herself up, she tried to drop the inhibitions she normally felt. She put aside the fear of rejection or of people thinking she was just a silly little girl who had no business traipsing about the country. Gradually, she stripped away the layers of protection, trying not to care what others would think. Then suddenly, she felt a shift inside her. As a key's turning opened a lock, she was immediately aware of Kas' presence. The tiny control threads steaming between the two of them filled the room and then faded from her awareness as the strong sense of pride coming from Kas filled her mind.

That is the first time I have ever felt you reach out to me.

Stephenie wallowed in the feelings she was picking up from him. *I've been practicing for days and days and days. Perhaps I am just more relaxed, but somehow I just did things a little different. I can't explain it.*

Well, you did a good job. Always improving. Just be careful if you do this with someone else; if they know what they are doing, they could push their way into your mind and take control of you.

Stephenie listened to what he said and knew it to be just concern for her, not the reprimand she might have heard at another time. A blissful grin filled her face; she did not believe it would be possible to hide anything or be false when communicating in this fashion.

Unfortunately, that is a significant misconception. One can be just as dishonest with mental communications as with any other. Perhaps the deception is even easier, if the other person believes there must be honesty.

I don't see how, she thought back at him.

It takes practice, but if one conditions oneself to believe something completely or is able to section off one's thoughts, dropping them to a lower level of consciousness, it is possible. Just something to remember.

Stephenie nodded her head, feeling warm and comfortable. Wrapped in his consciousness, she allowed herself to simply exist for a while, not exchanging words, just enjoying the emotions of each other.

"Beth, you're grinning like someone knocked the sense out of you," Henton said, drawing her attention.

Slowly pulling back slightly from Kas, she nodded her head. "Just taking it easy," she said as she noticed Will twirl a blonde girl probably a year younger than herself. John was trying to get his turn with her as well, but there were several more men than woman who were dancing.

You should go dance, Kas said, drawing back her attention.

But I am enjoying sitting here with you.

As am I, but I know you want to have some fun. I will not be jealous, not after having shared your feelings.

Stephenie let her admiration for Kas flow across their link and then got to her feet. Henton watched her wordlessly as she moved over to Will.

"Beth?" Will asked, as if she might not be real; his partner already forgotten.

"Just slide me into the line," she said, stepping around the girl; her feet still tapping to the drum beat.

Stephenie's appearance energized Berman, John, and what appeared to be a pair of local men in their twenties. She thought the older man was cuter than what was likely his younger brother, but that was only a casual appraisal. She smiled at the older man and started dancing as his partner. The music was more of a jig, and while she had been watching for a while, she did not really know the pattern for the dance. Everyone laughed at her missteps, but it was in good fun and no one minded, except perhaps the girl who's foot was stepped on.

Eventually, the partners switched and Will was linked forearm to forearm with her as everyone twirled in a circle. They switched arms and turned the other way. Laughing, Will leaned in with his sly smile and whispered, "You been eating with your left hand?"

Uncertain of what his comment meant, she had to wait for a full change of partners to get a chance to question him. "What did you mean?" she asked as the music changed and slowed to allow everyone to catch their breath.

"Just your left arm seems more toned."

Stephenie stopped in the middle of the dance floor and clasped both of her forearms with her hands. She rubbed them, feeling her arms through her heavy cotton shirt. Depressed with her body's appearance, she had not pulled up her sleeves in days. Feeling a definite difference in the muscles, she slid her sleeve up to her elbow and was startled to see her left arm as she remembered it from before the incident in the Greys.

Will had stopped dancing as well and the others tried to move around the obstacle they presented. "Beth?" Will asked, uncertainty in his face and voice.

She shook her head at him and quickly left the dance floor. The others slowed their dancing to watch her depart, but she paid them no attention. Her left arm had regained muscle tone while the rest of her body continued to exist in its emaciated form. *How, Kas?* She asked, reaching out her mind to him.

What happened? Kas asked, having moved to her side.

The muscles on my left arm have come back.

"Now that I think about it, my arm's not been so achy," she said to Henton who had discreetly brought her drink to her as she neared the table. A questioning look from him prompted her to continue. "My bones ache all the time, but I've kind of got used to it. My left arm hasn't. Not since..."

Connecting her current appraisal of her arm with what she said, Henton pondered, "not since that thing we don't want to talk about?"

She looked up to meet his eyes and was unable to suppress the smile on her face. "I think I may have found a way to heal myself," she whispered just loud enough for him to hear.

Henton glanced over her shoulder and met someone's eye, which she presumed was a signal for the others to continue dancing. Then he returned his attention to her, echoing her smile. "Well, if I can guess what you are thinking, I expect we won't be keeping that a secret from Will much longer."

Back in her room, she sat on the bed, still rubbing her fingers over the muscles of her left arm. She was uncertain when the tone and definition had started to return, but it was definitely something that had been gradual. Her left arm had been as emaciated as her right one when she had worn the dress to see the High Priest. Once that was over, she had gone back to the long sleeve shirts to hide her frail form.

Kas stood before Stephenie. "You've told me again what happened, but I am uncertain how that would have caused you to heal." Kas shook his head and looked to Henton, who was standing next to him. The others were still downstairs or in the other room with Tim.

"All I know is blistering hot, blue-white flames were shooting from her arm," Henton said with a shrug. "I'm not an expert in these things."

Stephenie looked both of them in the eyes. "Look, I am going to try doing it again. This time with my right arm, if it works, then I'll see about fixing the rest of me."

"Dumping energy through your body is not healthy. It could kill you or leave you severely burned. It kills mages every—"

"Kas, I know that, but there is something different about me— and no, Henton, you don't go getting all Will-like on me and thinking there is something divine about me." She reached over and unwrapped the book from the layers of oiled cotton, waxed burlap, and the inner wool blanket. It had been the only object that any of them carried which had been protected from the days of rain. "This book that you gave me, it talks about people who are able to transform themselves into other forms and even regrow limbs that were severed. You said it yourself, Kas, it was something rare, and most people didn't understand how it worked. I think I simply stumbled upon it. Perhaps drawing lots of energy through your body is what it takes to do it."

"Stephenie, I—"

"Kas, I have to try. I can't go on this way and unless we find another library that's been lost for a thousand years, we are limited in what we can learn by reading."

Kas lowered his head. "You were supposed to be practicing transforming that bronze Henton picked up for you. That is how you are supposed to learn to heal yourself. I fear what dumping energy through you will do. I do not want to lose you. You have to be careful." He turned to Henton, "can you offer any words of wisdom?"

Henton smiled at Kas and shook his head. "My suggestion is not to fight her, you won't win."

Kas' hands clenched before him. "I meant wisdom for her."

"Kas, Henton, please," she said, holding out her hands to them. "I do listen to both of you. I really do. But, I need to try this. I desperately need to try this. You don't understand what I am going through."

Henton shook his head and gestured to the small room. "Not here you don't. You melted gold and stone under Antar. You try it here, you'll burn down the building."

She nodded her head. "Yeah, I was thinking perhaps some rocky place without too many trees close by. Damned weather's made travel miserable, but with everything soaked, that should make sure too much doesn't catch fire."

"You don't want to do it near this town. Not unless you want people chasing after you. We have to do it somewhere that no one is going to notice. And," he emphasized, "we'll need to wait until Tim is better. We don't want to split up, and we're few enough that we can't leave anyone behind."

She held her breath a moment, but knew Henton was right. *Damn, so close. I hate waiting.* She let go of the energy she had been pushing through her body. It had started to burn uncomfortably and was performing no specific purpose. "Hopefully, he'll be feeling better in the morning."

"Stephenie, I would suggest that you take your mind off waiting and make good use of your time by continuing to try to transform the bronze. Parallel paths to the solution will give you more options."

Stephenie could see and feel the desperation in Kas. "I promise, I will continue to work on the bronze as well."

* * * * *

The next morning rain was still falling and Tim had not regained his strength, though his fever was lower. Douglas and Will went about the town to resupply the group, while the others took turns spending time in the pub or their rooms. Stephenie tried to contain her frustration, but despite what she had promised Henton and Kas, she could not get her mind off finding a place to see what drawing large amounts of energy through her body would do. The more she thought about it, the more she was certain it was the solution to her problem.

"I think that perhaps in the Greys I passed out and cut off the power before I was able to recover." She said aloud, triggering Kas to take visible form. "My body must have changed somehow to handle the energy, then didn't have a chance to go back to normal since I lost consciousness. I think that only when I'm exposed to enough energy, can my body change."

Kas shook his head. "I think you are trying to avoid learning to transform the shape of that bronze bar."

"Agreed," Henton added from where he was sitting against the wall. The other room was crowded enough, and with Henton pretending to be her husband, he was sleeping and waiting in her room as well.

She frowned at him and wondered just when she had grown comfortable enough with him that his presence did not feel like an invasion of her personal space. Camped out in the woods was one thing; it felt open. But to share a small room with someone else was something she had never felt comfortable doing. *Perhaps I always dreaded someone learning what I am.*

Putting Henton from her mind, she went back to staring at the lump of bronze on the bed next to her. Despite Kas' complaint that she was not trying to transform the metal, two days earlier, she had managed to make the surface a little droopy, like a candle sitting too long in the sun. However, she had not been able to hold the strange field in her thoughts for more than a brief moment since then. *For all the talk of my amazing abilities, nothing seems to come when I expect it.*

Knowing Kas and Henton were both sick of her talking about transforming her body through raw energy, a thought that honestly did scare her, she closed her eyes and went back to concentrating on the bronze. Breathing slowly, she opened herself up to the world and allowed everything to simply be in her awareness, as if she were a cat waiting to pounce as the secret meandered by, oblivious to her presence.

She felt the confines of the room, including the texture of the rough wooden walls, the scratchy cloth over her bed, the slick sheen of the leather of Henton's belt, the feel of the hairs on his arms and face. The very texture of his skin and even the strong masculine smell that filled the room.

She breathed out slowly, focusing her attention on the metal in her own hands; hands that were rough with calloused and worn nails, but still delicate and nimble. Narrowing her attention, the surface of the metal came into sharper focus and the rest of the world fell out of her awareness.

Despite the visually smooth appearance, the bar was actually quite pocked and irregular, like a worn road filled with countless holes after an army of wagons and horses traveled over it. Looking even closer with her mind's eye, Stephenie was again able to discern small gaps between what appeared to be small lumps of metal. Those lumps she could tell were not always the same; most were smaller, but there were some parts that were larger and not the same as the first. She knew them to be very small; smaller than anything she could even see with her eyes. And they were numerous, far too many to count in a lifetime.

Concentrating, she tried once again to sense the field that held these parts together. But, as had been her problem previously, the energy potential stored in the bronze blurred her senses. She knew from experience, that drawing off the energy would cause energy from other things, such as her hands or the air, to flow back into the metal. Kas had told her many times that everything tries to remain in balance, areas of high energy concentration flowing to areas of less energy.

Knowing that drawing away the energy had never been enough to see the field hidden behind it, she did not bother to try this time. Instead, she decided to ignore the energy she sensed, as if she were allowing her eyes to lose focus. Breathing in even more slowly, she focused not on seeing the field that had eluded her, but simply in disrupting what she knew must be there.

She sat for a long time, manipulating the fields by random instinct, hoping that something would happen. *Like jiggling the wrong key in a lock, hoping to make it work...is that what I am reduced to?* Slowly she felt a change, as if one piece finally slid into position. Struggling to hold the field in place, she reached inside herself to draw more energy. In the back of her mind, she knew Kas would complain about her lack of subtlety, but she could not risk losing the field before she had a better understanding of it.

Pouring in more energy, she expanded it further to envelope the whole bar, hoping that would give her a better chance to remember the look and feel of the field. She felt the metal growing slack as the forces holding the tiny pieces together grew weaker. Adjusting her field slightly, she wanted to make the metal even more pliable, but before she could finish the thought, the metal slid through her fingers and splashed over her feet.

She opened her eyes. Henton's mouth had dropped and Kas was wide eyed.

"Did it burn you?" Henton asked, already at her side, tentatively holding his fingers a few inches over the metal that had pooled between her feet.

Stephenie shook her head. "It just came apart." She knocked chunks of the metal from her boots that looked like bronze rain drops sitting on the surface; however, many parts of the leather retained a metallic sheen. The bronze on the floor had flowed into the cracks of the wood, spreading out as if it had been nothing more than a pool of cream. It was now as solid and brittle as it had ever been.

Kas moved closer to examine the metal. "I think you separated the bronze into pieces so small that they soaked into the wood itself." Glancing up, "the same for your hands. Some of it may have absorbed into your skin."

Stephenie sighed as she looked at her fingers and the metallic sheen. For a moment, she wondered if it was the same iridescence as she had seen on her arm after the blue-white flames had gone, but only a moment of investigation told her it was not. This was more like an ink stain, while the iridescence had been something almost shed from her skin.

"Well," Henton said slowly, "I see it as a positive step. Now you have something new to practice. Liquifying the bronze and extracting it from wood."

Stephenie frowned at him, but then looked down at the mess on the floor. It would be obvious to anyone who came into the room something odd had happened; metals did not normally flow as liquid without causing wood to catch fire. And, even getting a fire going in the room that would be hot enough to melt bronze was next to impossible. This would leave far too many questions. They would either have to try to dig it out, or she would have to figure out how to use her magic.

"Besides, if you don't, what will you have to practice with? We really don't have the extra money to buy more metal for you to play with."

Two days later, Tim was finally feeling well enough to travel and Stephenie had pried up the bronze from the floor with a dagger and gravity fields as best she could. There were scratches and gouges in the wood, but those could have been caused by something heavy being dragged over the floor. She had liquified the bronze a couple more times, but she had never managed to use a gravity field at the same time to control the form. The moment she tried, she would lose focus on the field that had separated the metal.

However, she no longer cared. The one thought that had been driving her night and day was the thought of trying to heal her right arm. Therefore, even though it was late in the afternoon, she led everyone out of town. Everyone knew it would not be possible to get very far before the sun set, but she drove them harder than at any point in the trip so far. She had promised Henton and Kas she would wait until they found a place that would not catch fire and was away from people, but she knew that whatever they found, it would simply be good enough for her. She would not wait another night.

By late evening, they appeared to have reached rockier terrain away from other people. However, it was still fairly wooded. Losing the light, she finally agreed to stop and camp, provided that Kas would explore for a rocky clearing while the others prepared the campsite.

The others avoided engaging her in conversation, aware that she was not in the mood for casual discussion, even if they did not know what she was planning. Stephenie was thankful for their forbearance and quickly consumed her dinner while pacing about, waiting for Kas' return. When he finally did return, she was on her feet and met him halfway into the camp. Still reserved with his emotions, she had no idea if he had found anything or not. "Well?"

He relented. "There is a place that will likely work. It is about a mile to the west." He slowly materialized as he spoke, "but we should not do this alone. We will need to take at least Henton with us in case you need to be carried back."

"What's going on?" Will asked.

"Just something I need to try," she replied with as much clarity to his questions as she had since they had danced.

"I heard Henton's name and while I don't speak the Old Tongue, I think I heard a distance."

Stephenie turned to Will and forced herself respond kindly. "It's something I need to try to see if I can heal the rest of me. It could be dangerous, so I want to do it away from everyone else to make sure everyone stays safe."

"Is there sex involved? I can help with that."

"Watch yourself, John," Douglas snapped. The tone of Douglas' voice was never really friendly to the man from the west country, but now held a cold promise of violence.

Driven to the point of frustration, Stephenie ignored the exchange and turned away from the others. "We won't be long. Everyone else stay here." She turned to Henton and switched back to the Old Tongue, "You'll come, yes?"

"Of course," he said and had to jog in order to catch up to her. Once he was close enough, he added, "Plus it will give Douglas a chance to work on John's attitude."

Stephenie nodded her head. "You'd think he's fresh off the farm, but he's almost as old as Douglas." She shrugged, "He's not the first to act like that to me. My mother's men were much worse."

"But you shouldn't have to hear things like that from the men who are supposed to keep you safe. I'll put an end to it once I get back."

Stephenie nodded. John was probably her least favorite person in the group; he had problems with maturity, but at the moment, the only thing she wanted to think about was potentially getting better. The prospect of regaining her physical strength was all consuming. Without recovering, she hardly cared what others said.

Kas eventually led them to a small clearing. The grass was green and thick from all the recent rain. While there were not many rocks about, a fire had long ago cleared the trees for at least fifty feet in all directions.

"You two stay here for now," she said as she pulled her shirt free of her belt. She slipped it over her head and then removed the binding from her chest, dropping the clothing to the ground. She glanced up at Henton and smiled at his surprise. "It's not like I have a lot of spare clothing to burn up."

Without further comment, she headed toward the middle of the clearing, taking to heart both of their requests for her to be safe. She had no desire to hurt herself further, but so far, this was the only thing that had seemed to make an impact on healing her body and she was willing to risk a lot in an effort to get better.

She started drawing in energy before she reached the center of the clearing. Once there, she inhaled deeply and made a concerted effort to pull as much energy from the ground as she could coax from rocks and soil. It burned and brought a grimace to her face, but she continued to pull in more and more. Just as when she fought the ghost, she could not contain the power she had brought into herself and so she directed it out her right arm.

Blue-white flames leaped into the sky. She tried to look at them, but the heat burned her face and the intensity of the flames blinded her vision. Pain from the effort of controlling the energy radiating through her whole body. In a detached part of her mind, she wondered just how long it would take. Fighting the ghost felt like ages, already the throbbing in her head made this effort feel as if the moon had passed across the sky. Though she knew it had just been moments. Trying to count to ten, she only reached four before sagging to her knees and at six, she could not bear the pain any longer and simply let the energy already in her flow out.

On her hands and knees, she opened her eyes. The ground was baked dry and the grass had been scorched away. Quickly she lifted her hands from the ground and sat backward away from the hot and dry soil. As soon as she was sure she was not going to fall over, she looked over her arm and again there was an iridescence to her skin. It was fading quickly and falling from her arm as if it was a fine coating of dust blowing into the wind.

With her left hand, she pinched her nose closed to try and stop the blood that started pouring down her face. Spitting, she emptied what had drained into her mouth.

"Steph, you okay?" Henton demanded as he rushed over.

Kas, already kneeling next to her was looking her in the eyes. "You have not damaged your mind further? I have always joked that you are a brain-damaged simpleton, but you give me cause to now think that may be true."

She stared back at Kas, somewhat hurt by his tone.

"Why did you persist in drawing so much energy through you? You should have started slowly. Do a little the first time. Experiment to see what it takes. You pushed way too much through you. Look at the blood running down your face and all over your chest."

Tilting her head back, she talked through the soreness of her throat. "We got stuck in Amil for far too long. We are behind schedule and I don't have time to take days seeing what will happen. Besides, I've already been trying low amounts of energy for days and that's not helped. I think it has to be something serious to trick my body into reacting."

"Did it at least work?" Henton asked.

Stephenie glanced over to Henton, who was staring at her clothing in his hand instead of her chest. She took a shallow breath, trying to breathe past the blood that was still trickling down her throat. She concentrated on her right hand, moving her fingers and twisting her wrist. The dull ache in her bones that she had grown so used to feeling was gone, but her arm and the rest of her was as weary as ever. "Yeah, I think it worked." She knew there was no visible difference in her muscle tone, but she hoped it would come back as her left arm did. "I just don't know how long it will take to rebuild the muscle."

He nodded his head. "I should have brought something to clean you up."

Still holding her head back and nose shut with her left hand, she stuck out her right. "Give me the binding. It'll be hidden under my shirt and heck, while I've never had big breasts, these have withered away to nothing now."

Henton cleared his throat. "You're still a woman, Steph. And having big breasts is not everything."

She laughed as she wiped the blood from her face and chest. "That I know. I always wanted them when I was younger, then they started to get in the way. But still..." Setting down the binding, she tested her nose to see if more blood would come. After she felt relatively safe from ruining her shirt, she took that from Henton and very slowly pulled it over her head. She was tired and feeling a bit faint from the blood loss. Struggling to stand, Henton helped her to not only gain her feet, but remain there.

"I should give you guard duty."

"What?"

"Perhaps knowing you need to stay up at night would keep you a little more reserved in your experimentation with your life."

When they got back to the camp site, every one was anxious and waiting for her. Henton waved away a series of questions until Will stood directly in front of Stephenie and crossed his arms.

"We all saw a gout of fire shoot into the sky and you look like crap."

"I don't know that it will fix me, so I don't want to go into detail, but I am really hoping drawing large amounts of energy through my body will trigger a reaction that reverses what's happened to my muscles and keeps me from feeling the need to eat everything in sight."

"We're here to help you, don't try to keep everything from us. We were worried."

She nodded her head as Henton helped her sit down. Kas remained at her side, watching protectively. "I know, and these two keep hounding me about keeping safe, but there are some things I just have to do on my own."

Will frowned, but gathered up a platter of food and a water skin. As he did that, John stepped forward.

"Ma'am?"

Stephenie sighed; all she really wanted to do was get some sleep, though the food Will was bringing over made her stomach rumble. "Yes, John."

"I'm sorry about earlier. I shouldn't say those types of things. It was not appropriate."

Stephenie noted a slight grin on Will's face as he came up behind John with the food. She turned back to John and nodded her head. "That's fine. Don't worry about it. I don't mind a good joke and the dirtier the better. And I consider you all my friends, so feel free to laugh at my expense. However, there will never be a physical relationship between me and any of you. My heart is already spoken for, so you can put that from your mind. And as far as joking about me being naked," she looked at Will and Henton, "well that's reserved for those who've already seen me naked." She took a bite of the bread Will had handed her. "I don't want people to fear upsetting me; I really wasn't that mad about your comment. But, I want to make it clear, don't expect anything of that sort from me. If you can find the time and a willing woman, please take advantage of that. Heck, tell me about it afterward if you want, I've heard plenty of stories from others, but Kas will take great offense if someone thinks to get me into their bed."

John nodded his head. "Of course, Ma'am. I didn't mean to imply we should have sex. It was just a bad joke."

Stephenie smiled at him as she refilled her mouth with food. "All's forgiven," she mumbled around the food.

Chapter 14

The next day they skirted around Ontic on their way north. They continued on without stopping and for the two days after that, they kept to the east of the main road heading northeast, remaining in the foothills of the mountains. During that period, Stephenie spent most of her waking time staring at her right arm to the point of distraction. She stumbled into nearly half of the team at least once, those that were more tolerant were stepped on several times. If Kas had not been so irritated at her reckless use of energy, he would have been proud of the meticulous measurements and the detailed notes she was recording.

By the end of the second day past Ontic, he had warmed his disposition. Her arm had visibly toned, adding muscle and her skin was much less blotchy. "I admit, you appear to have been correct about healing yourself. I have no explanation. You continue to do things outside of my experience."

"Does that make me sexy?" she teased in Dalish, her eye lashes fluttering up at his illuminated face.

He shook his head, but was still smiling. "I hope you did not flirt this way with others before me."

"Only you, my love." She hesitated, not wanting to destroy the mood, but her drive to be better was too strong. "I want to work on my legs tonight." She looked up at Kas, hoping he would understand her need.

After a moment, he nodded his head. "I am surprised you waited this long." He looked over at Henton, met the sergeant's eyes, and nodded his head.

"The two of you conspiring now?" she asked in the Old Tongue.

Kas turned back to Stephenie. "With regard to you? Always." He smiled at her again, "It was more of a bet as to how long you would wait."

Stephenie shook her head. "Who won?"

"It does not matter as long as you are careful."

"Henton won, didn't he?"

"He offered the first guess, but since his prediction was after mine, I am happy that he won." Kas turned to Henton who had come closer. "There is a cliff and creek about half a mile to the east. A rock slide has cleared most of the trees."

Henton nodded his head. "Ready. The others know to wait here."

Stephenie smiled at the two of them. For the first time she felt a clear sense of hope from both of them. "Thank you. Both of you."

There was no trail to the rock slide and the ground was filled with underbrush and boulders. Stephenie was tempted to fly herself and Henton to the site, but she knew they would argue about her overtaxing herself, and she did want to conserve her strength for the actual event. Instead, the two of them pushed their way through the rough vegetation, arriving at the clearing sweaty and slightly winded.

After a brief pause, Stephenie started stripping out of her clothing, dropping everything on a larger rock. "What?" she asked Henton who was trying to keep his eyes averted.

"Nothing," he responded, then added quietly, "One might get the idea you're rather something of a tease."

She smiled at him as she removed the last of her clothing. "Well, I'm not trying to be." Turning, she started slowly making her way across the sharp rocks and then after scraping her heel, simply flew herself thirty feet away from Henton, placing herself close to the cliff wall. When she landed, she took a few steps to find a place where she could stand in relative safety in case she was to fall down during the ensuing effort.

Once settled, she began to draw energy into herself, pulling it from the rocks all around her. The energy seemed denser in the rocks here than in other places and she wondered how much of a variance existed in different types of stone. She knew from experience different types of material, such as air, wood, and stone had different potentials and different resistances, but she had not paid close enough attention to notice all the variations within the same types of material.

Putting the thought from her, with the hope to remember it later, she started to slowly push the energy through her legs. She hoped Kas was noticing just how restrained she was being. It was difficult to keep from charging forward, but she understood the value of Kas' constant reminders.

Gradually, as the energy built up in her, she felt it radiate out from her legs. Almost instantly, her stomach and chest erupted in pain. She felt her skin burning and knew instantly she was in trouble as blue-white flames leapt upward from her legs, enveloping her upper body.

Knowing there was no way to shut off the flow of energy fast enough to avoid the severe burns that were already forming, she did the only thing she could think of, she pushed energy outward from her abdomen and upper body. Not even a heart beat later, she started pushing the energy out from her head and arms as they had started to burn.

The pain of the heat died off immediately, but the amount of energy coursing through her limbs was much less. Worried that she might not have used enough to trigger healing, she dug within herself and forced her body to draw in more energy.

Her heart beat was a rapid staccato, struggling to hold to the demands she was placing on herself. Abstractly, she knew she was unable to breathe. In fact, all the air in her lungs had been sucked out her nose and mouth; the flames surrounding her whole body simply consuming all the fuel they could.

Her limbs quivered. But the burning pain that had ridden up her body had not returned. Her insides were on fire with the energy, but it was dull and almost surreal. However, she knew she could not last much longer.

Already filled with energy, she stopped drawing in more. Her subconscious told her the ground was blistering hot, so as the energy started to drain away, she directed a field to move herself away from where she was standing. A moment later, she had the sensation of falling and when she hit the ground a sharp pain raced through her right arm and side. Her sight was already dim and a moment later she lost consciousness.

Henton bit his lip as he watched Stephenie first walk and then fly away from him over the rocky ground. The boulders here were large, with lots of gaps to catch one's feet. He hoped she would take it easy and go slow. Not only for her safety, but to keep her and Kas from arguing. Their up and down relationship was frustrating him, leaving him unable to decide what to think.

Once the flames started to form around her legs, he did not have a chance to finish cursing before he was scrambling over the rocks to reach her. The sickening cry of pain she issued just before the blue-white flames moved from her legs to consume her whole body told him something was wrong. When her burning body flung itself into the air, burned out, and then fell into a heap among the boulders, he feared the worse.

Night blind due to her flames, he reached her with several bleeding cuts on his arms and a sore ankle from hazards he had not seen. Kas was already there, having blinked across the distance. He had moved her to the flatter side of a rock twice as wide as Henton was tall, before Henton reached them. It was the only surface of size in the area that was mostly smooth.

"She lives," Kas said. The cold of his anger sucking the heat from the air.

Kneeling beside her, Henton quickly checked her over for injuries. With dark spots still in his eyes, he noticed only the obvious; the blood running from a deep cut on her upper right arm and that her forearm appeared broken.

The movement of her arm brought a moan from her lips and Henton tried for a moment to revive her. He cursed again when she did not respond. "I didn't bring many supplies," he said as he repeated a few curses he had heard Kas muttering over the last week or two.

Slipping off his shirt, he quickly cut away a sleeve and wrapped the cloth around her upper arm, hoping not to do more damage to the break, but still stop the bleeding. Once that was done, he took the bent arm and tried to feel the bone through her swelling flesh. The still slightly emaciated arm was not yet too swollen for him to work on it.

"She okay?"

Henton looked up, noting Kas had blinked halfway across the boulder field before stopping.

"What are you doing here Will?" he demanded, turning his attention back to her arm. His sight was improving, but his fingers had already told him what he needed to know. With a quick motion, he pulled her wrist away from her elbow and tried to align her bones.

"I wasn't going to be kept out of what was happening. She was on fire again!"

Kas had returned to Henton's side. "I was so focused on Stephenie, I had not noticed him following."

"Can you tell if her bones are aligned?"

After a moment of consideration, Kas nodded his head. "Almost, you need to twist her wrist a little more toward her.

Henton nodded his head and tried adjusting her bones again until Kas raised a hand to stop him. The effort brought another moan to her lips, but that was the only response. Looking up, he turned toward Will who was already halfway to them. "Go back and get her clothes."

Will obviously heard the reprimand in Henton's voice, but Henton still tracked Will with malice. *Damn her, why couldn't she have taken it slowly for once? Damn it, Steph, you are messing up too much lately.*

"Henton, can you not make her see reason?" Kas asked, mirroring his thoughts.

Henton looked up at the ghost, pain and frustration showing through his translucent face. Henton wished he had an answer. Ever since Kas had started turning to him, he knew the ghost was reaching the end of his tolerance for Stephenie's actions. Kas saw him as a rival, and sometimes Henton was certain Kas wished Stephenie would turn to him so the ghost could once again give up on the living and drift off into the trance of faded memories he had mentioned so many times before.

"Give her time." Henton looked around for a couple of small pieces of wood and noticed Will making his way over to them with Stephenie's clothes. "Get a couple of branches on your way. She broke her forearm."

Ignoring Will, he turned back to Stephenie and brushed her loose hair from her face. A little blood had run from her nose, but far from the gushing blood he had seen too many times. *Steph, wake up. We need to make sure you're okay.*

"Here you go sar...Henton."

"She'd be pissed to know you were here." He said, taking the young saplings Will had cut for a splint.

"I just wanted to see what she was hiding. Why should she hide this from me? I've seen it before."

Henton shook his head as he cut up more of his shirt. He started wrapping a few layers of cloth around her arm to protect her skin from the tree bark. "Think about it Will. What would you do knowing this?"

"She's healing herself with fire. It's amazing."

"And when others hear about that?" he asked, adding the splints to his wrapping. "What do you think will happen to others like her? How many more people will be cleansed by fire to see if they are Catheri's chosen?"

Will sighed as he bent down to put her shirt under her head. "I had not considered that. I've been focusing on doing what we need to do to support her and get people behind her."

"And she's worried about all the other witches and warlocks that will be set afire to see if they might be like her. Perhaps you can invent an alternate way to cleanse people."

"Really? Just come up with something? That kind of lie won't bother you?"

Henton tied off the ends of his ruined shirt and then sat back before turning to Will. "I told you, she changes things. Perhaps she can make it true. Perhaps the things the priests have always discounted as heresy actually have merit. I don't know, and I don't pretend to." He took Stephenie's pants from Will's hands. "You on the other hand are the one making claims. So perhaps you need to make some that are more in line with what she's been saying." Henton turned back to Stephenie and started working her pants onto her legs.

Chapter 15

Stephenie's head was thick, and it hurt like the time Joshua had allowed her to drink way too much ale mixed with that special spirit that had burned her throat. He had claimed he wanted to teach her the penalties for overindulging. She suspected he just wanted to make her suffer for having bested him at the game of tables twice the night before.

When she opened her eyes, she was certain someone must have dared her to finish a cask of wine and then proceeded to beat her head with the empty barrel. The light was way too bright and she was uncomfortable in every way.

Slowly, she tried to sit up, but pain raced through her right arm the moment she put weight on it. Rolling over into a ball, she tried to cradle the encased arm, but the pain was so intense tears rolled from her eyes. Time dragged on as the pain slowly receded. Gradually she became aware of others around her.

"You might want to take it easy," she heard Henton say. There was not much sympathy in his voice.

Taking a deep breath to keep from crying out, she moved to push herself up with her left arm. Sniffling back the congestion in her sinuses, she rubbed away the grime that was clinging to her lashes. "What happened?" she mumbled through parched lips. "And why are my clothes all bunched and cockeyed?" she added as she tried to straighten the shirt that was pulling uncomfortably at her neck.

Henton laughed. "Well, I thought perhaps you didn't want to expand the list of people who get to joke about seeing you naked.

Since you managed to knock yourself out, Will and I did what we could."

She looked up at him and Kas, who was standing a few feet behind Henton with his nearly transparent arms crossed. She swallowed, knowing Kas' appearance was a not-so-subtle reprimand. "I honestly was taking it slowly. Really, I was. But the flames started to burn me. I felt it searing my stomach and chest and the only thing that made sense was to push the energy out everywhere. I told you I'm not impervious to flame."

"Your skin changed," Kas said, floating closer. "It was changing back when I went to you. Some of it was shed away."

"That was skin?" Henton asked. "I thought it was a coating of ash."

Kas shook his head, which was already nearly solid in form. "No. It was decaying quickly, turning to dust, but I observed it close enough to know it was coming off her as she changed back to normal."

Stephenie nodded her head. The thought of being something else was disturbing, but she could not deny the truth of it to herself. However, the implications that presented were something she was content to ignore for the moment. *I can't explain it and neither can Kas, so unless it becomes a problem...*

Henton did not press the discussion. "Well, at least tell me that we didn't go backwards. Do your bones still ache?"

Stephenie took a moment to think about it and then shook her head. "No. I think they are better, aside from my arm." She could not help but let out a laugh that died quickly when it caused her arm to hurt from the movement. "I don't ache like I did. But I'm still starved."

Kas let out a sigh of relief. "You have slept until late in the afternoon, like a silly little princess. That is a record amount of time for you to go without food." He sat down next to her, "but please promise me, you are done with lighting yourself on fire. I do not want you to truly become a brain damaged simpleton."

She cocked her head to the side. "Me? Done making everyone panic, fearing that I'll do something stupid and cause trouble?"

Kas shook his head. "I would never ask that. That would exceed your capacity in every sense. I am just wanting to avoid seeing you on fire."

"You have my word Kas. Believe me. This headache is enough to keep me from doing that anytime soon."

"Good. So now you can go back to working on transforming the bronze and learning Dalish."

The next fifteen days started with difficulty. Stephenie was extremely tired and still quite hungry, eating most of their supplies within a couple of days. Her stamina was limited and they could only travel short distances before she needed to rest. However, she did nothing that either Henton or Kas could declare dangerous, and by the fourth day, her wrist was no longer broken and little more than a dull ache. More importantly, she could see visible changes in the muscle tone over her whole body.

By the sixth day, she was almost constantly giddy as she felt her endurance returning and she was once again able to march through the whole day without feeling as if a team of horses had run her down. This had a mixed response from the men, who while elated to see her happy, were not pleased with the extra effort they had to put forth.

On the eighth day, they crossed out of Midland and into Kynto. They did this along the main road leading from Feldspar to Perfection and at the border, there was a perceptible change in the mood. Where Midland had been fairly open and friendly, the people of Kynto were more guarded and serious. At the crossing, they were stopped and required to pay a toll. And then again, several times along the road to Perfection, soldiers demanded explanations of their travels, but the primary purpose seemed to be to exert a sense of control and extract small bribes from foreign travelers.

The one redeeming part of those days was the view of the Calis Mountain range to the east. The majestic peaks and ridges offered a dramatic sunrise as thin clouds rolled over the range, illuminated by the golden light of the early morning.

As they neared the large city of Perfection, Stephenie's claims to be the daughter of a Kyntian family, who married her off to Henton, a merchant from Cothel, was greeted with more respect and the extortion of unofficial tolls diminished. It caused her to wonder if the first eighty miles of Kynto was a test to ensure those who continued really desired to be in the country. Anyone lacking the funds or will would likely consider turning back at the scrutiny.

Despite the slight warming of the mood, they resupplied from merchants outside the walled city and continued north on the road to Wyntac, regretting the fact that the Calis Mountains fell away to the east. After two days, the continually white peak of Logan's Point emerged from a cloudy sky, giving them warning they were nearing the capital.

One day later, Logan's Point, which stood alone and isolated from the rest of the Calis range, but firmly inside the border of Calis, was behind them and the dirty city of Wyntac was visible on the lower plains ahead of them. They could not see the city of White Peak itself, which was roughly ten miles east, just over the border in Calis; however, from the high ground, they could see distant wood smoke from that city rising into the air.

The white and purity of Logan's Point stood in contrast to the coal fire smog that covered Wyntac and the surrounding countryside. The walled city appeared dirty, even from a distance. It was large and packed with people and the waste that accumulates from so many living so close together.

To the southwest of Wyntac were sewage fields and while they were favored with a westerly blowing wind, they were all glad not to be one of the king's slaves who had to handle the daily transport of waste out of the city.

Stephenie knew from her father that her uncle had forbid the dumping of sewage into Logan's River, which ran through the city and along the northern walls of Wyntac castle. It was not for the aesthetics or concern over the environment. Instead, it had been triggered by riots that occurred after many of the downstream cities and towns suffered plagues a couple of decades earlier. Restoring order, rebuilding the workforce, and restoring trade had cost him lots of money and so it became cheaper not to pollute the water.

As the afternoon waned, they passed quietly through the southern city gates and headed north along one of the many cobblestone streets. The city was filled with locals and foreigners moving about quickly, but with the subdued air that seemed to infect the whole country. There were definitely more lively conversations taking place in the streets of Antar than in Wyntac.

Once they reached a small plaza with several inns and public houses, Stephenie brought them to a stop and took in the scenery. The buildings, as in Antar, were mostly wattle and daub. Many here in the denser part of the city reached three stories high, sharing walls and roof lines with their neighbors. Occasionally, gaps between the first floors of the buildings provided for narrow, covered alleyways into what was likely a far less pleasant part of the city.

"Okay, so where do we go first?" Henton asked Stephenie in Pandar. "And everyone, keep to Pandar," he added quietly to the others. "Our accents will mark us from Cothel, but we are merchants, so stick to the trade tongue as much as possible."

Stephenie nodded her head toward Will, she hated to send both him and Douglas away from her, but she did not want to leave either one of them on their own with the new guys. "You, take Douglas, John, and Peter and buy a room in that inn over there. The rest of us will stay at the Green Leaf Inn we passed a short while ago. I think it will be best if we don't stay as one large group for now. I want the four of you to stay in your room for the most part. If you do need to go anywhere, stay in pairs. You might get some supplies, but we don't have a lot of spare money at the moment, and we don't know the situation yet. We'll meet up at that public house," she pointed to a three-story building across the plaza, "each morning and evening. Hopefully tomorrow we should have a plan."

Will nodded his head and tapped his pouch, which already had a portion of their funds. "We'll see you in the morning." With his knowing grin, he led the others toward the inn.

"Okay," Henton said to Tim and Berman, "let's head back to our inn and get ourselves cleaned up."

Kas, you good to start scouting out the castle?

Stephenie felt the smile in his emotions and then his voice, *yes, I will check out this nasty castle of yours. I will return in the morning or sooner if there is not much to see.*

"Kas is off," she whispered to Henton as she fell in line beside the man who would be playing her husband. She hoped the nine of them would be able to do what was needed. *Correct that, I'll just have to come up with a plan that nine people can pull off.*

The room situation at the Green Leaf was a little more crowded than she was used to. Staying in the room with Henton would not have been bad; she had accepted him into her personal space a long time ago. The other two made her feel cramped and uncomfortable and the smell of unwashed men was too pungent. Had their funds been a little better, she would have insisted on two separate rooms. However, that would not leave enough people to meet Henton's requirement that someone remain up to keep watch during the night. Without Kas, that meant they would all have to take turns this evening and she hated to admit it, but she had grown used to not having to do that.

By the time the sun was rising, Stephenie was glad the night was over and was ready to head to the public house for breakfast. When Kas appeared just before she was about to wake Henton, true relief filled her.

"What'd you find?" she asked, her voice effectively waking Henton and Tim. Berman, as normal, was eventually nudged awake.

"Well," Kas said slowly in the Old Tongue, still not comfortable enough with Cothish to speak it to more than Stephenie. "The castle is as you described. The old square tower is sealed on all sides except for the top level, which has one entrance. The vault is two levels below the ground, so that is six stories that you will have to haul up the gold."

Stephenie noticed Henton grimace. The seventy-five pounds he carried up from Arkani had worn him out by the time they had finally reached the surface.

"The good news is that on the fourth floor, there is a single passageway that leads from the old tower, through the newer

construction, to a room along the outer wall. A window large enough
to fit a person and the chests through exists in that room. The bad
news, there are several side passages off this main one. However, those
all have doors."

"Any guards?" Henton asked quietly as he picked up his blankets
from the floor.

"There were four on the top floor of the tower and four more in
front of the large vault door. It is reinforced and has what appears to
be a quality lock. I watched through the night, there was a single
guard change and not many people were about the fourth floor of the
castle. That section seems not to have bedrooms, mostly offices and a
few storage rooms.

"Your uncle, based on the size of the rooms and decor, sleeps on
the second floor of the castle, closer to the north side. The guards are
barracked on the first two floors of the east side. The window to use is
on the south side, overlooking the main road in front of the castle."

Stephenie pursed her lips. The fact that the road ran right past the
window could be trouble. However, it was good to know that what
Regina had bragged about was indeed true. Despite the confidence
she had projected, it had always been a concern to trust her sister's
bragging.

"There is another item to consider," Kas added as his mostly
opaque form sat on the bed. "There are a number of large chests in
the vault and enough gold, silver, platinum, and gems to fill seven or
eight of them. However, my guess is those chests would weigh at least
two hundred pounds or more when filled."

Henton actually grimaced. "That much?"

"The chests are designed for two people to carry. They have straps
that go over your shoulders and run under the chest. I however,
would not want to carry them myself."

"That's a lot more gold than I thought would be there." She
frowned, she had expected her uncle to have significant funds, but
not more than seven or eight people could easily carry away on their
backs. "Damn, I'll need to think about this." Switching to Dalish,
"my mother?"

Kas responded in like, "I did not see her. However, it does not
mean she is not present."

"What?" Henton asked, concern bleeding through his normally calm exterior.

Stephenie shook her head, her mind still racing, and returned to the Old Tongue. "I had not expected quite that much. We need to take it all or as much as possible, I just need to figure out how."

"What do you mean?" Henton's voice almost broke. "We take everything, he'll be sure to come after us and how are we going to carry it all away? I figured each of us could carry perhaps thirty pounds of gold plus our other supplies and that will still be a lot of weight...as well as a lot of gold. With eight of us carrying that much, it'd easily get Josh through the year or more."

Stephenie shook her head. "No. If we only took a little, he could afford to send men after us. We take all of it or at least most of it. We have to make him too afraid to come after us."

Henton raised his eyebrows and Stephenie had to laugh at his pathetic expression. "Let's wait until we're all together in a place where we can talk. I've got an idea forming in my head and need some time to work out the details. But I'm not crazy." She laughed again at Henton's pained expression that said he was not so sure.

Despite Stephenie's desire to tell the others quickly, it was not until late in the afternoon that they found a larger public house with a backroom that was available for their use. Sitting down to a late meal, Stephenie dismissed the servants and when she sensed no one was close enough on the other side of the door or walls, she leaned in and motioned for the men to do likewise.

"Okay, Kas' news has caused me to change my original plans. I was thinking that the eight of us would simply load up with twenty to thirty pounds of merchandise and I'd simply fly us over the city wall and we'd walk through Calis to the Sea of Tet and be on our way home."

"That'd be a long way to carry that much gold," John remarked. "We'd be rich, but that's a lot of weight to add to the pack."

Stephenie frowned at the interruption and John's face fell once he realized what he had done. "Well, it seems my uncle has more for us to take than I expected. If thirty pounds is a lot to carry, try dividing up and carrying more than fifteen hundred pounds, perhaps even as much as two hundred pounds each." Will's mouth dropped while the others started to grin as if they had just won the hand of the prettiest girl at the faire. "Before you piss your pants with glee, there are some things to overcome."

"Like how we would ever get that kind of material out of the city and will we even keep our heads?" Douglas asked, but his tone was more curious than negative.

"Keeping our heads is definitely part of the plan." Stephenie took a hard look at each of them, they were all actually older than she was, even if they did not always act their age. "My plan was always for Kas and I to go in and get what we'd take, then I'd fly it out, we'd divide up the goods and leave town, either over the walls, or when the gates opened at first light. The trouble is, we can't carry what's there and I think I will need help carrying it out of where it is currently stored. There are six flights of stairs to climb and seven or eight chests to fill and carry out. The chests are designed for two strong men to carry them. So I was thinking to bring some of you into the castle with me. In pairs, you can carry a chest up and I can still fly it out."

Henton cleared his throat. "My pardon, Beth," he said to emphasize their lax attitude in using her alias. "Getting everything out of the castle is not going to be the hard part. I am sure that will have a number of challenges, but I suspect getting away from Wyntac will be our biggest challenge. We can't fight the army that will be coming after us. We should only take what we can carry quickly."

Stephenie smiled, though Henton's direct challenge of her in front of the others spoke volumes to his concern. "There will be no army coming after us. I expect very few people will follow. That is why we can't take just a little bit, we have to take almost all of it."

Will leaned forward, "I believe you St...Beth, but I'm with the boss on that one, how is taking all of it better than taking just some of it? Won't that make him even more angry?"

Stephenie nodded her head to Will. "History lesson. For those who don't know, my uncle is an asshole. A right bastard with an attitude. He rules by fear. His nobles hate him, but are too afraid to do anything. The people are taxed, beaten, and threatened with slavery. He runs the country like his father had, with lots and lots of highly paid mercs. They keep his order and are as loyal as money can buy.

"He doesn't allow his nobles to have much of a standing force, mostly just a handful of soldiers to protect their property. He taxes the nobles heavily and says it is to fund the army, which he provides to each barony for their, and I quote, protection." She leaned back slightly, feeling a bit nostalgic about the discussion. It was a lesson her father had taught her several times. "And this keeps the dukes and barons on edge, always afraid someone is watching and ready to remove them. They are often pitted against each other with rumor and petty charges. This keeps them from trying too hard to work together to overthrow my uncle, because who knows if they can trust anyone else. He's strung up many a traitor as an example."

"And this helps us escape by..."

Stephenie turned to John. "It helps us escape because my uncle can't show weakness. He rules by fear, and if people sense he is starting to lose control, they might decide they can remove him from the throne. My father had the respect of the nobles and was well liked by the people. You can't easily go from a position of being hated to one of being loved. So my uncle is stuck, he's got to stay committed to this course."

"Easy to go from being loved to hated though," Will commented to no one in particular.

"Very," Stephenie agreed. "But that's not the issue. If my uncle admitted his treasury was emptied, and right out from under his own roof, that would show a lot of weakness. So he can't let people know it happened. If the mercs found out, they'd demand their pay in advance to make sure they didn't go without. If he couldn't pay, they'd probably sell themselves to the highest bidder, such as his nobles, or perhaps take over themselves. If he tried to quickly raise some taxes to fill the treasury, his nobles, I am sure, would find some way to delay payment. So it is important for him to keep it quiet."

"He doesn't have to tell anyone in order to send people to kill us," John protested, his initial thoughts of riches drowned out by fear.

"And you think he'd trust those highly paid mercs to bring back all that gold? They'd see the gold and they'd take it themselves. Even if they were honest and brought it back, my uncle wouldn't be able to take the chance. For they would talk, and word would leak out, and he'd have problems. If we take only a little, he will still have funds to work with and he could claim the money wasn't stolen, or perhaps stolen from someone else or at least some other place than his castle.

"So who's he going to send?" she asked, looking around the table. When no one answered, she nodded her head. "Well, my guess is he'll send some of the few people he actually considers to be loyal. But a man that rules by fear and intimidation isn't going to have many of those. And would you risk sending everyone you trusted away and leave your personal protection to people who were only there for pay? People who might be on someone else's payroll just waiting for a chance to remove you?"

She shook her head. "Not likely. So, my guess will be that we'll have a handful of men come after us. Probably a holy warrior or two."

She breathed deeply and relaxed a bit. "The other factor is we are ten miles from the border with Calis and while the countries are on friendly enough terms to allow trade, Calis won't let an army go through there. My uncle's father tried to take the western part and failed so there is a history of bad blood. The troops he sent to my 'father's aid' went directly through Midland with guarantees from my father. That means his neighbors don't trust him and once we are over the border, he can only send a small force that is disguised as merchants at best."

Will leaned forward, pursed his own lips, and looked at Stephenie out of the corner of his eyes. "Then what's the plan?"

Stephenie glanced at Henton, who had regained control of his emotions, and smiled despite herself. She always knew Henton and Will worked well together. Henton would often remain quiet in the group discussions, allowing Will to drive many topics. It allowed him to retain an appearance of neutrality, but sometimes she wondered if Will's mouth was driven directly by Henton.

"We get three wagons with teams of horses. We buy crates, and because of the mountain range and the cheap steel they have in abundance, we buy a bunch of steel stock. Bars and ingots and such. We'll have the wagons ready and put the gold under the steel in the bottom crates. We'll simply ride out of the city gates at first light. Mother always told Regina how merchants would compete to be the first ones out the gate with the hope they could get the best prices in Calis before anyone else could beat them there.

"That story always seemed a bit silly, but Kas did notice a line of wagons waiting at the east gates for sunrise. I suspect it has to do with getting on the road early enough to make it to White Peak to sell a few things before continuing on to the east. You might not get the best price, but you could unload some weight to make the rest of the trip to the Sea of Tet in good time and still make some profit."

"So your plan is to blend in," Henton said, "hiding our heavy metal under other heavy metal that would be too much of a bother to dig through for a tax collectors to notice. And then hope there is no army of men ripping through everything looking for what they lost."

"Exactly. If we are out of the gates before they even notice anything is gone, we should be able to make it into Calis with ease. It's only ten miles from Wyntac." She looked cautiously at Henton, "What?"

"Wagons cost a bit of coin the last I checked. Teams of horses even more and I don't want to think about the steel stock. How are we going to get the funds to prepare?"

"Steal it," Kas said in stuttered Cothish, materializing into a very faint transparency next to Henton. "Wealthy merchant. Steal it."

Douglas nodded his head. "That would be a good practice run."

Stephenie smiled at Kas. He had already been privy to her plans as she had worked out the details with him mentally while they had looked for some place private enough for the group to talk. The theft of gold from some rich merchant or nobleman was his idea to begin with. "Kas will scout out some of the wealthy houses tonight. They won't report the robbery for the same reason my uncle can't, it would make them appear weak and those who are in power only remain so because they appear strong enough that no one takes them out. The weak try to keep that appearance to avoid being removed early as a potential threat."

"And I thought life was hard in Cothel," Berman mused. "Glad I wasn't born here."

Stephenie nodded her head. "There are worse places. My father wanted to make sure Josh and I understood what we had and why keeping the trust of the people was so important. Once you take it to a place of fear and hate, you can't turn back. My uncle's father took it further than his father. I don't think my uncle is worse than his father. Heck, my father thought at one time Willard might not even desire this current state. But it's what he inherited and that's what he has to deal with."

Stephenie turned to Henton. "To go out buying wagons, horses, and lots of steel will take coin. We can't walk around dressed like this and pull off a wealthy merchant family. Tomorrow, the two of us need to do some discrete clothes shopping. You'll have to play an even wealthier merchant. I speak Kyntian well enough to pass as a daughter of a reasonably successful family that was married off to Cothel. We can explain the steel is going to be sold in Cothel for a good profit." She turned to the others. "And the rest of you will need to play up the role of bondsmen a little stronger. We'll need to get something that is matching for all of you to wear. Something uniform-ish, but nothing with any specific family colors. They have slavery here, but I won't go that far. Cothel, thankfully, has not had that problem for several hundred years. Your families simply owe my husband and I a sizable debt and you are working it off."

"Yes Ma'am," Will said with a smile. "I think we can play loyal to the two of you."

Stephenie shook her head. "That's the problem. You are bondsmen. You'll need to obey, but out of obligation and duty to your family, not out of a desire to please either of us." She leaned in and looked each of them in the eyes. She had felt good about the plan, but now that it was out there, some doubts started to creep in. "We all need to be careful and safe. After we get our new clothes, which we should have enough money to buy, we'll move to a new inn that caters to more wealthy merchants. We'll have to line up the purchases and make sure everything is done at the right time."

"Douglas is good at negotiating prices," Henton offered. "He can help arrange to get the steel and other supplies we'll need."

"And I'm good with horses," Tim added. "My family had a share in a carting business. Though I got tired of mucking stalls, so I joined the army."

Stephenie smiled. She was glad to see most everyone was feeling positive about the plan. "Okay, but we need to spread the purchases out. We should buy each wagon and team of horses separately. Buy the steel the same way, it might cost more, but it will be less noticeable."

"What of the time?" Henton asked. "We're already a long way behind your schedule."

She nodded her head. "I know. We'll just have to hope to make up some of the time, but we can't rush certain things." She sighed and sat back in her chair, "Let's finish eating, then start looking for clothes in the morning."

The next day, Stephenie found shopping for clothing a little easier than she had anticipated. Wyntac was divided into a number of districts and while there was bleed over of shops between the districts, many of the like shops still congregated together. And more importantly, while she was being measured for a new dress, she was able to review with Kas several of the houses he had investigated overnight. *We need to make sure they have a significant amount of coin on hand*, she thought to Kas. *We can't take the time or risk in trying to sell stolen goods.*

What do you propose? How are we to find someone with coins on hand to take?

Stephenie glanced in Kas' direction, though he was not visible, she could sense his frustration. She had basically told him his work overnight had been unproductive and was wasted. While he had found many homes of wealthy people, he either had not found where they hid their money or had found only a small amount of coin. Knowing Kas often felt useless, she hoped to divert the blame. *It was too late in the day yesterday to watch the markets, but why don't you scout for someone making a large transaction. It probably won't happen on the street, but perhaps you'll notice something. Or maybe a merchant who is doing a lot of business...now that I think about it, a large transaction probably would be handled by a note.* She smiled. *Forget a wealthy merchant, find someone acting as a money lender, they'll hopefully have a large amount of coin on hand.*

Kas gave her a mental nod of his head. *Unfortunately, neither idea is much help. What you are talking about is a matter of luck. However, I will attempt to rectify the problem and find a solution.*

Stephenie barely avoided sticking out her tongue as he left through the side wall, leaving her alone with a pair of women who had been recording her measurements. The idea to rob some wealthy business man or noble had a definite appeal to her. Not all of the ones she knew were abusive, but she had seen and heard her fair share of angry nobles that complained they were not able to maximize their own returns when her father had stepped in to mediate disputes. The blatant greed was often too much for her.

"Ma'am?" The nearer seamstress asked while staring at her.

Stephenie brought her focus back to the room and realized they had been waiting on a response from her. "Sorry, I was lost in thought," she said in Kyntian.

"Ma'am, I asked if you will need just the one dress or if you needed more."

"Yes, I will take a second one. Use the green cloth."

The second woman nodded her head. "Ma'am, I am sorry that your clothing was ruined on your journey. You have lovely hair and skin, it is a shame you are forced to wear such masculine clothing. Your husband should take better care of you. Do they not have any sense in Cothel?"

"Oh, he does a well enough job. Our bondsman was sloppy and he's been punished. The cost will be added to his family's debt. I expect I'll get at least two more years of service because of this." Stephenie puffed up her chest as she had seen ladies at court do, signaling an end to that line of discussion. "Of course, we must have the clothing as quickly as possible. I can hardy help my husband conduct business dressed as I am."

The roundish woman nodded her head knowingly. "Of course, My Lady, we will have the girls sew on it through most of the night. The first one will be ready tomorrow afternoon, since the dress is to be fairly simple. Would you like the green one to be more elaborate?"

Stephenie nodded her head. The cost would definitely make Henton cringe, perhaps even in a husbandly fashion. However, the story of them being wealthy merchants, who had their clothing stained beyond use, required a little bit of a snobbish attitude and while the plain dress would be functional enough to get some of the transactions going, it would be better when she could more look the part.

"It is too bad your good Kynto-blooded family had to marry you to a foreign merchant. You are fortunate to at least return to Kynto for a while," the second woman said as she shook her head. "I hope your situation remains better than that of our King Willard's poor sister. Accused of such things by that Elrin loving bitch of a daughter. And her very son turned to evil. Is it true what is rumored, that those heathens have actually declared the beast cleansed?"

Stephenie's chest was tight, but she did not detect any accusation from the women. "I've not heard all the details. I've been on the road for longer than was proper. Tell me what you heard."

"Not much Ma'am. We know the good King rescued his sister from those heathens—"

"And liberated their treasury," the second lady added with a snicker.

"Riders came through not too long ago stating that the High Priest of Felis declared that Elrin loving beast cleansed and marked with the sign of Catheri. Such nonsense. Likely that demon lover has taken over the High Priest's mind. At least Princess Elsia is back home and safe."

Stephenie forced herself to be calm. It had been a long time since she had heard her mother's actual name spoken and longer still since she had heard praise attached to it. It seemed those of Kynto had decided to accept her mother back as though she had never been married to her father at all. "Is the Princess here in Wyntac?"

The two women shrugged and the first one continued, "We don't know for certain. If she is, she's safely protected in the castle. But there are rumors she is out toward the west as well."

"She's been through a lot, she needs her rest," the second lady added.

Stephenie nodded her head as she stepped off the block where she had been standing to be measured. "My husband does not support the witch, but he is still a child of Cothel. It would be best to avoid those conversations with him."

"Of course Ma'am. We know how touchy foreigners are; useless beyond the money they bring."

Stephenie nodded her head despite her underlying anger.

When they got back to the Green Leaf that night, Henton gathered the remaining coins from Stephenie, Tim, and Berman and counted them out. "Will has one full crown and perhaps half of a silver crown left and we've got enough to make two silver crowns. That's basically only enough money for two or three days more of room and board, assuming we eat moderately and stay in these cheap inns."

Stephenie nodded her head. Henton had reacted calmly when he had paid for their clothing today, but she knew he was frustrated by the cost. "Hopefully Kas will find us a good house or two to rob."

Stephenie looked at Tim and Berman. Berman was already in the darkly dyed shirt they had found for the men. Tim's would be ready in the morning. Fortunately, Will and Douglas had managed to find a shop that had several used items of similar design. Tim, being a little broader in the shoulders, needed to have something made to fit.

"Ma'am," Tim said softly, "these people don't like us much. The merchants were quite rude when it became obvious we were from Cothel. I think they ripped us off with the prices as well."

"Just be polite and don't get drawn into anything. Even if they start it. Absolutely no bar fights. I don't want to have to pay a fine to get you out of jail, or worse, keep you from being made a slave of the king." Stephenie turned away from the others and looked into the corner of the room where Kas had just come through the wall.

Tim smiled. "Of course not, Ma'am. We're better disciplined than that."

"You better be," Henton said sharply. "Beth," he said turning back to Stephenie, "based on my conversation with Douglas and Will earlier, I think we are going to need at least a thousand gold crowns to pull this off."

Tim's mouth dropped at the number. "That much?"

Henton did not take his eyes from Stephenie. "To carry the load, we'll need quality wagons. I'm guessing we're probably looking at forty to fifty full crowns each. Three teams of horses, probably fifty to seventy each, perhaps more. We'll need feed and such, plus food for ourselves. Then twelve to fourteen crates per wagon, and steel to fill ten to twelve of those crates per wagon. Kas will need to find us a lot of money."

Stephenie smiled as Kas' form turned opaque next to Henton, startling the sergeant. "I did find a couple of possibilities. However, I do not think we will find that much coin easily in any one place save the king's castle."

"Which we can't rob until we are set up to do it," Henton replied in the Old Tongue. "If you have to rob several of them, should we spread the work out over a few days?"

Stephenie shook her head. "No. We take as many houses tonight as we can. Just in case anyone does decide to talk, we don't want them preparing for us the next night."

Henton nodded his head and pushed himself up from the floor. "I'll get my things together."

Stephenie put her hand on his arm. "No, this will be safer if it is just me and Kas." She smiled, "We'd still be paired up you know."

Henton forced his shoulders down. "All right, but if you are not back by morning..."

"Then you should get out of the city as quickly as possible. If in robbing a couple of houses, the two of us can't handle the situation, there won't be anything you can do to help."

"Come back to us," Henton said, patting her hand, "so I don't have to disobey your orders."

Chapter 16

A s Stephenie walked down the narrow streets of the poorer district to get closer to the large houses Kas had scouted, she noted the general sense of decay in the buildings and the resignation of the people. She had seen that kind of resignation before, in the eyes of those who had been trapped in Antar, too poor to escape the threat of the invading army. Fortunately enough for the people of Antar, she had derailed the Senzar's plan for Cothel, whatever that had been.

For the people of Wyntac, she had no cure. The very act of stealing Cothel's stolen money back would likely make these peoples' lives harder. However, she had a duty to her own people first and she hoped that the suffering of the poor here would be minimal. *It's not for revenge*, she told herself. *Not entirely*, she admitted after a another block moved quickly under her feet.

She noted a few people watched her pass. Dressed in her masculine pants and with her hair tightly braided, she suspected the people might not be certain if she was a man or a woman. She had left her sword behind, wanting to avoid any weapons getting in the way. Wearing only a pair of daggers, she felt slightly vulnerable; however, she walked with enough purpose and confidence that no one pursued her.

She shifted the leather pack, stuffed with her cloak, from one shoulder to the other as she turned down a slightly better street with a series of houses that offered a buffer between the rich and poor. She planned to distribute the money around the cloak to keep what she stole from shifting and making noise as she moved from house to house.

Kas filled her in on the general layout of each of the four homes he had chosen and the general wealth to be had. *These people live like kings themselves, while so many of the others are scraping by,* he complained as they passed by a couple of men who were sitting in the gutter and looking up to Stephenie expectantly.

She left them with only a sad shake of her head. She truly had no money with her, but even if she did, until she knew they were fully funded to do what was needed, she would not be able to offer anyone a handout. *I can't help everyone directly.*

Eventually, they turned onto wider streets where the cobbles were more even and there were fewer holes and broken stones. The buildings were whitewashed, with a very few painted in bright colors to attract attention. Signs still hung over most doors and many of the second and third story rooms extended at least partially over the street.

She noticed a patrol of soldiers coming in her direction and she turned off into one of the narrow alleyways. A crude door a few feet into the alley was intended to stop most traffic, but a quick blast of gravitational energy broke the lock and allowed her to pass through the doorway without pausing.

Stephenie knew the avoidance of the soldiers was probably unnecessary, but she had never been a true criminal before. Her nighttime chases with Joshua and his friends around the castle had been less than prudent for a young girl, but not something she would have gotten in trouble for. Here, if she was confronted, she might have to resort to using magic and that would draw too much attention and perhaps give people and her uncle cause for concern.

After the soldiers had passed, she returned to the main street and continued on toward the first house, which was furthest from the Green Leaf inn. After another quarter turn of the glass, she was now walking through a section of town where there were five-foot-high walls that separated the buildings from the street. Gardens with trees surrounded the large three and four story stone homes. These were the properties of lower nobles and wealthy merchants.

None of these look like a money lender's shop, Stephenie thought to Kas as they walked along the line of walls.

No, those had numerous guards on duty around the vaults. And from what I could tell, many of them were trading notes and not coins. Kas eventually stopped her, *this house belongs to a man who appeared to be head of one of the lenders. There is an office on the third floor, through the window on the right hand corner.*

Stephenie nodded her head, remembering Kas' earlier descriptions. Aware there was no one close enough to see her, she did not pause to look around. With practiced ease, she warped gravity fields around her lower body and quickly flew herself up to the corner window. Unlike when she was flying the others, her body conveyed instant feedback to the pressures she exerted and so she barely had to concentrate on the fields.

Hovering thirty feet above the gardens and shrubs, she kept herself steady just outside the window. Real glass panes, not mica, was used in homes of this quality. A normal thief might be required to break one of the expensive panes, but Stephenie simply moved the interior catch with her mind and lifted the window so she could climb inside with hardly a sound.

She could sense people sleeping in an adjacent room, so she moved lightly about the room, lifting herself partially with magic. The thick carpet that covered the wooden floor deadened any sound of her boots on the floor.

A desk and many book shelves, stacked high with ledgers, filled the far wall. The wall to her right had an oil lamp on a marble stand between two large windows that afforded a view of the neighbor's large house and garden.

Kas motioned Stephenie toward a second wooden stand that appeared to be a solid piece of maple at least one foot in diameter. A marble platform, with an exquisite wooden carving of a horse, topped the stand. The horse was crafted with care and an obvious eye for detail. Standing ten inches tall in a proud trot, Stephenie could not help but pick it up and examine it more carefully in the dim moonlight coming in from the windows.

That is not what we are after, Kas scolded playfully. *Though it would be something pretty to put in your tower, considering how bare your rooms are.*

Stephenie smiled and put the horse back on the stand. The legs were far too delicate for her to even think about trying to carry it back to Antar. And Kas' initial statement was correct, it was not what they were after.

Bending down, she looked closer at the polished, but still natural-looking base. There were many smoothed over nobs where branches had been removed from the trunk and even a couple of natural splits that appeared very artistic in their placement.

Closing her eyes, she could sense the different energy potentials coming from within the base and knew there was a hollow with metal inside the stand. After listening to Kas' explanation of how the lord of the house had pressed on a part of the base to allow a section near the natural split to come free, she repeated the process. With the outer panel removed, she pulled free two small leather bags of coins. They jingled as she shifted them to the floor. There would be several hundred coins in those bags, but the value would depend on how many were gold instead of silver or bronze.

After replacing the panel in the stand, she placed the two bags of coins in her backpack, locking them in place with the excess fabric of her cloak. She quickly went back to the window and checked the street to make sure there was no one who would see her. Finding it clear, she slipped out the window and hovered long enough to close the window and engage the catch. A couple moments more and she was back on the sidewalk as just another innocent pedestrian walking through one of the better parts of town in the middle of the night.

The second house went even easier than the first one. In that one, the money had simply been kept in an unlocked desk drawer.

The third house that Kas led her to was smaller than the first two, just a two story building. However, the grounds were larger and numerous well-developed trees filled both the front and back yards. Considering the cost of land inside any large city, especially one as crowded as Wyntac, Stephenie knew this house would be for an even wealthier family. *Hopefully, that wealth's not all tied up in the land.* She did pause a bit with momentary concern for what these wealthy people would do to the servants, who would be obvious suspects. However, at the same time, she could not let people know there was someone in town who was daring enough to rob from the very rich.

For the third house, the room with the money was in the back and there were no windows to the room. Stephenie again entered from the front and was able to use a central hall to approach the back room. This door, however, was locked and the other rooms on this floor held bedrooms with sleeping people.

Taking a calming breath, she knelt in front of the door and reached out with her mind, trying to sense the internal mechanisms of the lock. What came back to her was a jumbled confusion of small metal parts. She had never taken a lock apart before, so she lacked a full understanding of the subtle functions of each piece. Conceptually, she knew how it worked, but she did not know what parts to move to unlock the mechanism.

Kas, if I force it, I'm afraid of how much noise I will make.

Kas floated closer to her and generated a field to effect the illusion of his hand on her shoulder. *The hinges are on this side, but the pins look to be flattened on both sides. You may simply have to force it.*

She exhaled softly. Trying not to exert too much force, she put pressure on a small piece, hoping to force the lock to open. A slight grinding emanated from the lock before the piece snapped. *Damn.* Fairly certain she had just rendered the lock useless, she closed her eyes again, this time placing her hands on the metal. Breathing slowly and concentrating all of her effort on the task, she drew more power into herself. She started to look at the components more from their elemental state and not as anything more than just an oddly shaped piece of metal.

Trying very hard to limit the field she was creating to adjust the internals of the lock, she applied more energy and modified the field to weaken the bonds between the tiny bits of metal. She sat on her heels for several minutes, waiting, watching, and adjusting her field as she pulled more and more energy through herself. Fearful she would have no choice but to give up or simply make noise, she continued adjusting the field, hoping to weaken the bonds without overdoing it.

Suddenly she felt all the internals of the lock slump away as the metal turned fluid. As quickly as she could, she stopped the flow of energy and the field she had created. Opening her eyes, the exterior of the lock was mostly unchanged. There was a slight sagging around the key hole and dim depressions where her hands had been in contact with the metal, but she noticed this more with her senses than with her eyes.

A sudden change in Kas' presence drew her attention and she was immediately aware of someone opening the bedroom door just a couple feet from her. Panic filling her, she barely noticed the person was a young girl as she slapped a field over the girl's mouth. Turning the person away from her with her magic, Stephenie hoped the child had not seen her face clearly.

Unable to breathe, the girl immediately started to struggle and Stephenie noticed small tendrils of energy emanating from the child; reaching out in an uncontrolled manner. The power was weak, but before Stephenie could counter the girl's magical struggles, the door bounced away because of those fields.

Moving quickly, Stephenie wrapped her arms around the child and bound her tight, still keeping her from breathing. *Shh*, Stephenie thought toward the girl, hoping she would hear her. *I won't hurt you, but you need to sleep.*

Keeping the girl held tightly with both her arms and magic, Stephenie managed to contain the child, though the girl's panic and terror threatened to overwhelm Stephenie's mind. It was similar to the panic and fear that Oliver had felt, but it was also the more primal sense of the young: filled with confusion and uncertainty, and mixed with a desperation for her mother and a need for safety.

Stephenie sagged to her knees as the child finally passed out. It was several moments before the girl's emotions drained from her. Finally becoming aware of her surroundings, Stephenie carefully set the girl down and checked her breathing and heart to make sure she had not harmed the child.

The girl's breath was shallow and her heart was racing, but her mind was still functioning as close to that of a sleeping person as Stephenie could tell. *The girl's a mage,* Stephenie sent to Kas, a quiver still in her mental voice. *I'd take her away from here, but that won't work. I hope no one finds out what she is, they'll burn her.*

Stephenie, are you sure she is a mage?

Didn't you sense her energy threads?

They were not strong enough for me to notice. Regardless, you should get the gold and leave. The girl could wake up at any moment and you'd have to do that again.

Stephenie stood up slowly. She was completely drained, not only from transforming the lock, but more so from the after effects of the girl's terror. Being in contact with the girl allowed far more of the emotional energy to pass into her than she had experienced with the soldiers she had knocked unconscious. She could now say she understood something of suffocating and did not want to ever experience it herself.

Pushing aside what happened, she opened herself further and was relieved to not sense anyone else awake and moving about this floor. She went back to the office door and pulled the door open. It stuck just slightly because there was a thin layer of metal that congealed between the jam and the door, but that fractured and flaked away with little noise.

Where is it? she asked, not quite remembering.

There is a loose board under the chair.

Stephenie quickly went behind the desk and moved the chair with her magic. She lifted the rug and examined the floor. The room was quite dark without any windows and not much light made it all the way down the hall. Sensing where the money was below the floorboards, she simply tugged at the section with her magic until a piece lifted free. Continuing to use her powers, she elevated three bags of coins and quickly stuffed them into her backpack with the other money she had stolen this evening.

Knowing the melted lock and girl would give away the theft, she left the opening exposed and headed back to the door. *Damn, this lock could entice them to bring in a holy warrior to check out what happened.* Scared for both the girl's welfare and maintaining the secrecy of magic being involved, Stephenie paused at the door. She took a deep breath as she pulled energy through herself. Holding the door with one field, she smashed another into the lock, tearing the transformed block of metal free of the wooden door.

The crack of the wood echoed through the floor and walls. She immediately felt people stir in their rooms; however, she had caught the lock in the air with a third field, which kept it from bouncing down the hall.

Sensing the girl start to stir as well, Stephenie bolted for the open window at the end of the hall. She grabbed the floating lock as she ran past it. When she was close enough to the window, she leaped head first through the opening, allowing herself to drop quickly from view. As she plummeted toward the ground, she warped a field around her whole body, flipped over, flew herself over the garden wall, and onto the sidewalk. The moment her feet were under her, she started to run, keeping her head down below the five foot high stone wall.

"Are you okay?" Henton asked.

Stephenie had long ago wiped the blood from her nose, but there was still a red smear on her cheek. "I'm fine. I just can't get that girl out of my head. I know if we were to run into each other on the street, she would instantly recognize me. Not by sight, but by feel. She's like me, she's a mage, just very limited in power right now."

"Because she is young," Kas added. "Stephenie, you are very sensitive to energy fields. I doubt anyone would notice the magic you normally use, let alone what the girl can do, considering I do not notice them. As long as she does not demonstrate her abilities, I do not believe anyone would learn of her capabilities."

"Perhaps," Stephenie conceded. "However, if they call for a priest to read the girl's mind with regard to what happened, they might find out what she is."

Henton shook his head and put his hand on her shoulder. "You can't save everyone. You just have to trust that your assessment of them will hold and they won't want to draw attention to the robbery."

"Well, in that house, at least I don't have to worry about them thinking the servants did it."

Tim looked up from the floor. He and Berman had been putting the coins into piles, as they were not certain of counting numbers more than fifty. Henton and Kas had been watching, but Stephenie was now feeling a little uncomfortable about the money and feared they might not have enough with robbing only three of the four houses.

She knew there was no better option and had even liked the idea originally, but the actual theft left her feeling unclean. *I won't feel that way about taking back our money from Willard and the extra to cover our costs and the damages he did with Mother's help, but I don't like stealing.* She sighed mentally, but kept her thoughts to herself. Kas had tried to reassure her about the righteousness of the robberies on their way back to the inn, but after what she had done to the girl, she was not ready to be comforted yet.

"It looks like we have over nine hundred crowns," Henton said, counting up the piles of coins. "Kyntian crowns, which are a touch smaller than most countries', but if we are careful with expenses, we might have enough."

"Good, because I'm done until we visit my uncle. And that will be the end of it."

"You sure, Steph?" Tim asked.

"BETH," Henton growled.

"Beth," Tim repeated meekly. "We could fund a lot of things in just a few nights."

"Yes. My uncle and that's it," her voice was as hard as the lump of metal that had been the lock and was now sitting on the bed. Knowing they needed a justification they could understand, she added, "It was easy tonight because they expect only traditional thieves. If they realize what I am, that would change. Besides, if word got out, it would make people fear me even more, and that is not what I want."

Chapter 17

The next morning, Kas and Stephenie remained at the inn to catch up on their rest, while Henton led Tim and Berman to meet up with the others. They did not eat breakfast at the public house designated as the meeting point. Instead, they went to the building with the private backroom. Not able to sense people as Stephenie could, Henton had to hope no one was trying to listen at the doors or behind the walls.

"Okay men, Beth was mostly successful and we have the funds, though she didn't get out of the last place completely unnoticed. So, let's be careful, but still keep an ear out for news that could describe what she did last night. We need to make sure her thoughts on the way people will react are true."

"Well, that's still great news," Will said. "I knew she would be able to do it. With everything else, I think she will be able to bring some justice to what was done to her, her brother, and our people."

"I think she's feeling unjust about what she did last night," Tim said. "She might need to find the justice in what she had done. Perhaps Catheri was questioning her actions."

Henton cleared his throat, silencing the conversation. If Stephenie was here, he knew her skin would be crawling to hear the others talking like that. There would be a confrontation between her and the others at some point if things continued to progress as they had. He just hoped it was something that could be put off until this was all done. *Unfortunately, I know which side I will be on.* The more Will persisted in his belief and the more followers Will made of others, the more questions Henton felt. *If it is so easy to create such strong believers in such a short time, then what Steph and Kas have said could be right. The Senzar definitely did not live by the rules that were preached by the gods, or more correctly, the priests of the gods.*

Henton put the thoughts out of his mind and turned back to the men. "We have to be careful what we talk about." He was feeling rather angry at having to constantly repeat himself. The discipline he was used to expect from his men had yet to be instilled into those that were added to his group and Will was starting to lose some of the discipline he had. Douglas, the ever quiet man, was the only one he truly felt he could completely count on. Will had always been sharp and smart, but tended to push boundaries, mostly when appropriate, but occasionally, his judgment was off. *Lately, his judgment's been off the mark too much.*

"I want this group acting like the soldiers we are," he said softly. "We have to play our parts and play them well. If anyone screws up and let's something slip that should not be heard by someone, we could all end up dead. Which then means, Beth's brother doesn't get the money he needs and our families back home end up in the middle of turmoil. So get the focus back."

Henton nodded his head. "Douglas, you are in charge of negotiating prices and supplies. Tim is the only one without his clothes yet, so he'll stay with me. The rest of you, I want you to find several places to purchase the supplies we will need. Don't go making any deals yet, but get started on finding good places to get what we'll need for the wagons, horses, crates, and steel. You might wait on the horses for Tim to be ready.

"Also, look to get a feel for the town. Beth was wanting to use the east gates and head to White Peak. Get a feel for the roads between the gate and our expected departure point. I want all of you to know how to get to where we are going in case things go badly. We'll trust in her, but we have to be able to provide support in case things don't work out as planned. She can't always take care of us."

The men nodded their heads. "Good. Let's quickly finish our food and get busy. We're already behind schedule and this delay is not helping. We'll hopefully meet you for dinner with our new clothes and a new place to stay for the night."

"Yes, My Lord." Douglas said with a quick bow of his head.

Henton smiled at him and made a mental note to talk with Stephenie about giving him a field promotion to corporal.

Henton's arrival at the Green Leaf woke Stephenie from her sleep. She had dreamed of drowning, something she had never feared before, but after the little girl's terror, the times she had held her breath when swimming came back to her with a vengeance.

"I took the liberty of having the men start checking out the city to get a feel for what is there. I expect it will take us a couple of days to make all of the purchases, so they will have time to spare." He sat down on the bed next to her, handing Stephenie a mug of water he had brought up to the room. "I've got Tim waiting in the pub, he's ordering us something to eat."

"Okay. We'll go pick up our clothes and then we can look for a larger inn that caters more to wealthy merchants. I hope, like in Antar, there are some with places to store wagons that are getting ready to leave town. If we time it correctly, we can purchase the wagons tomorrow morning, then go about town and pick up the supplies during the day. Get a little sleep and then get the real goods and be at the gates just before they open."

"Well, I've got the others checking for places to buy the supplies. I figured you'd want to choose the inn."

She grinned up at him until he handed her a brush. Sighing, she got to her feet. "I guess that is my cue to get ready."

After they ate a midday meal, the four of them went to pick up Tim's shirt before retrieving Henton and Stephenie's new clothing. The dress was ready as promised and Stephenie had to admit she actually liked it. It was well fitted and while she still had a minimal chest to fill out the bodice, it was much better than just a couple weeks ago when she was little more than skin and bones. The idea of being able to remake her chest a little larger passed through her thoughts, *but I sure am not willing to go through all of that again.*

Once their clothing was attended to, Stephenie took them deeper into the city and closer to the castle where she hoped to find a new inn for them to make a fresh start as more wealthy merchants. She had seen some of these parts of the city the prior night and was surprised by the subtle beauty in the architecture that she had missed. Most buildings were depressed and sullen by Antar standards, with very muted colors where paint had been used. However, many of the upper levels of the buildings had small decorative trim and molding that slipped past casual notice.

Tim tried to stare at the buildings just as Stephenie was, but lacking her senses of the surroundings, he stumbled and bumped into her and Henton.

"I'd hold your hand to help you along," she whispered to him, "but that would be unseemly." More loudly she added in Pandar, "Pay attention to where you are walking. You don't want to owe me for new shoes as well."

Crestfallen, Tim dropped in line behind them and kept his face to the ground, though the slight smile he had given her let Stephenie know he understood.

Eventually, they crossed onto a large carriageway that was filled with many carts and carriages moving up and down the tightly cobbled street. To the north, she could see numerous barges tied up along the banks of the Logan River, who's route the street mirrored.

She knew from her research that only four bridges provided access across the river within Wyntac. None of them were near the castle for security reasons, but they would have to cross over one to get to the eastern city gates when they left in a couple of days.

Turning the group to the east, they followed along the southern edge of the busy street. The wider northern side, near the river, was filled with crates, wagons, and people who were actively moving cargo on and off the barges. A few wooden cranes were actively working on heavier cargo and one barge was unloading what appeared to Stephenie to be a whole herd of sheep.

After half a mile of walking along the twisting road, Wyntac Castle came into view. The area around the base of the castle was mostly clear; two hundred feet of cobblestone to the south, west, and east. The Logan river ran along the northern wall, providing protection through the deeply channeled waterway.

The walls of Wyntac Castle were made of thick stone blocks, all neatly dressed. Over four stories high, the castle dominated the area, making the waddle and daub buildings look small and insignificant. Unlike Antar Castle, however, Wyntac Castle had no outer curtain wall at all. Every exterior wall was part of the main structure. The interior did have a small courtyard, but surrounded on all sides by tall stone, that small bit of nature would be dark and uninviting.

"So it's true; they coat the walls of the castle in blood," Tim mumbled softly.

Stephenie looked at the reddish-brown stains that ran down all the stone surfaces, staining even the cobblestones around the base of the castle. "That's a popular tale, but not true. My father explained the truth to me when Regina tried to scare me." Stephenie looked away from the castle to the rows of two story buildings just across the street, the first level of these were shops of various natures, with residences likely above them. She turned back to Tim and Henton. "That stone is quarried from the area around Logan's Peak. There is a lot of iron flecks in the stone. The stain you see is the iron rusting."

Henton nodded his head. "Makes sense."

"And better than being blood," Tim added.

Stephenie agreed silently. The castle had a foreboding appearance with the stain, which seemed to fit in with her uncle's style of leadership. "Let's go find a place to stay."

There were no inns that Stephenie approved of in the immediate vicinity of the castle. However, they did explore the side streets directly across from the castle and there were a number of places she felt they could park wagons during the night while the gold was removed from the vault.

The first inn she considered suitable was three blocks from the castle, but it lacked sufficient space to hold the wagons for a couple of days. The second inn was called the Emerald Stone and it was almost half a mile from the castle. However, the inn looked to have been recently whitewashed and there was a large barn in a fenced off courtyard.

When the three of them entered the inn, Stephenie noted the presence of a guard standing half a dozen feet from the door. She could smell lamb and something with spiced apples cooking in a backroom. To their left, through a pair of sliding doors was a large dining room that had table cloths over the tables.

Henton raised his eyebrows to Stephenie, obviously skeptical, as a woman in a black dress, with light red trim, approached. "Good day," she said quickly in Kyntian.

Henton bowed his head slightly as the woman curtsied. The calm expression on her face did not hide the fact she was scrutinizing them heavily. "Ma'am," Henton said in Pandar, not having understood the woman. "We are looking for lodging for myself, my wife, and a handful of bondsmen. We will also have need of some of your barn space to store three wagons and their teams of horses while we are here."

Stephenie's expression hardened. She could sense the disdain coming from the woman; it was more severe than the narrowing of her eyes would indicate. "That will be a lot of money for a simple merchant from Cothel. You should look to find lodging, as you call it, in one of the hovels outside the walls."

Henton was for a moment speechless, but Stephenie used that moment to step forward. She glared at the woman, perhaps in her late twenties and looked her up and down as if the woman had a foul air about her. It was easy to mimic the look Stephenie had often received from Regina. "Get your mistress here now," Stephenie growled in Kyntian, throwing in a little heavier draw on her consonants, like she had heard from her mother's troop of soldiers that had come from the west. "I will not stand here and let the likes of you insult my husband, and therefore, me." The woman looked abashed and stood frozen in place. "Get! Bring your mistress at once!"

The woman curtsied more deeply and then scampered off quickly to talk briefly with an older woman of about forty, who was already on her way over to investigate the disturbance Stephenie had caused. The older woman nodded her head to the first one and then continued over to Stephenie where she curtsied. Stephenie simply stared at the woman.

"Ma'am, I understand you have an issue with Miss Clem," the woman said in very proper Kyntian.

"I had heard good things about the Emerald Stone, but the moment I walk in, I am insulted in every manner possible. This is intolerable."

"Ma'am," the older lady said, clearing her throat. "We are accustomed to people in a little better dress. Additionally, your husband greeted Miss Clem in Pandar and is obviously from Cothel. She simply assumed you were as well."

"I am Lady Calvar, though I was born Lady Urivar of Retmir," Stephenie said, using the common surname and one of the larger cities in Western Kynto they had planned to use. "We have had a rough trip from my Husband's lands, having one of our bondsmen ruin much of our things. The worthless man's been dealt with, but you look to add further insult to my injury."

"My Lady, as I stated, Miss Clem was not aware you were paven for your family. If you will calm down, I am sure we can find you accommodations that are more to your normal standards."

Stephenie's mind raced, she had heard the word before, but could not place the meaning of paven. However, the differential tone of the woman made her think it was not meant as an insult. She nodded her head, "We need a room for ourselves, a room for our six bondsmen, space for three wagons, and the horses to pull them."

"We have accommodations above the stables for servants, I am assuming that is acceptable?"

"Quite. They are only men from Cothel after all."

The woman smiled. "Your husband does not speak our language I am guessing."

"No."

"Is this your first time in Wyntac?"

Stephenie nodded her head, not exactly sure where the woman was going with her line of questioning.

"We are quite proud here. I would expect that of Retmir as well, but I believe that is a port town, so perhaps you are more accustomed to foreigners. As a bit of friendly advice, I would recommend that you perform any trade negotiations instead of your husband. Things will go more smoothly for you."

Stephenie nodded her head. "Thank you. It is one of the reasons I came along for the journey."

The woman smiled. "Well, for what you requested, the rate will be three full crowns a day."

Stephenie raised one eyebrow. She was not exactly sure of the going rates in the city, and room to store wagons was expensive, but that rate seemed way too high. "You do recall that I am Kyntian, yes?"

The woman smiled. "Of course, you are paven for your family. Had you been from Cothel, the rate would have been five crowns a day."

Stephenie took a deep breath. "I see," she said pausing. The woman was radiating quite a sense of satisfaction. *If only I could read minds.* "I understand quite well the need for different rates; however, I think a rate of two crowns a day is far more in line with what is considered acceptable."

The woman lost some of her sense of satisfaction. "We are not an establishment for common merchants."

"And I am hardly common," Stephenie said with her best Regina voice. "Do not make me comment on my treatment here to my family."

The woman frowned. "How many horses do you plan to have?"

"Three pairs."

The woman smiled. "Ah, well, I think that is likely our misunderstanding. I thought your wagons would take up more space and that you planned to have six pairs, not just three. For that number of animals, we can say two crown, four."

At six silver crowns to the gold, that was hardly a discount. "Two crowns, two, for three days, and we can pay you now for the accommodations"

The woman bowed her head. "Very well."

"Husband, please pay the madam seven crowns," Stephenie said in Pandar. "I am going to take a seat while you deal with the details." The woman was still a little too satisfied for Stephenie, but far from joyous. Finally remembering the meaning of paven, Stephenie plopped down in a large overstuffed chair that was sitting as part of a group of five in the middle of the room. *Pity me will they, well, they should give a better rate then.*

What is it? she felt Kas ask.

It's a fairly common practice to marry off daughters to other countries with the intent to have them bring as much wealth as possible back to Kynto. Expendable gold diggers. Gilded slaves. The pitied. Those that don't conform or are not successful in bringing back wealth are considered pariahs. The scorned and unnamed. The undeserving.

They returned to the public house where they were to meet the others. After the issues at the Emerald Stone, Stephenie's attitude was poor and she just wanted to get back to her men. However, they were a little late, having gotten turned around in one of Wyntac's more confusing burrows. When they arrived, her mood did not improve, as she could not sense any of the men. *Do you see them Kas?* she asked as they entered the public house.

No, none of them are here, he said after a moment of quickly moving about the dark room filled with just under twenty patrons.

She acknowledged a greeting from a man serving one table and continued to another group of tables where they had normally been meeting. "They should know better than to leave, we are not that late," she said to Henton, who had also noted their absence.

"If anyone did go in search of us, I would expect that at least two would remain behind."

Stephenie could hear the concern in his voice. Tim, fortunately enough, was acting his part and not adding to the conversation, as someone who felt they were considered an equal might. "They better not be in trouble." She released the fist she had clenched. *Kas, do you think you can go looking for them? Perhaps check the inns.*

I will not take long, he said and then paused as a servant approached.

"Sir, Ma'am, anything we can bring you?"

Stephenie turned to the young lady who had served them the night before. "Have the rest of my group been here recently?" she asked in Kyntian.

"No Ma'am. I've not seen any of those you were with last night."

Stephenie nodded her head. "Thank you. Please bring us some drinks and whatever you have for dinner."

The young lady bowed her head and quickly departed. Stephenie gave Kas a mental shake of her head, which caused him to also depart quickly. "We might as well eat," she said to Henton. "The inns will be checked. Hopefully they are just delayed like we were."

Henton helped her to sit in a chair before he and Tim took there own seats. "I had a bad feeling about us splitting up. Wyntac is very large. Finding them will be hard. If something happened, hopefully at least one of them will make it back here to tell us what is going on."

Stephenie wanted to agree, but talking about it was simply making her more anxious. She hoped they were at the inn and that would be the end of it. *And if they are, I'll knock their skulls together for making me worry.*

Their food was brought out fairly quickly, and while they were all hungry, Stephenie could barely eat half the stew. She kept looking up, hoping to see Kas or all of her men, but no one else entered the pub. Giving up on her meal, she turned to Henton. "I might need to go looking around part of the city."

"We need to give them more time. I take it there was no luck at the inn."

"Don't know yet." She turned back to the door, sensing several people approaching the building. She knew they were not her men even before the first soldier entered. When the five men dressed in the black and dark red uniforms of the King's Guard entered and began looking around the room, Stephenie's blood froze. While she could not read their thoughts, she sensed a purposefulness from them.

Henton, also on edge, moved his hand to his dagger. Tim was the only one of them wearing a sword, as none of their blades were fashionable enough for a lord to carry and it would be unseemly for a lady to carry one at all, no matter how fancy the blade. Tim picked up their focus and turned his head to see what they were looking at as the guards took notice of them.

"Don't do anything foolish," Henton said just above a whisper as the soldiers approached.

The lead man, who's black hair was pulled back in a queue, looked at the three of them and after a moment's hesitation, addressed Stephenie in Kyntian. "Lady Beth Calvar?"

"Yes," she responded evenly. "How may we help you?"

The guard smiled, but it was not friendly. "We half expected this to be another wasted trip. However, the lieutenant insisted we come back. You were not here earlier when we were told you would be."

Stephenie schooled her expression, uncertain of what was occurring and not wanting to make it worse, especially when Kas was not present. "We were delayed. Can you tell me what is going on?"

The sergeant shrugged. "Ma'am, the lieutenant wants to speak with you about the men who claim to be your bondsmen. When you were not here earlier, we assumed they had lied about you. I guess we gave up waiting too quickly. You will need to follow us to answer a few questions for the lieutenant."

Stephenie's heart stopped for a moment. That answered the question of where her men were, but not what had happened and what they faced. She was about to look for a means to stall them when Kas floated through the outside wall.

What is happening?

I'll tell you in a bit, she thought back to Kas. "Very well, we will follow you."

The journey to the guard house was long enough that Stephenie found herself fretting over the others. She did not know what to expect and she could not bare to lose anyone to the Kyntian justice system. Her friends would end up as indentured servants or slaves if it was simply a petty crime they were accused of. If it was more severe, they might be incarcerated or even executed.

After being led halfway across the city, they were escorted to a large complex of stone buildings inside a small curtain wall. A three story barracks was off to the left, the red-brown rust making the stone look nearly black in the fading light. To the right, was a long two story building with bars on the windows and a set of gallows by the main door. The soldiers led them into a smaller building adjacent to the prison.

The interior of the smaller building was actually more pleasant than Stephenie had expected. Whitewashed walls brightened the rooms, which had quality furniture and an overall sense of discipline. Numerous oil lamps illuminated the room, chasing away most shadows.

"Please follow me," the sergeant said in Kyntian, primarily to Stephenie.

She gave Tim a quick glance, signaling him to wait and he responded with a nod of his head. To Henton, she motioned for him to follow; he was, after all, supposed to be her husband.

The lieutenant's office was decorated similarly to the rest of the small building. There was a man seated behind a large oak desk that was covered in neat stacks of paper. Four chairs sat in front of his desk and Stephenie and Henton took the center two as indicated.

"Lieutenant, please tell me what is going on," Stephenie said, more concern than she wanted bleeding into her voice. They were no longer in a position where she could fight their way out. At best, she and Kas would be able to escape and her escape was by no means certain. If the soldiers had some holy warriors in the area, their chances would be that much less.

"Ma'am, I understand you are Lady Beth Calvar and this is your husband, Lord Henton Calvar," the man said in Kyntian. "You may call me Sir Jeral."

"Sir Jeral, I understand you have my bondsmen in custody. What did they do?"

Sir Jeral teepeed his hands, "Ma'am, they were reported as being suspicious. They were in the southwest district and were seen watching a couple of different stables and wainwright shops. A couple of them had made some general inquiries about prices, but they do not appear to be sufficiently funded to be making any purchases. This led some concerned citizens to report the incident."

"Sir Jeral, I asked that they look into locations for us to purchase some wagons. I assure you, my husband and I have sufficient funds. We have no intention of having our men steal anything." Stephenie's tongue felt thick and she wished she had something to drink.

Sir Jeral smiled and his brown eyes twinkled. "My Lady, not all of us automatically assume the worst about foreigners. Unfortunately, I suspect I can easily count the number who would give your husband a fair trade on one hand. I have spoken at length with your man named Douglas and I was fairly certain their actions were honest, but I am often at the mercy of politics that are greater than myself." He pulled a small stack of papers out from under a worn book and spread them before him. "If you will confirm some details about your family, we can close out the incident and I will have your men released."

Stephenie swallowed. "Certainly. What is it you need to know?"

"Your maiden name was?"

"My father is Lord Urivar. He lives in Retmir."

"And your husband's lands are in Cothel?"

"Yes. In Antar. We came here as quickly as possible with the intent to buy raw steel and bring it back. With Cothel in a bit of turmoil, weapons are in demand and if we can move quickly, we should be able to make a good profit. Which is why we did not bring our own wagons. We planned to simply purchase additional ones here. The extra profit would cover the extra expense and then give us a larger fleet."

Sir Jeral made a couple notes on the paper, taking his pen back to the ink well several times. Stephenie tried to sense his mood, but just like Henton, the man was guarded.

After a few more moments of writing, he set his pen back in the holder and looked up. "I think that will cover the details. However, can I ask where you are staying in case additional questions come up? I assume you are not staying at the public house you were to meet your men at."

Stephenie smiled. "Of course not. This is our first time to Wyntac and we arrived late yesterday, so we stopped at the first place we found. Today we have acquired accommodations at the Emerald Stone."

Sir Jeral's left eyebrow rose slightly. "That is a nice establishment. Though I would say it will cut into your profits a bit."

"Well, my cousin Darrel recommended it, so I promised him I would try it. We won't be there very long and they have room for wagons and horses inside the city."

The lieutenant nodded his head. "Before I get your men, may I offer one last bit of advice. With all the turmoil our Princess Elsia has been through, people of Cothel are not particularly popular at the moment. Things will go better if you handle the negotiations. Most of us will understand your situation. I even have a younger sister, a Miss Evelyn, who is married to a young Lord. He's only a third son and won't inherit much, but it was the best option for the family. It just saddens me that I never get a chance to see her anymore. She's in Cothel as well; all the way south in Easting."

Stephenie nodded her head. "It it hard to lose family. If you ever come through Antar on your way to see her, we would be happy to have you visit."

He smiled at her, genuinely pleased. "Be careful, I may just take you up on that."

Chapter 18

Stephenie remained stoic with her men until after they were well away from the city guards and on their way back to their current inns. Once they retrieved their belongings, she would take them to the Emerald Stone, but until then she worried about how everyone had been treated and if anyone had been hurt.

Eventually, she could not hold in her questions and she pulled Will and Douglas to her. "Everyone okay, no one hurt?"

"Ma'am, no one was hurt," Douglas said with slightly downcast eyes. "Everyone told the truth and while the guards that took us in were unfriendly, no one had cause to be violent."

Stephenie smiled; Douglas' version of the truth had been beaten into everyone for several days. Based on what happened, it was definitely a wise use of time. *Something else to give Douglas credit for.* "Good, I wanted to make sure no one was hurt, and making sure things don't suddenly take a turn for the worse will help make sure everyone stays safe."

She looked back and forth between Will and Douglas. "Any luck finding some wagons and horses?"

Will shrugged. "I think I know who complained, so we can definitely not do business there. We found three or four others we could buy the wagons from."

"I think we still want to get the wagons from different people. We didn't come into the city dressed that nicely. At least not nicely enough for someone who has the money to buy as much as we do. Let me know the places to go and Henton and I can go make the purchases tomorrow. I was hoping not to have to be involved in every transaction, but too many people have commented to the effect that if we don't want trouble, it should be me."

"Well, aside from your red hair, your Kyntian heritage is evident in your face," Henton said from behind her. "That and your fluency with the language."

"Well..." She stopped speaking, feeling Kas reaching out to her mind.

You should move this along and off the streets, I believe there are some guards following you.

Thank you, Kas. How close are they?

Less than a block. They are trying to make it look like they are not following you, but it would be very coincidental for them to patrol the exact route we are taking to the inns.

"We have some friends," she said quietly so that only Will, Henton, and Douglas would hear it. "Let's get going. We don't have anything to hide at the moment, so let's hope they get bored and forget us."

After they retrieved their goods from the inns they had stayed at previously, Stephenie led everyone back to the Emerald Stone. She and Henton went up to the room they had rented, while the others were shown a single room in the barn with cots for their use. The bed was large and quite comfortable, the furnishings of high quality, and most importantly, everything was clean. It was indeed a room that would be acceptable to most merchant families as well as lower nobility. For the first time in several days, Stephenie slept soundly, even with Henton sharing the bed.

Kas woke them in the morning. "Your friends have changed, but they are down the street watching the front door."

"Well, let's give them a tedious day and perhaps they will go away."

"I thought the lieutenant was sympathetic," Henton remarked as he washed his face. "I didn't follow what was said, but he seemed kind in his mannerism."

Stephenie shrugged. "I have a hard time sensing some people's emotions. If his job is to investigate things, he's probably quite adept at putting people at ease so he can catch them unaware."

"Well, I'll go down and make sure the men are ready," Henton said, dropping the towel he had used to dry his face back onto the side table.

After he left, Stephenie finished getting ready, using Kas' help to cinch and tie her dress behind her. *You are lucky I trust you. Most men would take issue with their woman spending the night in another man's bed.*

Stephenie smiled at Kas, sensing the playfulness of his jibe in their mental link. *I'm surprised it's taken you this long to notice. Think of all the nights I've been laying around seven other men. It's safe to say my reputation is ruined beyond all repair. My mother warned me that my behavior would lose me any chance of a good match.* She flipped her loose hair over her shoulder and through Kas' face. *I guess I will just have to settle for you.*

I so wanted to be associated with someone of such low standing. Kas seemed to pause a moment, *but that does raise the question, I did not find your mother and I think that is for the best. Will you accept that and focus on our primary goal and not revenge? At least as a favor for me?*

"Kas, I want my mother dead. She needs to die. It would bring justice to my father and so many others who suffered or died because of what she did." Stephenie sensed the concern Kas was feeling. "However, it can wait. Let her live for a while, knowing that her little shit of a daughter came and stole back all the money she removed from my father's treasury. Let her feel beaten for a while. You are right in that it is going to be hard enough to get out of Wyntac without getting caught as it is. Adding the complexity of killing her to the list of things to do might be more than we can handle."

And I do not think she is in the castle, he added, trying to cover the relief that was obvious to Stephenie.

She looked into his eyes, her own eyes large and tilted upward toward his face. *I love you Kas. No matter how difficult I am and the challenges we face, I love you.*

Of course you do. Now let's go buy your wagons so you can try to get yourself killed robbing the king.

* * * * *

The wainwrights that Douglas and the others had assessed the previous day were on the far west side of the city. After they had all eaten an early meal and crossed the city, half the morning was gone and Stephenie was growing concerned they may not have enough time to make all the arrangements in one day. They were already too many days behind where she wanted to be and the journey across Calis would be slower, not faster than she had predicted. If they had to spend too much more time in Wyntac, she feared the ship Joshua had agreed to send might give up on them.

When they finally reached the first wainwright's shop, she had already grown a bit too irritable to deal with a stubborn man. "Yes, our plan is to haul steel stock, so I want one of those heavier built wagons I see there. But, again, not the largest one. My drivers can handle a team of two, but they are not good enough to manage more than that."

The wrinkled old man looked at Stephenie with a scowl and shook his head. "You'd better get better men, if you'll haul large loads."

"Look," she said, her voice getting even harder. "That wagon there and a team of drafts, what will it cost me?"

Henton stood just behind her, his own scowl had deepened, but the master of the shop continued to disregard him as if Henton did not exist, despite the fact that Henton was at least a head taller than the old man. This inconsiderate disregard of him because he was from Cothel was irritating Stephenie as much as the man's continual evasiveness. "I'll be buying a wagon and horses today," she said, ready to turn around and walk away, "but if you are not interested in my coin, I can take my business elsewhere."

"Fine. You want a wagon and team to drive it, it'll cost two hundred and thirty full crowns."

Stephenie shook her head. "You ask me for more than one hundred and my family will have you blacklisted. I told you I am Lady Beth Calvar and while we primarily do business in the west, my Cothish husband plans to do lots of business in Wyntac."

The man stood straighter. "Don't threaten me. You can't get more than a couple nags and rot for one hundred and any Lady knows that. I'll sell you a rig for one seventy."

Stephenie was uncertain exactly what the man was feeling, but she could not afford that much and still have enough to purchase the steel. "One hundred and thirty."

The man's anger was growing. "One fifty. That is the lowest."

Stephenie looked to the wagon and pursed her lips. She wished she had a better frame of reference. These Kyntian coins were smaller and the market here was different than she was used to. Even in Cothel, she knew her father would arrange to have agents buy different things in different cities from time to time because of price variations. However, she was sensing the man was becoming tenser or perhaps firmer in his position. "Fine, though I will have one of my men pick the horses."

After a moment, the man nodded his head.

She turned back to Henton. "Please pay the man one fifty," she said, switching to Pandar. Turning further, she nodded to Tim. "Go pick out two drafts and hook them up to that wagon." Looking about, she walked over to a block of wood that would make a good seat and made a point of sitting down. *I would never make a good queen,* she thought to Kas. *I don't have the patience to deal with things like this all day.*

And all day is what I expect it will take.

Once Henton had paid the master wainwright and Tim had hitched the horses, Stephenie had Will and Berman drive the wagon back to the Emerald Stone, while everyone else continued to shop. They had to stop at four more wainwrights to purchase the two additional wagons. The second one did not have anything suitable for sale and the third one refused to do business at a reasonable rate. However, none of those shops were as difficult to deal with as the first one had been; the third one simply turned them away without wasting their time.

Once the wagons and horses were purchased and heading back to the Emerald Stone, Henton, Kas, and Stephenie continued to shop. This time, to purchase a number of crates. Based on the sizes, they planned for sixteen large crates per wagon. Two layers of six stacked three across and a top layer of four crates. The purchase was easy and the crates were ready to go, but Stephenie arranged to pick them up in the morning after putting down a deposit on them. On the way to find the steel, they requested several bags of grain for the horses as well as a number of bundles of hay, knowing they would have to acquire more throughout the journey.

As the afternoon was wearing down, they reached the northwestern side of Wyntac, where much of the smelting was done to convert iron into steel ingots, bar stock, and finished tools. The cloud of ash and smog was thicker in this part of the city, covering everything with soot. The stench of rotten eggs was always just on the periphery, as the sulfur-rich coal heated the fires of the numerous blacksmiths. It was a busy section of the city, with numerous laborers, dirty from days of endless work, pounding away on their tasks. When well-dressed businessmen or Lords and Ladies walked or rode down the streets, most of the lower classes knew to clear a path. The heavy presence of soldiers and city guards ensured everyone respected their position in society so the steel trade would continue without hindrance.

At the foundries, Stephenie and Henton were quickly taken into well kept buildings and offered refreshments and a clean place to sit to conduct business. Those they negotiated with were dressed well, but not too well. The volume of material that Stephenie was purchasing was not large enough for them to merit negotiating with someone above that of a well placed bureaucrat. In the end, they had enough money to purchase four hundred and fifty full crowns worth of steel, which they would pick up the next day with the wagons.

"I am glad this is over," Henton said as they walked once again across the city. This final trip before heading back to the inn was to get Stephenie's green dress. While it might have given her more negotiating power, and would not have darkened as noticeably from the soot as the white one, they simply did not have the time to wait the extra day.

"Not as glad as I am."

"Yeah, well, I was the one handing over money all day. That was more money than I have ever personally held before. I didn't like carrying it, always worried we'd get robbed, but I also didn't like spending it that much either. I must be cheap. The men always said I was."

Stephenie smiled. She knew how stingy Henton liked to be when rationing anything. However, she also knew that he'd always be more than willing to give anyone enough to survive. He had been more than generous with his own share of food when she had eaten so much right after escaping from Arkani. *Perhaps he's just more generous with me,* she realized thinking back over their travels. Not wanting to think about the reasons, she looked down at her feet as they walked quickly on the side of the cobblestone street.

The next morning, Kas reported their friends were still watching and following as they drove the wagons down the crowded streets. The first stop was to pick up the forty-eight crates, each just under two feet wide and five feet long. There was a little extra room from side to side in the wagon bed, but the last half foot of the second row of crates hung out over the back edge of the bed. However, Stephenie had chosen wagons with large rear axles and sturdy wheels. She was assured the wagons could hold the weight, not only by the wainwrights, but also by Tim who was turning out to be quite helpful with the wagons.

She was given permission to take as much of the wood shavings and dust as she wanted from the pile of scraps the crafters had dumped outside their shop. She had the men fill the center two crates on the bottom layer half-full with the shavings. Her hope was to deaden the sound any of the coins might make when shifting about on the rocking wagon.

After the crates were loaded, she and Henton directed the team across the river to where the steel was waiting for them. It took six stops to retrieve everything that had been purchased. In taking extra time and care to balance the weight across the three wagons, it was late in the afternoon when they were fully loaded and heading back toward the Emerald Stone to wait out the evening.

"Can you lift all that?" Henton asked as they pulled the wagons into the inn's back yard. Although he only watched and supervised the men loading the steel, it was not hard to see how much effort it had taken and how tired the men had become. Even the horses had to work a little to get the wagons up the gentle arch of the bridge that took them over the river.

"I won't know for certain until I try, but worse case, I move them off one crate at a time. The point is to keep any tax collectors from digging down to the bottom crates." She looked back over her shoulder to where Kas was floating invisibly. "Our friends have remained far enough away today and we made enough stops that no one should have noticed we left the center ones empty."

Henton nodded his head, but Stephenie could see the doubt in his eyes. He was afraid, but was hiding it well from the others. He trusted her enough to share his concerns, and she would never dismiss them outright, the risk was too great.

"Yeah, I know," she said in acknowledgment. "Let's get some dinner, and we can all discuss the plan."

"If we still have people watching, we won't be able to get into the castle undetected." Berman's eyes darted around the small room in the barn, quickly glancing from person to person. "We'll need to kill them and hide the bodies. Kas said they get changed out just before first light. The only choice is for Steph to take them out just before we head off to the castle. But then they'd still suspect us when their replacements can't find them in the morning. They'll come for us. They'll know who to look for. We have to wait."

Stephenie took a deep breath, drawing everyone's attention to her. She and Kas were monitoring to make sure no one came close enough to overhear the discussion. "We are loaded and ready to go. If we wait, then that will look suspicious and they'll have more people watching us, not less."

"Then we have to kill them and get out of the city before anyone notices. Perhaps we just call off the castle, we've got a lot of valuable steel. Sell that and bring back the money. Or rob some more nobles, that turned out well."

Unclenching her jaw, Stephenie pulled her shoulders back. "We are not calling it off. Josh needs the money, so we don't have a choice.

And I am not killing these watchers. They've done nothing to us. Murder is not how we operate here."

"They're just Kyntian soldiers," Peter added. "They abandoned us in the war and many of our brothers died because of that. They're all traitors. I've heard you talk about killing your mother, what's the difference here? Look how we've been treated. Locked up and then followed all around the city for simply looking to purchase wagons."

She shook her head. "No. In the war, they were ordered to abandon Cothel. Ordered by people like my mother. The blood is on her hands and the hands of my uncle and the generals. But regardless, I am not here to do anything about her. Not this time," she added softly. Looking around the room, she met everyone's eyes. "I don't like how rude they are, but the truth of it is, I stole the money we used to buy our supplies. So we are not innocent in this. They don't likely know that and to be distrusted simply because we came from Cothel is an insult, but I'm not going to kill because of it. They've done nothing to deserve such a permanent treatment. We kill to defend ourselves only."

"They could get us killed. Justify it as preemptive defense," Peter said with a shrug. "No one has to know it was us that did anything to them."

Stephenie shook her head no. She missed Fish so much. Josh had insisted she needed more men then Henton, Douglas, and Will, and while she generally liked these men, they had not been trained by Henton and so lacked a certain set of morals Douglas and Will had. "No. I will knock them out and tie them up. We'll stash them somewhere out of the way, but not somewhere that no one will ever find them."

"It's a risk," Henton said, "but one I agree with. We act responsibly, not without a conscience. Otherwise, we are simply bandits and rogues and those who were with me in Antar near the end of the war know we hunted that type of person down to face justice."

Stephenie looked to Henton and nodded her head. His proclamation seemed to quiet the others. "Alright, everyone get some sleep. We'll wake you when it is time to go. I'll have taken care of our friends by that time, so it will be straight to the castle, lots of wealth, then out the east gate with the sunrise."

Stephenie could not sleep. She tried for a while, then simply gave up, resolved to lay in bed with Henton sleeping beside her. He was more pragmatic than her. 'Sleep when you can, you might not get a chance later,' he had told her. However, sleep just would not come. Her fear of what would happen before the morning sun would shine ate away at the back of her mind. *If Berman and Peter were right and the guards watching them did get out an alert and people died because of it...* She did not want to consider the results. She had promised herself no one else under her command would die. Not if she could do anything to prevent it.

Do not fret, Kas interrupted her thoughts. *You are doing what is correct. We all knew there would be risks and this is one you must accept if you wish to remain who you are.*

Thank you, Kas. She took a deep breath and allowed herself to be bathed in Kas' mental image of herself. It was something she knew she had to live up to. *It's amazing how quickly I started to second guess myself.* She let out a mental laugh, *At least I can talk to you about these things without Henton listening in anymore.*

That does not give you leave to cease learning Dalish. However, that will have to wait, it is time for you to rise and tie up the watchers. I have found a place for you to put them that will hopefully give you until mid-morning before anyone finds them. It is in the basement of a nearby public house, which closed for the night a little earlier.

She nodded her head, getting the mental images of the location from Kas. Reassured that her decision was correct, she tried to slip out of bed without waking Henton. However, he was always the lightest of sleepers. Without a word, he slid from the other side of the bed and started getting ready himself. While he would remain at the inn until she returned, he needed to rouse the others and be ready to move out the moment she did return.

Both of them had lain down to sleep dressed in dark breaches, boots, and shirts. To this, she strapped her dagger on her waist, grabbed a length of rope, included wads of cloth to use as gags, and headed to the window. "Be safe," Henton mouthed as she carefully pushed open the shutters. She smiled at him, then slipped out the third floor window, dropping soundlessly to the ground.

Chapter 19

Stephenie walked ahead of the three wagons. It was well past the middle of the night and the streets were mostly deserted, leaving the clomping of the horse's hooves echoing between the buildings as the only sound. She had managed to knock out the two watchers and store them in the basement of Dermin's Pub without trouble and without being seen even by them. She had robbed them in the process, so there was a chance they would not be suspects.

That was what she had repeated to herself as she turned down a side street that paralleled the main road in front of the castle. They were still several blocks away and although there were many cross streets that allowed access to the main road, she hoped to be able to keep the wagons out of direct sight of the castle while they emptied the vault.

The buildings along this parallel road belonged to upscale merchants, with living quarters above the store fronts below. The proximity of the castle kept the less savory public houses further away and the few public houses this close to the castle closed quite early so as to be respectful of the King.

"We can stop here," Stephenie finally said as she reached a corner that had a direct view of the castle window Kas had identified as the one they should enter through. The building they had stopped in front of was a silversmith and it was early enough that no one was awake inside. She walked back to the wagons as the other two pulled up behind the first one.

Once the horses were settled and the brakes set, she gathered everyone around her. "Okay, we need to keep the noise down, we don't need attention. Henton, I want you and Douglas to stay here with the wagons. If anyone questions what's going on, you've sent the others off to find a wainwright to fix the wagon and you are waiting for them."

"I'd rather be inside to protect you."

"I need you here to protect the wagons and you are the one playing at being a Lord." She turned to the others. "Everyone will need to stay behind me when we are in the castle. We don't want to stumble across anyone and set off an alarm."

Everyone nodded their head and Stephenie smiled at all of them. "We'll get through this and be out of Wyntac with the sun. And we'll be richer than the King."

She turned her head as Kas approached. *I have checked the floors, things are as they were the last time I checked. Four on the top floor and four more in front of the vault door. The coins and money are essentially the same.*

Thank you, Kas, she said, letting her feeling flow across their link. *I just hope nothing goes wrong.*

You can handle it.

"Okay, Kas says things are ready for us. Let me take care of the wagon and we can head out."

She walked to the last wagon and knelt down next to the rear wheel. Drawing in a small amount of energy, she formed a gravity field around the springs that were already heavily compressed due to the weight of the steel in the wagon. Expanding the field, she lifted the bed. Using a new flow, she heated the head of the pin holding the ends of the leaf spring together and finally she pushed out the pin, allowing the spring to separate. Slowly she lowered the deck of the wagon, leaving everything dangerously tilted.

She let out the breath. She had not lifted the full weight of the contents, but she felt comfortable she would be able to lift all the steel in one effort when the time came. It seemed to her that the effort to lift something heavier was far less than proportional to the weight difference of a lighter item. She stood and turned to Henton. "Well, no one can doubt you that there is a problem with the wagon."

"Let's hope we don't need to make a quick escape," Henton said just loud enough for her to hear.

She nodded her head and started back to the crossroad. "Let's go," she told the others as she passed.

"Be safe," Douglas said quietly from where he stood.

"Yes, everyone come back safely," Henton added.

Stephenie gave them both a wide smile. "You too, don't attract attention." Turning down the cross street, she drew in energy again, this time, wrapping a field around her legs and that of the five others who would be coming with her. Without stopping, she lifted everyone quickly into the air, flying them across the open space with incredible speed. Eyes tearing from the wind, she brought them to a sudden stop just outside the window Kas had moved to as she crossed the wide courtyard between the castle and the main road.

The window was older in style, with many small glass panes. Kas had left it open after his last check of the castle, and sensing no one inside the dark room, she quickly flew her men through the window, bringing herself in last. Inside the office, she could see several chairs, a table, a desk, and a number of shelves laden with books and papers.

Although she could clearly see in the limited light, she could tell the others were having trouble. After opening herself to check that the surrounding area was free of people, she moved to the door and slowly opened it to a dark hallway. Grabbing the oil lamp from a small side table, she pushed energy into the wick until flames burst forth, bringing light to the room. Handing it off to Will, she went out into the hallway.

The hallway had a wooden floor, but the walls were made of stone blocks, neatly dressed and tightly mortared. To both her left and right, the hallway teed off in each direction, eventually leading to wooden doors at each end. Directly forward, the hallway went for forty feet before ending at a heavy, reinforced door. Several doorways could be seen along that forty foot passage. She took a deep breath, knowing that she was about to take herself and her friends further over the precipice. Each step forward was further risk. Until they were safe in Calis, she knew her chest would be tight.

I love you, Kas.

I love you too, Stephenie.

Feeling better with Kas' sense of confidence in her, she turned left and went to the door. As Kas had described, the doorway, like the walls, was made of stone with the wooden door opening toward her. *Please let this work this time,* she thought to herself as she reached up to put her hand on the lintel. While she was not overly tall, neither were these doors and she was easily able to lay her hand flat on the cold stone. Taking a deep breath, she pulled energy through herself to generate the fields that would disrupt the bonds holding together the tiny bits of stone that made up the lintel above the door.

Breathing slowly, she continued to focus on the stone, adjusting the field in subtle ways, as if she was trying to jiggle chain mail armor until all the links simply separated and fell apart. After just a few moments, she felt the stone start to slip and decay into a fluid. Immediately breaking the field, she froze the sagging stone in place, leaving it dropping down a couple of inches over the top of the door.

Carefully, she tried to open the door and while the latch was released, the top of the door held tightly. She sighed and smiled at Kas who had come over to watch, even though he remained invisible. "I'll fix the other doors, then we can take out the men on this floor."

Kas drifted ahead of her as she went to the door on the right side of the tee. For that door, she found the effort even easier, as the stone likely came from the same quarry and had similar enough properties that she did not have to hunt as hard for the proper field.

Once those two doors were secured, she quickly jammed the four doors along the longer passage. By the time she was done, she was starting to feel the effects of the concentration. The amount of energy she had drawn through herself had been limited, but her head ached from the constant change of focus from the very small to a more normal perspective. She wondered if the masters of Kas' time had similar issues to deal with or if they had found a solution to the dizzying effect.

Turning to the reinforced door separating her from the guards, she knew she had remained quiet so far, barely making a sound as she moved from door to door. She avoided the chance of the floor creaking by countering much of her weight with levitation. Now that she was standing at the final door that led into the old square tower, she allowed her weight to sink back into the floor.

The door was likely locked from the inside and although she could feel the presence of the men, she was now numb enough that she only had a vague sense of the room. *Kas, can you unlock the door for me?*

I will see what I can do, he replied as he drifted through the door.

Stephenie waited for a couple of moments before she heard Kas in her mind again.

The key was next to the door, it took me a moment to put the key in the lock without someone noticing. By the way, they are sitting on chairs facing the door, but three of them are focused on a card game.

Stephenie exhaled deeply and acknowledged Kas' comments, giving him her assent to turn the key. She heard the lock release and immediately pushed the door open with her mind, but also used a second field to block the door from slamming into the wall and making noise.

The men looked up, surprise on their faces and radiating from their minds. Without pause, she wrapped a field around each of the men, spinning them around and away from her, but preventing them from otherwise moving while at the same time cutting off their air. Unlike when she put the girl in the merchant's house to sleep, she tried to keep a mental distance from these men as she had when she knocked out the watchers. However, despite her mental deafness and reserve, she still felt overwhelmed by their combined panic and terror. Only when the last of them finally fell unconscious did the dread in her fade.

Breathing deeply to try and clear her head, she waved the others forward. Will came first, carrying the lamp. Tim was right behind him and went to work with Berman, John, and Peter to bind, gag, and blindfold the four soldiers.

Stephenie nodded her head to the stairs set into the floor of the far corner of this twenty foot by twenty foot room. The walls in the room were much rougher in form than that of the hall. They also had a slightly pinker hue in the flecked stone. Wishing she could take the time to truly appreciate the construction, she spared only enough time to consider the oppressiveness that the old tower seemed to radiate with all of the windows and arrow loops bricked over. It seemed the tower itself was depressed and sad, radiating out a mournful plea to go back to its original beauty. It left her with a feeling of malice that was just out of reach. There was a darkness that was more than just the lack of light.

As soon as the four soldiers, still unconscious, were secured, she picked up one of the lamps the soldiers were using and started to carefully descend the steps. The longer she was here, the more she wanted to be away from this old tower, but the only way to do that was to first go further into it.

As they descended, the wood treads of the stairs creaked slightly, but the ends of the treads were embedded in stone walls, lending strength and security to the worn wood. On the next floor down, there was a landing that opened into what was an empty room. Just after the landing, the stairs turned ninety degrees at the corner of the tower and continued further down. The next two floors were as empty as the third floor had been.

When they descended below what had originally been the ground floor, the sadness of the tower seemed to fade slightly. The walls were no longer marred with bricked over sections and the stair treads changed to stone as the stairwell opened slightly, offering Stephenie enough headroom that she could stand upright without risking her head hitting the ceiling.

When they reached the second level underground, she stopped before another heavily reinforced door. Kas simply continued through the door and quickly reported back to Stephenie. *The four men are eating. Two are quietly talking, but I do not see a key to the lock.*

Alright, I'll get the door open, she responded as she knelt down, placing her hands on the metal of the lock. Reaching out, she tried to sense the mechanics of the lock, but just as it had been with the merchant's house, she did not understand the workings inside the mechanism. However, unlike the merchant's house, buried two stories under the ground she could afford to make a little noise. This time, instead of liquifying the locking mechanism, she simply generated an intense gravity field. A moment after the field formed, the lock collapsed upon itself, sucking the bolt from the jamb. The collapsing metal and wood creaked and squealed slightly, but the noise did not carry far.

Flinging open the door, she managed to catch the men before they had a chance to truly react to the sound. The four men struggled, but were no match for her magic and in a short time, all were unconscious.

Stephenie leaned against the open door as the others moved past her and into the room. They quickly bound, gagged, and blindfolded the guards as she caught her breath.

"The other door looks a bit thicker," Will said, as he examined the six foot tall, steel reinforced door set into a stone wall that divided this room into half the size of the rooms on the floors above.

Stephenie walked over and examined the lock. The steel looked thicker and felt denser than the other door. With a quick thought, she stepped back and formed another gravity well inside the lock. The steel resisted and Stephenie increased the flow of energy, intensifying the gravity until the lock screeched as it collapsed. After a solid blow, the door swung open, revealing a dark room beyond.

She heard John laugh in anticipation. "Damn, that's a lot of gold," he said as the lamp light reflected off the valuables inside.

"And we get to carry it up all those stairs," Will chided.

Stephenie ignored the banter and headed into the vault. Every moment longer they delayed, the greater the chance something would go wrong. Inside the vault, there were many shelves with different boxes, bags, and many stacks of coins in neat order. On the floor, and against the wall, was where most of the coins were stacked. As Kas described, many chests with straps for carrying were stacked up against the left hand wall.

"Kas, can you go up and watch the hall above to keep an eye out for trouble?"

"Of course," he responded in the Old tongue, briefly becoming visible before disappearing again.

To the others, she pointed to the chests. "Okay, let's start loading. Will, you're the slimmest, so if you can stay here and load up more chests while the rest of us carry them up the stairs, that will help keep things moving."

Everyone quickly moved a chest closer to the stacks of valuables. The flat topped chests themselves were heavy, having a reinforced bottom and thick straps that fit into the harnesses that would go over a man's shoulders.

"Go for the gold crowns first, the gems may be worth more, but they'll be harder to convert to money," Stephenie said, seeing John empty a box of small gems into the chest at his feet. "Leave what you have in there, just focus the first effort on the coins. And don't fill it full," she added, "even two of you won't be able to carry it."

Once her own chest was filled quite a bit more than what the others would be able to carry, she took a deep breath and generated a gravity field to lift the chest from the bottom. It was not too heavy for her, so she quickly gathered a second chest and filled it. Using her powers, she stacked the second chest on top the first one as the men were strapping on the harnesses. "Follow as you can," she said, heading out the vault and up the stairs with the two chests floating in the air ahead of her.

By the time she was to the second floor above the ground, she felt sweat running down her forehead and into her eyes. The weight was not so much the problem, but the concentration needed to sustain a prolonged period of careful maneuvering was starting to give her a headache. Once she reached the top floor, she walked past the men who were still tied up, two of them had regained consciousness, but they stopped struggling against their bonds when they heard her walk across the floor.

Kas was down the hallway, but moved immediately in her direction. *They have not been making much noise, so I decided to leave them for now. However, it might be worth knocking them out again.*

Stephenie nodded her head as she moved past Kas and into the office at the end of the hallway. She set the chests down against the wall and walked back to the guards. *I'm glad I don't have to lug those up by hand,* she said to Kas as she cut off the air to the two who had woken. *However, I suspect I will need to bring up most of the rest and that wasn't easy.*

You will need to conserve some strength to fly the chests down and load them into the wagons, as well as fix that one wagon you broke.

"Don't remind me," she mumbled aloud after the two men had fallen unconscious. She had hoped talking to Kas would have distracted her from the panic and terror the men felt, but it had not. "I'll be back."

She encountered Tim and John on the third level of the tower, winded and taking a break, a lamp on the top of the chest. Berman and Peter were almost to the second level and were moving a little slower, but they were still moving. She gave them some encouragement and quickly went back to the vault.

"Cothel won't need to worry about funds for a long time," Will said when she entered the vault. He had already loaded up the rest of the chests and was waiting quietly.

"Let's hope so," she replied. "If there are a couple of small sacks that are not too heavy, you might carry those up by hand."

He smiled and patted the bulging pouches at his waist. "I'll grab a couple more."

She grinned, and then drew energy into herself. Again, lifting one chest on top of a second one, she briefly considered adding a third chest. However, it would be too tall to maneuver up the tight stairs with the limited head space. By the time she was in the stairway, she sensed Will had quickly outdistanced her and was moving out of her range. By the time she reached the second floor above the ground, she was feeling truly drained and took a short break to catch her breath.

When she could sense Tim and John coming down the stairs above her, she picked up the chests and resumed her ascent. The two men slid past her with giant grins. She suspected they were thinking about what kind of reward they would be getting for bringing back all of this money. *It's not in Cothel yet,* she thought to herself as they almost skipped down the stairs and out of her view. *But, I'll make sure all of you can retire after this.*

By the time she reached the top floor, Berman and Peter were heading down. "One more for us, right?"

"That'd be all of it," she said with smile, while wiping the sweat from her forehead.

She was only halfway down the hallway to the office when she felt someone approaching the other side of the door on her right. *Kas, we have trouble.*

He did not respond, but having sensed the person approaching himself, he simply drifted through the door. A moment later, Stephenie felt the slight draw of energy and pain from Kas.

What is it? she demanded, letting the chests nearly fall to the floor. She sensed Kas retreating away from the man. She now knew it to be a man as she sensed a brief layer of emotion when he tried to push open the door and failed as the stone she had transformed held it tightly at the top. *Kas!* she called out mentally.

Instinctively, she formed a field to repel the door fragments that exploded in her direction. The debris flew around her, sliding off her shield, and crashed into the chests and the wall behind her. On the other side of the open doorway, a man wearing steel-blue robes stood with a holy symbol of Ravim prominently displayed on his chest. However, Stephenie could sense numerous threads of energy coming from his mind and none coming from the holy symbol.

She did not have time to contemplate the observation as the man unleashed a quick series of attacks, driving narrow beams of force at her from numerous angles and directions. She blocked the initial attacks until pain ripped through her side.

Losing focus, she was whipped around by the force of the blow and knocked to her hands and knees, facing the doorway to the office. Knowing she would not be able to keep up with the speed of his attacks, she unleashed one of her own, sinking a gravity well under his feet.

Stephenie poured energy into the field, but the man was compensating. He quickly formed a control thread to her head in preparation to unleash what she knew to be lightning. Just as he unleashed the bolt, she linked it back to his control thread, hoping to end the attack quickly, but unlike the others she had fought previously, this man was too fast and he broke his control thread, shifting the lightning into the doorjamb instead of his head. The blackened stone stood out in her vision as she looked up and over her shoulder, still on her hands and knees. The only hope Stephenie had was that the man's sense of cavalier certainty she had felt a moment before was now gone.

Distract him, she heard Kas say in Dalish.

Without hesitation, she unloaded a series of quick attacks, trying to be as random as he had been, but none of them broke through his defenses. However, it did occupy the man's attention enough that he did not sense Kas' approach through the ceiling until Kas was already on top of him. The man tried to duck and avoid Kas, but Stephenie unleashed another gravity well under his feet and caught between the two attacks, he failed to avoid Kas' hand as it passed through his skull. A moment later, the man's body crumbled and broke as it slammed into a bloody mass on the floor, which was now splintered and crushed where the gravity well had compressed the wooden floorboards.

Still on her hands and knees, she tried to take a deep breath, but it sent agony through her side. She felt the blood draining across her belly and soaking into her shirt.

You need to heal yourself, that is a bad wound.

She nodded her head. Will had come out of the office to see the commotion, but the whole conflict had lasted just a few moments. "Kas, quickly, get the others, tell them to leave the chests." Almost in tears, she added mentally, *get them up here quickly. No idea how much noise that was. We can't take the time for what's left.*

Without a word, he dropped through the floor.

"You okay," Will asked, already kneeling at her side.

She nodded her head again and closed her eyes. The pain was intense. The blow had gone deep into her side and had ruptured many internal organs in her abdomen. She could taste the blood coming up her throat. Without magic to heal herself, she knew the wound would be fatal. Holding her breath against the pain, she drew in energy and focused it on allowing her subconscious mind to heal the wound.

She felt the warmth of the energy flowing through her. But as flesh knitted itself back together in an explosion of rapid healing, she felt herself grow weak and lost all sense of which direction was up. A moment later, she was looking up at Will's face. Concern radiated from him, but somehow he maintained a subtle charm.

"Steph, don't die on me. You've got to fly me down to the ground."

She tried to return his smile, but her side still hurt. The wound was no longer fatal, but it was not completely healed. After taking as deep of a breath as she could muster, she had him help her upright. "Thank you," she mumbled, as she continued to use him to lever herself into a standing position, hoping her nose would not start bleeding yet. "I need to get these chests into the office."

She sensed Kas coming up through the floors as she prepared to levitate the chests down to the office. She conveyed her sense of appreciation for his help as he reached her and Will.

"Others coming," he said in Cothish after he mentally confirmed her state of injury. *I will check if Henton and Douglas are prepared for the chests,* he added, as he headed through the office and out of the castle wall.

"Kas, can you not at least let us know when you are around? It unnerves me when you talk and I don't know you are there."

"Will, he's gone to check on Henton."

Will shook his head, but was grinning. "Would have been nice to know that as well."

She smiled at him, knowing that if she could not sense Kas, he might disturb her as well. *But not as much as that mage disturbs me.* She took another breath. *He might pretend to be a holy warrior, but he sensed Kas and he was worse than fighting the Senzar.* She needed to talk to Kas about what that would mean.

Feeling strong enough to continue onward, she put her thought of the mage out of her head, and drew in the energy from the stone walls to move the chests into the office. She set them down next to the four that were already present. "I just hope we are not leaving too much behind."

Kas returned about the same time the four others reached the top floor and rushed to the office where Will and Stephenie were waiting.

"Shit, what happened here?" Berman said, looking back down the hall to where the crumpled mass of a body lay just out of sight in the doorway.

"Clear," Kas' voice echoed in the darkness.

She nodded her head. "There was a mage that came upon us, we have to leave the rest and get away. I'm taking all of you out of here first and will come back for the gold we have."

"But..."

"I'll risk the gold, not all of you, Tim." With a deep breath, she drew in energy, picked up the men one at a time and slowly slid them out the window. Her body was aching now, not only the wound that was not fully healed in her side, but also her mind from the cumulative use of power.

Picking up herself, she flew all of them across the open space, over the road, and down behind the building where Henton and Douglas were waiting. Setting them down carefully, she sunk to her knees after she released the flow of energy.

"You okay?" Henton asked.

"A little trouble with a mage," she responded, forcing herself back to her feet. "Nothing too bad, you?"

"We had a little trouble with some thugs who saw horses and wagons, but we were able to convince them to leave us alone. I would have send someone in to get you if I could have. I smell blood, that better not be yours!"

She shook her head no, "I'll be back with the chests, we'll need to move quickly." Not waiting for Henton to call her on the lie, she lifted herself into the air and quickly flew back to the castle.

You need to be careful. That injury was bad.

I will, Kas, she said to him as they flew together across the open space to the castle. *As soon as we get the gold, we'll get ourselves to the gate and this damn place will be to our backs with the rising of the sun.*

Flying back through the open window, she set herself down in the office. She could taste the blood in her mouth and knew the toll on her body was growing. She looked at the six large chests and the straps that were sprawled across the floor. These were far heavier than her men, but in the open space outside the castle, she could maneuver them with less concentration.

Don't forget loading the wagons and fixing the one you broke.

I haven't but, I don't think we will have until sunrise before this is discovered. Someone might already be coming to investigate. She swallowed the blood in her mouth. *I may have to use one wagon as a diversion, we don't have as much gold as we planned, so the weight hopefully won't be a problem.*

What are you planning?

You won't like it, she said as she started to lift the chests one at a time and float them out the window. Trembling slightly in her hands, she lifted herself and flew out the window. Feeling the blood draining from her nose, she hurried to the wagons as quickly as possible, setting the chests down rather roughly.

"Steph?" Henton asked when she staggered before leaning against one of the wagons.

"I'm fine," she forced herself to say. "We have to get away quickly, but I fear if an alarm is sounded they might lock down the gates. I'm going to lead them west to the docks and hope that will keep them from blocking all the gates."

"Steph?" Henton's voice rose.

She shook her head and took a deep breath. Reaching down into herself, she forced energy into her body and directed it to lift the top two layers of crates from the first wagon. She floated them to the side, avoiding any of the men. Douglas quickly leaped into the wagon bed and removed the tops of the two center crates.

Struggling to hold the crates of steel floating in the air, she quickly lifted the nearest chest, flew it over the wagon, and dumped the contents into the sawdust filled crate. She set the empty chest on top of the crates on the broken wagon, then emptied two more chests into the crates. Douglas quickly slid the lids back on and got out of the way, allowing Stephenie to place the two very heavy layers of steel-filled crates back on to the wagon.

Blood flowing heavily from her nose, she took the cloth that Henton handed to her. She smiled at him for having the decency not to say anything about her state.

After just a few moments, she repeated the process with the second wagon. Once all the gold was hidden nicely under the crates of steel, she turned to Henton, the cloth still covering her bleeding nose. "I want all of you to get these two wagons across the river and to the east gate. I'll fix the third wagon, then take the empty chests down to the docks. I'll dump the steel in the river so hopefully no one will know what we are carrying, then leave the wagon and empty chests by an empty slip. Hopefully, any searches will be directed at the barges and not us."

"Steph, this—"

"I love you Henton, but I'm in charge of all of this, and I have the best chance to escape if I am caught with the chests. I'll not see any of you die if I can help it. Don't worry, I'll join up with you as quickly as

I can." She took a deep breath through her mouth and removed the bloody cloth from her face. "I'll have Kas with me, we don't have time to argue. We are in danger of getting caught and killed, so, no delays."

She could tell he wanted to argue, but after a moment, he nodded his head. "Move out, we need to be at the gates and leaving by first light, which isn't far away."

Douglas tossed her a leather bag of coins. "I grabbed a couple as you dumped them into the crates. You never know if we'll need them for bribes or not."

"Thanks," she said as she turned to the third wagon and the broken spring. She felt a pang of fear as the others quickly started to mount up and prepare to pull away. There was a great risk in splitting up, but things had gone wrong and she did not see a choice at this point.

You capable of fixing the wagon? Kas asked, his mental voice filled with concern, but still very gentle and caring.

Unable to lie, even though Kas said it was possible, she shrugged. *I hurt so much. This is going to be hard, but that's not the worst of it, once I leave the diversion, I still have to get back to everyone else and make sure we all live.*

Let's hope there is no pursuit and you can get some rest on the wagons.

She did not bother to respond. The others were already moving down the side street, trying to avoid any notice by anyone who might be watching from the castle. With a deep breath, she levitated the wagon bed, grunting from the effort. Drawing in more power, she forced the springs back together and then slid home the pin that held it together. She did not bother to flatten out the end of the pin, simply hoping it would remain in place long enough to do what was necessary.

She released the energy with a whimper and the horses took a step forward until they were blocked by the wagon's brake. Holding the cloth to her face, she quickly mounted the wagon, released the brake, and nudged the horses forward. They struggled a moment to get the wagon moving, but once it was underway, the two draft horses moved the load fairly easily.

Instead of following the side road, she turned down the crossroad and headed directly toward the castle. She nudged the horses slightly faster as soon as they were on the main street, sending the sounds of the loud clomping of hooves echoing into the night.

Once past the castle, she looked over her shoulder to see if there were any signs of pursuit, but it was unneeded, as neither her nor Kas sensed the presence of anyone coming. They did sense a few people moving about in the businesses on the south side of the street. The north side held the wharfs and numerous barges and vessels, but most of the people Kas sensed as he flew over them were asleep.

Once they were nearly three quarters of a mile from the castle, she drove the wagon onto the shoulder, where goods were stacked while loading and unloading. There was no gap here between the ships, but she wanted to unload the steel away from where she would leave the wagons and chests.

Taking a deep breath and leaving the cloth held to her nose, she drew in enough energy to move the six empty chests to the ground, then she gathered her strength to lift all of the crates from the wagon bed. Her whole body trembled with the effort and it took several moments before she could actually lift the heavy mass. Once they were in the air, she rushed them to the river, just skimming the top of the barge they flew over. She tried to gently set the crates into the water, but the distance from where she was to the crates made it impossible to hold the field in her condition and they crashed into the river, shifting and shaking all the barges in the area.

That was not good, Kas said, having moved the empty chests back into the wagon while she had unloaded the steel laden crates.

Too tired to respond, she whipped the horses into motion and quickly set off down the road. After another half mile, she found a section of the wharf with many empty slips. She pushed herself to fly the empty chests into the water, leaving at least one to rest partially exposed in the shallow water near the shore.

She staggered from the wagon and with Kas' encouragement, she used the last of her strength to fly herself the fifty yards over the river and into the narrow streets on the north side of the city. This would keep her from having to cross a bridge to leave, something that could lead to someone trying to stop her. Relying on Kas to help her keep her feet, she disappeared down a side street, heading toward the east gate.

Chapter 20

Stephenie had caught up with her men just as the east gates opened. Henton and the others were relieved to see her, but quickly grew concerned at her appearance. Her lips were blue and her face pale as snow. The blood stained shirt had not yet attracted attention because the sky was only just beginning to brighten and the shirt was dark to begin with, but that would not get them through the gates. Despite their early arrival, more than a dozen other wagons were lined up ahead of them.

"My pack," she mumbled. "I'll...change in that alley."

Douglas had already anticipated her request and was standing at her side with it before she finished asking for it. "I'll go with her to help. Henton, you need to be the respectable one if they come by the wagons." No one objected, as the first wagon in the line was heading out the gate and the others were starting to move forward.

Once in the alley and hidden from view, she quickly removed her blood stained shirt and used her dagger to cut away her ruined pants. "Don't have time...to pull off boots," she explained to Douglas who had turned his head away to give her privacy. Standing in her undergarments, she cleared her throat, "you're going have to look...I need your help."

"Sorry," he said, holding the green dress open for her to step into it. "Just watching the wagons, two more have moved past."

She tried to give him a reassuring smile, seeing the embarrassment on his face. She had never caught him trying to catch a glimpse of her undressed in their travels and wondered if his desire to help was more to protect her from the others ogling her. The sudden desire to find him a good woman filled her for a brief moment, but she dismissed it. *He's more than capable of finding someone if he wants to. Besides, who do I know?* she asked herself, feeling slightly better for the happy thought, despite her incredible exhaustion and pain.

With his help to cinch her into the dress, they stuffed the bloody clothing behind a water barrel and headed back to the wagons. Henton was next to go through the gate, but she did not have the strength to run, nor would it be appropriate for a lady to do so. By the time they arrived, Henton had already explained their cargo and was negotiating the taxes with the assessor. Stephenie heard the rate, but was too tired to join the discussion and so Henton simply handed over the amount and they were allowed to leave Wyntac.

She felt a weight lift from her as they passed under the stone gate house and out of the city. There was a similar line of people waiting to enter the city; a few glanced in their direction, but most were more eager to get inside than to watch those that passed. She sat back in the seat of the second wagon, the one that Tim was driving. Will and Henton were in the lead wagon, with the others walking beside them. Without even realizing it, she closed her eyes and fell asleep.

Stephenie woke briefly when they passed through White Peak around mid day. Douglas quickly sold four crates of steel for a loss, but lightened the load from both wagons. They picked up some additional hay and grain for the horses and were out of White Peak with the sun still in the the sky.

By the late afternoon, Stephenie forced herself to get up and walk, hoping to put some energy back into her body. She kept yawning until Will gave her one of his special pills he had been saving. Once that bitter concoction hit her blood, her eyes widened and a sense of dread and anxiety came over her. It was worse than normal, as she felt her heart racing and every little sound amplified.

I have told you not to take those things from him, they affect your mind.

She shuddered, trying to push aside the unpleasant feeling. "It'll pass...hopefully quickly," she mumbled in the Old Tongue. She did hate taking the pill, but she just had not been able to fully wake herself without it.

After half a turn of the glass walking beside the wagon, she started to calm down and feel closer to normal. Henton and Douglas kept forcing food and drink upon her as she walked, which Kas suspected had done more to clear her head than anything else.

By early evening, she was back on the wagon and other than a few merchants and travelers, they did not encounter anyone else on the road. Once late evening descended upon them, her neck was stiff from constantly looking over her shoulder.

"We're good," Tim said, adjusting his position to relieve the tension from having sat most of the day. "I was afraid at the gates, but we're miles east of White Peak, we're good."

She forced a smile; Tim had told her that more than thirty times already and after the first few times with nothing happening, she was beginning to hope that his confidence would not come back to haunt them. Peter, who was walking close by always cursed and made some odd gesture to ward off evil whenever Tim made that comment. She was getting tired of his superstition as well as her own desire to knock on wood. Of course, while she did not want to be attacked, the fact that they had seen no signs of pursuit was also worrying.

Sensing Kas' hasty approach, from where he had been acting as their rear guard, froze her heart. *What is it?*

A dozen men on horses, riding hard. At least one can use magic and I think he sensed me. They picked up speed as soon as I moved to warn you.

"Henton," she called out, "keep the wagons going and don't stop. We're about to have company and at least one of them can use magic."

Henton rose from where he was sitting on the lead wagon and nodded his head. He called out a quick command to those near his wagon and everyone quickly jumped onto the back as the wagon picked up speed. Peter and Berman jumped on her wagon as Tim coaxed the tired horses into a trot.

Stephenie climbed on top of the crates just as she started to feel the soldiers galloping toward them. The lead man sneered when their eyes met and Stephenie knew these men dressed in blackened scale mail were the men she had been dreading all day. Sensing control threads leap out from the man, she instinctively drew in more energy, hoping to counter what would come. But his attack was so swift, that she was still caught off guard and just barely blocked the narrow beam of force that was aimed at her chest.

Kas closed the distance on the leader and the group of riders slowed as the leader looked up and directed his focus at the ghost. Stephenie's eyes widened when Kas cried out in pain as the mage started to draw off Kas' energy, just as she had done to the ghost outside of Arkani. "No!" she roared with a deep rumble; rage flowing from her as she sensed Kas struggling to retreat. Leaping into the air and off the back of the wagon, she unleashed a blast of energy at the mage, but the line of horses had started to rear and buck. The leader's horse took the brunt of her attack. Undaunted, the man leaped easily from the horse as it fell, but Stephenie's only concern was that his assault on Kas had stopped.

Kas, get out of here! He knows how to kill you! Keep Henton and the others moving. I can't protect you and fight them.

Seven of the soldiers had been dismounted by the terrified horses. The remaining four were fighting to keep control of their mounts, which were trying to run back the way they had come.

Stephenie sensed Kas retreating quickly toward the wagons, which were still moving east. She stood in the middle of the road, the only obstacle between her men and these attackers. The lead man calmly stepped away from his horse that was writhing on the ground.

"Interesting," he said in the Old Tongue. "I had not expected someone so limited to be so effective against the horses. And what you did in the castle, that shows potential for one so young." He grinned at her as his men picked themselves up from the ground, two of the four still mounted had regained control.

Stephenie noted energy threads coming both from his mind as well as the medallion on his chest. He was too far away for her to see the details, but he was likely wearing a symbol of Ravim, Kynto's primary deity. Before she could identify what he was doing, she felt the crushing impact of a narrow beam of intense gravity. The force knocked her back several feet, but her body had reacted faster than her mind and the blow had not ripped through her flesh.

Feeling more control threads reaching out to her, she unleashed raw energy along one of those threads as she flung herself back to her feet, stumbling slightly because of the constraining dress. The mage diverted her flow of energy, causing it to strike a man standing next to him.

Stephenie did not attack again, wanting instead to conserve her strength, which was quite depleted from her efforts overnight. She waited and watched, noting how calmly the soldiers took the death of one of their own.

The lead man pursed his lips. "Quite interesting."

Stephenie was tensed, ready for his next attack, but he had pulled back his control threads, keeping them away from her. "You're no priest," she said, trying to buy time. "You might wear a holy symbol, but you're not using it to fight me."

The man laughed. "Oh, I am so much more than a simple priest. If you think to turn these men against me, you are not as smart as I was beginning to think you were. However, you have a pet ghost and you seem to know too much for someone so young in this day. Perhaps it was a good thing your mother failed to carry out those rituals I invented for her."

Stephenie flinched ever so slightly. She had known there was a good chance her uncle might assume it was her who had stolen back the gold. "You told my mother to cut my heart out and eat it?"

The man smiled again, stepping further around his horse and moving closer to her. "I told her far more than that. I am always curious how depraved a person will become when they desperately want something. I must say, I was quite creative with the things she would have to do in order to lift the curse. Much of it before she actually could kill you."

Stephenie felt her anger rising. She could sense no emotions from the man and the other men were almost as muted. *I've bitten off more than I can chew.* She did not turn her head to the trees, but she extended her senses, wondering if she could make an escape before he hit her with magic strong enough to kill her.

Stephenie swallowed as she took a slight step backwards. "Look, how about we split the gold. I really only need what was stolen from me back. You can have the rest."

The man shook his head. "That gold was mine in the first place. I will not settle for just a part of it." He smiled at Stephenie's confusion. "Silly little girl, who do you think is the power behind your uncle. He does as I wish and I leave the running of the boring bits to him. The same with the High Priest of Ravim. This is my country and my gold and you will pay for the theft. None of you will see the morning."

Stephenie subconsciously drew more energy into herself. The men were in a line behind the mage, many with crossbows readied. She hoped Henton and Kas would do as she had instructed. *They better keep running, because if they don't, they will die.*

He pursed his lips again. "Perhaps I should make you a pet. Your ghost; you called him Kas and spoke in accented Denarian. That is an unusual name. I think you should tell me more about him and how you learned what you have."

Stephenie's panic peaked. This man had heard her mental communication and if he found out about Arkani, he would undoubtedly go there and unleash a city full of ghosts on Antar and her brother. If she died and Henton was captured, the secret would be out as well. She knew the woods were clear, but the distance was too far. They would bring her down if she ran. "I don't think—"

Her words were cut off as a bolt of lightning sprung up before she even realized he had formed the fields to direct the energy. The bolt hit her leg and spun her around. Instinctively, she pulled the energy from the lightning into herself, hoping to prevent it from burning a hole through her flesh. Before she hit the ground, the mage unleashed a second attack, sinking a gravity well under her and slamming her with incredible force into the hard road.

Breathless, Stephenie detached herself from the pain and quickly countered the field while at the same time shooting lightning back at the mage. However, the impact had left her disoriented and she hit one of the soldiers instead of the mage.

Almost unable to keep up with the quick actions of the man, she just barely sensed the forming of another lightning bolt. Flinging herself into the air, the lightning streaked across the ground, missing her by inches.

Flipping herself around to face her attackers, she unleashed several more brute force attacks, hoping to push through his defenses, but each one was easily countered. Depressingly, she became aware that most of the energy he was channeling was through external fields and not through his own body as she was doing. *And he's not touched the power from the medallion yet.*

"I'm two hundred and thirty five years old, you think you can beat me?"

Stephenie thrashed about, both physically and mentally as small attack after small attack struck her. Nothing was strong enough to truly hurt her, but each one took more and more effort to defend and she felt blood running down her nose.

Then suddenly she was struck in the head and knocked back to the ground. The blow made her dizzy and she could no longer focus on her surroundings.

"Put some poison in her to pacify her, but not so much to kill her."

Stephenie struggled to move. Her body ached from the physical injuries as well as all the energy she had used. Unable to rise, she continued to draw energy into herself. Laying on the cool ground, she felt the massive potential from deep below her. She remembered feeling something similar in the Greys.

Sensing the firing of a crossbow, she reached out and pulled at the energy. Just as in the Greys, it was sluggish to start, but this time it came much more readily once it started to flow.

Desperate to avoid the poisoned bolt, she blasted back a wave of gravity, throwing everything away from her and even bouncing herself a foot from the ground. Unlike when she was in the Greys, she did not hold the energy in herself, but instead used it to drop a massive gravity well under the mage and his soldiers.

Three more crossbows were fired, but the bolts slammed into the ground inches from the bows. The men screamed in pain as they collapsed to the ground, their bodies rupturing like bugs smashed by a boot. The force she had unleashed was so large and powerful, a thirty-foot diameter section of the ground sunk more than a foot, compacted by the immense weight of the gravitational attraction.

For the first time, Stephenie felt a rise of emotion from the mage. He alone lived in the middle of the destruction. Brought to one knee, he remained on a raised section of ground, struggling against her field.

Feeling her body burning from within, Stephenie reversed her field, launching the mage, dead soldiers, and a large section of the ground thirty feet into the air. Feeling her body weakening, she flung rocks and dirt at the mage, enjoying a moment of clarity for her surrounding, feeling the location of every stone, of every leaf. She feared this. That kind of clarity had only happened once before, in the Greys, before she had set herself on fire.

However, the mage blocked the attacks and unleashed one of his own. Stephenie knew a hole had ripped into her chest and she struggled to minimize the impact, keeping the blast from reaching her heart.

Aware of the loose and broken crossbow bolts flying around the mage, she threw several more rocks at the man as she let go of the energy that was keeping the chaos in the air. Directing all of her remaining strength to the task, she drove three crossbow bolts through the scale mail and into the man's side, burying the fractured wood completely inside the man's chest.

The man fell to the ground, but managed to hold his feet. "Bitch! I'm sixth gen, you can't do that."

He swallowed and Stephenie sensed him pulling energy into himself. Crying from the pain and choking on the blood running down her throat and out her nose, she reached out and tugged at the energy in the ground once more. Fearful of breaking her body again, she hesitated for a moment. However, the thought of Kas and Henton and the others having to face this man pushed her forward.

Die, you piece of shit! She thought at the man as she channeled a wave of energy up from the ground and along one of the threads he was using to draw energy into his body. She felt fear come from him as she forced even more energy into his body and mind. The man started to stagger and she unleashed a lightning bolt at his head from where she lay on the ground. The lightning crackled and burnt away skin and hair. She unleashed another bolt, her own body quivering from the pain of drawing the power through herself.

After a moment more, she opened her eyes. The darkness of the evening was settling in around them, but she could see the devastation clearly. The ground had been turned over as if an army of giants has brawled in the road. Weak and unsteady, she forced herself to her feet and stumbled across the ground. Body parts, smashed and flattened, were strewn about; some were partially buried. The mage lay on his back, a rock forcing his hips above his head.

Stephenie looked into what was left of the man's face. Most of the skin and one eye was burned away by the lightning, but she still sensed a small amount of consciousness from the man. With a ragged breath, she drew his sword and took his head with a solid blow.

The effort brought her to the ground. After a moment, she forced herself back to her feet. Seeing the holy symbol of Ravim had fallen to the ground when she had removed his head, she picked up the bloody medallion. She considered throwing it into the woods, but she lacked the strength. Not wanting to ruin her pouch, she put the medallion over her head; her green dress was already ruined.

Weak from what she did, and the blood that was still running from her nose and chest, she put limited pressure on her wounds and hobbled after the wagons on one burned leg.

Chapter 21

Stephenie did not have to go far before Kas swooped in to help her. Then a few minutes later, Henton arrived to pick her up and carry her to the wagons that were waiting just a short distance down the road.

"I told you to keep going," she managed to mumble, dropping her head against his shoulder and trying not to cry from the pain in her body.

Henton simply shook his head as if to say, 'You don't know me very well'. When they got to the wagons, he handed her up to Tim, who was still in the driver's seat of the second wagon. Henton followed and moved her to the top of the crates. Without word, the wagons started up with a jolt and she allowed the rocking to lull her to sleep.

She woke in the morning with a headache and an incredible stiffness throughout her whole body. Her leg throbbed and burned with an intensity that brought tears to her eyes. Her chest ached and she wondered if she had really survived or if she was actually a prisoner of the mage.

Stephenie, take it easy, you are suffering from extreme exhaustion. You will be disoriented for a while.

In too much pain to respond to Kas, she reached out and drew energy into herself. The act burned every nerve in her body, as the additional energy scorched her already raw internal organs. However, she held out as long as possible, directing the energy into healing the burn on her leg and the shallow hole in her chest. Once she could stand the pain no more, she released the energy and let out the breath she had held.

"You okay?" Henton asked, coming over to kneel next to her.

She opened her eyes slowly; she was under one of the wagons. Turning her head, she noticed the dark circles under Henton's eyes. Reaching out to Kas, she asked, *he hasn't slept has he?*

No, Kas responded. *We expected you would pull through, but after I described the damage in the road, he insisted we take the wagons as far away from the destruction as possible. We took a side road and then found a field out of the way to camp. Aside from Henton and myself, everyone else is sleeping.*

"Henton, you need to get some sleep," she forced herself to say, despite the rawness of her throat. Coughing, she did not protest when he rolled her onto her side before handing her the water skin that had been in his hand. After a long drink, she slid it back to him and sighed, "I hope I don't look as bad as I feel."

"Worse," he said as he brushed some loose hair from her face. "You ruined your green dress. Burns and holes and blood and dirt. I think you are down to just the white one for clothing."

She laughed once, but that started her coughing until her chapped lips cracked. "Ouch," she whimpered, dabbing off the trace of blood on the sleeve of the expensive dress. "Everyone else?"

"We're good. I'll let everyone, especially the horses, rest a while more. We'll head out around midday, probably go south along this road. I think it will lead to a smaller town, perhaps we can sell a few things, then get back on the main road to the capital in a day or so."

Stephenie nodded her head. "I'm sorry. I miscalculated. I never expected what happened."

"It didn't seem to be a miscalculation. They have not sent an army after us, just a few men and a holy warrior, but you handled it. I'm angry that you almost killed yourself doing it, but you survived."

She switched over to the Old Tongue. "That man was not a priest. Neither was the one we fought inside the castle. The man who came after us claimed he was two hundred and thirty-five years old. He claimed my uncle is just a puppet and he actually ruled the country."

"Was he the High Priest of Ravim? I took off that holy symbol around your neck once you were asleep. I hope that was okay."

She shook her head. "No, not the High Priest; I've seen a painting of the High Priest. Yes, taking it off was okay." She swallowed. "Those men were just like me, just mages. The holy symbols were real, but neither of them used them much. They knew full well what they were doing, and I'll be damned, but they were more skilled than any of the Senzar I encountered. The first one Kas killed when I distracted him, the second one, I did like I did in the Greys, I just pulled everything I could from the ground and dropped it on his head."

"Have you damaged yourself again?" Kas asked, materializing in a kneeling position next to Henton so his face was visible to Stephenie, who was still under the wagon.

She shook her head. "No, I...I didn't hold the energy in me this time, just poured it out. I don't think he expected that I could move that much energy." She took a deep breath and coughed. "He was far more skilled. I was no match for that, but I overwhelmed him and managed to get some poisoned arrows into him. That tipped the balance." She took a deep breath and thought to Kas, *he was surprised I overpowered him. Does 'sixth gen' mean anything to you? The only thing I can think of is he's the sixth generation. But the sixth generation of what and how could he be over two hundred years old?*

Kas raised his eyebrows and shook his head. *I don't know. The elves used to live to two hundred years and sometimes more. A couple of really powerful humans have lived as long. However, most very powerful humans usually only lived for one hundred or one hundred and thirty years.*

"A hundred and thirty years?" she asked aloud.

Henton looked between the two of them. "Am I interrupting?"

She turned her attention back to Henton and began to panic at the hurt in his voice. "No. Sorry, I've just got so used to thinking to Kas. It's faster most of the time and my throat is hurting." She coughed once more. "I asked Kas about the mage claiming to be a couple hundred years old and he was saying most humans topped out at one hundred and thirty."

"I would expect you to live at least that long," Kas said, glancing between the two of them. "You have more raw power than most of the people of my day." He turned his focus back to her, "that is, provided you do not manage to get yourself killed or burn yourself out. I would expect each time you do this, you are taking years off your life."

"One hundred and thirty?" Henton asked.

"And for nearly the whole time," Kas said, turning to Henton, "she will likely not age much beyond her current appearance." He paused for several moments. "Regardless of that, if the man Stephenie killed really was ruling the country, I would expect there will be confusion and I doubt any additional pursuit will follow. That would be a positive change in our situation."

Henton nodded his head, but there was a slightly distant look to his eyes. Eventually he focused back in on Stephenie. "Get some sleep, you need it. I'll wake Douglas and Will to take over for me."

In the early afternoon, they were back on the road and traveled well into the evening, making only one stop at the small village. However, with the wagons, Stephenie's original goal of covering twenty to thirty miles in a day was not going to be possible. On a normal day of travel, they could manage only ten to twelve miles. And while there was no sign of pursuit, they stopped often enough to let the horses rest, fix issues with the wagons, and to purchase more supplies. She had planned to take perhaps six or seven days to cross Calis, but now it would likely take twenty days or more. She had known things would be delayed when she had changed the plan to use the wagons, but she feared the ship Joshua should have sent would not wait that long. The thought of having to trust a merchant vessel to take them safely to Antar was frightening. She could not afford to allow the gold to be stolen out from under her while at sea, but Joshua could not afford the time it would take for them to bring the wagons overland to Antar.

It took nine days to reach the capitol of Calis, which was a city with the same name. They sold a couple more crates of steel to help lighten the load a little further, but they still wanted to maintain enough weight on top of the coins that no tax collectors would want to look through the bottom crates. In all, they spent one night and part of the next morning in the city renowned for its white marble buildings. Everyone's spirits were lightened somewhat by the architecture and even though Stephenie knew they would be a full month late arriving in Wilm, she still gave everyone half a crown and a turn of the glass to buy a couple souvenirs to take back to Antar.

Douglas and Will, who seemed to have had a little more money than the others, bought her a necklace with a piece of polished blue-grey stone that was supposed to have come from the slopes of Logan's Peak. "You get your strength from the ground," Will said, in reference to the more detailed descriptions of the events she had shared with everyone over the last nine days. She thanked them, giving the two of them each a hug and kiss on the cheek. But the comment made her think about just how true that statement had been and she wondered about any possible affinity she might have to rocks and dirt.

Don't tell me you are reverting back to being a simpleton. Kas' tone was not entirely playful.

No, but I've been able to pull so much more power from the ground. It's what's saved me several times so far.

Kas' mental voice sighed. *Stephenie, think about it. You know the answer. What has a greater density of energy? What has more potential to give up its energy? The air or the wood of the wagon? The soil over there, or the stone under your feet? What about the steel you are carrying in the back of the wagons?*

I get it. I guess I was just getting nostalgic for old stories and myths.

Kas' mental voice carried a smile. *Stories and myths are fine, just don't confuse them with reality.* He paused for a while. *I did not get you anything as it is rather hard to make purchases without a body or money.*

Kas, you already give me so much. I don't need you to buy me things. She took a deep breath, *but I would like your help destroying the holy symbols.*

Of course, I have been waiting for you to ask.

Henton offered Stephenie a hand up into the drivers seat of the second wagon. "I did not manage to go shopping for nicknacks," he said, almost mirroring Kas' conversation. "You want me to go buy you something?"

Stephenie shook her head. "No. I love the necklace Will and Douglas bought," she said, holding out the stone for Henton to see, "but you saw my rooms before they were raided, other than weapons and gear, I really didn't keep much. If you want to give me something," she lowered her voice and leaned closer to him, "stop calling me Beth."

Henton chuckled. "Stop putting yourself in positions where I have to try to keep you from getting yourself killed and I'll consider it."

That evening, away from the others, she found a quiet spot in a copse of trees and sat with Kas, listening to him explain how the medallions worked in an effort to help her destroy them. "I don't know exactly how, but they feel funny when I hold them," she said holding out one of the holy symbols. "There's some odd field, I just can't quite make out what it is."

Kas nodded his head, which he had made just barely visible in the darkening light. "You amaze me more all the time. Your ability to sense fields is beyond any."

"Fields yes, but as you say, I'm still deaf to thoughts and emotions."

"Well, you should not need to establish a mental link with it. You are not wanting to use the device, merely destroy it."

"I can establish a mental link with something that's not alive?"

Kas smiled slightly. "Well, at some level, those medallions are alive or at least have intelligence. Anything that is magical has to have at least some rudimentary intelligence to persist the object's ability to use magic. It's done by fabricating specific latices and structures as part of what will be enchanted. The more it does and interacts with the environment, the more intelligence it must have.

"To be able to use these devices, you have to have some ability to establish a mental connection to it. At least that was the way they designed them in my day. The thought was that they did not want people without magic to be able to gain any significant power. This way, control was maintained by those who already had power."

"And it is why the priests of today need to be witches and warlocks, only no one knows the truth of it."

"You do not have to have significant power to use it, just enough power and skill to activate it. However, it is capable of defending itself. Probably more than most enchanted objects because it can pull power from the relays and not just the environment."

"Relays?" Stephenie shook her head and put the book she had pulled from her pack aside.

"The medallions, though they were not always fashioned as such, were designed to conduct energy. The early devices were weapons or armor or other metallic objects. The alloy they are constructed from was the best they could find at conducting and holding the complex latices needed for the intelligence."

"But what are these relays you are talking about?"

Kas moved slightly, shifting as if he needed to make himself more comfortable on the ground. "In the temples I have looked at and you have described, there are large statues made of the same material."

"Yes. There are temples scattered about the land. The further the priests get from their temples, the less power they have. Sometimes, they will take a smaller statue of Felis with them, such as on a ship or when they go to war. However, there are a finite number of these. Probably less then forty since the Senzar captured several. I probably buried at least two under the mountain top that collapsed in the Greys. Maybe more."

"Those are the relays. The original two medallions you have will be connected or entangled with one or more of those relays. Small sections of the object will have a link to a specific relay and the overall structure funnels and controls the flow of power from those individual sections. The design was well thought out, providing a way for a person to move about a large area, drawing power from one or more of the relays at any given time, hopefully never going out of the range of at least one relay. The medallion you took from the wizard from Kynto, that one is probably entangled with a different set of relays."

Stephenie pursed her lips.

"What are you wondering?"

"Well, by relay, if the word is being used as I think it is, that would mean the power comes from somewhere else and is passed on?"

Kas smiled. "Indeed. There is going to be a large block of metal somewhere that is the physical construction of the trap in this world. That device projects the trap into the other world. Each of the relays are entangled with the trap so that they can extend the range of transmission and protect the trap. Large portions of the relays are entangled with the trap, allowing for a large flow of energy. Only small parts of the medallions are entangled with the relays, in a way, distributing the total potential energy across many smaller devices."

"So much thought went into this. Not really magic at all."

"Well, if you consider the manipulation of the energy as performing magic or using magic, then yes it is. If you simply are using the word to describe something that cannot be comprehended, then no. Enough study and research will allow one to learn how just about everything works."

"So, how do we destroy them?"

"You have to generate a field that blocks the entanglement, then it will be possible to push past the defenses of the medallion, since it will have limited power to draw upon. Otherwise, the medallion will be able to draw on the relay and it will have more resources than you do. You will need to create a field unlike the others you have created. The other fields you have been creating are more direct. The entanglement allows for the transmission of energy across space without having to pass through the intervening area. However, these medallions can also draw energy from the surrounding area as well. Which is primarily for its own use in protecting itself, but that was usually limited."

"Protect itself how?"

"Well, in my day, they would absorb and transmit extra energy directed at them back to the relays. A protection against being overloaded. They could also attack you or counter your attacks with lightning, gravity, heat, or cold; things you are already familiar with. I am assuming those making them today, or whenever they were crafted, followed instructions laid down from prior generations. Given your people's nearly complete lack of knowledge about almost everything, I cannot imagine them being able to develop this technology or really even improve on it themselves."

Stephenie shook her head. "You have so much faith in us."

"I do not need faith. I have seen enough of what you know and the ridiculous ideas you have been raised upon." He leaned closer. "Destroying these devices requires that you sever their connection to the relays; blocking their ability to send and receive energy. Then they will lack a place to expend energy directed at them and often they can then be melted down or perhaps transformed to destroy their internal structure."

Stephenie nodded her head and then sighed. "And, I am guessing that I need to figure this out on my own."

Kas forced a smiled. "Unfortunately. However, I am hoping your ability to sense fields will help you."

They traveled hard the next eleven days, dealing with occasional rain and mud, but the road out of Calis heading to Wilm was well tended and solid enough that the rain only slowed them by a couple miles a day off their prior pace. Most days were pleasant enough and Stephenie found herself walking beside the wagons most of the time, silently trying to get a feel for the holy symbols she was carrying in a satchel over her shoulder.

For the men, excluding Henton, Douglas, and Kas, each time they passed through a town or city, they made a game of buying Stephenie little trinkets, each one trying to give her something more unique than anyone else had previously given. At first, she thought it was cute and enjoyed watching the men try to jovially compete for her affections, which everyone knew was not a serious pursuit. However, as the days went by and her pack filled with strange items she would never use, some of the thrill of the game started to diminish for her.

She silently hoped Will would stop lending the men money, which he had obviously kept on his person from when he was alone in the vault. However, he seemed to have an endless supply of coins and no hesitation in lending them out. Fortunately, no one was using large denominations or buying expensive items. That meant people would not question the purchases, but it also meant she did not have an excuse to justify telling the others to stop. She had hoped Henton would have put a stop to it, but he had remained somewhat distant of late.

In the evenings, she would divide her time between reading the book Kas had removed from the library and actively trying to destroy the holy symbols. Two days out from Wilm, while sitting on the ground and rubbing her fingers over the exquisitely carved miniature of a wolf Tim had given her early in the day, she finally had enough and tossed the holy symbol of Felis aside.

Her left hand still ached from the burns she had received the night before and she was tired of trying. Every attempt to block the energy flowing into them had failed and every time she tried to damage one of them, the medallion bit back. The worse part was that the medallion's defenses kept adjusting, almost predicting what she was prepared for and doing something not quite the opposite.

Closing her eyes, she noticed Will and the other five talking about what they were going to do with their share of the reward when they returned to Antar. Their plans ranged from exploring the beds of women to buying land and in Tim's case, getting married to the prettiest girl in Antar. For a while, she listened to descriptions of feasts they would eat and the clothes and horses they would buy for themselves. Berman was certain he would get enough to build his own castle.

And what about you darling Stephenie? What more do you plan to buy with your riches? Kas asked, having sensed she was no longer concentrating on the medallion.

She shook her head. *I want to get back the blades my father gave me and my mother's men stole. I'll probably want to buy some paper and ink; I've got a lot to write down.* She shrugged. *I don't have much I want to buy. You?*

Kas sat down next to her, still invisible to everyone's sight. *I can buy nothing. I might see if the library has settled down after all this time running across country after country.* She set aside the wolf, which she sensed Kas had been watching her rub. *But I hardly have use for such things, I am dead.*

She turned toward him, *you're not dead, you just lack a body.*

Not much difference from my perspective. Stephenie, do you really think there is a future for us? Honestly? Because, I fear you will just grow frustrated with the lack of me as time passes.

Stephenie picked up the medallion and put it back into the satchel. *Kas, until that happens, I am not giving up on us. So unless you no longer care about me, drop it until you have actually given up.*

She got to her feet and turned around. "Enough about what you plan to do with your shares. I promise you will get a big reward, every one of you, even Oliver's family. But the money will first go to Cothel's treasury to keep the country running, so you can forget about having enough to buy a castle. They cost too damn much."

She turned away with a huff and stalked just outside the campsite. She felt bad as soon as she was by herself, realizing how much she had overreacted, but she could not bring herself to go back and face anyone.

The trees just off the campsite were tall, if not overly dense. She flew herself high up into the branches and looked out across the surrounding area. To the west, she saw the campsite of a wagon train they had passed a little before dark. To the south, she saw lights from what was likely a farmstead. Otherwise, the night was clear and so she found a slightly comfortable position in the crook of a series of branches and leaned back to watch the night sky.

As the waxing Mother Moon slowly rose, she thought about Kas' concerns and wondered just what could be done. The relationship she wanted was likely impossible. She did want to be held and comforted and loved just like anyone else. Kas' lack of a body could not be ignored, but when they shared their minds and feelings, it was unlike anything she had ever experienced and she knew whom she wanted. *The problem is that Kas remembers what it was like to share that intimacy and still have a physical body to bring it to the next level.*

She closed her eyes, feeling no better than when she had stormed off. If anything, she felt more alone and hollow. Looking up, she noted the Mother Moon was now more than halfway across the sky. She dropped to the ground and went back to the campsite. Henton acknowledged her approach, but said nothing. Between him and Douglas, they both seemed to always know when to give her space and when to offer the right words to lift her spirits, only both of them had not been talking to her much of late.

She looked around; everyone else was sleeping and Kas was somewhere else. *Damn, well, at least there is one thing I can fix.* She walked over to the nearest wagon and reached out with her powers to lift the heavy steel off the crates of gold. Moving the load with more dexterity than she normally used, she removed the lid of one crate of coins and flew out a large handful of money. Being careful to keep the noise down, she put all the crates back the way they had been and dropped the coins into the satchel she held open with her hands.

"You should wait until this is done. Giving them money now will just entice them to spend more."

She frowned and then shook her head. "They'll likely just give it all to Will to pay him back." She met Henton's eyes, "Please put a stop to their giving me things. I don't want them to buy me anything else, but I don't know how to tell them without seeming rude."

Henton came closer, turning her to face him. "Can I offer some advice?"

She looked up at Henton, unsure if she was ready to hear what he had to say, but eventually she nodded her head.

Henton took a deep breath and indicated they should sit down. "I know I should keep out of it, but I think you are getting yourself into trouble and I don't want to see you hurt." He nodded his head when she did not protest. "You need to be clear about what you want and what your intentions are. Will and Douglas' necklace was a nice gift and given our history together, probably just okay enough with Kas. Everything else and the flirting you are doing with the others would make even me angry."

"But if I tell them to quit, they'll all think they've done something wrong. I don't want to hurt them."

"Steph, they are doing something wrong and you are just as much to blame for allowing them to do it. I know it was all in good fun, but Kas is excluded from being able to participate and he's the one who wants to the most."

Stephenie bowed her head. "I..."

Henton reached out and lifted her face. "You've got more balls than most men. I know you are trying to be nice to them, but tell them to stop. It will mean more to Kas if you do it than if I do it."

She nodded her head. "I guess the two of you've been talking a bit of late."

"Look, Steph, I know you are having a rough time right now, but so is Kas. I shouldn't say anything, but he's been hinting a lot lately that I would be a better match for you and wanting me to try to convince you of that. Saying that someone without magic can often extend their own life by being close to someone with strong magic. I told him to quit trying to convince me."

"Why? You not able to handle the idea I might stay young for years? Does that make me too much of a freak?" She shook her head. "I doubt I'll live anywhere near one hundred. I'll probably get myself killed in a matter of years as it is. I never expected this. Kas never said something like this would happen."

Henton chuckled and shook his head. "For someone usually so observant...no Steph, let me let you in on a secret, I don't know of a man who wouldn't at least consider jumping at the chance to have a young woman their whole life."

"That's rather sad."

He shook his head. "It's not that men don't consider other attributes as important, and I'm not saying everyone would pursue it, but the thought will occur in our minds. Think about it; I might have someone that looks like you at my side when I'm fifty and all wrinkled and saggy. Don't tell me women don't take a closer look at a firm young man as they get older. That I won't believe. I've known women who have."

Not Ladies, she wanted to argue, but the thought of everyone she knew growing old and dying when she was still a young woman caused her chest to tighten, and she was forced to fight back tears. She cleared her throat. "I don't want to see you get old and wrinkly. Or any of you die of old age, ever."

Henton chuckled again, just like when she had first met him. "Hey, don't worry, you planned to get yourself killed way before that." He drew her eyes to him again. "Look. Kas is having a worse time than you right now. Don't make him come to you. You need to go to him and make sure he knows where he stands with you."

She swallowed, knowing the truth of it. Searching with her mind, she still could not sense Kas anywhere within her range, and she started to stand.

"He'll be back before morning," Henton said, pulling her back to the ground. "Give him time to cool off and spend tomorrow talking with him like you used to."

She nodded her head and then cast her gaze around the campsite. All the others were still sleeping quietly. Taking a deep breath, she dumped out the coins from her satchel. "I still can make this right," she said as she started dividing the coins into seven piles. "In the morning I'll tell them to stop." She added the extra coins that did not divide evenly to one pile and gave that one to Henton.

"You know I'm not doing this for the money."

I know, she told herself as she rose to put the coins next to the others. *I know, I just don't know what to do about it.*

Chapter 22

Stephenie talked most of the next two days with Kas, but neither of them could find a complete solution to the problem. Eventually, the discussion changed to safer topics, such as magic theory and how to be more effective with channeling energy or controlling temperature.

When they finally reached Wilm, the sun was falling behind them, setting the high clouds ablaze with a deep red hue. Stephenie felt it somehow appropriate, as if they were leaving a broken wreckage of waste to burn behind them. They had managed to get the wagons from Calis to Wilm and no one else had died. To Stephenie that was significant, but the future was not clear.

The city of Wilm was larger than many of the port cities in Cothel. It was filled with people of many nationalities, and the sounds and smells of diverse cultures filled the busy streets. By the time they reached the main road that paralleled the wharfs, the sun was partially below the horizon, and all the people rushing about were trying to finish up their tasks before the sun finally set and darkness took over.

"What ship are we looking for?" Will asked from where he was sitting on the top of a crate.

Stephenie patted the horse she was walking beside and turned back to face Will before shaking her head. "I doubt it will still be here, but I don't know which one Josh was going to send. He wasn't going to arrange for it until we were supposed to be heading here to avoid someone finding out what was going on. If nothing looks promising, we'll need to find a place to stay and hire a merchant as quickly as possible."

"Ho, Sarge!" Douglas called from the wagon ahead of them. "Damn, that's a good sight!"

Stephenie heard Will laugh and slap his leg behind her and so she turned back to him and the grin that filled his face. "Which one?" she asked, quickly scanning the ships that were moored across from them.

"No, way down there," Will pointed with his hand, drawing Stephenie to look at a three masted frigate. It was flying Cothel's colors over another flag baring a yellow otter on a green field; both flags were flapping very lightly in the breeze. "That's not a coincidence," Will beamed.

"I don't recognize the ship."

"It's *The Scarlet!*" Will said, deadpanning mock astonishment that there could be anyone in the world who would not have known what the ship's name was.

Stephenie grinned, "The one you, Douglas, and Henton served on."

Henton came up behind her, putting a hand on her shoulder. "The very one, but everyone hold your tongues until we've confirmed they are here for us."

Stephenie joined Henton in leading the two wagons to *The Scarlet*. A sailor watched them approach the gangplank, which was rising and falling slightly with the ship as it bobbed up and down in the calm harbor.

"Permission to come aboard?" Henton asked in Cothish.

"We're not for hire," the sailor responded crisply. "In case you didn't notice, we're not a merchant ship."

"Captain Darelin still in command?"

The sailor perked up slightly, studying Henton and the others more closely. "Who wants to know?"

"Please fetch the captain. I have a message for him."

After a moment, the sailor called out to another man on deck and before long, a weathered man in fine dress came to the rail and surveyed the situation before grinning widely.

"Sergeant Henton, how is it that I find you in Wilm?" He waved them forward with his hand. "Come aboard so we can talk. Corporal

William? Private Douglas, do my eyes betray me? Where are the others?"

Henton stayed Will and Douglas with a quick gesture while he held his hand out to allow Stephenie to go up the gangplank first.

"Captain, it is good to see you. The White Peak is beautiful at sea."

"Squid tastes of shit."

Henton clasped the captain's hand around Stephenie at the exchange of the pass phrase. "This is not Beth," he added too quickly, stepping aside to introduce Stephenie.

"Noteth?" the Captain questioned.

"Not...Beth, as in, I am not," Stephenie said, stepping forward. "Believe me, it is an improvement," she added at the quizzical expression on the Captain's face.

"I think I understand." Captain Darelin inclined his head slightly to Stephenie before turning his attention to Henton. "Then the rumors I heard about your activities are true."

"They are. You should know that Douglas is now a corporal." Henton paused a moment, "and unfortunately, I lost Fish."

The Captain nodded his head. "I am sorry to hear that. Perhaps we should talk more in my cabin."

Stephenie cleared her throat. "Captain, I would like to have the cargo brought aboard as quickly as possible. If we can set sail at first light, I would feel better."

"Of course, I will have my men help bring on what you have, though we don't have much cargo space." He glanced at the wagons and nodded his head, "but those few crates don't look too bad."

"My men can sleep with some of the crates and we can sell what doesn't fit. I don't care too much about a loss, I just want to get back to Antar as soon as possible. We got delayed in route."

The Captain nodded his head. "Come, let us talk somewhere a little more pleasant. The men can get things loaded." After summoning a couple of sailors over, both of these recognizing Henton on sight, he quickly delegated the task of loading the cargo before escorting Stephenie and Henton to his cabin.

The Scarlet was not overly large, and while it boasted subtle details in the woodwork, it was obviously an older ship that had seen many

years at sea. The Captain's quarters were smaller than Stephenie had
expected, but it did have a dining table that six people could squeeze
around.

"When I received my order directly from His Majesty, I was
uncertain what to expect. He provided no details, only the pass
phrase and that we were to wait in Wilm until our passengers arrived
with some limited cargo. I had no idea to expect you, Your Highness."

Stephenie took the seat she was offered in front of the captain's
desk. Once she was seated, Henton and Darelin sat as well. "My
mission was, and still is, secret. Now that it is complete, I want to get
back to Antar and report to my brother." Stephenie tensed at the
apprehension she was feeling from the Captain. "What is it?"

"Ma'am, I am guessing you have not heard the latest news." He
continued when Stephenie shook her head no. "Antar is under siege.
It has been for a while. Duke Burdger's son is reported to be leading
the siege. Antar's port is blockaded by a handful of ships and there is
no chance we can bring *The Scarlet* to berth there. I hate to bear such
bad news to you, but I have continued confirmation from other
sailors who have passed Antar in the last week."

"When did this happen?"

"We left on the twelfth of the prior month, just ahead of the naval
blockade. Burdger's boy had taken the field the night before. His
Majesty ordered me away instead of trying to help the fight. He said
he had a more important mission for *The Scarlet* and to not return
until I had my passengers or there was no longer any money for slip
fees. None of us knew about the naval blockade at that time, but as
The Scarlet took to sea, we saw them coming."

"Damn it! Damn it!" Stephenie turned to Henton. "I told you
Elard would be trouble. He should have been hung not freed." She
balled up her fists

There is nothing that you could have done, Kas said mentally from
where he floated behind the captain. *This was inevitable, freed or hung,
there was too much momentum to stop the civil war.*

Yeah, well, if that was true, we should have hung him for certain. To
the others she said, "Let's get under sail at first light. Can we make
Antar in four days?"

Captain Darelin leaned back. "Ma'am, we cannot reach the port. There is nothing you can do to aid your brother directly from Antar and *The Scarlet* by herself cannot hope to stand against the other ships. We don't have any holy warriors to defend us."

Stephenie took a deep breath. "You have me. But we don't need to come into port, just get me close enough to the shore and I'll take care of the rest."

"Ma'am. I have always been loyal to your family and I accept the fact that you have been cleansed. However, I am not certain everyone on board is as firm in their agreement with the High Priest. I am sure others will come to the conclusion of who you are, if word has not already spread, as it was not a secret that Sergeant Henton was working as your body guard."

Stephenie nodded her head. "I understand and I plan to stay out of the way. But I need to get to Antar as quickly as possible."

Morning did not come early enough for Stephenie. Although the captain had given up his quarters to her, she found no rest. Her night was fraught with terror and dread, as she worried about what Elard was doing to Joshua and her country in the nearly thirty days that had passed since the siege had begun. As a single person, she knew there was not a lot she could do to stop the armies. What happened in the Greys had been a fluke, even against the man who said he was two hundred years old, she had only managed to turn over the ground. There was no way she had the strength alone to bring down a mountain.

"But the average person does not know what you are truly capable of." Henton handed her the bag of coins Douglas and Will received for selling the horses and wagons late the night before. "They have only heard the rumor."

"The money will do little good now if the armies have already turned to Elard."

"Steph, you need to keep hope. No one wants to bring down Antar Castle. The cost to repair it would be enormous. This will be one of those waiting games and your brother should easily have more than thirty days of food. Let's get there, and we can figure out what to do."

She nodded her head; there was little point in arguing. *Besides, Henton is essentially right; we don't know enough yet.* However, rational thought did little to ease her worry and so she soon went out onto deck to give herself something to do.

On deck, Stephenie watched as a number of sailors were preparing to kedge *The Scarlet* away from the docks. Henton, who had come up with her, nodded his head to the men who were working to move a dingy into place to be lowered with a light anchor and a long rope.

"The wind is too calm and not in our favor, they'll use the anchor and winch us away from the wharf until we can take sail."

Stephenie frowned, unhappy with the delay that would come from this laborious process. Slowly, she drew energy into herself. The whirlwind she had created around the mage and his men was a result of her pushing against the air with her power. It had not been intentional, but it had shown her that even something as limited in substance as the air could be moved with her magic.

Any suggestions, Kas? She asked, conveying in thought, instead of words, what she planned.

Do not tip over the ship. You will have to be very careful, I would suggest generating your fields well away from the ship itself; just rhythmically drive the air. Especially since you were thinking to avoid others knowing what you are doing.

Stephenie grinned. She was again getting a strong sense of approval from Kas whenever they communicated mentally, but it worried her as well, since they had not fully resolved their issues yet.

Putting aside her darker thoughts, she quickly formed the short lived fields just over the wharf, driving the air toward the ship. At first, the only change was the light breeze blowing from the east disappearing. However, as she increased the frequency of her effort, the breeze quickly turned.

Henton glanced in her direction and shook his head, but there was a grin on his lips. Calling out to the officer on deck, Henton pointed to the flags. "I think our winds have changed. You might hurry and get us under sail before it fades."

* * * * *

Once they were underway, Stephenie added some subtle wind to the sails, driving *The Scarlet* to the south. When evening came, the first mate directed the ship closer to shore and dropped anchor for the night. In the darkness, Stephenie climbed the mizzen mast and slid herself amongst the guy ropes and onto the open crosstree. It was dark even for her eyes, as both moons were new, leaving only the twinkling of stars in the sky.

There were no towns or cities to light the land, which was now nothing more than blackness against blackness. A handful of lamps, turned down low, provided some illumination on deck, but she was tired and exhausted from driving the wind and was happy to be able to disappear into the tangle of ropes supporting the mast. Henton knew where she was and that would keep everyone from worrying.

After some time, Will and a number of sailors gathered on the quarterdeck just below the mizzen mast. This surprised Stephenie, until she realized many of the sailors were officers and an invitation must have been extended to the common sailors to come onto the quarterdeck. She almost decided to descend, but no one had seemed to notice her and she would definitely be noticed if she climbed down.

"We heard what the High Priest had said, Daniels had even attended the service. But for those of us at sea...well, we see things land lubbers just don't. You know what I mean, Will; you were on board long enough. You sure she's some prophet of Catheri?"

Stephenie could hear the cocky smile in Will's voice as his words carried up to her on the calm night air. "You all know me, well most of you do. Damn, we've fought drunken brawls together in Rawner and that's dangerous...those damn purists there." He shook his head, "I've seen her in action. I've seen her in private. I've seen what she can really do."

"You see her take down the mountain?" interrupted a heavy set man hidden in the shadows. Stephenie could only see the top of his head, which reflected slightly in the lamp light, indicating a bit of balding.

Will nodded his head. "I witnessed that. I was there when the flames consumed her and the dozen Senzar warlocks. Burned them away, leaving nothing behind. Her Highness was left pure and whole,

the black mark of Catheri on her left breast, just over her heart."
Someone snickered, but quieted when Will turned his gaze. "She's
perfect. Unflawed. Beautiful. But those aren't her best qualities."

She watched as Will moved about the quarterdeck, mesmerizing
the sailors who were listening with his subtle gestures.

"No, her best quality is her sense of justice. Her sense of purpose
and knowledge of what is right and wrong." Will took a deep breath.
"You all remember Fish?" he asked, and then nodded his head in
unison with the sailors around him. "Well, Fish died because of
treason. Zac found out Steph had powers. She saved Zac's life, as well
as Fish's, and the rest of ours. She killed several Senzar; blew apart the
head of one. Like a watermelon exploding off the deck when dropped
from the masthead."

Stephenie frowned. Will was embellishing his tale; one he had not
even been there to witness.

"Well, Zac betrayed us to the Senzar. The stupid shit was directly
responsible for Fish's death. Couldn't handle that Her Highness might
have been sent as a gift from the gods and simply turned all of us over
to the evil heathen bastards that were killing our brothers and fathers.
Bastards that were raping the land for their own greed and would
have turned us all into slaves. Zac sold us out to them."

"Bastard," said someone who had a voice like gravel. "Should have
drowned that piece of shit when I first saw him."

Will simply nodded his head. "They had us. The Senzar that Zac
had summoned overwhelmed us. They had taken us by surprise, and
through Steph's strength of will alone, she bested another dozen while
we were fettered and bound with blades at our throats." He paused a
moment before continuing. "When it was over, she ordered Zac
hung, and she carried out the justice swiftly."

There was a small chorus of affirmations.

"That was before we even reached the Greys, where she routed the
Senzar, but you've all heard about that. However, I want to tell you
about something else. After the Greys, when we were all back in the
castle and the High Priest had declared her cleansed of Elrin's taint,
that very night, she was attacked by a young serving wench. A slip of
a girl, not really even a woman. The girl had committed treason,
trying to kill a member of the royal household in front of the King

and dukes and other nobles." The audience leaned slightly forward, waiting for Will to continue. "Steph demanded her brother allow the girl to go free. Said the girl had done nothing to harm anyone else and had no intention to. Said the girl had no chance of being able to harm her, she was just manipulated by nobles and the rich who didn't want someone like Steph interfering with them. So they went looking for someone to cause trouble. The cowards convinced the girl to do it, knowing she'd not have the chance and would hang for the crime. Well, Steph refused to let that girl hang. She'd not take no for an answer, and the King only banished the girl from Antar instead of dangling her from a rope or removing her head."

Will took a seat on the quarterdeck railing. "That's Stephenie. That's Her Royal Highness. That's the tenet of Catheri: justice. Not revenge. Not greed and hate. But give each person their due, regardless of birth and rank. Yes, the girl did wrong, but a child striking out because some manipulative people convinced her to do it did not deserve death and Steph recognized that and stood up to the King to get it."

"This is all good and well, but if she's Catheri's priestess, why doesn't she claim it. I've not seen or heard one thing from her declaring her relationship to that goddess."

Will shrugged. "She's humble. She doesn't want to declare it herself because she doesn't feel worthy. I know what I've seen. I know what she's done and the honesty she exudes." He rose back to his feet. "She's not perfect, but I'll support her until I die. I'll stand up for her, and where she's too humble, I'll cry out for her. It's my honor to protect her and spread the word of what she does."

"Ma'am, we'll be in Antar by late afternoon at this pace. The wind's been good to us."

Stephenie turned her head away from the sea to look at Captain Darelin. "Head further out to sea, away from shore. We don't want the ships guarding the harbor to see us passing. Then head south of Antar. We'll turn around and come back from the south."

"That will add time. We won't likely be able to return to Antar before nightfall."

She nodded her head. They had made good time with her countering the strong wind coming from the south, avoiding the need to tack back and forth quite as much as they would normally need to do, but there was only so much she could do. "That's fine, if we can come at Antar in the early morning, so much the better." She turned back to the sea, leaning over the port side railing to watch the waves roll by.

After a moment, she felt the captain turn away, leaving her visibly alone, as she had spent most of the trip so far. *Kas, what would happen if I dropped the medallions over the side? Would they force a fish to carry them to shore?*

Kas, who had also left Stephenie alone for parts of the journey, moved a little closer, as if his invisible form was also leaning over the railing next to her. *I do not believe they were made to be that intelligent. They are meant to serve, but I do not believe they are driven to be used. Their defense is to prevent destruction, but they should accept simple idleness.*

She pulled the two holy symbols of Felis from the satchel that was slung over her shoulder. She knew there was no one close enough to see what she was doing. *Nothing I've tried has allowed me to block the power they can access, even when we were so far away in Calis. I can feel their defenses getting even stronger now that we are coming back to Cothel. I am sorry I failed you in this.*

They would be pretty ineffectual if their source of power was that easy to block. Do not fret. I had hoped that you would be able to sense a way to do it. I had no intention of making you feel worse for not succeeding immediately. Do not think that you have failed me. I have failed you in causing you to feel as such.

She turned her head in Kas' direction, despite the fact he was not visible to her eyes. However, she sensed his energy clearly. *Kas, come on, you know me.* She sighed and looked back out to the sea. *I fret about everything, but while these are driving me crazy, it's Josh that I worry about. We were a month late getting to Wilm. What's been happening in Antar all that time? Can I even do anything to save things? I'm just one person.* She closed her eyes, fighting back tears. *I can't imagine having to use my powers against citizens of Cothel, even if they turned against Josh. I can't wipe out an army of people.* She sighed, *even if I had the power to do that, I would not.*

Then what do you plan to do in Antar?

Stephenie heard some of the reproach in Kas' mental voice. He did not understand what she was planning to do in Antar anymore than she did. She shrugged. *I'll get Josh out. Perhaps even Lady Rebecca, since Josh is attached to her. Perhaps a few more. Maybe fly them back to The Scarlet. If Elard's going to take Antar anyway, then I want his victory to be hollow.* She looked back to the sea, "I'll get Josh away safely and we can figure out what to do from there." Looking down into her hands and the two holy symbols of Felis, she swallowed and then watched as they fell straight down and disappeared into the waves with a splash that could have easily been the sound of a stray wave crashing against the hull. The medallion fashioned into the holy symbol of Ravim, she left in her satchel. That one she would keep working to destroy.

Chapter 23

Stephenie stood at the prow with the wind blowing through her loose hair. The eastern sky was a dim glow above the gentle curve of the sea. It had taken some convincing to get the ship's crew moving before sunrise, but she assured everyone that she would be able to sense any rocks well before the ship ran aground. At full sail, and this close to shore, she hoped she was right. However, Kas was flying well ahead of them and was the actual watcher.

Henton, fully armed and in boiled leather he had acquired from the ships armory, stood beside her. "I thought we had a deal. I stop calling you Beth and you don't do things that make it hard for me to protect you. I started in good faith, remember, we came aboard, and you were not Beth."

She grinned at Henton's latest attempt to change her mind. For once, she could clearly sense his desperation and that emotional energy coming from him was almost enough to change her mind. *Almost.* "Henton, I need you here to protect what we have. We can't let it fall into our enemy's hands and while I don't have cause to distrust our group or Captain Darelin, I trust you to protect it much more."

"It won't do a bit of good if you are dead."

She smiled at him and raised one eyebrow. "Really? Well, if it was me, I think I would set myself up as a virtual king somewhere and live a quiet life. But, if you want a suggestion, there's enough there to hire a large army of mercs. You could come back and take over Cothel."

"And who'd you suggest rules? You'll be dead, remember."

"I'll never rule this country or any country. I'm not fit, but if Josh is gone, then I would suggest Baron Arnold Turning, but you'd make a good leader as well."

Henton snorted in derision and shook his head. "Don't be ridiculous." He sighed. "Steph, I really think I should come to protect you."

She felt her jaw tighten. "Henton, you are staying and that's an order. Don't push it further. Kas will be with me, and when I am ready, I want you to bring *The Scarlet* back near Antar, and I'll join you with Josh and perhaps a few others. I need someone I can trust to do that."

Abashed, Henton dropped his eyes and nodded his head. "Of course. I just..."

She softened her expression and put her hand on his arm, looking up into his down-turned face. "I'll be back. Do you think I will let you get away with calling me Beth for all that time and not get back at you for it." She smiled, trying to lighten his mood. "I'm not leaving you behind to be nice to you. It's just what needs to happen."

She turned her head, Captain Darelin was approaching with another sailor. "Your Highness," he said, bowing his head. "We've got a strong wind blowing. We'll be passing Antar at speed at this rate. We'll need to start dropping sails if you want us to slow."

She shook her head. The sun, still not yet over the horizon, had brightened the sky significantly while she had been talking with Henton. "No. I'll be able to get off without trouble, just sail us close to the castle, then turn out to sea and away from the harbor. No use fighting a group of ships when there is no point. They'll likely have been at anchor and with the wind already in your sails, they won't have a hope of catching up."

"And then what are your orders, Ma'am?"

"Circle back around to the south and hopefully the winds will be in our favor tomorrow morning. Come back past the castle and hopefully I will re-board with my brother and a couple others."

"At speed?"

"Captain," Henton interjected, "trust her, she can do it."

Darelin bowed his head to Stephenie and then to Henton. "I expect we will be near the harbor and the castle just after the sun is over the horizon. If there is nothing else, I will leave you to finish your discussion." He bowed his head once more and then turned away quickly.

Stephenie turned back to the prow and watched as the high cliffs sped by. She had loved walking the edge of those cliffs as a child, looking down at the surf and the rocks that had fallen into the sea. Looking up, she only hoped Elard had not positioned siege weapons where they could fire on *The Scarlet* from above.

Time seemed to slow for a while, then suddenly she could see the ships that were blocking the harbor and the towers of Antar Castle standing tall near the edge of the granite cliffs. She called Kas to her as Henton tensed. She turned once more to the large man who had done so much to protect her. "Keep yourself safe. Perhaps if things had been different..."

"Keep yourself safe," he interrupted.

She smiled. "Get them turned away," she said as she launched herself up and over the side of the ship, moving fast enough to avoid the foresail. She dropped low, flying just over the waves as she raced toward the rocky cliffs, only changing course and launching herself skyward moments before striking the rough stone. Flying only a couple feet from the cliff, she hoped to avoid notice by any of the ships in the harbor.

Kas followed Stephenie with a more parabolic arch, joining her flight as she rose above the top of the cliff and the castle wall. Flying faster than she had ever flown before, she was forced to create a field to shield her eyes and face from the biting wind. A moment later, she lurched herself to a stop atop the new keep. The four guards standing watch along the crenelated walls at the west edge of the keep had not noticed her approach or landing.

She considered calling out to them, so they would not be alarmed. However, having landed next to the northern structure containing the door that led into the keep, she simply slipped inside and started down the stairs. *Let them wonder how I got in.*

Stephenie reached the fourth floor and headed quickly to another set of stairs going down to the third. She was not exactly sure where

Josh would be, it was early, but he was an early riser and it was likely he could be out surveying the walls or reviewing reports in his offices.

She had caught only a glimpse of the siege force as she had flown in. There had been no one between the castle and the sea, that ground was too narrow to put anyone, but she had seen the forces on the other three sides and guessed there were at least six to seven thousand, *perhaps more.* The castle's defense would hold if the holy warriors stayed out of the conflict, but she doubted that would happen when autumn started to turn to winter.

On the third floor, she extended her senses, hoping to feel Joshua or anyone else she recognized. She could tell there were a number of people on this floor, as well as the floor above and below. However, she was not sure who was present.

Of course, Kas replied to her unvocalized request that she had not fully formed into a coherent thought.

He broke off to search outside as she walked slowly down the hallway, uncertain of what she sensed. There was someone in obvious pain, but it was muddled and incoherent. Slowly, she realized it was coming from the area where Joshua's room was located. Without thought, she charged down the hallway, her sword bouncing off her hip. She turned a corner and slowed as a pair of guards raised their crossbows to chest level.

Recognizing one of them, but not remembering his name, she stopped and raised her hands. Enough power was flooding through her, she would easily stop both bolts if they were released. "Where's my brother?" It slipped out as more of a demand than the question she had intended.

"Your Highness," the one she had recognized responded slowly. "What are you doing here? When'd you arrive and how?"

She shook her head, growing more certain her brother was in the rooms these men guarded, and he was in immense pain. Kas floated through the wall, confirming her fear. She moved forward, heedless of the crossbows.

"Ma'am, there were assassins, until we confirm your inten—"

She wrapped a field around them, preventing them from moving or raising an alarm verbally. Pushing through the door, she moved into her brother's outer chamber and then through the next door into his bed chamber. She absentmindedly released the guards when she saw Joshua and Lady Rebecca laid out in his bed. A frightened nurse dropped the pan she was holding.

"What happened?" Stephenie was at the foot of the bed in an instant.

"Poison," the nurse said. "Are you here to finish them?"

Stephenie looked up, the fear on the woman's face was nowhere near the amount she was radiating. "Of course not! Fetch a priest. They need to be healed!"

The woman stepped back, "Ma'am, they're all dead. Lady Rebecca is the last one in the castle."

Stephenie looked down at the trembling and sweaty form of Lady Rebecca. She noticed now the priestess' mind starting to stir.

"Steph?" Rebecca's eyes barely focused. She tried to raise her hand out from under the blanket, but she lacked the strength.

Stephenie to the side of the bed and met the priestess' eyes. "What happened?"

On the other side of the room, the nurse replied, having assumed the question was asked of her. "Two days ago, holy warriors broke in. They killed the High Priest and his acolytes, then came here for His Majesty. Lady Rebecca killed the assassins, but not before she and His Majesty were poisoned."

"Steph...you must heal him," Rebecca choked out.

Stephenie swallowed. "I can't. I don't know how. Rebecca, you have to heal him."

She coughed up blood. "Been doing that...I'm dying...won't last much longer...then he'll die."

Stephenie looked around the room. Finding the nurse's eyes, she paused. "Fetch someone. Anyone who can heal!"

The nurse took flight and ran from the room, almost knocking over Sir Walter, head of Joshua's personal guard.

"Your Highness, there are no others. Elard does not yet know that, otherwise he would have attacked already. He grows weary demanding Joshua respond to his latest demand for surrender. I think he is trying to see if His Majesty still lives. We can't hold off his demands much longer." Sir Walter took a deep breath and brushed back his dirty hair, which had obviously not seen water in days.

"With you here, Elard may have second thoughts about attacking the walls. It might also give the men hope. Would you take the walls and respond to Elard?"

Stephenie clenched her fist. "My brother is the King, I am not going to trade insults with Elard. We need to find someone to heal them." She turned back to Rebecca as the priestess coughed once to clear her throat.

"Steph...not enough time. I'm using all my strength...to sustain him. I'm barely holding..."

Stephenie lowered herself toward Rebecca's face. "I do not know how!" She closed her eyes. "I killed Oliver trying to heal him. I won't kill my brother as well."

Rebecca spit some blood from her mouth and cringed in obvious pain. "Then...practice on me. I'll...direct you."

"I'll kill you if I try, and then Josh will die."

"I'll...dead before another day...Josh soon after."

"Kas!" she called aloud, sensing the ghost just on the other side of the bed.

I cannot help you, Stephenie. I did what I could with Oliver, but that was not enough. I wish I could do more.

"Steph, this hurts...I...getting weaker." Tears streamed from Rebecca's eyes. "Please...save him."

Taking a deep breath, feeling the tears of frustration running down her own cheeks, she clenched her hands. *I won't live if I kill him.*

It will not be your fault either way. I would say not to, but if you do not try, you will regret it forever; therefore, you must try.

Without further delay, she opened herself, grabbed Rebecca's wrist, and reached out to the priestess' mind. "Help me," she whispered both verbally and mentally.

After a moment, she made initial contact with Rebecca's mind, felt the torment that raged just below the surface, and knew with complete certainty that Rebecca cared for Joshua as much as she did.

Rebecca, help me.

Stephenie felt her own self stretch and expand and then snap back with a painful contraction. She sensed Rebecca and knew she had made full mental contact. However, the priestess was trying to shield her from pain or something else; she could not be certain.

What do you know about healing, Stephenie heard from Rebecca. The priestess' voice once again strong and complete, but with an underlying agony.

I can heal myself, was her reply, but with more than just words, Stephenie unintentionally transmitted some portion of her memory of healing her arm the first time Kas had shown her how.

Rebecca seemed to sigh, not one of exasperation, but one more of relief. *You have the basics. You just need to do the same thing, but let the other person's body direct you.*

Sensing the weakening of Rebecca's mind, Stephenie released her memory of healing Oliver in a flood of pain and emotion. She felt Rebecca reel from the intensity.

Stop! After a moment, she felt Rebecca try to arrange her thoughts. *Do not flood someone with memories like that, especially strong ones. You could really do damage.*

Stephenie's abashment flowed freely. *I don't know what I am doing.*

And that is fine. It is expected. You've never been trained. It takes time. Let me guide you. But you have to trust me.

Stephenie gave her assent, dropping the barriers she knew she had raised to protect herself. She would subject herself to any humiliation, if it would save the ones she loved.

Reach out to my subconscious. Let it direct you as your own directs you. For this injury, though, you need to know that you have to do two things. You have to try and draw off the poison. It impacts the body and mind, blocking our ability to control power, which limits our ability to heal ourselves at the same time it continues to do damage.

Stephenie accepted the memories and complex concepts that went along with Rebecca's words, taking them into herself, but not fully understanding them. Sensing the pain Rebecca was in, she tried to reach deeper into Rebecca's mind, looking for her subconscious, hoping to use that internal knowledge to direct her powers. After just a moment, and with the sense that Rebecca was guiding her, she found what she was looking for.

Pain filled her own body as she absorbed details from Rebecca. Reacting instinctively, her body pushed energy into Rebecca.

The priestess screamed and Stephenie started to retreat immediately.

Wait! Stephenie was certain Rebecca was in agony. *Like this.*

Her own terror of killing when she tried to help threatened to overwhelm her, but she could also sense Kas' subtle contact, reassuring her. Having trouble keeping track of whose thoughts were whose, she pushed back into Rebecca's mind, this time more gradually and greatly limiting the flow of energy to a more consistent trickle instead of the massive wave she was capable of handling inside her own body.

She sensed organs and tissue, though severely damaged, start to knit back together. However, she also sensed traces of something alien; something that did not belong. She knew that Rebecca was not able to fully conceptualize just what Stephenie sensed. Not trying to force anything, Stephenie simply existed for a moment, aware that Rebecca's pain was still intense, but there was a slight euphoria coming from her as she continued to focus on the poison.

Kas, Stephenie thought, but she did not wait for the ghost's response. Instead, she watched with her mind's eye as some of the poison appeared to slowly transform. It was on the microscopic level, just as when she had transformed the shape of the bronze and the stone in Wyntac castle. Visualizing the very narrow and specific field, she tried to speed up the transformation of this alien substance. The very thing that Rebecca's body was working so hard to fight.

Stop!

Stephenie withdrew herself, fearful of having done something terrible to the priestess. *Please, I didn't mean to harm you.*

You weren't, but my body is too weak for you to force more healing. You can only do so much at one time.

Stephenie realized Rebecca's pain had subsided and there was a contentment she had not felt since the last time she had shared her bed with Joshua.

Stephenie retreated completely. She shuddered and tried to forget the memory of Joshua's face close to her own, breathing on her neck. *His hands...* Coming back into her own head and closing out everyone else, she slipped to the floor, telling herself that the memory had been Rebecca's and not hers. After a couple moments, she felt Rebecca's hand reach down and touch her shoulder.

"It is not polite to rummage through other people's thoughts."

Stephenie pushed against the memory again, hoping the feeling would go away. She eventually took a deep breath and then looked up at the priestess. "I don't want that memory. I didn't ask for it." Then she softened. "I'm not judging you, but..." she shuddered and rolled her shoulders. She exhaled slowly and felt the memory fading away as she realized just how exhausted she was.

"You need to heal Josh. At least enough to stabilize him. I don't have the strength. If you can do that, I can continue later."

Stephenie nodded her head. She forced herself to her feet and went around the bed. Hoping desperately that she would not pick up any memories from him that would disturb her even more than what she had found in Rebecca's mind.

After taking a deep breath, she grabbed her brother's hand and delved into his mind. His consciousness was much weaker and she feared she might not be able to save him. But the fact that he lacked any conscious resistance made her effort that much easier. Rebecca's voice eventually came to her from what sounded like the outside of a cave. Realizing she had done as much as she could, Stephenie retreated from Joshua's mind. She had picked up some unconscious memories, but did her best to forget them immediately without allowing herself to know what they were.

She opened her eyes and looked around the room. Sir Walter was still standing by the door, but now there were at least five other guards and half a dozen nurses and servants as well. She felt her legs trembling and only managed to stay upright by leaning against one of the posts at the foot of the bed.

Rebecca called out to Sir Walter from where she lay. "She's saved the both of us. We'll need more rest...and some food."

A murmur ran through those standing at the door, which was overridden by Sir Walter. "Ma'am, I can see you are tired. But, if His Majesty is still too weak to respond to Elard, would you at least be willing to do so?"

Stephenie looked around. Separated again, and the only one in her own head, she was gradually feeling her senses and strength return. There was fear and also hope coming from the people watching. Eventually, she nodded her head. "But first, get me a white tunic. Something without any colors on it. And get me a brush and as much ink as you can." She watched as Sir Walter subdued his desire to question the purpose of her request.

"I will have it here as soon as possible."

"And some food and water for me as well. I need something to eat."

"What are you doing?" Sir Walter asked as Stephenie slid a shield between the layers of the tunic and flattened the material.

Stephenie swallowed the meat that she had stuffed into her mouth. "What needs to be done." She grabbed some more meat from the platter and stuck it into her mouth. Sir Walter nodded his head and left the bedroom, closing the door behind him.

Kas materialized, sitting on the floor across from Stephenie. Rebecca inhaled slightly at his sudden appearance, having never seen the ghost. "You are going to give into Will's desire?" Kas asked in the old tongue.

"Until I give the people something different they can believe in, I will be a problem." She pulled out the stone Will and Douglas had given her from under her shirt. "We slowly substitute one for the other. Change things gradually."

Rebecca cleared her throat. She was now sitting up with pillows behind her. "You have my approval." The lines on her face concealed the content, but not the presence of deeper emotions. "I just do not know what my approval is worth anymore."

Stephenie dipped the small brush in one of the ink reservoirs and started drawing the outline of a hand on the tunic. "You were the last Master Priest, which means with the High Priest dead, you are now the High Priest."

"Of a fractured and divided church. Stephenie, give them a way not to hate you and I think many will follow you."

Stephenie shook her head. "They can follow Will. I'm just trying to do as you say, give them a way they can accept me." She looked at

Kas as she grabbed another reservoir so she could quickly fill in the center of the hand.

He smiled at her and nodded his head. "That is a poorly drawn version of my hand print," he said aloud in Dalish.

She grinned at his jibe, but said nothing further. Once she finished inking the hand, she dried it with a little energy, and then did the reverse side. Grabbing a couple more pieces of meat, she quickly ate them as she pulled the tunic over her head and strapped her sword belt around her waist.

I sense that we are not going to retreat to The Scarlet in the morning.

She shook her head. *They tried to kill him. Cothel will not be whole while Elard lives.* After a quick glance in Joshua's large mirror, she ran her hand through her loose hair and then left the bedroom.

No one said anything to her as she strode through the castle and toward the gatehouse. She carried herself in a manner that forbade any conversation, but a wave of comments followed in her wake. Word spread like water crashing against the shore. When she neared the gatehouse, she could hear Elard's voice, shouting through a speaking trumpet, taunting the soldiers on the wall while demanding someone take the wall to negotiate a surrender.

Stephenie flew herself up and over the gatehouse, landing on the downward sloping road. The bulk of Elard's army was just outside of bow range of the walls. She had caught a slightly better look at what they faced as she flew over the gatehouse and she knew the few hundred troops inside the castle walls would never be able to route the forces encamped here.

Her anger boiling over, she cupped her hands and using Kas' trick to make his voice heard, she amplified her own voice well over that of what Elard had achieved with the trumpet. "I am coming to parley with you. Stop your noise."

She started marching the four hundred yards toward Elard's position with Kas holding invisibly just behind her. She saw Elard begin to respond, but then step away from the large trumpet he had been using to convey his demands. The soldiers on the leading line moved about nervously, uncertain of what they should do. When she drew closer, she noticed Lord Evens at Elard's side. At least four other holy warriors stood behind them.

I will be ready to strike them dead if they start to attack, Kas said as he moved quickly ahead of her.

Stephenie resisted the urge to say anything until she was within a dozen feet of Elard and his line of men. She would not stoop to the indignity of yelling, no matter how much she wanted to rip off Elard's head with her bare hands.

"So, it's the witch," Elard sneered. However, Stephenie could tell many people were staring at the black hand on her tunic.

"Where's your father?" she asked, looking around, but not sensing or seeing him.

"That's none of your business. You here to accept our terms? Though I would be surprised if you do, since the terms involve your burning."

Stephenie shrugged and looked about with indifference. "I am here to talk with the Duke." She turned back to Elard, "Unless you had him killed to make yourself the Duke?"

Elard took a step closer, his sword, which had been in his hand since she had landed on the other side of the gatehouse, swinging before him, but with the tip only inches from the ground, it lacked any real threat. "My father is not your concern. I am leading this force!"

Stephenie kept herself calm, despite the fact there were a lot of armed men standing before her. If Kas could help keep the holy warriors busy, she knew she could deflect the first rounds of arrows and force the soldiers back. That would give her enough time to retreat, even if it would be less than impressive. If that happened, she would have no choice but to abandon Antar, as they would then appear too weak to ever drive this force away.

She smiled at him. "I suspected so. Your father seemed to have more honor than to go back on his word. I guess as soon as you get the castle you'll have him killed if he's not already dead, just like you tried," she emphasized, "to do with Joshua."

This made Elard grin. "Your brother is dead, isn't he? That's why he's not been on the walls to respond." Elard turned, raising his arms and sword over his head. "The King is dead! We are victorious!"

"No, Joshua is just fine. He doesn't waste time on cowards who send in assassins to do their work for them. He sends me instead."

Elard, turned back to Stephenie. "That is a convenient story, little girl. But we all know Elrin is the god of lies. Witches should burn and we'll do that shortly."

Stephenie waited until he was done ranting, then shrugged again before looking down at her tunic. "I've burned once, didn't hurt that much. Not sure you'd have the same experience, such is the pity we don't burn traitors." She pursed her lips. "Your cowardly assassins did not kill Joshua, though they did attack him. It turns out, Lady Rebecca Cole, Master Priest of Felis," she added, looking directly at Lord Evans, "killed the assassins. Assassins that used spells."

"Well, so what if they could? It seemed appropriate with you around."

She could tell the news surprised Lord Evans and she began to hope she might not have to kill the priests as well. Turning back to Elard, she continued, "Really? Which god's priests did you find to kill the High Priest of Felis?"

Elard smiled. "The puppet of your house is dead."

"Elard, what did you do?" Lord Evans asked from his side.

"Removed the tainted corruption!"

"You should have consulted with me."

Elard turned toward Evans. "We could not have that weak puppet send priests against us! The troops would have rebelled."

Stephenie's jaw hardened. "You have done more to harm Felis' priests and church than I ever have. By my authority, I declare you a traitor and strip you of all your lands and titles. Your life is forfeit."

Elard started to sneer, but Stephenie closed the distance and removed his head before anyone realized she had drawn her sword. Using her mind, she pushed his head and body backwards, sending the spray of blood over the holy warriors who had stood behind him. The crowd immediately cleared from where his head had rolled and body lay.

She looked around, meeting the eyes of everyone nearby. Raising her voice and augmenting the volume, she addressed the immediate crowd. "I, Her Royal Highness, Princess Stephenie, cleansed by fire and declared prophet of Catheri, have executed Elard Burdger for crimes against Felis, myself, his own followers, Cothel, and His Majesty, King Joshua." She continued to watch the stunned crowd. "I cannot speak for His Majesty, but I will recommend amnesty to anyone who quits this field and never again takes up arms against Cothel and its rightful rulers. Any who choose to remain, upon first light, you will face my full wrath. The death I dealt to the Senzar will be pleasant in comparison."

Without another word, she turned, used her mind to fling the blood from her sword, slid it home into its scabbard, and walked with measured strides back to the castle. With her heart racing, she hoped her outward calmness would not be ruined by the gatehouse guards making her fly over the wall. Just as she began to wish she had brought Henton with her to offer needed suggestions to the guards, she heard the portcullis start to rise. Slowing slightly, she reached the doors just as they swung open to permit her entrance.

Chapter 24

When Stephenie heard the doors shut behind her and the portcullises lowered, she gave a sigh of relief, but before she could take in the fact she was once again safe in the castle, a crowd of soldiers had gathered around her. She looked up, uncertain of their intent, but glad for Kas remaining beside her. After an uncomfortable moment, the gathered soldiers cheered and Stephenie felt the tension drop from her bones. Had Elard or any of the soldiers tried to call her bluff at any point in the confrontation, the best she could have hoped for was a cowardly retreat. The fact they did not was likely more due to the legends around her than anything else.

She truly smiled at the men who had gathered, many of them rejoicing at what she had just done. Of course, she sensed others far less impressed, but she decided to ignore them for now. "I just took Elard's head," she said to confirm what was done for those who might not have seen. "We have to wait until morning to see if the armies will give up the field."

Someone behind her called out over the crowd, "No Your Highness, the army is breaking up now. Word of what you did must be spreading."

Kas rose above the gatehouse and then floated back down. *It's as they say. At least the parts I understand, but the army appears to be breaking up.*

Stephenie shook her head and raised her arms, trying to quiet the crowd. "Keep an eye on them and make sure it is not a feint that is meant to put us off guard." She slowly made her way through the crowd, still feeling uncomfortable with dramatic displays of power, and climbed the steps to the wall. From there, she watched Elard's armies pulling up camp and disbanding. She thought she could see some people trying to organize the soldiers, but there was obvious chaos on the field.

Once the midday bell rang and the watch started to change, Stephenie joined those who were going off duty and went back to Joshua's keep. No one had dared to bother her while she had watched and no one challenged her as she moved through the keep. Somehow that left her feeling more alone than anything else that had happened. There were smiles, but almost everyone still feared her.

She checked on Joshua and Rebecca, who were both sleeping, and then went over to her tower. From that vantage point, she could see the ships in the harbor were taking sail and appeared to be tacking out to sea, likely in an effort to head south toward duchies that had favored Elard.

"Kas, do you have trouble traveling over water?"

"No," he responded from where he was sitting behind a crenelation, partially visible, but hidden from view. "Are you asking me to find Henton and the others?"

Stephenie returned Kas' smile. "The sea is pretty big, I don't want you to wander too far to find them. Perhaps we'll have to wait until morning, but I want to let them know the situation has changed."

"I'll head south along the coast later in the day, once we get a better idea of the situation."

She nodded her head and kept watch from the tower. When the evening bell rang, most of Elard's soldiers were gone and those that remained were actively working to leave. She noticed several groups of people come to the castle gate and she headed down to find Sir Walter.

She did not have to go far, as he was waiting for her at the base of her tower. "I debated sending someone up to fetch you, but to be honest, Your Highness, no one wanted to disturb you."

Stephenie shook her head. "I was just watching the armies clear off; I don't bite people's heads off. I'm still just Josh's younger sister who used to follow everyone around. We played games together, Walter."

Sir Walter's face said he did not entirely agree, but it softened none the less. "No one ever disturbed the High Priest when he was busy, not even his own acolytes. I did—"

"I am not a High Priest," she injected. "What's the situation in Antar?"

Sir Walter accepted her changing of the subject with grace. "The soldiers that had remained neutral during the siege have sent emissaries to find out if they are to be punished or are required to leave. Many of them call Antar home."

She pursed her lips. "What do you think? Did they do things to hurt you or Josh?"

Sir Walter shook his head, his red hair still not washed. "They did not offer help to either side. Their presence did keep Elard from rampaging Antar proper. I can't say all of them remained completely neutral, but as a whole, they were somewhat a deterrent."

"Would you trust them under your command?"

Sir Walter hesitated a bit more. "Some, perhaps. Elard came with overwhelming odds and the men had nowhere to go for safety. It was a reasonable move."

"Josh will have to have final verdict, but I won't attack them for remaining here."

Sir Walter smiled and seemed relieved. "Catheri was always one people turned to for justice." He saluted her, bowed his head, and then walked away quickly.

Frowning, she wished Kas had not left already. Lacking anyone else to talk with, she went back upstairs to her room, barred the door, and climbed into bed.

"Wake up sleepy head," Kas' voice burrowed through the haze of her sleep and Stephenie opened her eyes. "The morning sun is already in the sky and you are still in bed."

Looking around the room, she frowned, realizing she did not have any water to drink. Based on the angle and color of the sun coming through the window, she knew it was not too late in the morning.

"I have been keeping watch since I returned; there are some men, the knight, Walter, is one them. They are debating who should wake you. I believe Rebecca wants to speak with you, based on what I understood of their conversation."

"You need to learn more Cothish," she said in Dalish, to punctuate her efforts compared to his.

"You have a knack for language that I cannot come close to matching."

"Henton knows it is safe?"

"I stayed around long enough to watch the crew suspect Henton of witchcraft because he 'somehow' just 'knew' things had changed in Antar. The assumption is he has some sort of crystal ball or link with you."

Stephenie laughed as she got out of bed, "Of course he does, it's you." Removing the bar from the door, she started down the stairs. "Now let's make the people below wonder if I'm psychic."

Disappointed there was little to no additional information to be reported regarding the armies, Stephenie went over to the keep and up to Joshua's rooms. He was still sleeping, but Lady Rebecca was sitting in the chair at his desk. She was still just in a dressing gown, but much of the color had returned to her face.

"Stephenie, I am glad you came over before things got too busy this morning. I wanted to talk with you."

"The only memory I picked up from you was..."

"Something quite personal, but I am sure it has you more disturbed in seeing that than in me knowing you saw—"

"Experienced," Stephenie corrected, "something that should not be experienced by a sister. Let's not talk about it ever again."

Rebecca smiled and nodded her head. "Stephenie, I want to apologize."

Stephenie took the chair that Rebecca offered her. "Why?"

"Because I did not trust you. I knew the reasons why the High Priest had declared for you, so I simply assumed you to be the witch everyone else believed you to be." Rebecca looked down. "I was wrong."

"Because I put on a tunic and claimed to be a follower of Catheri you changed your mind?"

Rebecca raised her head and shook it. "That was probably the best thing you could do to get the support of the people behind you. But that is not the reason." Rebecca removed a large leather bound book from the desk drawer. "Just after you left, the High Priest, his name was Richard by the way, not sure if you knew that." Stephenie shook her head no. "Well, he asked me to attend him. He was old and while I was not his original choice to succeed him, there was no one else left he could confide in. He handed me this book." She placed her hands on the cover. "It is written in a code that is shared only among the master priests and the high priests through the ages. The book was locked away in a secret vault only for the high priest to know about. That was to protect it from others. It contains the secrets of the office. He..." Rebecca swallowed. "He was a good man and hated so much of what the priests had become, but he was not in a position to change things."

"What things?"

"Steph, the things you have described to Josh in the mountains, the things that were relayed to me of what you have said, about how the gods are not what we currently believe...they have been described in this journal for hundreds of years." Rebecca closed her eyes. "I supported you before, for love of Josh. I did that, though I thought the worst of you, fearing you would be his ruin. I even wondered if you had warped his mind to make him so devoted to you." She met Stephenie's eyes. "I know this is not the case. A lot of you bled through when you healed me." Rebecca shuddered slightly. "Too much, I need to work with you on that. But I have a better sense of your character and feel so ashamed to have thought ill of you, especially after I read this over the last month."

Stephenie bit her lower lip. "I thank you for the apology, but what you believed was a product of hundreds of years of lies. You cannot fault yourself for that."

Rebecca nodded in agreement. "Yes, but I have done terrible things over the years. I have sentenced people like you to death. I have tricked people into revealing themselves as witches and warlocks when I was just like them. I am a horror of a person. I should be burned for my crimes."

Stephenie saw the tears falling from Rebecca's face and while she felt for her brother's lover, she knew that Rebecca had sanctioned and participated in many murders, all in the name of protecting the people from an imagined evil.

"Rebecca, I am not sure what to say." Stephenie looked around the room. "You're now the High Priest of Felis. Put a stop to it."

Rebecca wiped away the tears that had reddened her eyes. "I'm sorry. I should not have burdened you with this."

"Rebecca, if you are looking for forgiveness from me, you are looking at the wrong person. I can't undo all the people who died. You know I'm nothing more than a witch. I'm nothing more than what you are. Now you simply realize it. The question really is, what do you plan to do next? Are you going to explain it to Josh and everyone else?"

Rebecca shook her head. "It would destroy your brother. He truly believes in Felis. As do most of the people. I am the last Master Priest. No one else knows most of our secrets. I can put a stop to how the testing is done, where we trick people into revealing themselves to be a witch by using a fake holy symbol and ask them to call upon Felis' powers. I will put a stop to that and then anyone who is a witch or warlock and can use the holy symbol will be accepted and they will never need know the truth." Rebecca took a deep breath. "You have to realize, I truly believed I was weeding out evil when we only kept those that couldn't use the fake one, but could call forth flame from the real one."

Stephenie shook her head. "That only proved they had minimal power. If you keep using the holy symbols, that will continue to kill the creature that is caught and being bled to death slowly every time you use the medallion. Like watching a deer covered in a thousand ticks struggle and finally collapse. That is what happened to Catheri's priests almost a century ago. The creature they were killing died and their source of power went away. It will happen to the church of Felis at some point too."

"What would you have me do? We can't survive as a nation without priests and healers. We would be prey to our neighbors and overrun."

Stephenie pulled the stone Will and Douglas gave her out from under her tunic. "I doubt most people can sense the fields or even the sources of power. I doubt even you are aware of them, the look on your face says you have no idea what I am saying. Simply make fake holy symbols and teach the mages to use their own powers. They'll never know the difference."

Rebecca shook her head. "They will know the difference, since the holy symbols respond to us. Any of the current priests will spot the fake the moment they hold one. Add to that the fact that I don't know how to teach people to use their own powers."

"The war caused us to lose many holy symbols, correct?" When Rebecca nodded her confirmation, Stephenie continue. "Then simply say a new batch of symbols was required to be constructed and they work differently. If you know the truth of what I said about the current process killing a creature in another world, how can you condone more death if you so regret what's already transpired?"

Rebecca lowered her head. "I can't. But I don't know how to lead people beyond what we have today."

Stephenie was wondering how this woman, more than five years her senior, could suddenly be turning to her for advice and help. Stephenie was the youngest, the baby of the family; now they were expecting her to hold everything together and put the world right. She sighed, "I will teach you as best as I can. I might even be able to convince Kas to help, but that won't happen if you continue to use that cursed device."

Rebecca nodded her head. "I can't promise it will happen right away. I need to heal myself and Josh and get things under control, but I promise I will stop using it as soon as I can and I will support you. And if you teach me, I will try to convert as many new priests as possible."

Stephenie felt Kas give her a mental smile, and so she gave one to Rebecca as well. "Take care of Josh, and we can sort out the rest over time." Knowing Joshua was still asleep, Stephenie rose to her feet. "I've got to check on my men. Plus make sure the treasury is restocked. I've brought back everything my mother stole and then some."

"Really?"

"Yes." Stephenie pushed aside the chair. "Give Josh my love if he wakes before I get back." Without waiting to be given her leave, Stephenie turned and quickly left the room. She knew that one day that woman would technically be her Queen and Joshua was still her King, but she was not sure she could be differential to them anymore, *at least not Rebecca.*

Stephenie reached the wharfs with a large contingent of soldiers as *The Scarlet* was pulled against the dock. Sir Walter had refused to allow her to leave the castle without protection and because of the cargo she had to transport, she was willing to accept his offer.

"Henton," she called loudly, waving her hands and brimming with a smile she could not force from her face if she wanted to. Not waiting for permission to board the ship, she leapt from the dock, over the water and the railing, and onto the deck. "We've routed Elard."

Henton frowned. "Well, Beth, I was filled in on how you did that."

Stephenie glared at him until he raised his hands in surrender. "Okay, you're still alive, we'll try this again, Steph."

Smiling at her victory, she nodded her head to Douglas and Will, who were beaming smiles at seeing her tunic.

"I knew you would come around."

"Shut up and start unloading our steel. Josh's workers can use the metal." Then she smiles as she walked over to Will and Douglas and hugged them both at the same time. "I am glad to have you both safe. But, please shut up about the tunic, because you, Will, are going to be wearing it as soon as we get back to the castle."

"What?"

Stephenie turned away from Will and to Captain Darelin. "Captain, please come to the castle once you have *The Scarlet* secured. I would like to have you as my guest for dinner. Bring as many of the men as you can."

The soldiers Sir Walter had dispatched to her were already unloading the heavy crates and placing them on the elevator platforms that would be winched from the harbor, up the shorter cliff, to the waiting wagons. She turned back to Henton and with a nod of her head, led her men off the ship and down the gangplank.

"We going to get paid now?" Will asked as they walked up the switchbacks to the the city.

"Yes, but Will, you've just been made High Priest of Catheri, so you'll be too busy to spend your money, which you already collected directly from the vault." She frowned; Will seemed much too happy at that news. To the others she said, "You all get some paid time off. I don't plan to leave Antar for a while, so enjoy yourselves."

Tim, John, Peter, and Berman let out a cheer and did a small dance. "Money and free time!" they started to sing.

She met Henton's and Douglas' eyes, for a moment their concern was evident. "Okay, you two can keep working if you want." She smiled again at their relief and then simply shook her head, knowing she would not want either of them to be any other way.

What about me, do I get a holiday?

Kas, my love, you get the worst end of the deal. You get no rest, since you're going to help me find a way to give you more. I've been thinking about the living transformations described in the books from the library; I wonder if we can't transform you back to a living body.

Really? I planned to take a long holiday walking by the cliffs and watching birds glide in the wind.

Stephenie smiled. She could feel Kas' playfulness.